THE KING'S BOW

Jamie Roe is a senior video game designer with over seven years of experience in the industry, where he crafts engaging and meaningful narratives for gamers worldwide. He has contributed to hit games like Hogwarts Legacy, For Honor and Age of Empires IV. Hailing from the seaside town of Bournemouth in the UK, he now lives in historic Chichester with his wife. His debut epic anthropomorphic adventure, *The King's Bow*, is the first of many stories he plans to unleash upon the world. Keep an eye open for the next novel in *The Great Lighthouse* series and many other stories to come. You can find more detailed maps and sign up to his newsletter on his website

www.jamie roe.com

The King's Bow

Book I of the Great Lighthouse

Jamie Roe

The King's Bow by Jamie Roe.

Cover Illustration and Design: **Charles Utting**

Editing: **Lisa Gilliam**

Map: **Jamie Roe**

First published 2025

This edition published 2025

EBook ISBN: 978-1-0683003-2-5

Paperback ISBN: 978-1-0683003-0-1

Hardcover ISBN: 978-1-0683003-1-8

www.jamieroe.com

To everyone who believed in me, even when I didn't.

Thank you.

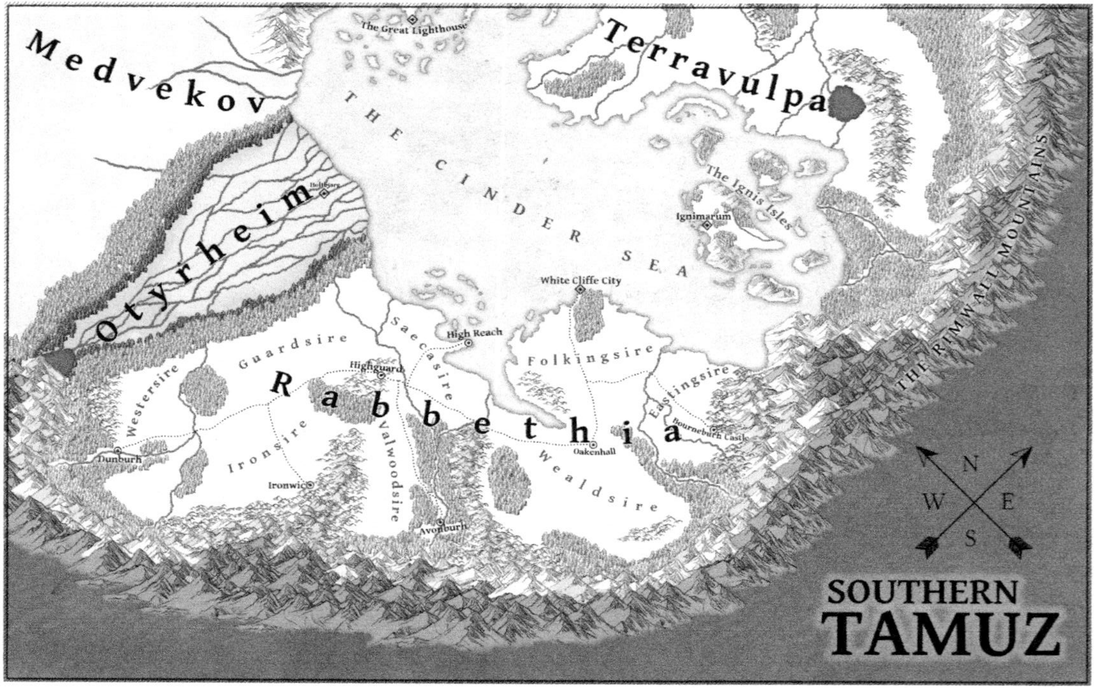
SOUTHERN
TAMUZ
Medvekov
Terravulpa
Otyrheim
Rabbethia
THE CINDER SEA
THE RIMWALL MOUNTAINS
The Great Lighthouse
The Ignis Isles
Ignimarum
White Cliffe City
High Reach
Highguard
Oakenhall
Bourneburn Castle
Dunburh
Ironwic
Avonburh
Guardsire
Saecasire
Folkingsire
Eastingsire
Westersire
Ironsire
Valwoodsire
Wealdsire
N
E
S
W

"Four to seal the power, four to release the fury, chosen by the Shepherd almighty. Stones of divinity, granted in aid, wielded with malice. Free once more what should be hidden and face the wrath of divinity."

Inscription on the Silver Coffin

Prologue

Silvana's fur bristled at the thought of what hunted her below.

She wasn't sure how long she had been climbing; she just knew she couldn't stop. The echoing sounds of her pursuers had forced her ever upward, their chattering teeth and scratching claws driving her aching muscles despite the biting cold. It had been a long hunt. She had lost count of how many times she had slept huddled within a metallic chamber branching from the oppressive stairwell. Time had lost all sense of meaning, but it didn't matter.

She was alive.

Please tell me that's it for bloody stairs, she thought as she sneered at the cold metal.

Her legs quivered as she took the final step. All that remained was the solitary metal door looming before her, denying her ascent. She gritted her canine teeth and moved to defy the malevolent architecture, her fingers tentatively wrapping around the rough metallic handle, her padded paws numbing the stabbing cold. What would she do when she walked through to the other side? It was foolish to proceed, stupid, idiotic, and crazy, but she had little choice. She couldn't go back down, not after what she had seen, and not with those Shangari stalking her from the darkened depths, her scent in their snouts.

She leaned into the door. The stairwell abruptly tilted with a heart-dropping lurch as her legs buckled beneath her, the metallic door approaching with alarming speed. With a quick turn, her shoulder collided hard against the cold surface, narrowly avoiding a broken snout. The echoing thunk bounced around the sullen space as if mocking her with juvenile joy.

Silvana winced as her shoulder began to throb, and it wasn't long before a prickling chill began to creep through her woollen cloak like an icy claw. She didn't move. She couldn't. Exhaustion was clouding her mind, draining her muscles and dragging her eyelids down with wrought iron weights. She instinctively wrapped her bushy tail around her legs to warm them. Hot breath rose from her long snout like a clouded wraith within the narrow stairwell, her chest rising and falling deeply, desperate for what little air permeated the space. Her pointed ears twitched as a muted wind surged beyond the thick metal.

'We'll be out of here soon, little one,' she whispered, resting a gentle paw on her stomach, and forcing a weak smile. 'I promise.' The frigid cold caressing her shoulder became unbearable. 'By the ancients, that's cold,' she said with a sharp breath, her thick white fur doing little to keep her fangs from dancing inside her mouth. She had to move.

With waning strength, Silvana tightened her grip on the handle and leaned into the door, wincing as old scars burned anew. The door eventually groaned open. The scraping metal shrieked down the stairwell, sending shivers down Silvana's spine as a freezing wind forced its way through the narrow gap.

They definitely would've heard that.

She gathered up her tail and squeezed through, into the frigid wind and onto a wide metal platform. What she saw took her breath away. Never before had she seen a view so beautiful and vast, a view that made her feel so utterly insignificant. Over a dangerously low railing, miles below, the world stretched away to the horizon, shrouded in a tranquil twilight. She stared in stunned awe. There were patchworks of dense forests, swathes of vast open fields, and networks of rivers that snaked from the mountains, eventually ending in the Cinder Sea. Cities dotted the land. Towering walls and mighty keeps rose high above the surrounding land, with smaller towns–and their far less impressive defences–nestled in the spaces between. On the horizon, the vast Rimwall Mountains encircled the world, enclosing both land and ocean within, their enormous size appearing tiny and faint, like faded ink streaked across parchment.

This was Tamuz.

This is the world I'm trying to save, Silvana thought as the weight of her task bore down upon her. *What could possibly go wrong?*

A deep rumble drew her back to the platform. The deep vibrations rolled like thunder within her chest, and she spun, her eyes growing wide. Before her stood a gigantic cylindrical mass, several stories high and a thousand times blacker than the darkest night sky. It was hauntingly beautiful. Silvana could feel her eyes begin to lose focus as she stared into its hypnotic tranquillity, her exhaustion begging her to give in. A warmth suddenly grew upon her cheek, pulling her from the all-encompassing void. She turned. A faint glow had begun to creep around the cylinder's far-stretching edge, its sudden light illuminating Silvana's world in shades of weathered black and rusted grey.

As she began to welcome the warming touch, the gentle glow suddenly erupted into titanic flames that licked at the cylinder's darkened edge. Silvana recoiled as the wind abruptly lost its chilling bite. The once-frozen railings began to drip with increasing fervour, the droplets scattering to the wind as soon as they had formed.

'It's turning,' she breathed, amazed. 'The whole bloody thing is turning.'

Like a colossal brazier, the flame's light cast a golden net across the world below, dispersing the tranquil twilight. A wall of light steadily crept across the land, bathing it in a warming embrace. Silvana smiled as she imagined people waking up fresh and ready to attack the new day, while the others kissed their loved ones goodnight.

Footsteps echoed from the stairwell. Her eyes fell to the doorway, and her smile faded as dread sank in. Hooded figures in white robes stepped out from the door's shadow, their breathing laboured, faces hidden within their hoods. They lingered with a menacing eagerness. Silvana shifted under their sinister silence, her eyes darting from one to the other, her mind racing to what she had seen them do to the prisoners below. This patient silence was definitely preferable.

'Why must you run, darling?' came a voice as soft as velvet yet sharp as a dagger. The sultry words announced a much taller figure who stepped from the shadows and almost floated to the front of the group. Her steps were light and purposeful, her robes elegant and pristine. While those around her wore simple white, this figure was adorned with ornate gold trimmings and covered from head to toe in intricate, swirling patterns, emulating the wild dance of fire. It was a lavish extravagance that could only belong to one who demanded supreme authority: the high priestess, Constance.

'You've run yourself ragged, my little light,' the figure mused softly as they pulled back their golden hood to reveal an elegant canine face. 'Come home, before you hurt yourself.'

Constance was a Vulpen like Silvana, but while Silvana's fur was an unkempt mess of white dusted with dirt, the high priestess's was a radiant red, expertly trimmed and silky smooth. Fur whiter than snow flowed like a waterfall from the underside of her snout and down the front of her slender neck, vanishing into her ornate robes. Sitting gracefully upon her head, glinting in the growing light, was a simple gold circlet, an unassuming, clear-cut gem embedded at its centre. The circlet didn't shift a millimetre as her hood came to rest against her slender shoulders. Her elegant tail flicked back and forth in erratic but controlled motions. Deep, emerald eyes looked down at Silvana with a look of superiority and mild annoyance. This woman exuded a regality that couldn't help but be respected, despite Silvana's best efforts.

'I know what you're doing!' Silvana snapped, unable to contain the spike of hatred rising within. Her mind raced to the cages she had seen below, and the faces of those inside.

The gem in Constance's circlet began to pulsate with a slow, rhythmic glow.

'W-What is that?' Silvana asked, taking a cautious step back.

Constance said nothing as a wicked smirk crawled across her snout. A sudden pain formed in Silvana's mind, like a pinprick between her eyes. She winced.

What in Thena's name...?

The pain exploded. It encompassed her entire skull, stabbing at her mind like a storm of searing needles burrowing into her mind. She clutched at her head, staggering backwards. Her back hit the railing, and she strained to glance over. Far below, a ring of clouds swirled around the tower's peak like churning waves, the stormy colours shifting to golden pinks as the brazier continued its unrelenting turn.

The pain in her skull increased, drawing her back to the high priestess. Silvana gasped. Constance's eyes were now ablaze with a white, radiant fire.

I have to get away. I have to get away. I have to get away.

She pulled herself from the reverent terror of Constance's stare and glanced back over the railing, a crazy, reckless plan forming in her mind.

'Don't be foolish, girl,' Constance snapped as if aware of Silvana's desperate thoughts. She furrowed her brow, and the gem began to blink with increased fury. Her voice took on an unworldly depth, heavy and ethereal. 'Now, come *here*.'

A thousand whispers echoed around Silvana's mind, each one reciting the priestess's command in a nightmarish cacophony of ghostly screams. It was as if something were clawing at her very being. It grasped with serrated talons at her thoughts, at who she was, trying with manic desperation to force itself into the deepest corners of her mind. It wanted to get in, shove Silvana aside and take control.

She screamed.

Constance's smile deepened as the wind howled around them. The air was growing hotter as the brazier continued its unrelenting turn, uncaring of the events unfolding at its feet. The ends of Silvana's cloak began to singe, wafting a burning scent up her panicked nostrils.

One of the hooded figures cautiously approached Constance. She waved a dismissive paw, and her robed followers hurried back through the door, leaving the two Vulpen women alone on the platform. Silvana could feel the last of her free will slipping through her paws. She had to do something, anything, or be lost to this mad woman forever.

'Please! Don't do this!' she cried, thinking of nothing better than to beg for what little mercy this woman had. Tears streamed down her cheeks, matting the fur. 'Mother!' Within the ever-growing inferno, Constance remained unchanged, deaf to her daughter's pleas. Silvana squeezed her eyes shut and prayed to the ancients.

Then she felt it.

For the briefest of moments, the pull in her mind weakened. She opened her eyes and found Constance wincing, a fresh wave of heat scorching her cheeks. It wasn't much, but it was enough. In a flash of pure desperation, Silvana pulled from her mother's control and vaulted over the super-heated railing.

Constance's startled shrieks faded into silence as Silvana dropped. The brazier's heat, once searing, cooled quickly against her back. The wind howled around her, sharp and merciless. Through bleary eyes, she glimpsed the black walls of the tower rushing past, a dizzying blur of blackened shadow as the wind whipped away her tears. Placing a loving paw over her stomach, Silvana plummeted down the length of the Great Lighthouse.

I

The Thief and the Horde

Asher's long ears trailed in the wind, cooling him in the cloudless midday heat. Dust erupted underfoot as each booted step thudded against the stone, kicking dirt onto his beige tunic and brown trousers. As he ran, he wondered why the small Otyren trader would be so angry over losing a single red apple, let alone why he would squeak to the palace guards to chase down the Rabbethi thief.

Yet here Asher was, sprinting past market stands at breakneck speed. His powerful legs propelled him ever onwards as he grasped the shiny apple tightly in his white-furred paw. His large hazel eyes found gaps between the muted tunics and hooded cloaks as a sea of tall floppy ears streaked by in a blur of brown, black, and white fur.

He glanced over his shoulder and beheld White Cliffe City's finest in pursuit. Three broad Rabbethi soldiers were making much slower progress through the crowd, weighed down by their heavy plate armour and overbearing sense of superiority.

'Out of the way! Move!' the leader bellowed, his flat pink nose furiously twitching as he attempted to swim through an ocean of absent-minded citizens, careful to keep his tall glaive pointed away from the crowd. The corner of Asher's mouth stretched into a cocky smile as he turned his attention forwards.

His smile dropped.

A huge, grizzly Medvedian blocked his carefully planned escape. The rotund trader stood before a wide market stand, attempting to entice the much smaller citizens to peruse his oversized goods. With a mighty paw, he thrust an enormous pumpkin, the size of which would take several Rabbethi to lift, into the path of a passer-by. Asher watched as the startled citizen sped on, avoiding eye contact and provoking an irritated growl from the overbearing trader.

A distant cry echoed from behind Asher. 'Y-you there! Medvedian! Stop that thief! The one with the patch!' The oak-coloured fur covering Asher's right eye had always been an easy way to identify him, and at times like this, he wished he had a hood that would actually stay up.

The Medvedian's short, round ears twitched, and he turned from the elderly Rabbethi he was berating. His beady eyes widened at Asher's approach. He adjusted the thick rope belt around his red tunic and squatted, spreading his arms wide. Asher could see the determination settle across his broad, fluffy face, as if catching this thief would prove he was meant for greater things.

As Asher was about to experience the tightest hug of his life, he dropped, ducking under the trader's thick arms and sliding between a pair of short, stout legs. The stench was putrid. Spending too long on the road without a proper bath seemed a common problem among Medvedian traders. It was as if the smell proved they had travelled hard, earning their way with strength and perseverance. To Asher, it proved they had no sense of hygiene.

His momentum carried him sliding under the stand, and he vanished with a flourish beneath the large white cloth. He reached out and kicked one of the stand's wooden legs. With a powerful crack and a spray of splinters, the whole stand began collapsing around him, the weight of the considerable produce threatening to crush him flat. Asher had just enough momentum to fling himself out the back of the stand in a cloud of dust, dirt and billowing cloth. Behind him, all manner of colourful fruits and vegetables cascaded into the market, rolling to the feet of the suddenly curious crowd. The trader dropped to all fours, attempting to gather his escaping produce. The excited crowd surged forwards, desperate to snag a free meal.

'B-back! All of you!' the trader roared, his yellow fangs on clear display as thick wads of saliva sprayed across the stone floor. His eyes shot from person to person, daring anyone brave or foolish enough to steal from him. The guards broke their chase from Asher and set about preventing the panicked trader from mauling the citizens of the city. Asher jumped to his feet. With angry roars and terrified screams echoing around the collapsed market stand, he brushed the dirt from his tunic and looked back with a satisfied smile.

Well, he thought, *my work here is done.*

With a skip in his step, he turned from the chaos and strolled through the market towards his favourite spot in the city, a quiet area in the southwestern corner of the stone plaza, where a cloud of green rose high above the slated roofs of the neighbouring buildings. As he walked, he noted the stalls manned by less observant traders. The easily distracted Otyren often made decent targets. Their short stature, stubby limbs and small black eyes made them far less intimidating than the Vulpen and Medvedian traders, though Asher always watched for their gnashing teeth. Used to tear into raw fish, they could easily puncture tough leather and pierce the skin beneath. He had the scars to prove it. Their powerful tails made them formidable swimmers, and it was well known that one should never try to swim away from an angry Otyren. Asher had the scars to remind him of that too.

***

It was quiet when Asher arrived. Before him stood a great oak tree, its trunk thick, its branches full and far-reaching. The workday was still underway, and the Rabbethi with responsibilities were working hard, making a living across the city. They had little time to relax beneath the tree's welcoming leaves, whose shade graciously provided a much-needed break from the afternoon heat. The only sounds came from the rustling leaves and quiet snickers of kits playing a game of Otyren's Fall.

'That's not far at all!' one laughed, pointing at a rock five metres away. 'You're a Cowardly Otyren!'

'I am not!' protested a little girl no older than five. 'At least I can make it to mine. Yours is waaaay too far!'

Asher smiled as he walked by, remembering when he'd played the same game with Henric. The rules were simple: Each player stood in a line, holding a stone. Everyone would throw their stone as far as they thought they could jump. Each player would then take turns jumping to their stone. If everyone made it to their stone, the player who threw theirs the shortest distance was the loser, or "Cowardly Otyren". Should a player reach their stone, they were the loser and named the "Fallen Otyren". These outdated titles were remnants from the Expansion War more than two hundred years ago.

Some traditions never change, Asher thought with a smile as he approached the tree's thick base.

He placed the apple in his mouth and found the usual grooves in the bark. With his muscular Rabbethi legs, it took no time at all to clamber up to the upper reaches and over to his favourite branch. He sat along its length, took the apple from his mouth, and leaned against the trunk with an audible sigh.

Below, the city was a maelstrom of activity, a cyclone of senses, chaotic, manic and overwhelming. Asher loved it. Within the market, a sea of long ears flopped and flowed around hundreds of stands. Travelling Medvedian merchants roared at the crowd, enticing them over for what one claimed was the "sweetest honey this side of the Lighthouse". Their words rumbled like thunder in Asher's chest, and he almost felt compelled to "purchase" some honey for himself. He thought better of it, taking a sizable bite of his apple with his impressively large front teeth. It was sweet, with a satisfying crunch, made all the more satisfying for the work he had put into obtaining it. Asher didn't need to steal, not really, but the way this particular trader had scorned some young kits for playing too close to his stand, well, someone had to teach him some manners. He hadn't expected the guards to chase him so feverishly. Petty theft didn't usually draw much life out of the patrolling soldiers, but the recent disappearances plaguing the noble families had them frustrated and on edge. Months without a single lead made the city's guards look foolish and weak. They wouldn't have been kind to Asher if they had caught him, though that just made it more exciting.

His eyes landed on the palace on the far side of the plaza, a massive stone structure atop a vast plinth. It loomed over the bustling market like a sentinel, its thick walls stretching along the plaza's width. Four vast square towers sat at each corner, proud and formidable. Statues of Rabbethi heroes and heroines posed triumphantly within the walls, earning their spot by dying in one of the many wars that had previously plagued the land, from the rebellions against their once Vulpen masters to the Expansion War against the Otyren.

At the far end of the palace rose a foreboding square keep built into the city's outer wall. On one side, the city lay before it; on the other, the Cinder Sea crashed against the white cliffs from which White Cliffe City drew its name.

Asher closed his eyes, feeling the Great Lighthouse's warmth upon his fluffy cheeks, the golden light radiating down upon the land from its lofty heights. The tower's black mass rose from the west like a needle into the sky. Its shape faded into the blue before appearing once more beneath a ball of blazing light. Both the tower and the light never failed to instil a sense of inner peace within Asher, and he released another satisfied sigh. While most his age preferred to live non-stop, bouncing from one task to the next, Asher always found time to sit back, relax, and enjoy the view.

Twenty-six isn't too young to take it easy.

The scent of cinnamon floated up his nose, rising from nearby pastries baked to perfection by the Otyren. The scent rose into the tree on a cooling wind, carrying with it fond memories of a life long ago, of love and laughter, of his mother. He reached into his tunic and lifted a tarnished silver chain from his chest. Attached to one of the links was a small silver bow. Like the chain, it was stained and badly scratched, years of improper care taking its toll on the precious metal. Asher fiddled with the bow's curve, running a soft finger across the imitated string.

I'll get it cleaned one day, he promised to the wind, the same promise he made every time he held the precious trinket. He was just proud he hadn't lost it.

A harmonious chanting roused him from his thoughts, making his ears stand tall. He placed the necklace back within his tunic and gazed over the market, the melodic voices drawing his attention towards the palace steps. A large group of hooded figures moved slowly and in unison through the market. Asher recognised them by their long white robes as acolytes of the Shepherd, a religious group whose practices seemed particularly dull. It was not uncommon to see groups trudging through city centres, chanting and gathering fresh recruits from the prisons, slums and other places that housed the city's "unwanted". Asher never understood why anyone would want to dress all in white, travel from city to city and do nothing but preach about a fairy-tale god destined to return. The idea that there was only one god was utterly ridiculous. Asher cast his eyes over the acolytes once more. There was something strange about these ones, other than their particularly terrible singing.

There's so many of them.

Asher had never seen so many white robes in one place before, and more were streaming into the central plaza from numerous streets and alleys. The market citizens continued their day, unaware of the surge of holy folk, but the palace guards began to shift at their stations. They turned to each other, shuffling anxiously.

Something wasn't right.

Curiosity forced Asher from his perch. He finished his apple in a few sizable bites, devouring everything but the stem, which he flicked into the branches. He scrambled down with little grace, jumping the last few feet and landing in the soft soil below with a thud. The children had left, leaving behind a collection of rocks some distance from a line in the dirt. One was over ten metres away, an impressive leap for such a young Rabbethi. Brushing himself off, Asher strolled back towards the market, tucking his tall ears down behind his tunic and pulling his hood over his head.

The crowd was easy enough to push through as he strode along the central walkway, and it didn't take long before he was at the plaza's centre. He glanced up at the statue there, which stood imposingly atop a stone plinth. A Rabbethi woman aimed a bow high into the sky, an intense expression on her face. This was Folka, the ancestor of all Rabbethi and the founder of Rabbethia. A church to her worship could be found wherever there was a population of Rabbethi, which was nearly every city in the world, other than Otyrheim. It was strange, but Asher's heart always grew warm whenever he passed her by. Whether it was a sense of pride or even belonging, he couldn't tell.

Around the plinth's base was a large pond. Giant lily pads dotted the surface like floating islands. Reeds bunched together around the pond's edge, breaking up the hard circular border. Two white carp, which Asher had grown fond of over the years, glided beneath the water's surface. They had resided in their watery home for longer than he had been able to talk, and he regarded them almost as friends, constants in his life that would forever be a part of his home, much like the stone keep that towered over the city.

He curtly saluted the statue and continued towards the palace steps, gazing up at the enormous wooden doors within the wide gatehouse. The thick wood was reinforced with impressively heavy iron plating. Two giant banners hung on either side, upon which was the Rabbethia sigil, a golden bow with three golden arrows pointing up from the bow's string, set on a cobalt-blue background. They flapped loosely in the cool breeze as the chanting persisted.

The acolytes at the base of the steps had grown into a horde, their numbers overflowing into the market. Heads began to turn as palace guards began to gather atop the stone steps. The chanting was growing intense, and it was difficult not to feel intimidated by the deep guttural voices projecting far over the market and into the city beyond.

Just as Asher reached the sea of white robes, the chanting abruptly stopped, and a graveyard hush filled the air. Asher waited, unsure of what to do. Worried whispers simmered around the market, and even the traders hurriedly packing their wares slowed at the sudden silence. The palace guards shifted with nervous energy, gripping their glaives and short bows tightly.

Eventually, a broad brown-furred palace guard stepped forwards, his deep-blue cloak marking him as a captain. He raised his chin, puffed out his chest, and cleared his throat.

'What is your business here, holy men?' Although his voice was firm and authoritative, a slight tremble betrayed his unease across the plaza. The market held its breath for a response, but the sea of hoods remained silent.

Asher's eyes drifted over the hoods before him. *Strange.* All the acolytes were shorter than he was. He had assumed the church welcomed all folk into its fold, but he couldn't see a single Medvedian, Vulpen, or Rabbethi in this gathering.

A light glinted across his eyes. He recoiled, blinking the spots from his vision. Something was glistening from under the acolyte's sleeves in front of him. He focused on it, and his eyes went wide.

Chainmail.

'I said, what is your—'

A whistle cut through the air, and the captain fell silent.

Asher's eyes snapped up to the palace steps, and his stomach lurched. A gnarled black arrow had plunged itself deep into the captain's throat, its jagged head protruding from the flesh, coating his fur in blood. The captain's eyes grew wide in stunned horror. He dropped his glaive with a heavy clatter and reached for his throat, a strained gurgle bubbling from within. His panicked eyes grew wider as his fingers found the arrow's pointed tip. He slowly turned to his fellow guards, eyes pleading, nose twitching faster and faster. The other guards stared, frozen with the same fear enveloping their now-dying leader. It seemed no one knew where the arrow had come from, and none would take a single step, lest they be next. The captain began to slow. His nose eventually stopped twitching, and he dropped to his knees, arms falling to his side, eyes rolling backwards. He collapsed to the hard stone floor with a thud, dead.

Blood cascaded down the stone steps like a dreadful waterfall, pouring under the white robes of the acolytes below. They watched, unmoving, uncaring. Asher trembled in stunned silence, too terrified to run, too bewildered to help. This was the first time he had witnessed anyone die, and his mind had just stopped.

Thud.

Something heavy fell from beneath the acolyte's robe in front of Asher and slumped over his boot. He pulled his eyes from the dead captain, stifling a gasp at what it was. A long, thick, hairless tail trailed up and under the acolyte's robe.

'Shangari,' he breathed as quietly as his fear would allow.

An ear-piercing screech made him jump, and he watched in horror as a sea of dense, scabby tails slumped to the stone floor, a chorus of heavy thuds echoing across the silent plaza.

Then it began.

The holy horde leapt into action. Gnarled fingers pulled daggers from deep sleeves, and the acolytes surged up the steps in a crazed rush. Still shaken from the death of their senior officer, the guards scrambled to form ranks and ready their glaives. Hundreds of manic footsteps thundered up the stone steps, accompanied by a cacophony of screeches and wails. To their credit, the guards assembled quickly. Archers at the rear leapt high into the air, unencumbered by heavy-plated armour, their strong Rabbethi legs propelling them to great heights. Arrows glinted in the afternoon light, each one nocked and ready to rain death from on high. The archers unleashed a volley upon the horde. The first Shangari wave crumpled halfway up the steps in a bloody roar of shrieks and cut-off cries, but it wasn't long before a fresh surge came writhing over their fallen comrades.

They quickly found the top of the steps and collided with a sickening crash against the guards' sharp glaives. Blood-curdling screams echoed across the plaza as the guards of White Cliffe City cut down the first attack, the men and women proving their worth. Their glaives danced and spun in fluid motions, slicing through white robes and black flesh like hot knives through butter. The guards' long weapons came to rest by their side, ready for the next assault.

The next wave came, followed by another, and then another. With less and less time between each attack, the guards slowly faltered, their swipes becoming cumbersome and wild. The heights at which the archers could climb were growing shorter. Shangari began scraping and clawing at each other to get past, their bulging red eyes radiating with a ferocious hunger from under their hoods. With a final surge, they swarmed over the guards' defences like a wave of white robes and rusty daggers, hacking and slashing at the overwhelmed guards, whose agonising screams carried far over the city. The Shangari crashed against the palace gates, then streamed back down the steps towards the now-fleeing market citizens.

Asher watched in horror as all around him, the city's inhabitants ran for their lives. Waves of Shangari surged around him, slaughtering everything in their path, unafraid of the soldiers that had put up a fight, unaffected by their kin cut down before them. Blood-curdling screams and malicious snickering filled the air, filling Asher's ears. He had to do something, anything to help. He cursed his natural instincts and took off running.

His heart was racing, his nose twitching, his breaths short and sharp with each frantic step. Nausea began to swell in his stomach as his tall ears thrummed with heat. The burning and screaming rushed at him, compressing his surroundings into a suffocating ball of nightmarish terror. He reached for the necklace at his chest, feeling the bow through his tunic. Asher heard his mother's calming voice.

'The next right thing...' A deep breath. 'The next right thing...' Another deep breath. 'The next right thing. The next right thing. The next right thing.'

Someone slammed into his left flank, hurtling him back to his senses. The pair crashed hard to the floor, kicking up dust as they tumbled together, separating as they rolled to a stop. Asher eased himself off the floor and raised a paw to his brow, wincing at the sharp pain. He stared blurry-eyed at the dark crimson now coating the white fur of his fingers.

Head swimming, he looked around, searching for who or what had taken him out. Nearby, a large Medvedian lay face down on the dusty stone, motionless, a grove of black arrows sprouting from his back like a scorched forest. Asher's panicked breaths returned with a fury, his chest tightening like a vice.

A sinister cackling came from behind a collapsed market stand. Two Shngari, robed in white, stepped out, poorly constructed crossbows in their black, scabby paws. Strapped to their backs was a quiver full of sinister black arrows. Their white hoods were caked in blood and resting loose upon their broad shoulders, revealing their contorted Shangari features: matted black fur, small pointed ears, and a long, crooked snout that ended with a bulbous black nose. A pair of razor-sharp teeth protruded down from the end of their snouts, perfect for gnawing through tough sinew and solid bone. Most striking and terrifying to Asher, however, were their eyes, which radiated a deep pupil-less red and seemed to lack any semblance of a soul. His heart sank as their cold, bloody gaze shifted from the dead Medvedian to him. Wicked grins stretched across their long snouts as they snickered like sinister children, drawing vicious arrows from their backs. Asher shifted on the floor, his eyes darting to his left and right as he searched desperately for an escape. Then he saw it, a gap in the stands. It was so close. He remained still, waiting for the right time to move.

The Shangari looked down to adjust their bowstrings, and Asher took his chance. He leapt to his feet and bolted towards the stands as fast as his Rabbethi legs could carry him. The Shangari screeched furiously, but the dreadful sounds faded quickly into the distance as Asher ran faster than he had ever run before.

He flew through the maze of broken market stands, steering away from the screams of the dying and praying to the ancients that the next turn wouldn't lead him into the maws of the hungry horde. Around every corner, mutilated bodies littered the stone floor. They stared at Asher, mouths agape in a tormented scream, their last moments immortalised upon their terrified faces. Tears began to form in the corners of his eyes as each one made a permanent home in his crumbling mind.

None of this made any sense. The Shangari clans were scattered, an incoherent mess of warring clans and blood feuds. There was no way such a number could band together, let alone disguise themselves as acolytes. Someone was behind this, leading them, but who? And, for the love of Folka, why?

He burst out of the market's eastern border and onto the cobbled streets bordering the plaza. Despite the questions circling his mind like a hurricane, one stuck firm in the centre of his thoughts: Were his brother and father okay? He had to find out. With a burst of speed, he sprinted towards the palace's eastern wall.

***

The statues within the palace's eastern wall passed by in a blur. Asher needed to get inside, and he knew exactly where the best spot was. To his right, tall, terraced houses and empty streets whipped by, the usual bustle of the city having come to a screeching halt. The residents had likely rushed home to cower with loved ones, fleeing as soon as the sound of battle erupted. He didn't blame them. The guards, sworn to protect them, had all been called to die on the stone steps or defend the royal family within the keep. Asher hadn't seen the streets so devoid of life since the great Shangari raids ten years earlier, the last time the Shangari had any semblance of coordination.

An image of his mother leapt into his mind: her long white ears, pink nose and caring blue eyes, her coffin as it was laid to rest within the burrows just outside the eastern gates of the city. His father changed that day. Without the loving embrace of Asher's mother, his father grew cold and distant, throwing himself into his ancient scriptures and leaving two young boys to grow up alone.

Asher shook his head. *Focus, for Folka's sake!*

He arrived at the section of wall he was looking for, where ivy branches crawled up the smooth stone to lay siege to the grounds within. Without a second thought, Asher leapt onto the ivy and began to climb. He could feel the rough vines scratching and rubbing the inside of his paws, but years of climbing had toughened them, and the bark could no longer pierce the padded skin. A cool breeze blew across the quiet fortifications as he climbed. Evening was descending upon the city, the bright light of the Great Lighthouse shifting to a rich orange glow. The deep-blue sky slowly began its transition into pastel hues of purple and pink.

Panting, Asher pulled himself up and over the battlement, crouching low to avoid the sight of patrolling guards. However, he found it eerily empty, with no sign of activity between himself and the towers that loomed at each end of the wall.

That can't be good.

He raced to the wall's inner edge and stared down into the palace grounds. Dropping fifty feet before him were the eastern gardens, a series of square, neatly cut lawns bordered by rose bushes that stretched the length of the eastern wall. The roses were in full bloom, with beautiful white flowers covering each bush like patches of snow.

Without a second thought, he jumped down, landing awkwardly in the bushes below. Careful to avoid the sharp thorns, he clambered onto the lawn. The intoxicating scent of roses filled his twitching nose, sending him into a daze of nostalgia. He pushed the memories aside and crossed the neatly cut grass, hurrying towards the stone-covered walkway that hugged the exterior of the central keep. Pristine white wisteria hung from the slated roof, swaying in the dying light like a white-veiled curtain. Asher pushed the hanging flowers aside and stepped onto the stone walkway, finding the thick wooden door that led inside.

He reached for the iron handle and froze. His long ears stood to attention as a heavy rumbling began reverberating deep in his chest. He waited.

BOOM.

It had come from the front of the palace, specifically, Asher knew, the giant wooden doors leading into its central courtyard. Someone had opened them. The acolytes would be pouring into the palace courtyard any second, and it wouldn't be long before they surged into the royal hall. His father was in trouble.

His heart pounding, he threw the door open and raced inside.

2

A Home Invasion

Asher's throat burned, his legs were aching, and the gruesome images of a hundred slaughtered faces now plagued his mind. He could still see them staring at him, sheer, unimaginable terror exuding from their wide-open eyes. He shook the vision from his mind and willed himself onwards, his rapid footsteps echoing against the stone around him.

The keep was a maze of corridors and sporadic dead ends, dimly lit by wooden torches fastened to the walls. It was a construction principle used since the days of old when Asher's ancestors dug elaborate burrows that twisted deep underground, protecting them from the world's predatory species. It also felt right. Fortunately, the world no longer resorted to such barbarism, and now all meat-based diets were sourced only from the "lesser developed" creatures: wild boar, grazing deer and fish. The idea of eating such meats still made Asher's stomach turn, but he preferred it to being on someone's dinner plate himself.

Onward he ran, bouncing off the walls at full speed as he navigated the keep's inner workings, his shoulders bruising with each corner and junction. It had been a long while since he had passed through these halls, but something inside pushed and pulled at him, telling him which corner to turn, which archway to pass through.

All sense of urgency evaporated as he stopped at one of the junctions. A floor-to-ceiling portrait of the royal family loomed over him, painted with delicate brushstrokes and set within an intricately carved wooden frame. Panting, he stared, heart aching as he gazed at the faces.

It's been so long.

All the figures were finely dressed in their smartest attire. Queen Aethel, a beautiful Rabbethi woman, peered down with ghost-grey eyes, her regal blue dress embroidered with shining golden threads. Two tall ears stood to attention from within a slender crown that sat gracefully on her white-furred head, the gold intricately set with blue sapphires. Around her neck was a dazzling silver necklace, the centre of which shone a silver bow and arrow, the painted strokes bringing the piece's beauty to life with just a few simple colours. Asher raised his paw to his chest and felt his bow through the thin material of his tunic. His eyes found the queen's. They were kind and caring, but had an unspoken mournfulness that made Asher's heart sink.

Next to her, in all his glory, stood King Hengist of Rabbethia. A broad and handsome brown-furred Rabbethi in dark leather armour, the kingdom's sigil etched into his chest piece. A cloak of deep blue rested at his back, the epitome of heroism, and his ears were bound in a traditional warrior's topknot. They passed through his regal crown and were fastened with a large golden ring. His cold, blue eyes stared down at Asher, stern and disapproving, a look Asher knew all too well.

With a pang of immature spite, Asher averted his eyes to the two children standing before the monarchs. They were young kits, a few years apart, both dressed in matching tunics of deep blue, thin golden circlets resting across their much smaller brows. The younger stood before the king, whose paw rested heavily on the young kit's shoulder. The boy had the same dark brown fur as his father, with large blue eyes to match. He had a quizzical gaze. Asher had always loved answering Henric's questions, and had envisioned the energetic lad would've become a fine scholar one day, if only he could've learned to sit still for two seconds.

The other child was older and taller, with an oak-coloured patch covering the left eye. His posture was straight and tense as he stood rigid before the queen. His white fur was clean and well-trimmed, a sense of obedient pride glowing within his hazel eyes. There was so much hope there, so much naive pride and aspirations. What a different life he would end up leading from the one he envisioned.

With a sigh, Asher stepped back and gazed at the royal family—his family—preserved so many years ago. All were present, all but one. His father had once had a brother, Horsa, but there were no paintings of him anywhere in the keep. Asher had learned long ago not to ask questions about the man. Over the years, his interest in the stranger all but faded from his mind.

Asher took a step back and looked at the eyes of his family before him, envying the lack of pain within. A deep yearning for older, simpler days began to swell in his heart. He shook his head, angry at himself for lingering so long.

That was then. This is now.

With a last loving look at his mother, he planted his foot and took off once more.

Memories flooded his mind like a broken dam as he ran. He couldn't help it. Long ago, he had chased his younger brother down these halls, pelting him with wooden arrows from his training bow, laughter echoing around the cold stone. Henric was a few years his junior and, as such, was always the one who had to flee; it was the law of brotherhood. After their mother's death, however, Asher began spending less time with his little brother and more time outside the palace walls, away from the cold, mournful keep. Their father became absent, choosing to spend his time in the library, even making it his bedchamber and taking every meal within. He seldom noticed that his sons were absent from court and never knew, nor seemed to care, that they spent their time out in the wild. It was a bittersweet freedom for the young kits.

Asher sped down another hallway, the ground beneath him becoming soft underfoot. He was now racing down an expensive blue carpet that masked each footstep with a dull thud. The change in furniture marked the approach to the throne room, with shields showcasing the Rabbethia sigil now lining the walls, and empty suits of armour flanking the hallways. Asher's ears stood to attention as the faint sounds of battle began to emanate before him.

The horde was inside the keep.

He picked up the pace, not knowing what he hoped to achieve. He didn't have a bow and was still in his simple street clothes, yet something compelled him to run. Whether it was the remaining love he had for his father, a sense of duty to his king, or even his mother's memory, he didn't know. He just hoped his brother was nowhere near the city.

He eventually reached a large wooden door. The loud clang of metal striking metal rang out from the chamber beyond, quickly followed by something wet splatting against the stone floor. A heavy thud then followed.

'Back to the sewers with you!' a booming voice spat. 'Snivelling rodents are not welcome in my hall!'

Asher recognised his father's voice in an instant. He had to get in there, fast. He went for the handle, but footsteps behind him made him pause. If he had to fight through a few bloodthirsty Shangari to get to his father, he would.

He turned, lowering himself into a boxing stance, legs apart, fists raised. There was no way he could fight a whole horde out in the open, but in the narrow corridors of the burrow-like keep? Against a few? That he could handle.

'What sort of stance is that?' a voice rasped from the shadows. A wave of relief swept over Asher as he recognised Harold, the captain of the guard. An old war scoundrel of a Rabbethi, he was as big as a small Medvedian but ten times as agile, with coarse grey fur. Age and combat had taken their toll on his once proud ears, and now they flopped down the side of his head, emerging like wilting flowers from the top of a battle-ready top knot. An old cut ran deep into Harold's right ear, leaving a sizable wedge missing from the tall, thin flesh. Harold had told Asher with pride how he got the wound fighting off one of the fabled Muuraki assassins of the northern continent, though, like many others, Asher never believed him.

A trail of blood followed him as he limped forwards, staining the blue carpet with intermittent pools of crimson. His bloody paw held his left flank tightly. Deep cuts marked his leather chest piece and right armguard.

'You look like a common boxer,' he strained through gritted teeth. Dried blood stained the corner of his mouth. '*Not* what I taught you.'

He stumbled forwards, and Asher rushed to his side, catching him under the arm. He was heavy, but Asher was able to help the aged warrior to the floor, leaning him against the wall.

'Harold...' Asher breathed, staring at the battered veteran. Fresh scars covered his body, adding to the existing lines of furless pink skin; fatal blows of battles long past, denied their mark by Harold's formidable prowess. Asher checked the old war veteran over. He lingered as he always had when he was younger, on the strange scars around Harold's calf. They had always been there, a curved shape carving down his right calf with another circular wound within its centre. Asher had learned long ago not to ask about it, lest he receive a smack for being as nosy as a Cozati. That never stopped him from sneaking a peek whenever he got the chance. Asher pushed the distracting memories from his mind and moved away from the scars.

'Is that stance what they've been teaching you down at the docks?' Harold strained as his eyelids heaved themselves open. 'I swear to you, boy, I'll shut down those fighting rings once and—'

Asher wrapped his arms around the old soldier, squeezing him tight.

'Ah, hey now,' Harold winced. 'Those bastards did a number on me, but they're nothing compared to a Muuraki assassin. Did I ever tell you—'

'What's going on?' Asher blurted. He had no patience for the old man's stories today.

'I don't know, but it has something to do with your father and that damned church.'

'Father!' Asher sprang to his feet, his ears standing to attention, listening for the sound of battle. He could still hear the conflict. His father was putting up a valiant fight, but Asher doubted he could last much longer.

'Don't... there's too many,' Harold pleaded between laboured breaths. A coughing fit racked his body as blood sprayed the front of his leather armour. His dark brown eyes began to close.

'I'm sorry,' Asher whispered, 'I'll come back for you, I promise.' He turned to him, tears forming in the corners of his eyes, but there was no response. Harold's eyes had closed. His head was slumped forwards, paws limp at his side. With a heavy heart, Asher tore himself away, reached for the door's iron handle, and threw it open.

***

Asher's footsteps echoed in the grand hall, bouncing off the marble pillars that flanked the hall's length. With horror, he watched King Hengist fall to one knee, panting, blood dripping from his ornate glaive. Shangari lay dead at his feet, thick pools of hot blood spreading across the stone floor from where they fell. He raised his head towards Asher, weary eyes growing wide. A warm evening glow bathed the king's face as the last light shone through the round window high above the fractured grand doors. Panting heavily, with bodies all around him and the golden light upon him, he looked like one of the heroes of old, a magnificent warrior of the forgotten days.

'Father!' Asher slid to his knees as his father fell limp, catching the wounded king and easing his head onto his lap. His royal glaive clattered to the ground with echoing clangs. Tears gathered in the corners of Asher's eyes as he stared down at the king, his father. A lump caught in his throat at what he saw. Now that he was closer, he realised this was not the man he remembered. His once vibrant brown fur was now faded, and a dense scattering of grey spread from around his mouth up his cheeks. His tall, strong ears limped at the tips, and his piercing blue eyes were dull and clouded. It had been longer than Asher realised since he'd seen the old man. A heavy guilt wrapped itself tight around his heart.

A fresh wave of robed Shangari poured in through the broken doors. Asher's eyes snapped to meet them. His heart was pounding, his nose twitching, tears streaming down his white cheeks. He clenched his teeth and narrowed his eyes. If he were to die, he would take as many of the bastards with him as he could. They didn't attack. Instead, they crept into the hall and formed a wide circle around Asher and his father, a wall of bulbous red eyes bearing down on him from within a sea of white hoods.

Rough paws suddenly caressed Asher's face. He jumped as he realised his father was holding his cheek gently. Asher leaned into the embrace. He looked down and found his father's eyes staring up at him, tears welling in the corners.

'Horsa, Aethel... I'm so sorry,' the old king breathed, his voice strained and hollow.

'What? N-no, it's me, Asher. Remember? Your son?' His father's eyes began to close, his nose slowing. 'No, no, no!' Asher shouted, panic and despair taking hold. 'Don't you die on me! You owe me that!'

But the king was gone, along with any chance of making amends, of swapping desperately needed apologies, of forgiving each other. With his father's final breath evaporating into the blood-heavy air of the throne room, the closure Asher had always wanted but had always run from vanished with it. He bowed his head and began to weep.

A soft voice floated into the hall from the broken doors. 'Seize him.'

The Shangari pounced, kicking the glaive away and sending it skidding across the stone floor. Asher lashed out as they tore him from his father, landing several heavy kicks on his attackers. He kicked one in the stomach, which began vomiting blood, and cracked another across the face, snapping its snout gruesomely out of place. They eventually restrained the rabid prince and brought him down hard on his knees next to his father's body, tying his paws tight behind his back. Asher stared at them through puffy red eyes, a red-hot fury burning a hole in his heart.

Somewhere deep inside, within the bottomless pit of rage and sorrow, something awakened – a spark, no, a fire. It wasn't the usual fire that burned when he got into trouble or tried to survive a few rounds in the boxing ring, but something entirely different. It felt like it had always been there, and yet, was utterly foreign at the same time. It raged within him, burning with the injustice done to him, to his people.

The voice spoke again. 'Well, well...' Slow, gentle footsteps echoed against the stone floor, drawing closer. 'Such vigour and spirit you have for one so young. Still wasting your talents stealing apples, hm?' The voice's owner entered the Shangari circle. Her tall, slender frame set her apart from the vermin around her, her beautiful, red fur vibrant against the dark crimson seeping into the stone floor. White fur cascaded like a river of snow from under her cheeks down into her robes. Her perfectly trimmed tail flicked behind her as she watched Asher with a smug curiosity. The air of superiority this woman exuded was intense. She was clearly someone who either had little respect for the authority of others or deemed herself above it.

Unlike the other church members, her white robe was adorned with the finest golden trimmings, spun into intricate, flowing patterns as if a great fire had been frozen in gold upon her person, the flames immortalised in shimmering threads. In contrast to the ornate clothing was a simple golden circlet that sat perfectly around her brow. At its centre sat a single clear gem.

She was Constance, high priestess of the Church of the Shepherd, and oh, how Asher hated her.

She looked down at Asher with cold emerald eyes, her pointed ears flicking at the slightest sounds. 'I am sorry about your father,' she said solemnly. 'I did enjoy his company... for a time.' Although her words were soft and kind, the smirk forming across her lips betrayed her true feelings. 'I think he enjoyed my company too. It was the least I could do, considering how... lonely he was. You see, no one was there for him, and I was more than happy to be someone he could rely on.'

Asher gritted his teeth. It was true that, in recent years, an increasing number of acolytes from the Church of the Shepherd had visited the palace. Constance called often, arriving with dusty scrolls and fresh bouquets of beautiful green flowers. Whispers of relations began circulating among the upper nobility. Asher knew better, though. Even so long after his mother's death, his father was wholly and deeply committed to her. He would have crossed the Rimwall Mountains for her, to whatever lay beyond.

'You'll pay for this!' Asher snapped. He hated her with every fibre of his being. She had appeared soon after his mother's death, and he was sure she had encouraged the grieving king into the library to search for who knows what, fuelling his descent. Now, she was attacking his very home? Asher couldn't take it anymore.

Constance no longer attempted to hide her smile. With a wicked grin, she raised her arms and proclaimed, 'When I'm done, the people of this land will not remember who lived and who died. They will remember those who brought them their salvation.' She looked down at Asher and then at his father. 'And those who tried to keep them from it.' She gestured a black paw towards Asher. Gnarled black claws dragged him to his feet. 'Come now,' she beckoned, maintaining her wicked smile as she turned towards the grand doors. There was a shove at Asher's back, and he was moving, following the high priestess, surrounded by a pack of chuckling Shangari.

'Why are you doing this?' Asher demanded through gritted teeth.

'It's simple, really,' the priestess replied, not missing a step. 'Your father wanted us gone, but we weren't quite ready. Unfinished business, you see. It is a shame he had to die for his arrogance, but alas, nothing will stop us from achieving everlasting peace.'

Slaughtering my people seems far removed from peace. At least Henric's not here. Despite Asher's burning anger, he was relieved to see no signs of his younger brother in the palace. Henric was likely out in the wilds somewhere, hunting or fighting the locals. *Better than being here.*

They stepped out onto the courtyard of the main keep, an expansive lawn divided into four quadrants by two stone paths crossing at the centre. At the far end, the two massive doors that defended the palace were open, undamaged. It was as if the palace guards had simply invited the Shangari inside.

Someone must have let them in, Asher thought, deeply troubled at the implications.

He silenced the paranoia as his eyes landed on a mound of dead guards piled near the base of the inner wall. Their throats were a ragged mess of muscle and sinew. Beside them was a metal grate built into the floor, the bars twisted and pulled apart like a metallic maw. Hundreds of deep scratches scored the stone floor around it.

They did it. They actually came up.

Shangari inhabited the sewers of White Cliffe, but it was beyond Asher's wildest nightmare that they would ever surface en masse like this, especially not within the palace itself.

Asher stared at the bent metal bars anxiously. It must have taken a Shangari of titanic strength to contort the thick iron enough to pass through. He prayed to the ancients that he would never meet who or what had been capable of such brutal strength. More Shangari flanked the growing group. They led Asher through the gatehouse and onto the broad steps that led to the stone plaza below.

The smell hit him first, like a fist to the gut.

Asher retched as he breathed in the metallic scent that hung thick in the air. With each step, his boots made wet slaps in pools of dark blood. It was everywhere, trickling down the steps and accumulating in pools at the plaza below.

Crunch.

Asher turned, and his body went cold. A wave of nausea enveloped him. It took everything he had not to vomit at the gigantic heap of bodies amassed atop the stone steps. Not just guards but civilians and traders of all races lumped onto one another, their eyes wide, mouths agape as if screaming in a never-ending re-enactment of their final moments. It was as if Asher could hear their cries in his heart.

Slurp.

A group of Shangari stood before the pile, talking in their harsh, guttural language. Beside them lay blades, saws and other tools, all dripping with blood. Asher stared in horror as blood dripped from one Shangari's scabby lips, the padded foot of a Rabbethi protruding from its long mouth. It tore the flesh from the bone with ease and only ceased its gluttony to join the conversation. It brought its jagged teeth down on the bone with another mighty crunch.

Asher couldn't take it anymore. He averted his eyes, wishing to scrub the image from his mind, the nausea making his stomach churn.

'Animals,' Constance scoffed as an entourage of much taller acolytes formed a protective circle around Constance. Their stiff and straightened postures were clearly not that of Shangari in disguise, but of actual church acolytes. Their lack of any foul stench all but confirmed this.

They reached the bottom of the steps and crossed the market plaza. The stands were a mess of torn cloth and splintered wood, and bloody, half-eaten bodies littered the floor. Asher's tall ears could still detect the screams echoing from the far corners of the city, but the market plaza itself had fallen eerily silent.

The dying were now dead, and the victors feasted on their flesh.

They approached the statue at the plaza's centre, the water dark and murky at its base. One of the fish was dead and floating lifeless on the surface, a gnarled black arrow penetrating its flank, blood oozing from the wound. The other carp swam in frantic circles, unable to escape its dead brethren.

Constance pointed down at the water, not breaking her stride. Without a word, one of the acolytes reached into the water and grabbed the dead carp by the arrow.

'Put it down,' Asher demanded, Constance's arrogance becoming unbearable.

Constance stopped, released an exasperated sigh and turned. She bent forwards like a parent patronising a child, 'Darling, it's just a fish.' The gem within her circlet began to pulse a brilliant white. Then, suddenly, her eyes erupted into glorious, radiant flames.

Asher stumbled back, bumping into the acolyte guards. They were beautiful, yet utterly terrifying. It was like staring into the fire atop the Great Lighthouse, yet wrong. Asher couldn't explain it. The fires in her eyes were glorious, but the power behind them, the intent, filled his heart with a sinking woe.

'What are you—' A tremendous throbbing erupted throughout his skull. He doubled over in agonising pain, unable to hold Constance's stare any longer.

'It's easier this way,' she said, her voice becoming deep and ethereal. 'Now, sleep.' Her words echoed a thousand times in Asher's mind, each time crawling deeper into the back of his thoughts, pulling at everything they found along the way. Then it stopped, and a chronic wave of exhaustion surged over his body like a heavy blanket. He tried to fight it, glaring up at Constance in stern disobedience, but it was too much.

The last thing Asher remembered was Constance's chuckle, hounding him into the dark.

3

The Silver Coffin

Asher awoke with a groan as something large pressed against his stomach. Whatever it was, it must have been there a while, as his abdomen was cramping horribly from the prolonged pressure. A gentle bobbing churned his stomach and caused spikes of pain to pulsate through his head. Had he been out drinking again? It wouldn't be the first time he had awoken with no memory of the night's revelry. A chorus of marching footsteps, hushed whispers and guttural grunts filled his ears.

Wait...

A sea of dead, screaming faces flashed into his mind, their corpses piled atop a set of stone stairs before the palace. Asher's eyes snapped open. His breaths became short and panicked, his nose twitching uncontrollably. It hadn't been a nightmare. It had really happened. It was still happening.

There was a jolt as the weight pressing into his stomach shifted. He looked down, and, to his horror, realised he was slung over the heavy-plated shoulder of a titanic Medvedian. He tried to move his paws to push himself away, but they were bound tight behind his back, the thick rope rubbing the skin raw as he twisted. He was well and truly trapped. His mind began to race with the awful things these people might have in store for him. Would they feed him to the Shangari? No, they would have done that by now if that was the plan. They wanted him alive for some reason. With a few deep, steady breaths, he tried to calm himself. He began examining the Medvedian's armour to distract from the fear and gather as much information as possible, just as Harold had taught him.

The armour shimmered in the flickering torchlight and was etched with fine golden details. A white cape billowed behind, the golden threads dancing into Asher's eyes. He focused on the symbol at the cape's centre: two shepherd crooks crossed over a raging fire, the mark of the church's elite soldiers, the Knights of the Holy Fire. Asher's eyes widened. The knights were notorious for the brutal enforcement of the church's zealous ideals. They were ruthless and without mercy. The church's few holy wars throughout history had been swift and bloody. Although the religions that followed the ancients were left alone, no other faith dedicated to the Lighthouse had survived. The Shadri, a whole race of people, had been nearly wiped from the land because of their competing faith in the Shepherd. Their black-and-white striped faces were seldom seen anymore, with only pockets surviving in nomadic groups that steered clear of larger settlements. At least, that's what Asher's tutors had told him before he stopped attending his princely education.

Careful not to draw the knight's attention, he strenuously raised his head. It was dark and damp wherever they were, with only a few flickering torches for light, held by individuals within a sea of marching acolytes. Above, he found nothing but inky blackness. The air was cold, as if untouched by the Great Lighthouse's fire.

We must be under the city, he realised.

It reminded Asher of the dark, watery caves and abandoned burrows he and Henric explored as young kits, though they had never found one this cavernous.

'Be ready,' came a hushed voice.

Asher's eyes returned to the acolytes, landing on one following close behind his captor. The shadow of their hood hid their features, but from the softness of their voice, they were not Shangari.

'Who—' Asher began, but the acolyte abruptly slowed, disappearing into the sea of hoods.

'Ah, you're finally awake,' came a familiar yet all too unwelcome voice. Constance appeared at Asher's side, a smug look about her well-trimmed face. 'I must say, you disappoint me, Prince. You didn't put up much of a fight. Still, we got here without any more outbursts, didn't we?'

Asher scowled. He was about to reply when the procession came to a sudden stop, and two large brown paws lifted him off the knight's shoulders, dropping him onto the ground. Asher stood tall and stretched his back, relieved to no longer have solid plating pressing into his stomach. He then gasped as his eyes gazed upon the massive structure before him. A huge, circular arch, at least forty feet wide and the same in height, had been cut into the solid rock, its frame made of a strange black metal and completely smooth. A hive of activity hummed from the chamber beyond as Constance stepped through without a word. A paw shoved Asher forwards, not the heavy press of a Medvedian as he had expected, but a gentler touch.

'Stay calm,' whispered the same voice from before.

'Who are you?'

'That's not important; you just have to trust me. Now, quiet.'

Asher obeyed, and he and the mysterious figure entered the chamber. The knight and a few other acolytes followed quietly behind, bowing their heads in reverence as they passed beneath the foreboding arch.

The immediate area beyond was square and as wide as the arch itself. Numerous acolytes of varying races busied themselves around wooden tables covered in ancient scrolls and dusty manuscripts. They conferred with excited voices, pointing enthusiastically at the papers and nodding in agreement. Cracked murals covered the walls to Asher's left and right, though some were difficult to decipher. Time had taken its terrible toll on the artwork, and vast sections of the coloured figments had flaked away, revealing a metallic surface beneath.

These are old, Asher realised as he was guided deeper into the chamber. *This whole place is ancient.*

He followed the images as he walked. They depicted a strangely joyous scene for a space so ominous, full of smiling faces and warm colours. Rabbethi and Vulpen embraced in brotherly affection, and Medvedians shook paws with a Fenrathi. It had been a long time since Asher had seen a Fenrathi. Their long snouts, broad frames and bushy tails always reminded him of a larger, more predatory version of a Vulpen.

Asher stared in amazement as they walked past the final mural. It depicted a tremendous golden city at its centre, the paint shining as if emitting light. Buildings of all shapes and sizes covered the ancient artwork, and the windows and doors were filled with people kneeling towards the painting's centre, where a silhouette of a hooded figure stood, arms outstretched, a golden light outlining their frame. What looked like five golden stones, or possibly gems, were painted between the figure and the worshipping people.

It must be the Shepherd, Asher realised. Behind the figure rose a vast tower. At its peak shone painted rays of gold, the simple strokes contrasting brilliantly in front of a mysterious, vast circle of solid black.

Asher's tutors hadn't mentioned anything like this, though he hadn't actually finished his education. The structure was the Great Lighthouse, which was obvious, but he had only heard of the black circle at the back from Medvedians and the occasional Rabbethi trader who had ventured east and returned. They told of a shadow that rose and fell as the Great Lighthouse turned its radiance towards that part of Tamuz. The Medvedians called it Lochoten; the Fenrathi, Fearsgaile. Both races claimed divine ownership of the dark shape that lumbered across their sky. Asher and the rest of Tamuz, whose lands this dark stranger did not visit, simply called it the Wanderer.

It was all beautiful, but Asher was sure it was just religious imagery created by acolytes in ancient times to help spread their faith. The artist had done an excellent job of evoking emotions with this piece, and Asher could imagine waves of church acolytes passing by, their faith invigorated.

Stifled whimpers distracted Asher from the painting. He turned and found a group of citizens huddled back near the arch, their fine linen clothes torn and stained with blood.

They're no ordinary citizens, Asher realised, noting the expensive jewellery still on their persons. These were members of the high nobility, distant relations of his, ranging from young kits to the elderly. Their arms and legs were covered in cuts and bruises from where the church had dragged them into the city's darkest corner. Why were they here? To be used as hostages for ransom? No, that didn't make any sense. None of this made any sense.

The eldest, a scraggly matriarch with wiry white fur and long drooping ears, stood apart from the huddled group, conducting a quiet sermon. She held a long silver chain. The chain dangled from her paws, and at its end hung a small bow crossed with a single arrow, the symbol of Folka. The metal glinted in the flickering torchlight as she murmured words of prayer. Asher shifted, relieved to feel his own chain rub against the fur around his neck. The matriarch's eyes drifted across the group, the words trembling from her mouth.

'T-trust in Folka, my children. Her k-keen eye will guide us always.' She forced a thin, reassuring smile, but the congregation looked at her with nothing but sorrow and despair. Asher turned away, unable to bear the misery.

The group eventually came to a stop. Asher looked up and found the chamber had expanded, becoming vast and spherical. The floor before them fell away into a gaping abyss. A wide walkway extended precariously over the void, ending at a large glass sphere resting at the chamber's centre. It was beautiful, at least twenty feet tall, with black metal supports surrounding its transparent surface, as if grasped from below by colossal claws, the wrist fading into the inky blackness below. A glass door sat at the sphere's base, framed by the same dark metal. It was an incredible piece of ancient architecture, but it was what lay within that made Asher gasp. Standing tall and thick with swirling patterns that flowed like golden estuaries etched onto its surface was a coffin of pure silver. Four hefty clasps clung to its edges, two on each side, keeping the lid sealed tight.

What on Tamuz...?

A blood-curdling scream suddenly erupted around the chamber. Asher's eyes dropped to a figure writhing upon the metallic floor before the coffin. It was one of the nobles, a brown-furred Rabbethi, her face twisted in a contorted expression of unrelenting agony. Asher watched with a mixture of horror and awe as the woman fruitlessly swatted at a haze of swirling white fire churning about her body.

He snapped to Constance. 'What is that? What are you doing to her?' She paid him no mind as she observed the crying woman with an inquisitive smile. Asher returned to the Rabbethi woman. Terror and pain exuded from her wide eyes as she desperately searched the orb's interior. Her eyes met his, recognition sparking within. She shrieked a torrent of muffled pleas or possibly curses; Asher couldn't tell... until the last words.

'Help me...'

His heart sank as he stood there, helpless. The poor Rabbethi unleashed one last harrowing scream as she erupted into a fiery inferno, her fur, skin, muscles, and finally, her bones burning to ashes. Every layer of this poor woman was put on show, accompanied by a wail that would haunt Asher for the rest of his days. She had seen Asher, her prince, had begged for his help, and he had done nothing.

After the last terrible echo finished reverberating around the chamber, nothing remained of the poor woman but a small pile of unassuming ash. The fiery mist faded to nothing. Asher stared in disbelief, tears rolling down his cheeks. This was magic, *real* magic, and it was nothing like his mother's bedtime stories.

'Bring him to me,' Constance commanded, not taking her eyes off the orb. An acolyte shoved Asher towards her, and he stumbled to her side before being brought down hard onto his knees. 'Do you like it?' she asked with pride.

'What... what was that?'

'Why, this is my life's work!' she said in surprise, as if the answer was obvious. 'A search for those with ancient blood and an untainted fire. They will help me forge the world anew.'

Asher continued to stare at the ashes, wondering how many people had succumbed to such a horrific, painful death. How many had burned for this woman's zealotry?

'Your church is supposed to help people,' he breathed.

Constance smirked. 'Did you ever wonder what happened to all those criminals and homeless we take in? Did you honestly think we would waste our time trying to save the unsavable? The unworthy?' She let slip a patronising giggle. 'Oh, how naive the young are. Your father knew, of course. He would have done anything to see his precious queen again.'

Asher's eyes widened. 'What does this have to do with my mother?' he snapped, turning to face her.

Constance stepped in front of Asher, blocking his view of the orb. 'Oh, I may have told him our work would bring back those that had fallen. It's not my fault he thought I meant his whore, and who am I to correct a king?'

Asher's anger burned like an inferno in his heart. The binding around his paws tightened as he strained against it.

'Then why kill him?' he demanded through gritted teeth.

'It may come as a surprise, little prince, but that was never my intention. I had plans for the old fool. No, his bravado killed him. Luckily, you came along and, oh my yes.' She stared deep into his eyes, her smile growing. 'I've got a feeling you have just what I—'

'Asher!' came a sudden, recognisable cry from the entrance behind him.

Oh no, Asher thought. *No, no, no, no!*

Constance glanced up to see who had interrupted her mocking, but Asher knew who it was. 'Ah! The family's all here,' she said, her smug smile turning wicked.

Asher turned to find his beaten and bruised younger brother, Henric, stumbling towards them, surrounded by a pack of equally battered Shangari. His short brown fur was a ruffled mess, and he had a fresh cut running down the left side of his chin. His dark green cloak was torn, and his leather armour was caked in mud and blood.

'Where's father?' he pleaded as acolytes brought him down beside Asher, his voice equal parts anger and fear. 'What do these bastards want?'

Asher's eyes fell to the floor, unable to meet Henric's desperate gaze. 'Father's gone.'

'No...'

'In the orb with him,' Constance suddenly ordered. In a terrifying moment of motion, the knight lumbered forwards, gripped the back of Henric's collar with a giant paw and hoisted him off the ground.

'No!' Asher cried, fearful of what was to come.

Henric struggled against the Medvedian's overwhelming strength. 'Get off me, you bastard!'

'I'll go!'

The knight hesitated. He turned to Constance, but she was locked on Asher, eyebrow raised, head tilted, her expression that of sinister contemplation. 'Such an honourable gesture, my young prince.' She addressed the knight, 'Retrieve the *noble* prince.' With a nod, the knight dropped Henric with a thud against the metal walkway.

Asher's eyes met Henric's, and all Asher could muster as tears filled his eyes were the breathless words, 'I'm sorry.'

The knight grabbed Asher from behind, lifting him off the ground with ease. He carried Asher down the narrow walkway, opened the orb door and threw him inside. Asher tumbled through the pile of ashes, which erupted in a plume of choking dust. Spluttering, he opened his eyes and gazed out of the glass door. Everyone beyond was holding their collective breaths. Even the acolytes who had ignored the woman before had quietened their heated debates and now watched anxiously. Asher's nose twitched. His heart was thumping. Filled with regret and terror, he waited for the fire, for the searing pain that was sure to come.

But nothing happened. Asher just lay there, untouched by the white fire that had burned the others. There was a warmth in the air, a hum as if the area around the coffin was vibrating with energy, but there was no mist, no burning fire that had incinerated the poor Rabbethi woman before him. He raised his head, turning to the coffin. It loomed over him, bearing down with an ominous presence. And yet... something in his chest urged him closer.

'He is ancient-touched!' came Constance's muffled cry from beyond the glass door. She raised her robed arms high and turned to the acolytes around her, who erupted in cheers and yelps as all raised their paws in celebration.

Asher suddenly felt a desperate urge to leave the orb, worried that whatever force present could change its mind and decide to roast him anyway. He rose and approached the glass door, pushing down the handle with his knee. He stumbled out, falling heavily onto the walkway. As soon as he hit the metal, a thick paw grabbed his back, and he was once again weightless.

'What now, your holiness?' asked the knight as he returned to Constance's side, dropping Asher at her feet.

But Constance was gone, lost in a frantic display of plotting and calculating, mumbling to herself as her eyes darted back and forth. 'We just need the bow, and we'll be one step closer. Yes... Then there's the mask and the fist...' She spun and gestured to someone back towards the entrance.

Slow, heavy footsteps echoed throughout the chamber, accompanied by the strange sound of objects clacking together. They grew louder until Asher looked up and found a monstrous Shangari standing beside him, far taller and much broader than any he had ever seen. His fur was tar black and wiry, his skin mangled with old and new scars. Two long, serrated teeth descended from the end of his upper jaw, and one of his sinister red eyes was coloured a milky white. His chest was bare, except for two belts crossing his chest and over his shoulders. They were lined with huge rusty daggers specked with dried blood. A thick black rope around his waist held up torn, grey shorts and was decorated with skulls that clattered together like a horrifying wind chime. Asher had heard stories of this Shangari when he was a kit, stories intended to stop him from venturing too far into the woods and to make sure he went to bed at the proper time, lest he be fed to this monster. This was Nin-Kilim, the high chieftain of the most brutal and infamous Shangari clan, the Blood Tooths —a nightmare come to life.

The titanic Shangari trudged past Asher, not paying him the slightest mind, his long, thick tail snaking across the floor behind him. For a Shangari, Nin-Kilim was huge and stood nearly as tall as Constance despite his hunched posture.

She stood straighter as he approached, lifting her nose to maintain a facade of superiority. 'I need you to gather more of your men,' Constance ordered, unblinking. 'Tell them to prepare their vessels.'

Nin-Kilim peered at her for a time as if considering whether to obey her or eat her.

Constance held his gaze. 'There will be corpses to feast upon,' she added, tilting her nose a little higher.

Nin-Kilim eventually made a sound resembling a grunt of approval and turned before trudging back towards the chamber entrance.

After the last echoing footstep had faded and the lingering oppressive air had ebbed away, Constance released a held breath. Composing herself, she turned to Henric, malicious intent in her eyes. 'Now, I'm afraid we don't need a—'

'You're sick,' Asher spat, interrupting whatever smug mocking she was about to spew. 'Evil.'

'Evil? Don't talk to me about evil, boy!' she exclaimed, her voice rising in a snarl. 'Evil is the senseless war between the Fenrathi and Medvedians, and the countless Ruadrae sacrificed beneath the Wanderer! Evil are the thugs and bandits that roam the roads, preying on anyone they can find!' Her distressed voice began to echo around the chamber as her canine fangs revealed themselves from under her curling lip. 'Evil are those that take innocent children from their mothers!' Constance took a deep breath, adjusting her robe. 'This world is evil, and its people cannot be trusted with their own freedom. Nothing but a holy paw can guide them towards peace and prosperity. As it was before.' Before Asher could respond, she turned to the acolyte at his back. 'You there, bring the prince to his feet.'

There was no response.

Constance turned slowly to the acolyte, her eyebrow raised. 'I gave you an order,' she spat.

Silence.

Constance's eye twitched as she struggled to maintain her composure. She gestured to the knight beside her, who nodded and made for the acolyte.

'Hold your breath,' whispered a voice into one of Asher's tall ears. He didn't have time to register the words before the acolyte stepped between him and the approaching Medvedian. A large red tail unfurled as they pulled a small vial of black liquid from their sleeve and threw it to the ground. It smashed, releasing a plume of choking black smoke that filled the entire walkway. Cries of panic and racked coughing erupted all around.

'Henric!' Asher cried, inhaling the darkened smog. Henric was the only family he had left; he had to save him. His lungs burned as he began coughing up thick wads of soot-clogged saliva.

'Don't let them escape!' came Constance's rasping cry, followed by a hoarse coughing fit. She was close, and Asher's focus shifted. If he could get to her, maybe he could end all this. He could stop her from hurting any more innocent people. Something pressed into his back. Looking over his shoulder, he saw a slender black-furred paw reaching through the smoke and grasping his beige tunic.

'Ready?'

Without a chance to reply, the paw threw Asher through the air, sending him spinning out of the black smoke. He closed his eyes, expecting to collide hard against the metal walkway.

But the impact didn't come.

Wind began coursing through his fur, and he opened his eyes. To his horror, he found himself staring at the underside of the walkway, watching as it grew smaller and smaller, the light from the chamber above becoming faint and distant. A thunderous sound of surging water grew with intensity, filling his ears until it was utterly deafening.

'Henric!' he screamed as the darkness enveloped him.

4

Blood and Leaves

Gentle waves crashed against an unseen shore as sand shifted beneath Asher's back. A fire crackled nearby, the flames warming his face. It was peaceful and reminded him of when he and Henric would sneak out of the city to explore the many rock pools of the jagged coastline. Their mother would always get so frustrated when she found out.

'It's dangerous out there, my darlings,' she would say, her white ears flopping as she shook her head. 'The shadows are home to monsters.' The boys would always apologise profusely, only to sneak out the following night.

'Henric!' Asher cried, bolting upright. His nose twitched wildly as his eyes darted around the campfire, searching for his brother, praying he'd find him in a peaceful slumber nearby. He wasn't there. Instead, he found a red-furred Vulpen woman leaning back against a large piece of driftwood, her bushy red tail flicking lazily by her side. Her long snout protruded from under a black hood, revealing white fur that ran from under her jaw, down her chest and under her black leather armour. Asher could feel her intense, dark brown eyes staring at him through the flames.

'I suggest you calm down,' she ordered, her words echoing around them. 'Unless you want Shangari scouts to find you?'

Asher recognised her voice. She was the acolyte from the city, the one who had thrown the smoke vial and then thrown him into the chasm. Asher watched the woman warily through the fire, unsure what to make of her. Judging from her actions under the city, she was clearly no friend of Constance or the church. That was good enough to trust her for now, he decided.

He took a deep breath and took in his new surroundings. Wet rock in all around reflected the campfire's flickering light as fine sand shifted between his fingers. Unseen waves lapped against a nearby shore. The mysterious Vulpen began sharpening a curved sword with a whetstone, her black paw gliding over the blade's edge with a satisfying ring. Two of her slender fingers glinted with each motion of her arm, silver rings shimmering in the firelight.

'How long have I been out?' Asher eventually asked.

'Few hours.'

There was an awkward silence as Asher waited, expecting something more, but the woman said nothing and continued her work.

'Where's my brother?' Asher asked, fearing the worst.

The woman didn't reply, and Asher gritted his teeth, suddenly fearing the worst.

Whatever the answer, he had to know; he needed to know. '*Where* is my brother!'

The stranger sighed, laid her sword down and pulled back her hood to reveal the rest of her Vulpen features. Her face was hard and sharp and had the look of someone already dealing with a mountain of bullshit. A large nick was missing from her left ear, and she appeared to be a few years Asher's senior.

'I couldn't save your brother.' Although her words were cold and firm, they couldn't hide her defeated tone. She grabbed her sword and rose quickly, clearly having nothing more to say on the matter. Her black cloak fluttered to reveal a crimson lining. 'We need to move. Shangari raiders will be heading out soon to secure the rest of the kingdom.' She sheathed her sword at her hip and marched into the darkness, the sand shifting beneath her feet.

Asher rose quickly, marching to follow her. 'What do you mean you couldn't save him? Why not?' He found her standing at the cave entrance.

'I could only save one of you.' Her eyes remained fixed on the darkness beyond the cave. 'After what I saw in that orb thing, getting you out of the city became the priority. So count yourself lucky.'

'Lucky? You're calling me lucky? My father is dead, who knows what they're doing to my brother, and my people are overrun with Shangari and fanatics!' Asher's nose furiously twitched as he stepped before the Vulpen, his eyes narrowing on her.

'You're alive. That's something,' she said, unmoving.

'Well, I shouldn't be! You should have left me and saved Henric.'

The Vulpen said nothing and returned to the shadows outside the cave. Asher lowered his eyes with a sigh. He didn't have the energy to fight, and in truth, he was thankful to be alive.

He turned to the darkness as a cool breeze rolled across the sand. It coursed through his fur, chilling him. His eyes quickly adjusted to the shadows, and a narrow sandy beach materialised before him, stretching away before fading back into blackness at the edge of his vision. To his right rose a small cliff with a few hardy grasses clinging for dear life.

'Let's go,' the Vulpen said, setting off at a startling pace and forcing Asher to jog to catch up. They hurriedly marched along the shore, the mysterious woman leading the way. After a time, she turned towards a steep slope that climbed the rocky cliff, providing a much easier way of ascension. With grace and agility, she sprang from one large rock to the next, climbing the cliff in seconds. Asher took a more cautious approach, his body aching from the beating he had received the previous day. He slowly reached the summit and pulled himself to his feet. The Vulpen wasn't staring at him impatiently, as he had thought she would be, but with a look of dismay at what lay behind him.

'What is it?' Asher asked, worried. He turned, and his heart sank. Across a small bay and beyond several fields, White Cliffe City was alight with activity. Torches were racing up and down the city walls as horns sounded, their echoes filling the night air. Fires burned as screams whispered along the wind.

'They've taken the city,' she said coldly.

Asher stared in a wrathful silence as he watched the torchlights dance across the city walls. The burning buildings beyond illuminated the night sky in a sinister orange glow. His paws formed into tight fists as he thought of the Shangari inside, killing and devouring his people with malicious pleasure. His heart tightened as he thought of Constance, the one who let it all happen.

'We need to get to King's Wood,' the agent said, snapping Asher from his vengeful trance. 'I have friends waiting there.' She turned and began making her way inland, jogging through a field of tall grass and small shrubs.

'Wait!' Asher yelled, following after. 'You still haven't told me who you are!'

'My name's Cara,' the Vulpen called between breaths. 'And I'll tell you everything once we get to the forest.' They ran through the open fields under the light of a thousand stars, the glow of the city burning in the distance. Eventually, they reached a wide dirt road bordered by an old stone wall.

Asher stopped.

'What's wrong?' Cara asked, paws on the stone, ready to leap over.

Asher didn't respond. His ears were trained on something approaching from the city, something sounding like the rumble of a thunderstorm, rolling toward them with haste.

'Get down,' he snapped, dropping below the stone wall.

Cara followed, and after a few tense moments, the ground began to shake as the recognisable sound of galloping hooves grew louder and louder. A rider in black came to a sudden halt in a cloud of dust and dirt before Asher and Cara, their horse neighing in protest.

Cara slowly gripped the hilt of her sword as Asher held his breath. He peered through a hole in the wall, nose twitching. No distinguishable features protruded from under the rider's hooded cloak, but Asher swore he could hear rapid inhales through an unseen nose. The rider was sniffing, stalking, hunting. They pulled on the reins, and the steed moved in erratic circles. As the rider turned, Asher caught a glimpse of a sinister-looking crossbow strapped to their back. Whoever this stranger was, he had the distinct impression that they weren't friendly. Asher's instincts told him to stay low and quiet, to make himself as small as possible. The mysterious rider was close. All they needed to do was lean over the wall, and they would find Asher. Cara began to unsheathe her sword silently.

Without warning, the stranger kicked the horse's flank, taking off at startling speed, following the road south, and disappearing into shadow. The thundering hooves eventually grew quiet. All that remained were the chirping of crickets and a gentle breeze rolling through the grass. Several tense moments passed before Cara stood.

‘I don’t know who that was, but they weren’t Shangari,’ she said, peering into the shadows. ‘The smell wasn’t right.’

‘They weren’t Rabbethi either,’ Asher added. ‘We don’t use crossbows. They’re difficult to jump with.’

Cara frowned. ‘We need to be careful.’ With a swift motion, she was over the wall and racing across the road.

Asher followed, his muscles complaining at their sudden use. They leapt over the next wall and continued over the grassy fields towards the sentinel of thick trees.

‘So where are your friends?’ he asked as they eventually reached the treeline.

Cara raised a finger to her lips, ordering silence. Asher obeyed and listened. A moment passed, and then he heard it, the clashing of swords, the faint screams of the dying, the sound of battle resonating deep within the forest’s groaning blackness.

‘We’ve got to move,’ Cara said, frowning. ‘Now!’ They took off, sprinting into the forest and the darkness beyond.

***

Trees whipped past in a blur of reaching shadows as Asher and Cara raced towards the sound of death. Their path weaved through the forest like a snake. Asher couldn’t help but marvel at how gracefully Cara avoided the rocks and branches that would have tripped the most experienced hunter. He too showed an aptitude for navigating the maze of trees despite the crippling lack of light. Long days he had spent assisting the woodcutters and herbalists, gathering herbs and berries and dealing with dangerous boars or murderous packs of wild dogs.

Asher always declined their modest payments, and the villagers would praise him for his noble charity, not knowing his true identity as their prince.

An orange glow grew bright before them as a stone structure began to take shape between the trees, illuminated by flickering torchlight. They burst out of the trees into a wide-open clearing. Standing before a tall but crumbling stone tower was a titan of a Medvedian, clad in heavy-plated armour and a white cape that billowed behind him. Trimmed with golden threads, the image of two shepherd's crooks crossed over a fire flashed in the breeze. Asher's eyes went wide.

'The knight from the city...,' he breathed as panic took root.

Cara didn't respond. She was staring in horror at what the knight held aloft in one huge paw. Asher followed her gaze and found a much leaner figure suspended off the ground, thick fingers wrapped around its throat. They struggled uselessly against the Medvedian's monstrous grip as blood dripped from under their dark leather armour, their bushy red tail swishing erratically from under their black cloak.

With a wicked grin, the knight raised a colossal greatsword and jammed it through the Vulpen's abdomen. There was a short, sharp scream, and the Vulpen went limp. The knight's grin grew. He wrenched the blade free and watched as a torrent of blood poured from the gaping hole it left behind, then threw the lifeless body to the floor. He turned to Asher and Cara.

Asher then noticed the others.

All about the clearing were the mangled remains of numerous hooded Vulpen; each caked in blood, their eyes wide with fear, dead. His eyes snapped to the knight, who was now lumbering towards them.

'What do we do?' Asher asked, not taking his eyes off the knight.

No response.

'Cara?'

Her eyes were locked on the knight. Her fangs glinted in the torchlight as a deep snarl emanated from her throat. Asher turned back to the knight, unsure who he should be more afraid of. The Medvedian was close now. Just a few more steps, and he would be on them.

'Cara...?'

Cara moved faster than anything Asher had seen before. She stepped into the knight's space, drew her long, curved sword from her hip and sliced at the Medvedian's flank. Startled, the knight stepped back, glancing down to inspect the damage. Cara pressed the attack. She assaulted the other side, her blade connecting with the knight's armour, but harmlessly sliding against the metallic surface. He stumbled back a couple more paces and stared down at the Vulpen, fury spreading across his round face. Gritting his huge teeth, he swung his greatsword down. Cara nimbly stepped aside, and the massive blade narrowly skimmed her ear, colliding with the ground in an explosion of dirt and leaves. A second passed before a second mighty thud echoed in the clearing. Confused, the knight looked down to find his chest piece in the dirt beside his blade, the straps cleanly cut. Without missing a beat, Cara planted a foot into the soft soil, leapt forwards, and brought her elbow square into the knight's sternum. A sickening crack echoed about the clearing, and he released his sword, the momentum sending him stumbling backwards.

'You will pay for your heresy!' he roared, his words thunderous and full of spite.

Cara continued her assault, her eyes focused like a hawk. Quick as lightning, she stabbed at the Medvedian's exposed gut. He swatted the attack away and brought a massive fist across her cheek. It connected. She fell to the ground with a heavy thud, her eyes closing. With an unimpressed scoff, the Medvedian heaved a massive section of the broken tower above his head and loomed over the unconscious Cara, grinning with sinister intent. Asher knew he should do something, anything, to help, but his muscles refused to move. His stomach became a sinking well of despair and guilt. His eyes darted from Cara to the knight, then to the wall of trees surrounding them. Once again, his instincts pleaded with him to run, to stay small and unnoticed.

C'mon, you coward, he pleaded to himself. *Do something...*

The knight dropped the stone.

Against every fibre in Asher's being begging him to stay silent, he took a deep breath and screamed, 'Cara!'

Her eyes sprang open, and she rolled just as the stone collided with the forest floor. The ground shook under Asher's feet, the echoing boom resonating throughout the forest. A wave of relief washed over him as he watched Cara grab her sword and leap to her feet. The knight glared at Asher in fury, forcing Asher to step backwards instinctively.

Small rocks and pebbles began to rain down from the old tower, dislodged by the sudden quake. Asher pulled himself away from the knight's stare, and his eyes climbed to the tower's peak, watching it sway like a drunken sailor.

'The tower!' he cried, praying Cara would understand.

She nodded, not taking her eyes off the knight. Charging forwards once more, she thrust her sword into the Medvedian's huge abdomen. The knight scoffed again and made to slap the blade away, but as his paw reached Cara's, she paused. The mammoth fist sailed harmlessly between them, and she lunged again. This time, the blade found its mark, punching deep into the knight's exposed stomach. The knight roared in pain. Cara pushed with all her might, her powerful legs driving him back until he collided with the tower with a crash.

Cara wrenched the blade from the knight's stomach. Blood spurted from the wound, and the giant Medvedian fell to his knees, reaching to his stomach with both paws in an attempt to ease the flow. Cara stood over him, a look of hatred and disgust twisting her face. He stared up at her in defiance, his beady black eyes showing no sign of weakness or fear. Without a second thought, she ripped the blade across his thick, muscular throat. Blood flowed from the knight's neck, but his eyes didn't shift. They remained fixed on Cara in spiteful rage. There was a quiet pause as the forest held its breath, the stone above groaning as larger and larger stones thudded to the ground around them.

Then it went.

The sound of cracking and tumbling rocks thundered across the treetops as huge blocks began to rain down upon the pair. Cara hurried away, sprinting towards Asher. The tower crashed down upon the scowling Medvedian knight, and he was gone, buried under a mountain of carved, ancient stones. It was over in seconds. After the last pebble had rolled and the dust had cleared, an eerie stillness permeated the clearing, settling on the dead that littered the forest floor.

'Are you hurt?' Asher whispered as he stared at the rubble.

'I'm fine,' the exhausted Vulpen replied between heavy breaths. 'But we need to go. This place will be crawling with Shangari soon.'

Asher nodded, and they hurried across the clearing, passing the fallen tower. He glanced down at the bodies. They were all Vulpen, dressed similarly to Cara, all dead. He grimaced at the gruesome, bloody holes left behind by the knight's sword, lamenting as the fresh, nightmarish scene burned itself into his memory. A wooden bow and a quiver half full of arrows lay next to one of the bodies.

I'm so sorry, he thought as he scooped up the weapon and continued forwards. With a last sorrowful glance at her fallen friends, Cara dashed into the thick tree line. Asher followed close behind.

They ran over roots and under branches, through thorny bushes and past mossy boulders as fast as their battered bodies would carry them. It felt like an eternity before they eventually stopped. Asher doubled over, panting. He had never run so fast nor for so long in his life. Rabbethi were excellent sprinters, but their legs were not built for long distances, and his body was all but spent. He looked at Cara. Her tense shoulders rose and fell as rhythmic breaths emanated from deep within her chest.

'Are you oka—'

She exploded, drawing her sword and slashing with reckless abandon at a nearby tree. Large chunks of hacked bark sprayed in all directions as Cara stifled screams of rage, the poor, defenceless tree crumbling under her fury. Asher stepped back, remaining silent. Whatever this woman was going through, he was not going to get in the middle of it.

After a time, she slowed, her swings becoming lethargic. Eventually, she became still. Her long blade came to rest by her side as her breaths returned to their deep, rhythmic flow. Silence returned to the forest.

Those other Vulpen must have meant a lot to her.

He wanted to let her know; he too was in pain; he knew how she felt. "I'm sorry for your loss" was what people typically said in situations like this, but he couldn't bring himself to do it. There were no words for moments like this.

With a final sigh, Cara sheathed her sword, pulled her hood over her head and adjusted the straps on her leather armour. Without a word, she began walking away.

'Where are you going?' Asher called, her sudden movement catching him off guard. 'We need to go back and stop Constance!'

Cara spun, a stern look on her face. 'Listen, princeling, I know you're in pain and want nothing more than revenge, but there's a whole army of fanatics and Shangari between you and that bitch.' She began pacing, lost in her own spoken thoughts. 'Even worse, she's somehow managed to unite the Shangari clans, though it's doubtful she's united all of them. The clans on the outer rim are fanatical in their own right. They wouldn't dare bow to someone as godless as Nin-Kilim, and *definitely* not Constance.' She snapped back to Asher, her anger flaring again, renewed and burning. He jumped back. 'Not that I'd expect you to know much about Shangari, spending your days in luxury behind your palace walls!'

Asher couldn't help but cower as her fangs slowly emerged from under her curling lip. He was aware of the Shangari clans hiding beneath the cities of Tamuz. He knew all too well that they fought for control over the cities' underbellies, led by brutal and vicious warlords. However, he wasn't about to correct the angry predator on what he did and did not know.

Cara stepped forwards with a growl. 'You're not the only one who's lost people because of her, you know.'

Asher's back collided with a tree, a deep instinctual fear coursing through him.

Something then gave in Cara's glare, and with a deep sigh, she calmed her breathing, her fangs receding under her lip. 'Listen, we can't go back. You must know that, right?'

Asher nodded slowly, though he didn't want to admit it

'But I know someone who can help, someone with as much hatred for Constance as any of us.'

'Who?' Asher asked as his twitching nose began to calm.

'Tessina of Terravulpa. My queen.'

5

The Golden Leap

Asher and Cara moved through the midnight forest in silence, the peaceful quiet interrupted only by the nocturnal creatures rustling in the undergrowth. Asher's attention snapped to any sound that echoed among the trees. He was never usually this skittish within the deep woods, but his nerves were fried. Not to mention, it wasn't in a Rabbethi's nature to venture outside once the Great Lighthouse had turned its back. Instincts begged at him to dive for cover and wait for the protection of the morning light. He ignored it and pushed on.

After a time of careful marching and a few stumbling missteps, the pair entered a small clearing surrounded by a ring of tall trees. Cara quickly patrolled the area before gathering a pile of dead sticks and dried leaves, which she deposited in the centre. She drew the knife from her chest piece and a whetstone from the pouch at her side. With the finesse of someone accustomed to camping in the wilds, she slid the stone across the blade's edge, igniting the crisp foliage in a flash of sparks. The surrounding trees were instantly bathed in a warming glow. Without a word, Cara gathered and prepared a small meal consisting of wriggling grubs and woodland berries, of which Asher could only stomach the berries. They ate in awkward silence, with nothing but the sound of a crackling fire filling the space around them.

After the meal, the Vulpen warrior positioned herself under a large tree and pressed her back against its base, unhooking her scabbard from her belt and resting it by her side. Asher arranged himself as close to the flames as possible without burning himself. He was jealous of Cara and her warm, bushy tail, which she had wrapped around herself like a thick woollen blanket. How the Vulpen could so easily hide their tails within their clothing was a complete mystery to him, as was why any Vulpen would want to. His tail, by comparison, was small, ball-shaped and not much to brag about under his tunic.

'What was that thing on Constance's head?' he asked, gathering his courage and plucking one of the many questions that swirled in his mind.

'It's one of the relics,' Cara replied, not opening her eyes while she fiddled with the rings on her fingers. 'A tool used by the ancients in the old days.'

Asher's thoughts flashed back to the fires burning within Constance's eyes. 'Is it magic?'

'Not sure. It has something to do with the ancients and some stones. Julius would be the one to talk to about that. You'll meet him in Ignimarum.'

That only served to add more questions to Asher's already overflowing mind. 'Why were you with the church the day they attacked?' he asked, trying to get to an answer he could understand.

'I infiltrated their ranks to keep an eye on them, Constance specifically.'

Asher sat up and looked at her through the fire, his curiosity no longer allowing him to rest in peace. 'Why?'

'I don't know, but as soon as—'

'Did you know about the killings?' Asher blurted, catching Cara by surprise. 'About those people being burned alive in that orb thing?'

There was a pause before Cara sighed. 'Yes.'

Asher fell silent, frustration rising.

'What's wrong?' she asked, opening one eye.

'You knew and didn't do anything? All those innocent folk dead, and you just watched?' He stared at her with an intensity that cut through the campfire flames.

She opened the other eye. 'I was told not to interfere. Acting might have provoked Constance to attack Terravulpa. The Vulpen Queendom doesn't have the strength to take on the church alone, and the other kingdoms have their own problems to deal with.'

'My father would have put a stop to it!' Asher blurted. Though the words left his mouth with conviction, he didn't believe them. His stare dropped from the Vulpen to the fire, a wave of defeat and sorrow washing over him.

'Oh please,' she said, rolling her eyes as frustration carried her words. 'Your father knew what they were doing. He—' She cut herself off, seeming to notice Asher's lack of conviction. 'From what I had gathered, he cut ties with the church as soon as he discovered they were lying to him. The church attacked when he tried to banish them from the city.' She paused for a moment, her eyes growing softer. 'He did the right thing in the end.'

Asher unclenched his fists and met Cara's gaze. 'Thank you,' he said with a sigh.

She nodded thoughtfully. 'I'm sorry I couldn't save your brother.'

Asher rested his head back down behind what remained of the fire. 'I'm sorry about your friends.' With that, he turned and closed his eyes, ensuring the brave Vulpen agent of Terravulpa couldn't see the tears rolling down his soft, white cheeks.

***

As the first light stretched over the treetops like golden fingers. The birds of the forest stirred from their slumber and began singing cheerful melodies, much to the annoyance of an exhausted Asher, who reluctantly opened his eyes, expecting to see morning rays caressing the leafy canopy above. Instead, he found a red snout grinning down at him, wet black nostrils sniffing the air inches above his face.

'Gooooood morning, sleepy ears!' yelled the stranger in an all too pleasant tone. Asher rolled away in a fluster and jumped to his feet, raising his fists against this cheery attacker. 'Well, aren't you the feisty one? she said with a grin. 'And cute as a button, too!'

Standing before Asher, paw on hip, was a short Vulpen woman, a broad smile across her red-furred snout. Her face had a roundness to it and was gentle in its features. She looked to be of a similar age to Asher, and, despite her sudden and alarming invasion of his personal space, her endearing smile and cheerful demeanour were already making her more pleasant to be around than the cold, calculating Cara. The woman winked and he stared at her, bewildered.

'That's enough, Lucilla,' came Cara's voice across the clearing. 'I've told you before, an agent of the queen should not be so... brash.'

Asher noticed the woman was wearing the same dark leather armour as Cara, but without the black hooded cloak clasped at the shoulders. Where Cara wielded a long curved sword sheathed at her side, Lucilla had no such weapon. Instead, about her waist and chest were sheathed a wide array of small knives, all in different styles and likely possessing distinct, sinister purposes. Asher struggled to imagine what a friendly face would do with such gruesome-looking instruments of death.

'I'm not being *brash*, Cara. I'm being *friendly*. Maybe you should try it sometime?' the playful Vulpen said, sticking her tongue out. Cara shook her head disapprovingly and returned to her equipment. Lucilla returned to Asher, her bright blue eyes looking him up and down. 'I've never met a member of Rabbethi royalty before...' She stepped towards him and curtsied, pretending to pinch the corners of an imaginary dress. The smile on her face grew into a tremendous grin. 'I'm Luce, Your Highness. A pleasure to meet you.'

Entirely and utterly defeated by the charm of the small, bubbly Vulpen, Asher lowered his fists. 'Nice to meet you, Luce,' he said, unable to control the smile creeping across his face. 'But I'm not a king. My father is the—'

'Eh?' Luce exclaimed. She snapped to Cara, who was fastening her sword scabbard to her belt. 'You told me you were going to save the king! Did you grab the wrong guy, Cara?'

'No!' Cara snapped, looking up from her belt straps. 'This is Prince Asher. He just lost his father, the former king, making *him* the new king. Have some tact, for Thena's sake.'

The smile dropped from Asher's face. He could no longer fool himself that it had all been a nightmare, that his father was still alive, and the church's attack hadn't happened. The memory of his father's body flashed before his eyes, and he could feel the tears fighting their way to the corners of his eyes.

'Everything alright?'Luce asked, a look of genuine concern across her face.

'I'm okay,' he said, his go-to phrase for when he was most definitely not okay. He also reserved it for when he didn't want to be a burden, seen as weak, or when he needed to be a rock for someone else. An excuse for his not-so-happy demeanour usually accompanied it. "I'm just tired", was a favourite of his. He wondered if those around him worried about his sleep, considering how often he was "tired".

A weight pressed into his chest as slender arms wrapped around his torso. Luce had thrown herself around him in a tight embrace. 'I'm sorry for your loss, Ash,' she said softly. 'I lost some people too, last night in the forest.'

Her head rested against his chest, and he could feel the warmth of her fur pressing into his own, the faint scent of exotic orchids rising into his twitching nostrils. He was utterly taken aback. This complete stranger, someone who had just been told he was a king, had already given him a nickname and was showing him more kindness and affection than he had received in months. He would have thought most people would keep their distance after learning of his royal lineage, but not this woman. The relaxed air was refreshing. Almost instinctively, he wrapped his arms around her.

'We'll protect each other from now on, okay?' she said as they parted, a playful smile beneath her kind eyes.

'Okay,' he said with a forced smile of his own.

'Let's move,' Cara called, stomping out the campfire's dying embers.

***

The light cascaded through the trees like a golden curtain, basking the forest in a warming glow. The early morning dew was evaporating, creating a mystical fog that hung in the air like a hot breath on a cold day. At times like this, Asher remembered why he loved the woods. He adored the chaos of the city, but when he needed to get away and be alone with his thoughts, the forest was always there for him, letting him exist without any expectations.

Luce vanished regularly into the mist like a spectre to ensure the path ahead was clear. She would then reappear silently beside Asher, making him jump every time, much to the giggling delight of the petite Vulpen.

It was early afternoon when they broke the tree line. They found themselves standing at the summit of a grassy hill, the view before them a picturesque scene of rural quaintness. The morning fog had dissipated entirely, and above them, the sky was a vibrant blue. It stretched to the vast ocean below, separated by a thin line that marked the horizon. Tall grass covered the hillside, swaying in the wind. Asher's ears danced as the breeze swirled around him, and he took a deep breath, the cool air rushing up his nose.

He turned to Cara. Her eyes were closed, snout raised to catch the wind. The black hood of her uniform billowed behind her, revealing her short, pointed ears, the breeze coursing through her red fur. It was the first time Asher had seen her look peaceful.

'Smells like a fresh catch,' she said with an eagerness that failed to hide her hunger.

Asher looked towards the base of the hill, finding a collection of small thatched cottages extending towards the sea, ending at a wide cove. The curved wooden arms of a dock stretched around a good portion of the cove's width, with numerous boats and dinghies moored along its edge. Several more bobbed gently deeper in the cove. Some were unloading their freshly caught produce onto the docks, though how Cara was able to sniff that out from so far away was beyond Asher.

He sniffed the air but could only detect her heavy musk and a salty brine.

'I don't see a merchant ship,' Luce said as she squinted towards the docks.

Cara opened her eyes and peered at the quiet village. 'Neither do I. We'll have to ask around, see if any are passing through soon.' She turned to Asher and Luce. 'I think it best we remain quiet about what happened in the capital. We have a better chance of escaping Constance if we don't draw attention to ourselves.'

'But these people need to know!' Asher protested, his chest tightening at the thought of leaving more people to suffer.

'We can't save them if we can't get to my queen,' Cara snarled. 'Starting a panic will lead Constance right to us.'

Asher turned to Luce, who merely shrugged. 'They'll find out sooner or later, Ash. Why worry them now?'

Asher's eyes fell on the village below and the tiny figures scurrying about the dock. 'Fine.'

Cara nodded and set off, wading through the grass towards the dirt road at the bottom of the hill. Luce skipped down, a faint giggle trailing behind her as she picked up speed. Asher ambled, gliding his paws across the tips of the tall grass, thinking about the people of the village before him and the storm of teeth and daggers that would eventually be heading their way.

Starting a panic would draw Constance's attention, he thought quietly, though it pained him to agree with the Vulpen agent. Cara's words sounded like solid reasoning, and he couldn't deny the logic. That didn't stop the guilt from wrapping tight around his heart.

A crumbling stone wall at the hill's base kept the ocean of grass from flooding onto the dirt path beyond. Luce reached the wall first and, with little effort, vaulted over the old stones, landing with a silent flourish on the path beyond. Asher and Cara both mounted over with less showmanship. They landed with light thuds, small clouds of dirt rising from under their boots.

Before them rose a wooden arch carved with intricate patterns. Finely crafted figures of fish, whales and other marine creatures swirled around each other in a solid piece of beautiful carpentry. Asher knew it well. He had spent many a night drinking and brawling with the locals of this town, only to wake up the next day on the beach, covered in vomit and several gold coins poorer. This was the village of Saewic, and it had been a good while since his last visit.

A strange rumble caught his attention, and he peered at the base of the wooden arch. A guard lay slumped on the ground, his back against the wood, snoring heavily. His armour was typical of a White Cliffe City guard, and his standard glaive lay flat among the tufts of grass creeping under the stone wall. His helmet rested lazily on his head, pressing his long ears flat against his back.

Luce rushed over, grabbed a few strands of grass from the roadside, and began placing them delicately into the guard's drooling mouth. 'Must be boring,' she remarked as she put another blade between his protruding front teeth, 'being posted to a little village like this.'

'We should let him sleep. The fewer folk that see us, the better,' Cara said, not breaking her stride.

Asher hesitated before leaving the guard. The guard could probably do with a peaceful nap before things in the kingdom became… difficult. A giggling Luce caught up moments after.

The main road in and out of the village was wide, dusty, and flanked by a single row of short cottages, each only one floor high, enough space for a single occupier.

'Just so you know,' Asher said as they walked the quiet road, 'some of the folk here know me, but not as Prince Asher. Here I'm just Bill.'

'Bill?' Cara questioned, raising an eyebrow.

'What of it?' Asher asked, feeling a little embarrassed. 'It was the most common name I could think of. Plus, I think it has a local ring to it. Anyway, we don't have to worry about anyone reporting they've seen a prince back to White Cliffe.'

'I like it.' Luce grinned.

Before Cara could reply, one of the cottage doors slammed open and out from the dark interior flew a small, brown-furred figure. He sailed through the air before landing hard into the dirt, sliding until he came to rest at Cara's feet. Clouds of dirt erupted around the small body. Standing at the doorway was a broad, muscular black Rabbethi. Traces of wiry grey fur streaked across his face, and he wore the dirt-brown smock and loose trousers of a typical seaside folk.

'If I catch ya anywhere near my daugh'er again, I'll kill ya!' he bellowed as he reached for the door handle.

A young feminine voice called behind the outraged man, 'But, daddy, I love hi—'

The door slammed shut, and peace abruptly returned to the quiet street. The three looked at each other with curious expressions before turning to the small figure, who remained face-first in the dirt, unmoving.

Cara prodded the unconscious figure with her boot. 'Hey.' There was no response. She pressed a little harder, rolling him over. They peered down at the Otyren lying before them with curious eyes.

His clothes were lavish yet tattered and covered with filth and other unmentionable stains. Embroidered with fine yellow linen on his shirt was the image of a clam, under which were two tridents crossed at the shaft. Dried mud splattered his white trousers. The turquoise shirt had several patches of mismatched cloth sewn over it, and brown fingerless gloves covered each webbed paw. His black boots were encrusted with even more mud.

Like all Otyren, he had a short snout that ended in a flat black nose. Two short, rounded ears sat on the side of his small head, and white fur made its way down the underside of his chin and under his shirt. These features all contributed to an adorable facade, which was nothing like their actual disposition: short-tempered and proud.

'Who do you suppose he is? He doesn't seem like a local,' Luce asked, crouching down to poke at the man's soft, squishy cheeks.

'This is Jarl Erik,' Asher said with a heavy sigh. 'The local bard, adulterer and cheater of pub games.'

'*Jarl* Erik?' Cara asked, raising an eyebrow.

'That's what he calls himself. I guess it's a stage name?' Asher knelt and scooped up the unconscious Otyren with ease, cradling him in his arms and pulling his thick tail away from the prodding fingers of Luce.

'What's that?' she asked, reaching for a small pouch hanging from Jarl Erik's waist.

Asher pulled away sharply, turning to the quizzical Luce pointedly. 'Hey, don't touch that.'

Luce cocked her head, her smile growing as if the sudden motion had initiated some sort of game. 'Why?'

'What do you mean "why?" No one touches an Otyren's Oathstone without their permission.'

Luce moved closer, her eyes drifting hungrily back to the dangling pouch. 'But why? Is it valuable?'

'Because it's rude, that's why!' Asher exclaimed. 'The pebbles inside mean a lot to the Otyren. Some are even family heirlooms. Looking inside the pouch would be like looking under someone's dress without permission. How do you not know that?'

Luce's eyes jumped up to meet Asher's, a coy smile across her snout. 'I wouldn't mind that, depending on who was looking.'

'I... err...' Asher's cheeks flushed beneath his white fur as Luce's playful stare paralysed his tongue and made his thoughts slow to a crawl.

'That's enough, Lucilla,' Cara said sternly.

The petite agent giggled, turning. 'Oh, come on. You have to admit, he's pretty cute when he's embarrassed.'

Asher's thoughts quickly returned, though his cheeks refused to cool. 'We... err... we should get him to the inn at the docks. I have a friend there. She'll know what to do with him.' He nodded down the dirt road towards the glistening ocean.

The rumble of activity grew louder as the hill became flat underfoot. A wave of nostalgia washed over Asher as he saw the familiar sight of tall sails poking above the rooftops and the glint of the ocean expanding from the wide cove beyond. Gulls squawked frantically overhead. A thrum of voices began to rumble in the air, some in casual chit-chat, others booming to be heard over the crowd.

The dirt road gave way to wooden planks as the three entered the docks. The crowds were growing thicker, with more and more people appearing from side streets and shop doorways. Some hurried towards the next store, while others stopped and discussed essential events of the day, much to the annoyance of others who huffed their quiet protests as they squeezed past. This part of the town was alive, breathing with a gentle heartbeat.

Pushing through the growing crowd, they reached a junction by the water's edge. Before them lay the cove, its gentle waves lapping against the docks. Tall cliffs rose on either side of the cove's entrance, appearing as stone sentinels, guarding the quiet village from the stormy winds and violent seas. Vessels of various sizes bobbed in the peaceful waters, some moored along the dock, others resting further away, anchored in the shallow and protected waters. Asher breathed deep, letting his senses take in their fill.

He led Cara and Luce left and began following the walkway, ignoring the curious stares he and the unconscious Jarl Erik were receiving. Eyes also fell on the two Vulpen agents, who were following closely behind. Cara lowered her gaze to the floor, avoiding eye contact where possible. Luce, however, smiled and waved. This seemed to satisfy the villagers, who must have become convinced such a kind smile couldn't be up to anything nefarious.

Fisherfolk lined the docks in their market stands. Vast swathes of thick green kelp and other edible sea plants hung heavy on large hooks, dripping their salty brine onto the wooden planks. Traders from further afield intermingled with the locals, desperately attempting to keep their goods dry whilst convincing the hardy folk of the village to purchase their overpriced luxury items. Rabbethi and even some Vulpen and Otyren women perused each stand, searching for the evening's dinner as their children played unsupervised around their legs.

'Isn't there any fish in this bloody village?' Cara asked, her eyes darting from stand to stand, disappointment spreading across her face.

'Rabbethi don't eat fish... or any meat for that matter,' Asher said, pushing forwards. 'But you should be able to get some at Mia's place. She caters to a lot of outsi—'

'But that's my baby!' A woeful wail erupted beyond a gathered crowd before a small cottage. 'Have you no heart?'

Standing in the doorway was a young Rabbethi woman. Two kits, no more than five or six years old, cowered behind her legs, clinging tight to her dress. A third child, younger still, wailed in anguish as a guard in a deep blue cloak carried them away from the door. Just a few paces off, four more guards stood rigidly at attention, their eyes fixed ahead, unmoving.

'You know the law,' the guard insisted over his shoulder at the sobbing woman. He turned to the crowd and projected his voice. 'This child will be taken to the Black Rock Mines and placed under the stewardship of Earl Cuthred, where he will live the rest of his days. He will be provided for, but his rights are forfeit.' His eyes scanned the crowd, a hardness in his expression. 'Know this, citizens. These laws keep us safe from our enemies and ourselves. Follow them, and never forget the tragic cleansing of our forebears.' With a swish of his cloak, the captain led the way through the crowd. It parted without a sound, and Asher's eyes dropped to the wooden planks as the captain passed by.

'You talk of safety, but what of my boy?' yelled a strained voice from deeper within the crowd, anger and spite cutting the air. 'Taken from his crib by Shangari, he was. Nothin' but half an ear left behind. What are you doing about that?'

The captain said nothing, though his face visibly darkened as he marched.

Asher felt a motion beside him. He turned to find Luce straining forwards, her eyes wide in a quiet rage, her paws clenched onto the hilts of two daggers sheathed at her side. Cara's black paw was pressed against her chest, keeping her from lunging towards the captain.

'Control yourself,' she commanded with a hushed authority.

'But they're stealing that child from its home, from its family!' the smaller Vulpen snarled through gritted teeth.

'I said *stop*.'

There was tense silence before Luce eased, and her paws came away from her daggers. Cara eased her paw from her chest, and they watched in silence as the guards disappeared into the crowd, the child held within the captain's arms, crying for its mother the entire time.

'What was that about?' Cara whispered.

'I'll tell you later,' Asher said with a dour expression. The three continued walking in sombre silence, the murmuring crowd dispersing around them.

The mood of the docks had shifted, and a quiet sorrow now hung in the air. The town's citizens hastily retrieved what they needed from the market stands before heading straight home. The traders no longer boomed their voices; instead, they conducted each trade with quiet respect.

Asher eventually reached the end of the wooden walkway, where a large thatched tavern sat. An inviting plume of smoke rose gently from its chimney. Where most buildings in the village consisted of one surface-level floor, this building boasted a towering two with wide wooden barrels stacked on either side of a small door. The smell of urine and stale beer hung thick in the air as Asher's eyes glanced up at a familiar sight. A sign above the door creaked in the gentle breeze. Upon it was the image of a giant golden fish jumping out of the ocean. The name under the illustration read "The Golden Leap".

'You should be able to get some fish here,' he said, stopping before the door. 'There are some folk here that fish, and they usually sell what they catch to the inns of the area.'

'I thought your people didn't eat meat?' Cara questioned.

'We don't, but that doesn't mean we won't hunt or fish for coin.' He leaned his shoulder against the wooden door and pushed it open.

The inside of the tavern was dark and musky, yet had a welcoming air. The few windows there were did little to illuminate the open space, leaving the fire set into the eastern stone wall to do most of the heavy lifting. It bathed the interior in an orange flickering glow as several candles sat at each table, attempting to help spread the light, though they achieved little more than being decorative items. The scent of urine was far weaker inside, but the smell of stale beer was undoubtedly more intense.

After Asher's eyes adjusted to the dimness, he looked at the room around him. He had spent many long nights here pretending he was anything but a prince of the realm. The space was well-used by the town's inhabitants and well-loved by its owner, whose best intentions had seen to its attempted repairs. The coin spent had not matched the effort. Old wood chippings wedged in the right spot cost less than a new table leg, and blood was easier to clean if nobody knew it was there. A well-placed, half-melted candle and no one was the wiser.

Quiet murmurings caught Asher's attention, and he glanced towards the two tall armchairs flanking the fireplace, where the only two patrons had made themselves comfortable. They were deep in a hushed conversation, leaning close to avoid prying ears. One was a local Rabbethi, sporting the typical attire of fisherfolk, complete with a clay pipe held loosely in one paw. The other figure made Asher pause. They wore a black cloak–not unlike Cara and Luce's, but made of a thicker, more rigid material–dark leather armour, black riding gloves, and boots. The lowered hood kept their face hidden in shadow, and a clasp, glinting in the orange glow of the fire, held the cloak tight around their neck. The clasp was made of a dark metal and fashioned into a simple ring with a thin piece running vertically through its centre.

Cara closed the door behind them, and the strangers ceased their conversation, snapping towards the sudden disturbance. The fisherfolk regarded the group with a sneer, clearly not a fan of strangers. Asher turned to the cloaked stranger and found two yellow eyes staring at him from the hood's shadows, glowing with the intensity of the fire beside them. Thin black pupils watched him like a hawk, observing his every movement. Asher's nose began to twitch, his fur standing on end. The stranger's pupils widened at the fear. If eyes could smile, these were positively grinning.

A black paw fell onto Asher's shoulder, causing him to jump out of his fur, nearly dropping Jarl Erik. 'Are you alright, Ash?' Luce asked, stepping beside him, concern across her face.

'I'm okay,' Asher said, willing his nose to be still. He peered over her shoulder at the hooded figure, who had turned back to their companion.

'Do you know them?' she whispered, a sense of playfulness returning to her voice. 'Should we say hi?'

'Definitely not,' he said, clearing his mind.

With Luce and Cara at his back, the urge to flee slowly began to pass, and he continued his approach to the bar, floorboards creaking underfoot. Behind the bar, three huge barrels sat on their sides, with one end facing the tavern and a tap hammered into their base. Several bottles of various alcohols lined a shelf above the barrels, some covered in years of dust while others appeared brand new. He laid Jarl Erik down and knocked on the beer-stained wood.

'Hello?' Asher called, peering over.

A faint rustling came from a narrow passage at one end of the bar, followed swiftly by the sound of pots and pans clattering onto a stone floor. 'Oh, for Thena's sake!' came an agitated cry. 'One moment, I'll be right with you!' A moment passed, and out stepped a dishevelled young Vulpen woman, dainty when compared to the muscular Cara, with vibrant red fur, wearing a long-sleeved brown dress and beer-stained white apron. She hurried down the bar and stopped before Asher, wiping flour from her black paws onto her apron. 'Right then, what can I do… for you…?' She trailed off as she looked up, her bright blue eyes meeting Asher's.

'Hey,' Asher said with a faint smile. 'It's been a while. How are—'

Wham!

The barmaid raised her fist square into Asher's nose, sending him backwards onto the wooden floor. A small trail of blood trickled from his right nostril, and he winced at the sharp pain. Luce giggled, unable to control her excitement.

'Six months!' the barmaid yelled from over the bar. 'I tell you how I feel, and you just up and leave for six months!' She snapped to Cara. 'Who does that?'

Cara, who was smiling, now looked somewhat uncomfortable at being made a part of Asher's drama. She shrugged. The Vulpen stared up at Cara with narrowed eyes, examining her before turning back to Asher as he eased himself off the floor. She raised her fist again, ready to send him back down.

'Whoa! Easy, Mia!' Asher pleaded, raising his paws to guard against another assault. 'I'm sorry about before. I truly am. You deserve someone better than me, but a lot has happened, and I didn't know where else to go.' There was an uncomfortable silence as the angry barmaid stared daggers at him. 'We also found Erik face down in the dirt. Looks like he was messing around with Leofman's daughter again.' He gestured to the unconscious Otyren lying on the bar between them. She looked down at Jarl Erik and back to Asher, lowering her fist. Sensing an ease in the tension, Asher stepped towards the bar. Mia raised her fist again in a jerking motion, and Asher flinched, stumbling backwards and slamming into one of the tables.

Luce giggled once more, and Mia lowered her fist with a satisfied smile.

6

Mia's Wish

Evening descended upon the quiet village. The traders packed up their stalls and either headed home or out onto the open road, while the fisherfolk moored their small vessels and stored away their harvest. With nothing to steal and no people to aim their refuse at, the gulls ceased their endless squawking and found suitable perches along sails and rooftops for roosting. Their screaming and plundering would continue in full in the morning. As the Lighthouse turned from the sleepy village, grey clouds gathered overhead, darkening the evening sky as the air became damp and humid.

The tavern was busier now. After the working day had drawn to a close, the locals had poured through the doors and filled the empty seats. The mysterious figure had remained by the fireplace, lounging in one of the comfy armchairs, their friend having left some time earlier. They didn't ask for any food or drink. They simply sat in silence, watching others merrily enjoy their evening.

'He's giving me the creeps,' Asher said under his breath, bringing his tankard to his lips. He and Cara were seated on a pair of stools at the bar, nursing their drinks.

'Me too,' she replied, blowing on her tea. 'They don't have a scent, or if they do, they're taking great lengths to mask it.' She took a sip and returned her cup to the bar before turning to Asher. 'Once it's quieter, we can talk to your girlfriend about getting us on a ship to Terravulpa.'

'She's not my girlfriend. Well, not anymore. We—'

Cara raised her paw, silencing Asher. 'I really don't care.'

The evening had taken on a more serious atmosphere after Cara had ordered Luce outside to keep watch. With a considerable pout, Luce had left the tavern, vanishing into the dying light and slamming the door behind her. Asher promised they wouldn't have any fun without her. So far, he was right.

'If we're going to Terravulpa to see your queen,' Asher led with a hint of hope, 'does that mean we're going to Ignimarum?' He had never been to the Vulpen capital but had heard wondrous things about the layered city from his mother. Cara nodded, and a flicker of excitement leapt into Asher's heart. He never imagined he'd travel to the legendary city nestled within the towering spires of the Cinder Sea. Of course. Jarl Erik had claimed to have visited the isles many times, though this was a boast usually made before collapsing unconscious in his own vomit.

What's wrong with you? Asher thought, suppressing his quiet excitement. How dare he feel any fragment of happiness? Did he care so little that any slightly positive news would make him forget his father was dead? That his brother had been taken and his people were suffering? Guilt weighed down upon him like a rock on his chest, and he lowered his gaze to the ale sloshing about in his tankard.

Mia had taken Jarl Erik to her private chamber behind the bar, bandaged him up, and left a warm herbal tea for when he awoke. She then began rushing around the tavern, seeing to every patron's needs. Tankards were filled, and hot meals were served. Still spiteful from their last goodbye, she had initially refused to serve Asher any food or drink or even give him a room for the night. But after Cara had presented a heavy metal pendant, Mia begrudgingly gave them everything free of charge.

'What was that thing you showed Mia?' Asher scoffed. 'I want one if it means I get free food.'

Cara, unamused, reached under her cloak, pulled out a metal pendant and placed it onto the bar with a *thud*. It was black, circular, about four inches across, and made of solid metal. Engraved on its surface was the image of a Vulpen head facing to the left with many tails forming a flower-like pattern behind it.

'It's the mark of the royal household,' Cara said with a slight hint of pride. 'It is to signify that the bearer is on a mission from the queen and must be provided aid by all Vulpen.'

Asher stared at the pendant, at the intricate design and engravings. He reached out to inspect it, but Cara snatched it back and tucked it away under her cloak.

'Do all Vulpen have to obey?' he asked, returning to his ale. 'Is it a law for your people?'

'Any decent Vulpen would respect the queen's mark. It's how we agents work so efficiently. And besides.' She reached for the sheathed sword at her hip, placing a paw on the pommel. 'No one would dare refuse.'

As the night continued, Cara probed Asher about his homeland. He indulged her, though he wasn't sure whether she was genuine in her curiosity or just gathering information. He spoke fondly about how his people took great pride in their leaping prowess, boasting how he held the record for the longest leap in White Cliffe City and that his legs could out-kick a warhorse. His face turned solemn when she asked about the guard who had taken her child away.

'After we gained independence from the Vulpen some two hundred years ago, our population boomed, thanks to our... fertile nature. Our workforce grew, as did our armies, and we easily overwhelmed the raiding Shangari clans of the southern mountains. Then came the war with the Otyren. We ran out of room within our borders, so we pushed into their lands to the west. They, of course, fled into the dense forests bordering Otyrheim, and the expansion stopped. We ran out of space to grow. Food supplies couldn't keep up, and we starved. Disease ran rampant.' He stared into his beer, deep in thought. 'That's when King Beornraed ordered the weakest, oldest, and other "unwanted" folk be put to the sword. In the space of a year, our population dropped by half, either through slaughter or people fleeing to other kingdoms. And they call him a hero...' He sighed, pushing the horrific history from his mind. 'Since then, a strict two-child per household law has been in place. Any more, and they're branded as "Third Sons" or "Third Daughters" and sent straight to the mines either at Direbrook in the east or the Iron Hills to the southwest. If the population ever reaches too high a level again, the king, or queen, must enact another "cleansing" or face punishment from the witan.'

'That's awful,' Cara breathed.

'The alternative is far worse.' Asher raised his tankard and drank deeply before wiping the foam from his upper lip. They remained in silent contemplation as the tavern gradually emptied, unable to conjure any conversation capable of lifting their spirits. Asher glanced towards the hooded figure, finding the chair empty.

'Phew! Sorry about that!' came an abrupt and exhausted voice. Mia had seen the last patron out and now stood opposite Asher, a large tankard of ale on the bar. She looked up at Cara with a cocked eyebrow.

'Now then, what does an agent of the queen want with Bill here, hm?' She took a large swig and eyed Cara suspiciously.

'I need to get *Bill* to Ignimarum. I can't tell you any more than that.' She met Mia's stare with narrowed eyes, and the pair locked, each waiting for the other to break.

Mia conceded, turning to Asher. 'I don't know what you've done this time, Bill, but I wouldn't do anything stupid with an agent around. Best fighters in the land, they are.'

'Tell me about it,' Asher said, remembering how ruthlessly Cara had fought the knight in the woods. 'I wouldn't stand a chance.'

'Hey, don't sell yourself short!' Mia protested, pointing a clawed finger towards Asher. 'I've seen you take down a boar twice your size with a single kick! I heard you even outran a deer when your quiver was out of arrows. The family on the edge of town ate well for a week after that, all because of you. So stop the self-pity, okay?' She gave Asher a kind smile. Asher returned it with one of his own, feeling his spirits lift, even if he didn't believe her words of confidence.

'Yes, well, is there a ship that can take us?' Cara asked.

'Marius is your best bet – dark-furred Vulpen, tall and handsome, but he bloody knows it. He heads up and down the coast until the information is either old or unwanted. Should take you home if you flash your pendant at him.' Mia turned back to Asher. 'The Vulpen Queendom deals mostly in information, extracting and selling secrets to the highest bidders. They sell all sorts of gossip at high prices from army movements to market prices.'

'I know,' he said abruptly, offended that she would assume otherwise.

'How?' Mia asked, raising an eyebrow. 'I mean, no offence, Bill, but I can't imagine a forest boy like you knowing much about our culture.' She gestured to Cara and back to herself.

Asher stammered as Mia watched him. He knew quite a bit about the Vulpen Queendom from reports he had read in his father's study, not to mention the Rabbethi royal family had kept close contact with the Vulpen rulers since their independence.

'I just do,' he replied, thinking it best not to mention this to Mia. He also had no better excuse come to mind. He brought his tankard to his lips for another drink and hoped Mia wouldn't look further into the matter. Fortunately, she only gave Asher a suspicious look as she drank from her tankard.

Cara and Mia continued to discuss the Vulpen Queendom, their homes, and recent developments within its borders.

'I just want to sail over the Cinder Sea, squish my new nephew's little cheeks, and stroke his soft fur,' Cara said with longing in her eyes.

'You can come with us if you like,' Asher said, watching the two Vulpen reminisce. Cara shot him a look that made him regret every choice he had ever made.

'No, thank you,' Mia said with a smile. 'I've already made plans to sail there later in the month. I'm sure it'll be easy to get transport to my family's farm in Petrosa when I get there, or I might just walk the high road like I used to when I was younger. It's a quiet town on the island's north side.' She smiled down at her drink, a yearning in her eyes. 'I really can't wait, though.'

The three finished several more drinks before Mia retrieved rusty keys from behind the bar. She gave one to Cara, one to Asher, and kept one for herself as Jarl Erik was still fast asleep in her chambers. She doused the fireplace embers, plunging the tavern into a tranquil twilight, and locked the door, sliding heavy latches at the top and bottom for added security. They climbed the old, rickety staircase hugging the western wall up to the rooms above the bar, wished each other a pleasant night, then closed their doors.

Asher's room was small. He was forced to squeeze between a table to his right and a single straw bed opposite the entrance, cursing as he kicked the large wooden chest at the foot of the bed. A small square window looked out onto bare stone, the sound of the sea gently lapping against the rocks below. He laid his bow and quiver at the foot of the bed, fell back onto the straw mattress, and rested his head on the soft, feathery pillow. A moment passed in the unlit stillness. Although he fought against it, his mind thought of Henric, his father, and all who had died back in White Cliffe. He didn't save them, he couldn't. If he had just been stronger or in the keep like a good prince, he could have saved his father and fought back against the church. But no. He had been out having a wonderful time in the streets, away from his ailing father, away from his responsibilities.

Tears began to gather as, one by one, the faces of the dead leapt into his vision.

'What do I do?' he whispered to the darkness around him.

The shadows kept their silence. With rain starting to patter against the window, tears began to stream down Asher's cheeks.

***

There was a sudden banging against Asher's door. The frantic and panicked thuds reverberated around the wooden walls. Asher rubbed his eyes, dazed. It was early. The first light of the Great Lighthouse was just creeping over the small village and into the tavern.

'Wha...? What's going on?' he groaned, attempting to pry his eyes open from the slumber sand that sealed them.

'They're here!' Cara's voice was firm and commanding from the other side of the door. 'We need to go. Now!' Her booted footsteps padded away with speed until quiet returned to the small chamber.

Asher leapt out of bed, slung the quiver of arrows over his shoulder and grabbed the bow. He burst through the door and out onto the balcony. Cara and Mia were crouched by one of the dirty windows, peering through a clean patch they had made with their sleeves. Asher raced down the rickety stairs and crouched beside them, bruising his shoulder as he hit the wall.

'How'd they find us?' he asked, nose twitching.

'Take a look for yourself.' Cara gestured with a nod.

Asher looked through the window, pressing his pink nose against the glass. The sky outside was dull and grey, the docks devoid of people. The wooden planks were sodden, and puddles covered the uneven surface of the walkway while water dripped rhythmically off the thatched rooftops. A strong wind whistled in from the cove entrance, gently rocking the moored boats.

'It seems our creepy friend was interested in more than just fishing,' Cara continued. Asher's eyes followed the docks away from the tavern. Approaching from the main road was a host of hungry-looking Shangari, their chaotic marching and guttural chattering penetrating the early morning stillness. They were led by two individuals. Asher instantly recognised one of them, the black cloak and dark leather armour still fresh in his mind.

The stranger from last night.

Now standing, they looked about the same height as a Shangari, but that was where the similarities stopped. Where Shangari were completely ungraceful in their movements, lumbering from place to place, the mysterious figure walked with a nimbleness in every step, as if they could spring into action at a moment's notice. The second figure was a colossal bare-chested Medvedian. He took one giant step for every three of those around him. His furrowed brow had an intense look of what, Asher could only guess, was an extreme hatred for something or someone within the tavern. Asher's eyes widened as he inspected the Medvedian's metal-plated armour guarding his legs and arms. The gold etchings appeared dull in the grey morning, the silver shine scuffed and dented. A tattered white cape billowed in the wind behind him, and his neck was wrapped in a bandage several layers thick and soaked red with blood.

'No...' Asher said to himself in a sudden and horrific realisation. 'There's no way...'

'What is it?' Cara asked, becoming worried.

'It's the knight... from the woods...' Asher lowered himself from the window to let Cara look.

'He should be dead.' Cara snarled, white fangs creeping out from under her upper lip.

Asher felt a tug on his tunic. 'What in Thena's name is going on, Bill?' Mia demanded in a hushed voice. 'What's with the Shangari? And what is a knight doing here? Please tell me this isn't to do with you two.'

'I... err...' Asher realised he couldn't do justice to all that had happened in the little time they had. They had to think fast. Being captured meant certain death. 'I can't explain right now,' he continued. 'All I can tell you is that the Church of the Shepherd slaughtered everyone in White Cliffe City, and we need to get out of here.'

Mia's eyes widened in disbelief, a mixture of confusion and panic washing over her.

'M-Marius moored up earlier, before first light. His boat's called *The Silvi*. It's the red one.'

Asher pulled himself back up to the window, careful not to disturb Cara, and looked towards the ship floating just outside. He saw a sleek sailboat, much unlike its lumbering neighbours. The hull was a dark red, the railings a deep black, and its wide black sail was furled up and tied to the single mast's crossbeam with a thick rope. Just out of Asher's sight were the beginnings of a small cabin. With its smooth curved edges, the ship had clearly been built to cut through the waves at great speed, able to traverse rough seas quickly where few would dare chase it.

'That's it,' Asher breathed as he read the words *The Silvi* painted in black along the side of the hull. He was about to ask Cara what the plan was, but something made him pause. It was suddenly silent. All he could hear was the gentle creaking of ships and the continuous dripping of last night's rain from the rooftops. The sound of marching footsteps had stopped.

'Er... Bill...?' Mia pointed out the window. The hooded figure and hulking knight stood not twenty paces away, a host of vicious Shangari waiting hungrily behind them. The knight unsheathed his massive greatsword from his back and pointed it one-pawed towards the tavern. He puffed out his chest and bellowed, 'Come out now, or we slaughter every man, woman and child!' His voice was deep like thunder, but strained, as if each word arrived with tremendous agony. 'No one defies the Shepherd! There will be repercussions for your heresy!'

Asher turned to Cara in a panic. 'What do we do? If we don't give ourselves up, everyone in the village will die!'

Cara closed her eyes, shaking her head slowly as her teeth retreated beneath her lip. 'This village is done for regardless.'

'No...' Asher breathed, not wanting to believe it. 'There must be something we can do. It's our fault these people are in danger!' But Cara ignored him and peeled away from the window. She crouched beside Mia, who was brushing her red tail with frantic strokes and staring wide-eyed at the floorboards.

'Mia?' Cara asked, keeping her voice low. She tried to make eye contact with the panicked innkeeper. Mia gave no response. 'Mia!'

The absent Vulpen jumped. 'Y-yes?'

'I need you to focus, okay? We're all getting out of here, but I need you to show us how.'

Mia stared at her, bewildered, then blinked. 'There's a trapdoor behind the bar. That'll take you right down to the water. I-I haven't been down there today, so it might be stiff.'

'Thank you, Mia,' Cara said with a reassuring smile. 'You're doing great.' With that, she rose and dashed to the bar. 'Asher, help me with this!'

'What about Luce?' Asher asked, noting the bubbly agent's absence.

'She'll be fine!'

Asher rose from the window and, with his bow slung over his shoulder, sprinted to the bar, the arrows rattling in their quiver at his back. Mia followed cautiously. She stood to one side once she reached the bar, re-grabbing her tail and stroking it once more. Cara swept aside a small red rug to reveal a wide trapdoor with a large metal ring resting at one end. Asher crouched beside her, and they wrapped their paws around the ring. With a mighty heave, the door creaked open, landing with a heavy thud to reveal a ladder descending into a dark space below. The sound of waves sloshing against rock echoed from the shadows.

Cara jumped down without hesitation and landed silently on a stone floor.

'Come down. Quickly!' She then disappeared from view.

Asher stared at the hole, at the dark pit that led to safety. He felt movement behind him. Mia was edging closer to the hole, her legs pressing into Asher's back.

'Wait here,' he said with a quick, reassuring smile. 'I'll call up when it's safe.'

'But I—' she began with a tremble, her eyes darting between Asher and the hole.

'Hey, trust me. You'll be fine. I just need to make sure it's safe.' Asher's smile widened as far as his nerves could allow, his twitching nose betraying his calm words. Mia nodded and took a step back. She glanced back nervously towards the tavern door, tightening the grip on her tail. Asher turned and backed himself into the hole. 'You'll be holding your little nephew soon, I promise.' He descended the ladder, his eyes focused on the rungs at his feet.

There was a sudden sound. It was quick and quiet, like a tiny marble dropping to the floor. Asher almost thought it was a trick of the mind, but he was sure he heard it. 'Mia...?' he asked, thinking she might have kicked a fallen glass. He stopped his descent and looked up. She was still standing where he had left her, staring down at him. Strangely, tears were forming in the corners of her bright blue eyes.

'What's wrong...?' He trailed off as he saw it. A sleek crossbow bolt protruded from her neck, blood coating its black, pointed head.

A small trickle of blood trailed between her lips, falling down the white of her chin. Time slowed as a methodical dripping filled Asher's ears, forming a small pool at her feet. The world fell silent, save for her short, stuttering breaths. Their eyes locked, both terrified.

'B-Bill...?' she whispered, her voice barely audible.

Her eyes rolled to the back of her head, and she collapsed to the floor, landing right in front of the trapdoor and Asher. The world came crashing down like an avalanche as Asher screamed for Mia, a torrent of tears descending his cheeks like a broken dam. This wasn't happening, it couldn't. His heart was a maelstrom of rage, frustration, sorrow and guilt. A thousand deafening thoughts churned around in his head, unrelenting in their pursuit of his attention, but only one claimed it.

I have to save Mia.

He scrambled back up the ladder, but as he was about to leave the hole, he felt a hard tug on his back and was dragged into the darkness below, landing against the stone floor with a painful thud. Above him, he saw Cara's silhouette climb the ladder and pull the trapdoor shut, sliding a latch on the underside and locking it from within.

'No!' He leapt to his feet and made for the ladder, barely noticing the pain in his back and shoulders after the fall. 'She needs my help!'

Cara wrapped her arms around him and held him tight, restraining him. 'She's gone, and we need to go,' she whispered. 'Right now, we need to run. I promise there will be time to mourn.'

Asher fought with all his might against her, writhing in her arms, trying to break free and save Mia. She needed him, and he was the only one who could save her. She was innocent in all this. If he could just get to her, she would be okay, and he could tell her everything he was too cowardly to say before: that he was a prince, that he loved her, that he was sorry. She was the only one who believed in him, not as a prince but as a good person. Without her, he would feel like nothing; he would *be* nothing.

'She's gone,' Cara repeated slowly, calmly. 'She's gone...'

The fight in Asher evaporated, and he began sobbing uncontrollably into Cara's shoulder, burrowing into her tight embrace. She held on tight, keeping him close. Waves lapped against unseen rocks as Asher's muffled cries echoed in the shadows.

7

The Silvi

Quiet eventually fell within the darkness beneath the tavern. Asher was calmer now. His sobbing had slowed, becoming deep and rhythmic, interrupted only by the occasional sniff. His long ears flopped over Cara's cloaked shoulders as she held him close. Footsteps thudded above, quickly followed by a cacophony of excited screeches. The trapdoor began to rattle furiously. Cara snapped up. It appeared to hold firm, but it likely wouldn't last long.

'Asher?' Cara said softly. 'We have to move.'

Asher stirred, raising his head slowly from her shoulder, the fur on his cheeks matted against his skin. Cara met his gaze. For the first time since their meeting, her eyes appeared to show genuine empathy.

'Okay,' he whimpered, his voice hoarse and painful.

The pair separated and rose to their feet. It felt as if his shoulders now carried heavy chains, and Asher had neither the energy nor the fight to escape with any sense of urgency. With effort, he grabbed his quiver from the floor and gathered up the scattered arrows. He slung the quiver and bow over his shoulder. They felt heavier than usual. Reluctantly, he took in his surroundings.

Large crates and ale-stained barrels were stacked around them like the towers of a wooden keep, behind which were walls made of dark, rotting wood. The fourth wall was bare, uncarved rock, the ladder fastened to it with thick iron rings. A stream of faint light leaked from under a door opposite the ladder, bathing the stone before it. The calming lapping of waves echoed beyond, carried on a faint briny breeze.

Cara made for the door and pressed a pointed ear to the wooden surface. Asher approached and mimicked the agent, draping a long ear against the cold, damp wood. He heard nothing but the gentle waves and the creaking of ships as they groaned from side to side.

'I think it's clear,' she whispered, reaching for the handle.

Asher stepped back, and Cara cautiously pulled the door open. With a creak, light poured into the room, a gust of sea air following behind, carrying the salty brine up Asher's nose. Cara stepped out into the morning air, leaving Asher alone in the darkness. He hesitated, glancing back at the trapdoor in the ceiling, a cacophony of guilt and longing compelling him to open it.

'It'll be okay,' came a soft voice.

Asher turned and saw Cara silhouetted in the doorway, her paw outstretched. This was it. If he stepped through that door, he'd be leaving Mia behind. She was gone, he knew that, but if he stayed in that room, he could fool himself into thinking he could still save her. Leaving meant giving up, despite all logic telling him otherwise. His eyes rose to meet Cara's.

'I've got you,' she said, meeting his sombre stare. 'It's time to go.' Asher reached out, and she grabbed hold, pulling him through the door and into the light.

He stepped onto a stone ledge, wincing as his eyes adjusted to the morning light. The wind was chilly, the sky dull and grey. Clouds rolled slow and fat overhead, floating inland and threatening to unleash their load. Asher and Cara looked about the private stone dock. Loose rope and bits of broken barrels lay strewn across the floor as gentle waves splashed seawater into puddles and onto their boots.

'There,' Cara said, nodding to the back end of a red hull bobbing gently to their right. She pointed to an open square window in the ship's stern. 'That's how we get inside without drawing attention.' She took a few steps back, crouching low, then sprinted towards the edge and leapt onto the back of the ship, landing with a muted thud against the hull. She clung onto the wood as the white tip of her tail dipped into the sea below. With a nimbleness akin to that of the tree-dwelling Ruadrae, she clambered up the wood and through the small square hole, disappearing into the shadows beyond.

Asher took a couple of steps back. Any self-respecting Rabbethi would find such a distance trivial. Today, however, he didn't feel all that confident. Chains of apathy weighed heavy upon him, threatening to drag him to the depths with little more than bubbles to mark his grave. He pushed the dark thoughts from his mind and urged himself onwards. With a push from his powerful legs, he bounded forwards, leaping from the edge and aiming directly for the hole.

It was not a good take-off.

It was as if his body didn't care whether he made it or plummeted into the cold waters. He sailed low through the air, barely reaching the open window. His chest slammed into the wooden hull, and he grasped frantically at the window ledge. With a strenuous effort, he pulled himself through and into the dark space beyond, a flurry of paper and documents swirling around him. He clambered over a wooden table before collapsing onto a wooden floor.

The space he now found himself in was dim and smelled like a mixture of lavender and salt. In the corner of the cabin was a single bed, on which, much to Asher's relief, sat the grinning figure of Luce, who waved playfully at him as their eyes made contact. Try as he might, he couldn't bring himself to return her smile. Her smile faded, replaced by quizzical concern.

'And who in Thena's name are *you*?' came a startled voice.

Asher looked past Luce to find the owner of the profanity.

Pressed into the corner was a tall, black-furred Vulpen man. His long-sleeved white shirt hung loose upon his slender frame, covered by a crimson velvet vest. Black trousers fit tight around his slim legs, ending in knee-high black boots. Although slightly dishevelled, the clothes exhibited the class and sophistication of someone not accustomed to fighting, at least not fairly. His scruffy fur was as dark as night, with a faint streak of lighter grey running from his lower jaw down his chest, flowing like a river of silver. Orange eyes stared at Asher with a mixture of shock and annoyance.

'Calm down, Marius,' Cara scolded from beside a wooden door on the opposite wall. She returned to peer through a small circular window. 'He's with me.'

'Oh, is he now?' Marius said in a huff. He released himself from the corner and stepped over the unusually quiet Luce. His eyes narrowed at Asher. He crouched beside him and began gathering up the papers scattered about. 'Ya know, I don't appreciate having my home seized by agents, only to have their friend sprawl through the window like a drunken circus performer, messing up my merchandise!' He glared at Asher, who immediately scrambled to assist.

'I-I'm sorry,' Asher stammered, bundling up as much as he could and dumping it onto the table behind him.

Marius rose to his full height and dropped his armful of papers onto the desk with a thud. His imposing yet slender frame only just managed to fit into the cabin without ducking.

He sighed. 'Don't worry about it, patches. You look like you've had a rough day already.' He made his way to the bed, his pointed ears brushing lightly against the wooden beams as he walked. The tension in the room dissipated slightly, and Asher noticed something strange about the black Vulpen. He didn't have a tail. Where a big bushy mass of fur should gracefully flow behind like a voluptuous shadow, Marius had nothing. Asher averted his eyes from Marius's rear, feeling surprisingly sorry for the poor Vulpen. He shifted his attention to the rest of the chamber.

All manner of pulleys and levers covered the walls, attached to ropes that disappeared into the woodwork. It was a labyrinth of mechanical ingenuity that Asher simply couldn't follow, and although he had never been on a ship before, he was pretty sure it wasn't normal.

'You need to be more careful,' Marius said as he sat on the edge of his bed beside Luce, whose eyes remained fixed on Asher. 'Stunts like that could get people hurt or, worse, disrupt their business. Have you ever thought about how—'

'Leave him alone,' Cara snapped, glaring at Marius. 'Just do your job and keep your mouth shut.'

He raised his paws in surrender, and she returned her gaze to the window. 'And what job would that be then? What do you ask of my girl and me? Oh, great warrior, heroine of the queendom?'

'Your... girl?' Asher queried.

'Yeah, *my* girl.' He gestured all around him. 'The beautiful woman in whom you now find yourself. *Silvi*.'

'Who was she?' Luce asked, turning to Marius.

'Who?'

'The person you named your ship after.'

'Oh,' he said with a fond smile. 'Just a friend.'

A soft smile spread across Luce's face. 'She must have been very special.'

'She was.' The black Vulpen fell silent, deep in thought.

An unusual sound rumbled beneath a loose pile of blankets at the foot of the bed, the pile rising gradually before descending in a squeaky snarl. No one seemed to be paying it any mind, so Asher felt a measure of safety as he approached. He reached down to the topmost blanket and, with a swift tug, threw it to the ground. A gentle wave of relief filled him at what he saw. Jarl Erik, snoring loudly, appeared quite comfortable with a large empty bottle of whiskey in his webbed paw.

'I had barely moored before he was sniffing around, looking for that drink I owed him,' Marius said, glancing over. 'Went straight for my finest bottle. Next thing I know, he's passed out in my blankets.' His gaze turned to Asher. 'Best leave him, eh? I wouldn't want to wake up to this shit show.'

Asher nodded and gently placed the blanket back over the unconscious Otyren, keeping his head clear. He tried to take the empty bottle from Erik's webbed paws but was met with a stern grumble, the paws tightening their grip and pulling the bottle closer.

'Sorry to interrupt,' Cara interjected. 'But there's a whole horde of bloodthirsty Shangari after us, and you need to get us to Ignimarum.'

'And there we have it!' Marius exclaimed, pulling a white clay pipe from his vest. 'The job.' He raised the pipe to his snout and lit it with the stylish flick of a match, which he drew from another pocket. 'And what do I get out of this?' he asked, raising an eyebrow.

'You get to keep your life and this poxy little dinghy,' Cara snapped.

Marius chuckled. 'Hah! Good luck getting out of here without me.' He patted a beam that rose from the wall beside the bed. '*Silvi* doesn't play well with others.'

Cara shifted her cloak to reveal her sheathed sword and placed a paw on the pommel. A puff of smoke trickled out from the end of Marius's long snout like a spectre. An excited grin grew across Luce's face.

'Okay, okay,' Marius said, closing his eyes and raising his paws in surrender. 'I'll be your personal escort! As a favour to our queen, a most valued customer.' He gave Luce a nudge. 'She's so serious.'

'I know!' Luce giggled.

Cara let out a disgruntled huff and returned to the window, not removing her paw from the pommel of her sword.

'I was hoping to spend some time in the capital, but I'm guessing that's out of the question?' Marius asked with a knowing sigh. Neither Cara nor Luce responded, and Asher's eyes fell to the floor, unable to say the words. Another puff of smoke blew out from the end of Marius's snout, and he nodded. 'I thought as much.' He stood from the bed and made his way over to Cara. He stood over the Vulpen agent and waited with arms crossed. 'You're gonna need to move.'

She didn't turn from the window.

'Please,' he eventually said with a courteous smile.

Cara snorted, then stepped aside, allowing Marius to take her place.

'You might want to hold on to something. I haven't had to do this for a while.'

Asher sat on the chair by the desk and gripped the edge of the table while Luce held onto the edge of the bed, her face unable to contain her excitement.

'I'm fine,' Cara said flatly, standing to one side.

'Suit yourself.' After pulling several small levers, he rested a paw on a thick red lever and whispered, 'Come on, girl, you can do it.'

He yanked it down hard.

At first, nothing happened. The sound of waves lapping against the ship's hull continued to fill the cabin as all inside held their breath. Cara raised an eyebrow, distinctly unimpressed.

Ca-chunk!

A rumbling began to resonate around the cabin, and Asher scanned the walls. Ropes began pulling in all different directions. Gears turned, some slowly, others at a rapid pace, and he stared in amazement at the incredible display of engineering. All of a sudden, there were three loud snaps just outside, followed by three heavy splashes. The cabin lurched, and Asher turned to the window, finding, to his amazement, that they were now drifting away from the dock. Marius pulled another lever, and the ship began to turn until it eventually pointed towards the bay's entrance and the open water beyond. The rear window now faced back towards the docks and the doomed village. A throng of Shangari flooding in and out of the tavern, the sound of smashing glass and frustrated screeches emanating from within.

There's so many, Asher thought, his heart tightening in his chest, his mind on the village's poor inhabitants.

The two leaders stood before the gnarled horde, staring in disbelief at the ship drifting out of reach. Asher's eyes landed on the hooded stranger, specifically the sinister black crossbow held tight by their side. His mind flashed back to Mia, her blue eyes filling with tears, blood dripping from the black bolt in her neck.

Then he felt it, that fire deep within his heart coming to life, the fire he hadn't felt since the attack on White Cliffe City. It began to burn stronger than ever, fuelled by his grief, by the injustice done to him, to Mia. His muscles tensed, and his eyes became predator-focused. Without thinking, he grabbed his bow from his shoulder and nocked an arrow from the quiver, pulling the string tight to his cheek. He released his breath and loosed the arrow, watching it sail out of the window straight towards the hooded figure. It was the perfect shot.

Clang!

The knight raised his arm, and the arrow clattered against one of the metal plates running up his muscular arm. The hooded figure didn't even flinch.

'No!' Asher cried, reaching for another arrow. As his fingers wrapped around the narrow shaft, a paw gripped his arm, preventing him from pulling it out. His head snapped around. It was Cara.

'It's no use, Asher,' she said, looking into his eyes.

'But-but it was them! They killed Mia!' Asher was shaking. He felt so much fury, so much sadness, all at once, like a hurricane tearing him apart from the inside. The fire within him raged, begging for vengeance.

'I know.' Cara's grasp was firm, determined not to let Asher continue.

'Then get *off*!' He strained against her grasp again, fury overwhelming all senses.

'Asher, look at me.'

He turned to her.

'I've seen what anger can do to people. It... it turns them into monsters. Don't let it consume you.'

Asher stared into her eyes for a time and saw her own grief overflowing, saw the fear and worry that came from a past filled with pain. Slowly, he began to match her slow, rhythmic breaths, and the worst of his rage began to ebb away. Asher dropped the bow to the floor. He rested his head on Cara's shoulder and closed his eyes, fighting back the gathering tears. Cara raised her paw and rested it against the back of Asher's head. Her touch was warm, comforting, and what remaining rage he felt melted from his heart, releasing the tightness in his chest.

'I'm not as strong as you,' he breathed.

'I'm not strong,' she whispered back.

'Princeling!' came a booming cry from the docks.

Asher raised his head and turned to the window. Back on the dock, the knight glared at the back of the ship, a colossal fist raised high. It wasn't clear whether he could spot Asher through the small window, but his eyes were filled with rage. 'I am Umaloch, Knight of the High Priestess. Remember my name as you abandon your people! I shall rain death upon them and free their holy fires from their godless bodies!' With that, he dropped his fist to his side, and all the Shangari dispersed. They surged into the homes, and a chorus of blood-curdling screams began to echo around the cove. Asher could only watch in horror as the quiet village of Saewic was plunged into a nightmare of carnage and blood.

'Hold on to your asses!' Marius suddenly cried, and he pulled hard on the largest lever. The sails unfurled with a flurry of motion, and the ship burst forwards with tremendous speed. They surged between the cliffs guarding the bay's entrance and out into the waters beyond. Asher watched the tiny village shrink into the distance, the sound of slaughter fading until it was a whisper in the wind.

His entire life had been torn to bloody ribbons in such a short time. So many lie dead. He fought with his mind as it tried to convince him it couldn't be real. Everything he had seen, everything he had witnessed, it must have been a sick, twisted part of his imagination running wild. His paws tightened into fists so tight he could feel his nails cutting into his palms.

It was real.

His father's death had been real. Mia's death had been real. All those innocent people in White Cliffe and Saewic, their deaths had been so very real. He could still see their horrified, lifeless faces staring at him, eyes wide, desperately pleading for him, begging him to save them. And what had he done? He had fled to save his own fur. All his life, he had run from his responsibilities, assuming they would fall upon another. Now, he was the only one left, the only one his people could turn to. Constance had let loose a ravenous horde upon the kingdom, and now they rampaged through the land, devouring everything in their path. Someone had to put an end to whatever deranged plans she had. Someone had to stop her madness from killing any more innocent people.

My people.

He let out a held breath, an overwhelming resolve washing over him.

'I'm going to stop Constance,' he declared to the wind through gritted teeth.

Cara placed a paw on his shoulder. 'I know.'

8

Welcome to Ignimarum

Asher leant forwards in his chair, watching Cara as she slept. He did feel a little invasive, but her restless slumber had summoned him into the cabin, and now she murmured as if suffering from a terrible nightmare. He yawned. Sleep had evaded him this night, as it had the past couple of nights aboard *The Silvi*. The faces of the dead plagued his mind whenever he closed his eyes, howling at him to save them, with Mia leading the nightmarish choir. He turned back to Cara, thankful for someone else he could focus on.

'I had to...,' she whispered among a spew of incoherent murmurs.

Asher's leg bounced. Should he wake her from the visions that plagued her? Or leave her to rest and gather her strength? It was late, though Asher couldn't say what time. The Lighthouse had long shifted its light away from the vessel, and the cold night air now filled the cabin. From the desk, a small candle bathed the room in a soft orange glow. It flickered as a fresh breeze rolled in through the open window, out of which sparkling stars dotted the night sky, their light reflecting in the calm sea like a vast, endless mirror.

At the foot of the bed, wrapped in a heap of blankets, was Luce, sleeping peacefully where Jarl Erik once resided. Asher had yet to see where the little Otyren had scampered off to. One minute, he was unconscious; the next, he was gone, along with a bottle from Marius's supply.

'Luna!' Cara cried, bolting upright. She searched the cabin, her breaths quick and frantic, eyes darting from corner to corner, looking for something or someone.

'Whoa... hey... easy now,' Asher said softly, rising to his feet. 'It's okay.'

Cara closed her eyes and collected herself with a sigh. She rested her head on the plump pillow. 'What time is it?' she asked, her breathing now steady. 'Are we there yet?'

'It's late,' Asher replied. 'Marius said we'd be approaching the Blazing Gates soon.'

Cara said nothing, her mind seemingly elsewhere.

Asher looked to Luce, who remained undisturbed by the sudden outburst. Happy, or at least content that Cara and Luce were okay, Asher made for the door. 'I'll be at the wheel with Marius if you need anything.'

'Have you slept?' Cara asked, not opening her eyes.

'A little,' he lied with a forced smile. 'Honestly, I'm okay.'

He pulled the door open and stepped out, feeling the fresh, cold breeze roll through his fur. A single lantern hung from the central mast. It lit the deck in a dim glow, the sound of its warm crackle entwining with the gentle lapping of waves as *The Silvi* skipped across the calm water. Asher closed his eyes, breathing in the sea air deep through his twitching nose. It was a calm night, cold but peaceful. Fortunately, Marius had loaned Asher some warmer clothing, which he had accepted without question. He now wore a simple, long-sleeved, dark green shirt that fit tight around his chest, black trousers, black boots and a thin brown belt around his waist. Over his shirt was his old brown hood—a way to make the outfit his own. It was much warmer than his previous tunic and thin trousers, and he was thankful the strong breeze no longer had such a bite.

He turned and climbed the creaky steps leading above the cabin and onto the quarterdeck, where he found Marius standing behind *The Silvi*'s large steering wheel. He smiled at the approaching Asher, his orange eyes watching him, almost glowing under the dim light.

'How's our fearless leader doing?' he asked with a chuckle, though Asher could detect a note of sincerity.

'She's okay. Well, I think she is. It's hard to tell.'

The black Vulpen pulled out his clay pipe, placed it in his mouth and lit it in one smooth motion. He puffed a few times to get the smoke flowing. The tobacco-packed end emitted a warm glow with each drag, illuminating his long snout and dark fur.

'You know, you haven't told me why you're running to Terravulpa or why those friends of yours were after you.'

Asher hesitated, unsure how much to say. Sure, Marius had saved them, but only while under threat. He was in the business of selling secrets, and who Asher was and what had happened to his family would be worth a fortune to the right buyer.

'The church attacked after the king banished them,' he said. 'I don't know why they're after me.'

The end of Marius's pipe glowed, a wisp of white smoke flowing from his snout. 'Was it bad?' he eventually asked. 'In the city, I mean.'

Asher closed his eyes and nodded, too tired to talk.

'You okay? When was the last time you slept?'

Asher opened his eyes and found Marius's concerned gaze studying his solemn expression. 'I'm okay. I just... I just saw some things I'd rather forget.'

'Oh, right. Well, you know, I would have helped you with or without the threats,' Marius said with a light nudge of his elbow.

'Marius, I—' But before Asher could finish, Marius raised a paw over the wheel, gesturing for Asher to look over the ship's bow.

Dark shapes began to form on the horizon, growing tall and thick, like fingers grasping towards the sky. Massive burning braziers capped the two largest. They stood like titanic sentinels, keeping watch over the dark ocean before them. A colossal arched gatehouse lay between them, covered in a vast array of torches and smaller braziers, the glow reflecting in the water below as if the sea itself were on fire. Beneath the arch, colossal stone doors opened out towards the sea, spread wide like welcoming arms. Faint torch lights flickered between the other rocky fingers, marking the presence of the immense sea wall that enclosed Ignimarum. Hundreds of lights flowed beneath the vast gate like river lanterns during a harvest festival.

'Welcome to Ignimarum,' Marius said with pride. 'Crown jewel of Terravulpa.'

They sailed closer, and the air began to warm. The sentinel torches began to bathe *The Silvi* in an orange glow, their great might rising high, looming over the tiny dot that was their ship.

'It's... beautiful...' Asher breathed, his eyes staring up in awe.

'It's home,' Marius returned with a contented smile.

Tiny figures marched up and down the gatehouse's length, the light from their torches reflecting off their metal-plated armour. At each end were two huge ballistas, loaded with giant bolts, ready to fire down at any vessel deemed too threatening.

The Silvi, dwarfed by the enormous stone doors, sailed between the crowds of other ships passing under the stone arch. The structure was colossal, its thickness at least the length of three small vessels, and as Asher looked up at the inner architecture, his eyes focused on something much closer. Up in the crow's nest, dangling over the side, he spotted a small webbed paw. In it was an empty bottle.

Marius glanced up and shook his head. 'Sometimes, I think that damned Otyren is actually trying to kill himself.'

'Or he's trying to forget something,' Asher said thoughtfully.

Marius shrugged. He continued steering *The Silvi* with ease between the chaotic maelstrom of other vessels. They ranged from small ships like *The Silvi*, carrying only a few folk, to much larger vessels carrying cargo and other goods for trade.

The ship suddenly lurched. It took everything in Asher's power not to lose his footing and fly over the low railing and into the midnight ocean. Marius grabbed the wheel and pulled it hard, righting the ship.

'Sorry about that! Bastards don't give a shit about us smaller folk!'

'What was that about?' Asher yelled. His mouth hung open as his eyes landed on a hulking mass looming behind Marius. A colossal warship, at least ten times the length and three times the height of *The Silvi*, lumbered past their left flank. Hundreds of sails were fastened to five towering masts, propelling the behemoth forwards with overwhelming might. It forced all other vessels aside, lest they risk being trampled by the titanic front ram.

'What is that thing?' Asher asked, staring at its vast wooden hull.

'That is a royal Tail o' War,' came a voice from the stairs.

Asher and Marius turned to find Cara making her way up and onto the quarterdeck. She watched the warship crawl by with pride. 'It contains a large portion of Terravulpa's army on board, and sails the ocean on patrol, protecting our waters from pirates. It's also a deterrent, able to deploy its soldiers anywhere in Tamuz at a moment's notice.'

She turned to Asher, who continued to watch the warship as it faded into the night. 'Is this your first time at Ignimarum?'

He nodded. 'I've never travelled that far out of White Cliffe.'

'You're gonna love it,' Marius beamed. 'She's a beautiful city with the sleaziest of bars and the most proper of dining establishments.' He spoke the last words with an exaggerated accent, raising his snout to accentuate his mock grandeur. 'Yup, Ignimarum has everything you need, and it's where we shall be parting ways, I'm afraid. Thanks to this recent escapade, I'm late for a shipment, and I don't intend to be any later than I need to be.'

Cara straightened herself and faced Marius with a courteous bow. 'Your recent assistance has been appreciated by Her Royal Highness, Queen Tessina.'

'Yeah, well, appreciation doesn't put food on the table,' Marius huffed.

The Silvi sailed on, under the Blazing Gates and into the calm water beyond. The space opened into a vast bay, surrounded by hundreds of huge sea stacks and rising cliffs, enclosed by stone walls rising between each stack. Hardy plant life clung to the rock faces, and tiny black dots circled the upper heights, squawking relentlessly despite the late hour.

Asher gasped as their nimble vessel rounded the bay's curve.

A sprawling, multileveled city sat nestled within the rocky bay, walled tiers climbing the cliff like steps for a colossal giant. Torchlight from the city's countless homes and shops illuminated the night sky. The golden glow cascaded down the tiers like a waterfall, eventually reaching the water's edge, where thick stone docks stretched out into the bay. Each dock was crawling with life.

Asher's eyes climbed the tiers and found that as the city rose higher, the architecture grew more extravagant. Where the lower tiers featured many simple, square buildings stacked atop each other like a child's wooden blocks, the upper levels were filled with large, lavish-looking manors, several floors high and overgrown with lush greenery. To the left of the middle tier sat a large gatehouse nestled within a gap in the cliff, likely granting access to the rest of the island. Asher's mind returned to Mia and her family. His heart ached at the thought of telling them about her passing. He had to be the one to do it, though. It was only right.

His eyes reached the top tier, where an expansive palace took centre stage. It was a vast building enclosed by tall walls and featured several domed roofs across its length. An expansive balcony stretched out over the lower tiers. The supports descended to the levels below, where archways had been carved into the thick base to create passageways for citizens to pass through.

The Silvi sailed towards the city, passing between two protective walls that marked the entrance to the docks. The thick stone walls stretched out into the bay like massive arms, embracing the docked vessels and keeping them safe. Numerous Vulpen soldiers patrolled their lengths, their armour made of layered plates tinted red as if coated in blood. Each plate curved to a point, the edges trimmed black. Helmets covered the top half of their heads and stretched down to cover the upper jaw of their snout, giving them a mysterious, sinister appearance. Asher had never seen such intimidating armour. He had always imagined the entire Vulpen army comprised sneaking agents like Cara and Luce, not heavy soldiers in plated armour. He dismissed the idiotic assumption before Marius or Cara could see the mild confusion on his face.

Of course they need soldiers, idiot, he thought, chastising himself. *Kingdoms don't just function on spies and secrets.*

Long curved blades sat at the side of many, while a few had elegant short bows slung over their shoulders, tall quivers full of arrows strapped to their backs. On both walls were figures with crimson capes. They flowed behind the captains as they inspected the troops, paying no mind to *The Silvi* as it sailed past. Asher watched them with a fascinated stare.

Within the sea wall's safe embrace and anchored within a particular section of the docks was an armada of sleek ships not dissimilar to *The Silvi*, the largest being another Tail 'o' War. It lazed in the water like a sleeping giant. Hundreds of soldiers ran up and down its sloping planks like ants swarming a nest.

Marius steered *The Silvi* away and towards the dock's commercial area, where he found a suitable space to moor. He navigated the ship up to the stone walkway and tied her ropes to a small round bollard. Asher and Cara grabbed their things from the cabin, woke the grumbling Luce from her slumber and stepped onto the stone dock, thankful to be back on solid ground once more.

Asher stared up at the towering city before him, the atmosphere unlike anything he had experienced. It was chaos, glorious chaos. It reminded him of White Cliffe City, except... more. Everything was more: the buildings, the people, the sounds, the sheer scale of the city as it climbed higher and higher up the cliff face.

The docks before him were full of Vulpen hurrying about, carrying goods from their ships and rushing to the nearest tavern for a well-deserved drink. A chorus of voices filled the air. The scent of a thousand spices floated on the breeze, mixing with a salty sea breeze and filling Asher's twitching nose. Music drifted across the dock. The stringed melody had a vibrant beat that Asher couldn't help but nod to. He searched for the source. Looking towards the city, he found the swish of a ribbon breaching over a large gathering of people. Standing on the balls of his feet, he attempted to peer over the sea of dock goers.

Among the crowd, Asher found the familiar sight of tall Rabbethi ears bouncing their way above the heads of the locals. It was good to see his people thriving in this foreign land.

I doubt they consider this city foreign anymore, Asher thought as he observed their Vulpen clothing—loose shirts and slender trousers for men, and simple stola dresses for women. The Rabbethi here were likely descendants of refugees who fled Rabbethia during the great purge all those centuries ago. *I wonder if they have any love for Rabbethia anymore? For their homeland, their king...*

A hard shove brought him crashing back down.

'Watch it,' grumbled a broad Vulpen sailor stomping by. Asher rubbed his bruised shoulder and contemplated relieving the gentleman of his coin pouch, but a paw on his shoulder made him pause.

'It's not worth it,' Marius said as if reading Asher's intention.

'I don't know what you're talking about.'

'Sure,' Marius scoffed.

'What will you do now?' Asher asked, changing the subject.

'Well, I'll make a claim to the spymaster to cover the disruption of my business.' He gave a side-eye stare to Cara, who paid him no mind and continued to tighten her bootlaces. 'Then I'll stock up on new information and set back off again. Maybe I'll head north now that Rabbethia is a bit of a shit show. Errr... sorry.'

'It's okay,' Asher said. 'I don't know how, but I'll make it right.' The determination in his voice surprised even himself.

Marius smiled. 'I'm sure you will.' He placed a paw on Asher's shoulder. 'Well, this is likely the last we'll see of each other. Good luck on your journey, patches.'

'Thank you, Marius,' Asher said with a smile, a little sad at the Vulpen's departure. He had grown to like the man, his nonchalant manners, witty responses and all-around laid-back approach to life.

With a quick squeeze of Asher's shoulder, Marius sauntered along the docks towards the city lights, vanishing into the crowd.

'You ready?' Cara asked, standing and pulling her dark hood over her head.

Asher nodded, pulling his brown hood over and tucking his ears down his back.

'Ready as I'll ever be.'

'Then let's go!' Luce yelled with overwhelming energy, appearing suddenly. She skipped ahead through the crowd, disappearing into the sea of people and out of sight in an instant.

The enchanting music began to grow, rising in pace and rhythm as they neared the start of the docks. A flash of a white ribbon sailed above the crowd, then a purple one, until both twirled around each other like a duet of dancing snakes. It was utterly captivating, a dance unlike anything Asher had seen in White Cliffe City.

Cara veered away from the gathered crowd. Asher knew he should follow, but was utterly spellbound. He continued forwards, pushing through the mass until he stood just a few folk from the front. His heart skipped. Two lustful figures danced atop a high, rounded platform. One was a tall, slender, black-furred Vulpen dressed in fine purple silks embroidered with golden threads. Her face was kind, her eyes like orange fire.

The other, more petite figure took Asher's breath away. A beautiful white-furred Rabbethi danced next to the Vulpen, dressed in red silk trousers that flowed behind her as she kicked and danced to the music. A red silk sash covered her chest, and she held a thin white ribbon high above her head. Her eyes were the brightest blue Asher had ever seen, and her coy smile enchanted all who watched. The pair danced on and on, moving around each other to the music, laughing and smiling, gliding with elegance. At the platform's base, musicians spun a fast-paced tune. One played a viola, the other patted a small drum, their tall Rabbethi ears flopping to and fro as they strung their sweet melody.

Asher lifted his gaze back to the dancers and found the young Rabbethi staring straight at him. She smiled at his surprise, her eyes narrowing with purpose. She winked, and Asher felt his cheeks glow, but couldn't avert his gaze. The music and dancing continued to build until an eventual crescendo left the two dancers panting, frozen in an acrobatic pose.

Applause erupted around them, and all performers gave deep bows. The dancers descended the pedestal as the musicians removed their caps and began walking among the crowd, asking for tips and donations for their performance. Many dropped a few silver pieces, the occasional gold appearing, while most simply walked away, profusely apologising that they had no spare change.

Asher's eyes remained fixed on the Rabbethi woman, her shape and beauty muting all other senses. With a final smile and wave to the ogling fans, she turned, eyes locking onto Asher's. Her smile dropped. Her eyes darkened, and a deep worry descended upon her face.

She mouthed the word "Help" in a silent plea before vanishing into the crowd.

Asher's legs moved before he knew what was happening. He followed her deeper into the stone plaza, the crowd dispersing around him, their chatter and laughter growing louder in the absence of music. It wasn't a large plaza by any means, but Asher quickly discovered it was still easy to lose someone when packed full of lively citizens. It was enclosed by many flat-roofed buildings stacked on top of each other, with wooden walkways and stairs wrapping around the higher buildings, allowing access from the plaza below. The ground floor was an assortment of shop fronts manned by Vulpen or Rabbethi. They enticed passers-by inside with toothless smiles and special offers. Every so often, a street or alley would cut the stack of buildings in half and lead to other plazas along the lower tiers. Asher stared into each one, searching for the mysterious siren.

Just as he was about to convince himself she had been a figment of his imagination, he found her waiting by the entrance of one of the alleyways. They made eye contact, and she darted into the darkness beyond. Against his better judgment, Asher continued his pursuit. He reached the entrance to the alley and paused. It was dark and wholly uninviting, but the fragrant scent of something sweet floated up his nose, and he quickly pushed his fears aside. Determined to help this beautiful stranger, he stepped into the shadows of the narrow passage.

It wasn't long before the plaza lights faded behind him, the warm glow of the lanterns and torches becoming cold and distant. The pungent odour of sewage replaced the vibrant scent of perfumes and spices, and he could feel his initial bravery starting to falter. His fearless pace slowed as the pull of the plaza lights grew stronger. He came to a stop at the first junction. Straight ahead led to a long set of stairs that opened onto a bright, busy street. To his right was nothing but shadow.

'Hello?' he asked into the darkness, the sound of the bustling plaza now muted behind him. There was no sign of trouble, and he released a tightly held breath, almost thankful to find no one in need. A sense of guilty relief washed over him, and he turned for the safety of the plaza.

A blade edge came racing out of the darkness towards his neck. He stumbled back, pressing himself as far into the wall as possible. The sharp edge dipped into his flesh, and a small trickle of blood descended his throat. Asher held his breath as he looked down at the blade, feeling the warmth of his blood gliding down onto his chest. There was a white ribbon wrapped around the blade's handle, gripped tight by a petite white-furred paw.

'Hmm, you're not from around here, are ya?' came a smooth, delicate voice.

Asher's eyes ran up the paw, along the slender arm and into the shadows. A familiar set of bright blue eyes glared at him with dark and malicious intent.

'Welcome to Ignimarum, pretty boy.'

9

The Lower Tiers

The blade was sharp against Asher's throat. He dared not move. The slightest motion would undoubtedly be the end of him. His blood continued to trickle, leaving a thin crimson trail down his white fur.

'I'll ask ya again,' came the agitated voice of the beautiful Rabbethi woman. 'What gold have ya got?' Her bright blue eyes stared intently, her brow furrowing at the lack of response. Asher felt her eyes drift to his neck, to the silver chain of his mother's necklace that poked from his shirt's open buttons. 'What's this?' she questioned with a nasty grin, her annoyance dissipating with the sudden find of loot.

'That's a pretty thing. Where'd ya get something like that? Steal it?'

Asher motioned to the knife with one paw. The woman rolled her eyes with an exasperated sigh, easing the blade off his throat, not by much, but just what Asher needed.

'Now,' she continued. 'Where did—'

Asher raised his knee and planted his boot square into the woman's stomach. With a hard shove, he sent her hurtling backwards, crashing into the shadows, her shocked face vanishing into the darkness. Asher stumbled forwards, his breaths heavy, adrenaline coursing through his body. He peered down the alley and waited. A stupid part of him felt guilty for hurting the woman, and he almost wanted to see if she was okay, but the thin, matted line of red fur descending his neck pushed those thoughts aside. Hearing nothing and desperately wanting to be back in the safety of the plaza crowd, Asher moved.

'You bastard!' screamed a hoarse voice from the shadows. 'You'll pay for that! Boys!' There was a short pause before a door slammed open between Asher and the plaza lights at the end of the alley. Asher stepped back as a large shape stepped out. The silhouette approached with purpose, growing increasingly menacing as it drew closer. Asher turned, hoping to escape through the alley behind, but another door opened, blocking his path. Out stepped another figure, smaller than the first but equally as menacing. A sinking feeling settled in Asher's gut as he realised he was well and truly trapped. He backed himself towards the junction. On either side of him, emerging into the dim light, came two, unkempt Rabbethi, their fur scraggly, their frames broad and assertive. Asher hesitantly raised his fists.

'You hurt my sis, runt?' asked the larger of the two, glaring down at Asher with a look of unimpressed cockiness. His voice was deep, and his white fur exaggerated the sheer filth coating him. He stood a good foot above Asher and had thick, muscular arms bulging from the torn sleeves of his beige shirt. He crossed them expectantly in front of him. The other Rabbethi was shorter and much leaner, with jet-black fur covering his body as if he were a shadow come to life. He said nothing but stared at Asher with a sinister, calculating gaze. The weight of their presence pushed Asher back against the wall. He remained silent as his heart raced.

'Come on, mate, speak up,' the larger one encouraged, taking another step closer.

Asher couldn't help but shrink at the scope of this Rabbethi. Back home, he would have used some clever trick or distraction to avoid a confrontation with a beast this large. Today felt different. A slew of discouraging thoughts destroyed every quick and witty plan that entered his mind. They were new, foreign, and all too unwelcome.

I couldn't even save Mia. How can I save myself?

Fresh footsteps began to echo to his right, coming from the plaza, but Asher dared not take his eyes off the menacing pair. His nose twitched as adrenaline coursed through his veins. His mind was a cyclone of panicked thoughts, all shouting at him, screaming at him. Seeds of doubt wrapped their vines around his heart, squeezing, tightening. They had grown strong since Saewic, since his decision to descend the ladder first had gotten Mia killed, and now they extended to his limbs, attempting to root him to the ground. Nausea welled up from the pit of his stomach as Mia's sobs pierced through the cacophony of thoughts.

You were wrong.

'Let's just gut him and be done with it!' yelled the shorter one in a scratchy voice. His fiddling paw grasped onto something, and he began to pull what Asher now saw was a sharp, serrated shortsword.

It was halfway removed from under his cloak before a blur of black and red flashed before Asher's eyes. A gust of wind followed, and the shorter Rabbethi was tumbling away, enveloped by a shadow. They came to a sliding halt and untangled themselves. As the shadow stood, a large red tail unfurled behind them, its owner staring daggers at the Rabbethi, eyes stern and focused.

'Cara!' Asher yelled, a sense of relief overcoming him, but she didn't turn to face him.

'I told you to stay close,' she snarled, drawing her long, curved blade.

'It's an agent,' the larger Rabbethi said, a sudden worry creeping into his once overconfident tone. 'Let's just go, Marrick.'

Cara growled at the pair, her canine fangs revealing themselves from her curled upper lip. The muscular Rabbethi took a couple of cautious paces back before abruptly spinning and sprinting into the shadows of the alley opposite, his thunderous footsteps fading quickly. The shorter, black-furred Rabbethi glared at Cara, clearly the braver of the two despite his slighter frame. After a tense moment, he spat at the floor and backed away, fading into the shadows without a sound. Asher released a held breath.

Cara sheathed her blade, standing straight before turning to him. 'What were you thinking?' she demanded, as if chastising a child. 'It's not safe for outsiders like you. The dark places you're used to are nothing compared to the underbelly of Ignimarum.' She was right. The thugs of White Cliffe City were troublesome but relatively harmless and easy to handle. These criminals were something else entirely—dangerous. 'It's a good thing I noticed you were gone and came looking,' Cara continued. 'Have you seen Lucilla?'

'No, sorry,' Asher said, feeling foolish.

Idiot. I'm such an idiot.

Cara sighed. 'If she doesn't want to be found, then we won't be able to find her. Best we head for the palace. She'll end up there eventually.' Cara began marching down the alley towards the steps at the far end. Asher followed, but something on the ground caught his eye.

It glimmered on the cobblestone floor, the low light of the alley illuminating something small and sharp. It was the dagger held to his throat not moments ago, a thin trail of his blood still coating its edge. He picked it up. It was a fine blade, sharp and devoid of any tarnish or chipping. A white ribbon wrapped around its handle, giving it an elegance he hadn't seen in such a simple weapon.

He hesitated, then sheathed the dagger through his belt. He then picked up his fallen bow and collected the quiver of arrows before catching up to Cara. With a nod, she stepped out of the shadow and into the warm glow of the main street.

The cobblestone street was at least three carts wide and sloping. Heading left led deeper into the city, the street ascending towards an imposing three-storey gatehouse before turning and ascending the next tier in the opposite direction. Heading right descended back towards the water level and the bustling dockside plazas.

All around were more precariously stacked buildings. The upper floors were residential, with washing hanging between windows, people half-dressed leaning in doorways. They chatted merrily as they set about their nightly chores, while hordes of people flooded in and out of the shops and taverns occupying the lower floors.

The methodic sound of a hammer striking metal rang across the street, echoing over the bustling crowd. The scent of spices and incense had returned, and Asher sniffed deep, expunging the smell of sewage from his nose. The buildings opposite ran several structures deep before colliding with a gigantic rocky cliff rising high into the night sky. A large stone wall sat atop the ridge, following the cliff as it sloped upwards to the right. The immense scale of it all was overwhelming. Asher returned his gaze to the street, turning to his right where the road sloped down and curved into the bottom tier's central plaza.

'You see that building?' Cara asked, noticing Asher's wandering gaze. She pointed towards a structure at the curve's corner.

Asher followed her clawed finger and found a short stone structure with a reinforced metal gate and two heavily armoured Vulpen guards on either side, red capes adorning their shoulders. Gold patterns swirled around the stonework and gating, creating designs that imitated the dance of an inferno. It was strange to see something so intricate nestled among the more rustic establishments of the lower tier. Its single level stretched back to the base of the cliff, where it penetrated the rock like an ornate piton.

'That's the queen's Royal Run,' Cara continued. 'And it goes straight up to the palace.'

'I take it we can't use it then?' Asher queried, already guessing at the answer.

'No one uses it without the queen's express permission, and we don't have that.' She turned her gaze uphill and sighed. 'We'll be taking the long way.'

Asher followed her gaze and traced the stone street as it ascended some distance before curving right and under a large stone gatehouse. The stone wall that ran along the top of the cliff edge ascended from its flank, ensuring there was no way through other than under its stone arch. Beneath the gate, large wooden doors opened inwards. Crowds made their way through unchallenged by the observant guards.

'Let's go,' Cara said. She took off through the crowd and up the slope. Asher followed close behind, not wanting a repeat of the last time he didn't follow her instructions.

They weaved in and out of the bustling crowd as the citizens enjoyed their evening. A multitude of different shops lined the lower floors, ranging from food stands, apothecaries, and herbalists to blacksmiths, armourers, and general goods. Taverns roared with life. Laughter streamed out the open doors and windows, carried by the welcoming glow of fires within.

Asher and Cara eventually reached the gatehouse atop the first tier. Guards in curved crimson armour stood like stone sentinels on either side, with more atop the gate, though they were not so rigid.

They peered down at the crowd below, surveying the river of fur and frivolity. A few guards patrolled the wall ascending from the gatehouse, climbing with purpose and control, their armour clinking in sync as they stepped together. This was a well-disciplined force, an army of rules and order—much unlike what Asher had witnessed elsewhere in the city.

The buildings of the second tier were still simple stacked structures with walkways and stairs built into the stonework. The masonry, however, was more refined and made with less of a "that'll do" mentality. The topmost floors had sloping tiled roofs instead of the flat tops of the bottom tier, and the residents walked among the walkways wearing more upmarket clothing—clothing with fewer loose threads, fewer stains and the addition of yellow embroidery to imitate gold. Plenty of shops and taverns still lined the lower floors, but had an increased air of class about them. Their walls were cleaner and coated in less grime and other stains abundant in the lower tier. The occasional flower bed decorated the edges of the street, the gentle scent replacing the heavy spices and incense dominating the lower tier.

Guards were posted behind the metal gates of some of the more exuberant homes. They were not Vulpen guards, as Asher would have expected, but Rabbethi guards dressed in Vulpen-style armour. Colours adorned their shoulder plates, which Asher could only assume represented the families they protected. They watched the crowd passing by, more relaxed than the guards at the gatehouse, though their large eyes remained vigilant, watching individuals closely as they passed. Some lingered on Asher for an uncomfortable length of time before moving on.

'Rabbethi make better guards,' Cara said, noticing Asher's inquisitive stares. 'With your wider peripheral vision and natural alertness, you Rabbethi are tough to sneak up on. In a city home to the best spy network in Tamuz, that sort of talent comes highly sought after.'

'I know,' Asher replied, slightly annoyed at the explanation of his own people's anatomy. 'It's why our top secrets are still secret. I just didn't expect to see so many Rabbethi working here.'

Cara raised an eyebrow. 'You think we don't know your secrets?'

Asher opened his mouth to protest, but found he didn't want to know the truth.

'These Rabbethi have lived here their entire lives,' Cara continued, thoughtfully. 'Their grandparents' grandparents lived here, and they have just as much right to call Terravulpa home as I do. You'll have to get used to not every Rabbethi owing you their loyalty.'

Looking at the guards again, he did notice that they seemed different. All these centuries away from their homeland had changed them. Their fur was shorter and coarser than he was used to, and their ears were wider and taller than his own. The differences were subtle, but definitely there. Would they care that bloodthirsty Shangari had overrun their ancestral homeland? The descendants of those who forced their ancestors to flee during the great purge, slaughtered and devoured? A sinking feeling grew in Asher's stomach as he guessed the answer.

The crowd grew thinner on this tier, making it easier for Asher and Cara to proceed up the gentle slope, though Asher could feel his muscles beginning to ache. He gazed up the slope and then towards the towering cliff to his left, sloping walls towering above like rising waves of zig-zagging stone. He groaned quietly.

These people must have the endurance of a warhorse.

Still, they pressed on, drawing close to another entrance to the queen's Royal Run. The intricate gold metal workings around the strong iron gates shone under the warm glow of the city's lights. Unlike the iron gates of the lower tier, these were open. A stranger in clothes identical to Cara's stood before the gate, blocking Asher and Cara's path. A dark black hood covered their face in shadow, masking all but the hint of a white snout that poked out into the light. A white bushy tail curved around their hip, swishing to and fro expectantly. They stood in silence, their arms strapped in leather bracers and crossed before them.

Cara stopped, stiffening as she held out an arm to halt Asher. Without a word, the figure pulled its hood down to reveal the face of a white Vulpen woman, covered in old scars that criss-crossed her face, with pink skin exposed where the fur had not regrown. Her brown eyes were hard, and she stared at Cara with what Asher could only guess was utter contempt.

'Domina Cara,' she acknowledged with a stern voice.

'Domina Flora,' Cara replied with equal disdain.

'We have logged your return, and your presence is requested urgently in the throne room.' Domina Flora turned to Asher, looking him up and down with a cynical eye. She scoffed. 'He's needed too. It seems he has some royal duties to perform.' With a smirk, she turned and swiftly entered the Royal Run, the guards snapping to attention as she passed.

'Let's go,' Cara said with a huff. Before Asher could say anything, she was on the move, making for the gate, her demeanour taking on a prickly shell.

As they made their way into the dimly lit entrance of the Royal Run, Asher heard the iron gates creak shut and lock behind them. There was no escape, and his mind began to fixate on what these "royal duties" could be.

10

A Question of Duty

Domina Flora led the way, with Cara following in a brooding silence, her eyes boring into the back of the white Vulpen's skull. Asher walked quietly behind. The corridor was silent, save for the crackling torches fastened to the wall and the faint murmur of the crowd fading behind them. Asher cast his eyes down to the red carpet, growing anxious over expectations he had yet to receive. The air suddenly became chilled, as if they had passed through a wall of ice. Asher guessed they were now within the rocky cliff itself, where the Lighthouse's warmth never reached.

Still, no one spoke.

After what felt like an age, they came to another iron gate with two Vulpen guards stationed on either side. It was open, and beyond lay a contraption Asher had never seen before. A large wooden box hung over a black pit by a thick metal chain on its roof. It was hollow, at least twice the height of Asher, and large enough to hold six Vulpen soldiers. The side facing the gate was open. The inside was empty, save for a single lit torch fastened to the wooden interior. Asher's eyes climbed the thick metal chain as it ascended a broad rocky shaft, the metal disappearing into a groaning darkness, swaying from a sourceless breeze.

'When you're ready, Your Highness,' Flora said sarcastically.

Asher's eyes returned to the box, where Flora and Cara stood inside, waiting. Cara jabbed Flora with a glare, to which Flora responded with a coy smile.

'It's okay. It's safe,' Cara said, turning to Asher with an impatient nod.

With careful steps, he entered the strange wooden box, choosing to stand beside the stern Cara. It jolted as it took his weight. His nose began twitching, and he could feel the smirk forming on Flora's face. By the ancients, he missed Luce already.

After the wooden frame eventually settled above the abyss, the guards closed the gate. One guard returned to his post while the other walked to a great lever, placed both paws onto it and lowered the mechanism to the ground, leaning his whole weight upon it. It hit the stone with a heavy thud. Metal grinding against metal began to resonate from the dark shaft above, and with a sudden lurch, the box started rising, drawn by the chain on its roof. Asher steadied himself as the world outside faded into darkness. They rose slowly. No one made a sound, but each continued to stare at the cold black rock as it passed, illuminated by the single torch within the contraption.

After a long while of awkward silence, the air began to warm. Metal gates descended in the space before them, and the box slowed before stopping with a jolt. The gates swung open, and two more guards stood to attention on either side. The trio stepped out of the box and into the hall. Flora marched ahead, entering a well-lit, lavish hallway with a wide red carpet and many braziers lining the walls.

Cara slowed her pace to walk beside Asher. 'The queen will know how to proceed,' she said with an air of knowing pride. 'She is both fair and wise.'

'You think very highly of her?' Asher replied.

'I do. From the shadows, she steers the world towards peace and prosperity. Because of her, the Fenrathi and Medvedians are preparing for peace talks.' Asher had heard stories of the war to the north but knew little of the details, save for what he heard from Medvedian traders back in White Cliffe City. The Fenrathi rarely ventured out of Fenrath, so many of the tales he heard were very one-sided.

'You'll see. You will come to love her as I do,' Cara finished, standing taller than before.

Asher smiled and nodded. He had come to trust his Vulpen companion but decided to reserve his opinions on foreign rulers until meeting them in person. Still, he couldn't help but feel hopeful at her words.

They continued down the extravagant hallway, passing wooden doors decorated with pieces of iron worked into the shape of fire, appearing as if each door was ablaze with shining flames. They were beautiful to glance at but not as stunning as the massive double door at the end of the hallway, sitting heavy on the opposite side of a junction. Patterns of shining gold overlaid wood of deep red, glinting as the brazier's fire danced. Embedded in the wood were two large golden rings. Clearly, this door acted as a display of power and opulent wealth, intimidating guests before they attended an audience with the queen. It was certainly working.

Hurried footsteps to Asher's left caught his attention. A black-furred Vulpen approached briskly, wearing a white shirt buttoned up and slim black trousers. He carried in one paw a silver plate covered by a silver dome lid, which he held high, keeping it level as he hurried past.

'Pardon me,' he said as he hastily crossed the junction.

Asher stepped aside and sniffed, expecting the scent of something rich and mouthwatering. He recoiled immediately, unable to control his reaction as the smell of meat filled his nostrils. He understood the need for certain folk to eat meat and could appreciate the skill in preparing a large stag or fatty boar, but the idea of actually eating the flesh of another creature sent shivers down his spine. The scent lingered, assaulting his senses. Flora and Cara paid no attention to it as they stepped towards the door, clearly accustomed to the fragrance, but something made Asher pause. It was a vile smell, and yet so recognisable. It differed from the wild boar and deer he had hunted for coin, which had only made him feel a little queasy.

This smell was utterly repulsive.

'But Domina Flora, she is engaged with Jarl Vatn,' came a flustered voice by the double doors.

Asher broke from his thoughts, finding Flora debating with one of the guards before the grand double doors. The guard was fighting a losing battle.

'The queen has granted me permission to inform her when the Rabbethi arrived,' she informed him with an agitated snap. 'Now open this door. That's an order.' She turned from the guards to the door, signalling she would hear no more of the guard's futile pleas. Both guards shared a look. After a moment of desperate eye motions between them, they relented and grabbed hold of the door's great golden rings. They then heaved the heavy door open.

The crackling of a roaring fire floated out into the hallway as the trio relinquished their weapons to the guards and stepped through. They entered into a vast chamber. The carpet stopped at the doorway, and their boots echoed off the stone floor as they walked. A large roaring fire took centre stage, its warmth felt instantly upon entering the area, and the light it emitted reached the far walls to the left and right. A series of circular wooden benches surrounded the flaming centrepiece, each covered in soft sheep wool to soften the hard wood. They were several deep and stacked, ascending in height as they grew away from the fire. A singular gap allowed the court to watch visitors approach from the grand doors, judging them before they could plead their case. On the opposite side was a throne. It sat higher than the uppermost bench and lorded over all with an aura of supreme rule.

The chamber expanded on either side. More benches circled smaller fire pits and braziers and were covered in thick wool for comfortable decision-making. Behind the throne, where Asher had expected to find a solid wall, he was amazed to see the night sky. The entire area was a roofed terrace. As the realisation came to him, a cool breeze rolled through thick columns, swirling around the fire before coursing through Asher's white fur. The mixture of cool wind and warm air created a pleasant atmosphere, making him feel strangely calm and safe despite his anxious worries. Carried on the wind came two raised voices, battling over one another for the right to speak.

Flora continued forwards, making her way around the central benches towards the open night sky and the glow of the city radiating below. The grand doors closed behind them with a boom. They stepped out into the cool night air onto an expansive stone balcony that reached out over the city. Asher peered over the low stone railing and stared in wonder at the city below. The view was breathtaking. They were high above the city, taller even than the Blazing Gate, which stood strong and proud, flanked by the two sentinel rocks, their huge braziers shining brightly into the sea beyond.

The city's tiers zig-zagged below like a snake slithering towards the docks at the water's edge, the glow of a thousand torches dancing in the streets, illuminating the citizens as they scurried about like ants. He could see the city reflected in the bay like a shimmering mirror, dotted with the lights of hundreds of vessels as they moved through the docks.

'It's beautiful,' he breathed, intoxicated by the grandeur of it all. An agitated squeaking brought him back to the balcony, the sound making his fur prickle.

Towards the end of the balcony stood two figures deep in conversation. One was a stout Otyren with a build that exhibited a life of luxury and comfort. His brown fur was speckled with grey, and the white fur under his chin, braided to a point and kept together with a thick silver bead, was stained – with what, Asher could only guess. He wore a green tunic embroidered with swirls of silver thread that circled and snaked across the seams like a hundred rivers. Simple brown trousers wrapped around his short, stumpy legs, and black boots covered his small webbed feet. A black woollen shawl covered his shoulders, held at the front by a golden chain and large golden plates, and his pebble pouch sat on his hip, bulging with the weight of something heavy residing within.

Not your average Otyren, Asher thought, swallowing his anxiety.

A perturbed expression crossed the man's short-snouted face as he gestured a webbed paw across the cityscape below. 'My goodness, Tessina, if it weren't for us, you and your senate would be wasting away, or worse, feasting upon the vermin that scurry about your own city!'

The beautiful red-furred Vulpen woman he was talking to huffed in annoyance. A good two feet taller, she wore a delicate stola dress of midnight-black silk, with golden threads lining the edges, trailing their way up and inwards. Draped over one shoulder and wrapping around her slender waist was a beautiful palla shawl of deep red.

Around her neck was a thin golden necklace embedded with intense rubies, and atop her brow sat a delicate crown of gold, simple in its design but featuring a sizable clear gem embedded at its centre. Asher couldn't help but gawk at how every little detail was perfect, how, although agitated, she maintained an air of pristine grace. She was magnificent.

Beside her sat a majestic brown hawk perched upon a tall wooden stand. She caressed its feathers as she listened to the Otyren's complaints. The bird screeched as its large black eyes searched her person.

The Otyren continued, 'And what would your late husband think? He'd—'

The woman snapped towards him, her calm demeanour vanishing in an instant. She pointed an angry clawed finger towards him. 'You forget yourself! This is my queendom, and you are a guest here.' Hers was a soft voice and yet possessed a surprising bite to it. A snarl began to form at the corner of her mouth, revealing a set of sharp canine teeth. 'I know things about you that your wife would not be too pleased about.'

'And that is exactly why I have come when called,' the stocky Otyren snapped back. 'Though I now trust you will no longer use that particular information against my name?'

'Fine,' the fiery Vulpen conceded, pulling back her finger and crossing her arms. Her long tail flicked with added fervour.

'And as for your request,' he continued. 'The answer is no. I care not what other secrets you hold over me. I will not relinquish my people's prized possession.'

'But it is not yours to have. You must—' The woman noticed the three approaching and silenced herself.

Flora came first and fell to one knee before the woman. 'My queen, I bring before you Domina Cara and Prince Asher, as requested.'

'Thank you, Flora, you may leave,' the queen said softly, a stark contrast to her previous tone towards the Otyren jarl.

'But I—' Flora started, raising her head. She hesitated as her eyes met the queen's stern stare, and her gaze dropped back to the floor. 'Yes, my queen.' She rose, gave a low bow and turned, her eyes lingering on Cara before she marched past, storming back towards the blazing throne.

The hawk watched Asher as they approached, its excited screeches replaced by an almost calculated silence. Cara dropped to one knee, eyes to the floor. Not knowing what to do, Asher followed suit, his ears flopping over his head as he knelt.

The jarl scoffed as the queen floated towards Cara.

'You're late, Domina Cara,' the queen said. 'I heard about the church's attack long before you arrived. I almost sent Domina Flora out to collect you.'

'I'm sorry, my queen. I shall act with more haste on my next mission. It will—'

'Look at me when I'm talking to you,' the queen commanded, her words calm but sharp. 'It's rude not to make eye contact. Stand up.'

Cara rose, her eyes locking onto the queen's, her jaw clenched tight. Her fists squeezed themselves into tight balls. The queen's eyes flashed with excitement at Cara's frustration like a child receiving a gift, but as Cara breathed deep, calming herself, the queen's expression returned to one of mild disdain.

She turned to Asher, a kind smile growing across her snout as her tone shifted once more. 'Now, is this the young king I've heard so much about?'

He rose to his feet and gave an anxious smile. 'It's a pleasure to meet you, Your Majesty,' he said, attempting to remember his royal etiquette training.

'Oh my, so polite.' The queen smiled. 'You *must* be of royalty.' She gave a gentle chuckle. Her face was pleasant, almost hypnotising to stare upon, and it wasn't long before Asher lost himself in the oceans that were her eyes.

'This, Jarl Vatn,' she said, addressing the short Otyren, 'is King Asher the First of Rabbethia.' She grabbed Asher's paw and pulled him forwards, presenting him to the short, fat man.

Jarl Vatn stared at Asher for some time. His beady black eyes looked him up and down as if inspecting a new racehorse or fine cut of meat, and his long whiskers twitched as he sniffed the air around him. Asher started to feel like this was less of an introduction and more of an inspection.

'Well, boy?' the jarl abruptly asked as if his patience had already been spent. 'Are you the king? Come on, speak up!'

'Well... no. I mean, yes, but I... well...' Asher stammered. The question had caught him off guard. He wanted to do right by his people, but he had never considered leading them or taking the throne. It was the one thing he had been running from his entire adult life.

'See?' continued Jarl Vatn, turning to the queen. 'The boy doesn't know who he is. You expect me to relinquish a prized possession of the Otyren to this child because you asked nicely? I think not! Rabbethia has no king, and the sooner their witan takes control, the better.' A coy smile grew across his face as he turned to Asher, his beady black eyes brimming with a smug secret. 'I've heard they've received quite the offer from the church.'

'What do you mean?' Asher snapped.

Jarl Vatn's smile grew into a wicked grin. He turned back to the queen, ignoring Asher's outcry. 'Now, I have come when summoned, and I will consider the favour to you paid. If there is nothing more, I shall take my son and leave. I have heard the fool recently arrived in your city.'

'But of course,' Queen Tessina said through a forced smile. 'Please make your way to the banquet hall. My custodian will aid you in locating your son.'

With that, Jarl Vatn of Otyrheim bowed to Queen Tessina before shoving past Asher as he made his way to the grand doors of the terrace, the base of his thick tail bouncing off the stone as he stepped. As soon as the doors had shut, Queen Tessina turned to Asher and raised a black-furred finger to his face.

'You need to figure out who you are!' she snapped, her soft and pleasant demeanour abandoned. 'Your people need a leader they can rally behind, and you, currently, are not it.'

Asher dropped his gaze to the floor, ashamed. 'I'm sorry, Your Highness,' he breathed. 'I do want to help my people, but I don't know if I *can*, if I'm fit to.'

The queen lowered her finger and sighed. She turned and began walking to the end of the balcony. 'Come,' she said, her frustration all but spent. Asher followed.

Cara remained behind, moving to the stone railing and leaning against it. She gazed over the city below, her free paw fiddling with the two rings around her slender fingers. Asher approached the queen's side and stared out into the night sky. The cold breeze was invigorating, and the salty smell of the sea filled Asher's senses.

The queen closed her eyes and spoke as if deep in memory. 'You know, I didn't want to rule either. Nor was I meant to.'

Asher remained quiet, turning to face her. Her fur was fiery red, and the white cascading from her chin was like snow and trimmed to perfection. The breeze blew through her fur, causing her whiskers to flutter about her nose like river reeds in the wind.

'Sometimes, those sceptical of power come to use it most wisely,' she said, opening her eyes and turning to meet Asher's stare. He averted his gaze. 'You do not want power, but still, you yearn to help. That is exactly why you should have it.'

Asher summoned the courage to return her gaze.

'Thank you,' he said in quiet contemplation. 'I always knew I'd have to take the throne eventually. I just... didn't expect it to be like this. I thought I had more time.'

'I understand,' the queen said as a servant approached, bowed deeply and placed something small into the queen's paw. She smiled in thanks, returning to Asher as the servant approached the hawk. 'As royalty,' the queen continued, 'you have a responsibility to lead, to guide and make your people strong.' She held out her paw towards Asher, forming a small cage with her fingers, the fluffy thing moving about in panicked twitches. Its nose twitched wildly, and its tiny black eyes gazed outwards in a petrified stare.

'From the mightiest Medvedian to the smallest mouse, all things have a place in this world. Your people will need your guidance to find theirs.' She smiled at Asher with kind, understanding eyes, and he felt the weight of responsibility begin to ease from his shoulders. Like the mouse, protected within the gentle paws of the queen, Asher would protect his people. He smiled.

A swoosh made Asher jump as a blur of feathers and talons soared between himself and the queen. He flinched, shielding himself from the attack. A moment passed, and the flapping of wings faded into the night. His twitching nose eased back into a steady rhythm, and his eyes returned to the queen's open paw. It was empty, save for a small scratch against her palm and a few wisps of soft brown fur. His eyes jumped to meet hers. They stared at him, unmoving, unflinching, her smile still gentle and soft. She lowered her paw.

'Just as predators hunt prey, royalty lead the masses. You can't run from it or fight it. It is the natural order of things.'

Asher nodded, unable to summon words. He understood the queen's lesson, and it even made him feel better about what was to come, but what she did to make her point; it just seemed cruel.

'Well, you must be hungry!' she said, clasping her paws together. 'Speak with Leylan, my head servant. He'll take you to your room and make sure your needs are met. Now, I must discuss some important matters with Cara. I bid you a good evening.' She gave a courteous nod to Asher before turning to Cara.

Unsure of the correct etiquette, Asher bowed deeply and turned for the doors, unable to take his mind off the mouse. His appetite had vanished.

'Goodnight, Your Highness,' Cara said with a smile as he passed. Asher smiled in return and continued, his ears picking up the start of their conversation as he moved away.

'So, my darling, did you hunt well?' the queen asked, her eager voice becoming a whisper as Asher neared the roaring fires of the inner terrace.

A brown-furred Rabbethi stood waiting by the closed grand doors, dressed in similar clothing to the servant Asher had seen before. His posture was stiff and proper, and he clasped his paws tight behind his back. He bowed as Asher approached, one ear flopping over, the other ear being only a short stub at the base of his head. Asher dared not ask how he received such a horrible injury, but his mind raced.

Battle? A cult? Madness? Punishment? That last thought didn't sit well with Asher.

The servant straightened and spoke, his voice well-mannered and polite. 'I am Leylan, Your Majesty. I am to bring you to your chambers. Please follow me.' Before Asher could reply, Leylan spun and moved towards the doors. They groaned wide, and Leylan strolled through, making a sharp turn down the corridor. 'Right this way, Your Majesty.'

Your Majesty. Asher doubted he would ever get used to that.

They walked down the long carpeted hallway and around several corners before Leylan eventually stopped at a simple wooden door. 'Here you are, Your Majesty. Can I bring you any food?'

'Oh, some roasted vegetables would be great, thank you.' Asher's appetite had returned during the long walk from the royal terrace, and he could feel the pains rumbling in his stomach.

'Very good. I shall return shortly.' Before Asher could say anything more, Leylan was gone, striding down the hallway and disappearing from view.

'Right,' Asher breathed, turning to the door. The room inside was a decent size and well-kept, with a few bookshelves lining the walls, each filled with all manner of books. On the opposite wall rose a tall arched window, providing a sweeping view of the tiered city below. An elaborate candelabra sat on a wide table by one of the walls, bathing the chamber in a warming glow, and Asher felt his remaining energy drain from his body as the flickering glow lulled him to rest. He approached the bed beneath the window, noting his bow and quiver at the foot of it. He groaned with delight as he leapt onto the mattress. It was exquisitely soft, and he felt it would swallow him whole and take him away to a dream from which he would never wake.

A lump under the duvet prodded at him just enough to prevent sleep from taking hold. He lifted the duvet and found himself staring face to face with a vicious hawk—or at least a hawk made of thread and cotton. It was clearly well-loved. Its plumage was a faded brown, and it was missing one of its black button eyes, loose threads dangling where the eye had been lovingly sewn. Asher smiled, remembering the soft animals he had owned as a child, and placed it to one side of the silk pillows before lying face-first into the pillow.

Moments before he drifted off, there were three knocks at the door. He strained his eyes open and heaved himself off the bed. Staggering to the door, he pulled it open. Standing there was Leylan, holding a silver plate covered with a silver dome.

'Your vegetables, Your Majesty,' he said, passing the plate to Asher.

Asher took it. 'Oh right, yes, thank you, Leylan. Could I—'

But Leylan was already gone, marching down the hallway and out of sight. Asher began to close the door, but before he shut it entirely, he noticed a shape standing by one of the other doors down the hall. Keeping his door open by a crack, he peered out. The figure scanned the area, and as they turned to face Asher's door, he saw who it was. It was Cara. She looked flustered as she knocked on a door and waited. The door opened, and another figure leaned out: Domina Flora. Before Asher could guess what was happening, she grabbed Cara by her leather chest piece and pulled her in for a passionate kiss.

Oh, Asher thought. *OH!*

The realisation hit him like a charging Medvedian, and he quickly felt awkward spying on such an intimate embrace. He quietly closed the door, pretending he saw none of it, and carried his food to the table. He placed it down and lifted the silver dome. The array of roasted vegetables smelt stupendous, and his stomach growled in anticipation. There were roasted carrots, mashed potatoes, steamed cauliflower, honey-glazed parsnips, and green beans. No sooner had he laid the silver dome to the side than he began eating. It was exquisite and far more than he could handle.

With his stomach full of vegetables and his mind full of worries, he threw his clothes to the stone floor, ensuring his mother's necklace remained secure around his neck, and he tucked himself under the light silk duvet.

II

An Innocence Taken

Giggling echoed through the void. It circled all around and was yet sourceless. Cara opened her eyes and found she was no longer lying beside Flora's strong, elegant form. To her surprise, she was in a large square bedroom, floating several feet above the floor. She panicked and tried to reach out before falling but couldn't move her limbs—rather, she had nothing *to* move. No arms or legs, paws or feet. She just existed, formless and floating. After the initial shock, she found it to be a strangely calm and peaceful experience.

Her attention returned to the room. It was so familiar, as if plucked from a long-forgotten memory. Bookshelves lined one wall, each full of colourful books ranging from epic stories of gallant Vulpen heroes and heroines to dull histories of Tamuz. On the opposite wall lay a long table covered in an assortment of vibrant, tropical fruit imported from all over the Vulpen Queendom. Beneath a tall arched window sat a large luxurious bed littered with pillows and soft toy animals, a large brown hawk taking centre stage, black buttons for eyes.

She knew this room.

'Save me!' came a cry from below.

Cara watched as two Vulpen cubs leapt dramatically over an expensive purple rug, its exquisite threads scuffed and tattered from many a ferocious battle. One cub had vibrant red fur and wore an elegant red dress torn at the ankles, its white sleeves ripped at the shoulders. She wielded a large stick in her tiny paw and swung it with wild vigour.

'Help me! Help me!' cried a white cub, tumbling in an exaggerated fall. 'The monster's gonna eat me!' She was younger than the other and wore a robe of white, trimmed with golden embroidery and strange iconography. Upon her brow was the thin, golden circlet of a princess.

'Luna...' Cara's incorporeal form breathed, a conflicting wave of joy and grief filling her in equal measure.

'I'll save you!' the young red cub declared as she leapt over her fallen friend. She pretended to stab at some monstrous beast.

'My hero,' Luna swooned. Their loud and joyous giggles echoed around the chamber.

Cara hadn't thought of her friend Luna in a long while. Their unbreakable bond, formed a lifetime ago within the rooms of the royal palace, remained firm in Cara's heart and was ever present in her thoughts.

Someone new in the open doorway. With a soundless gasp, Cara watched a much younger Tessina wearing a beautiful silk stola dress of deep red glide into the room, her long white palla dancing in her wake. Around her neck was a thin golden necklace embedded with intense rubies, and upon her brow sat a golden tiara. She looked down at the young cubs with a smile, a sense of endearment and a smidge of jealousy in her eyes. Then she saw the state of the red cub's dress.

'Look at you! What would your parents think?' She reached down and brought the cub to her feet. She began inspecting the torn fabric and loose threads. 'You can't keep doing this to your dresses, Cara.'

Cara's non-existent mouth dropped as she stared at the visage of her youth, the innocence and naivety exuding from her younger self's smile, at the joy still present in her heart. Her disregard for dresses hadn't changed.

'I'm sorry, Princess Tessina,' the young Cara apologised, staring down at her fidgeting feet. 'It was too restricting.'

Tessina sighed and lifted Cara's head by her chin to meet her gaze. She smiled a comforting smile, to which the young cub responded with her own.

'Tell me, what were you playing?'

'Well, there was a monster, and it was going to eat Luna, and I needed to save her, but I couldn't swing Peleus 'cause of the dress. So I made it better for fighting!' Her excitement grew as she retold the account of her great battle.

Tessina raised an eyebrow. 'Peleus, you say?' Do you mean to say you were the mighty warrior, Silvana, fighting off the monstrous Shangari of Deep Hollow? And this...' Tessina reached down and picked up the stick, which in her paw was more of a dagger than a sword. 'This must be the mythical sword, Peleus?'

Cara nodded, a huge grin across her face. Tessina chuckled, turning to Luna, who had risen to her feet and stared at the pair. There was a sadness in her violet eyes, a longing for something unspoken.

'And how do you think she did, Princess? Did she save you from Nin-Kilim, king of the Shangari?'

'Yes, Princess Tessina. She performed admirably.' Luna raised her head, but her eyes danced around the room, refusing to make eye contact. Tessina's smile lessened at the sight of the sad little cub.

She sighed. 'Your mother has done well, raising you with manners, but please, call me auntie.'

There was a pause as Luna contemplated the request. 'That would be improper.'

Heavy, metallic footsteps began echoing around the room, and a gruff, black-furred guard appeared in the door frame. His broad, muscular frame was covered in black plated armour, each plate curving to a sharp point. A long red cape flowed as he walked—making his entrance into the chamber all that more dramatic—before coming to rest over his large, bushy tail. He whispered something into Tessina's pointed ear.

'I see. Thank you, Dario, that'll be all.'

The captain took a few steps back and bowed low before exiting the chamber, leaving the princess alone with the cubs.

She brought her fingers up to the bridge of her nose, pinching it in frustration. 'It appears my sister has returned from her pilgrimage and brought an alarming amount of friends with her.' She looked down at Cara. 'I have to go, darling.'

Cara giggled as the princess leaned down and kissed her lightly on the forehead.

Tessina then turned to Luna. 'I suppose I should see what new sermon your mother has brought from the Lighthouse.' She strolled out of the room, her tail flowing behind her like an echo.

Darkness suddenly blurred Cara's vision. She floated there for what seemed an age, contemplating what she had just seen and wondering when and if she would ever wake. Then she heard something, a faint sound somewhere in the distance. It was a voice, angry and screaming. She strained to listen to it, and slowly, it grew closer. It was as if the person was screaming mere metres away, yet it was muffled as if a stone wall lay between her and the source.

'The throne belongs to me!' the voice echoed. Despite the outrage, it carried a condescending venom.

'Mother has made her choice!' came another voice, softer than the other. 'Stand down your acolytes and cease this foolish behaviour! Think of your daughter!'

'My daughter is no concern of yours! She will inherit *my* throne and keep the *true* faith strong!'

With that, a chorus of muffled shouts began to echo in the darkness. The clang of metal clashing filled the void and the sound of men and women dying surrounded Cara. She tried with all her might to release her focus on the sounds, not wanting to hear any more, but they kept building and building. She attempted to cover her ears, but she had no paws and no ears to cover. It was all too much. She was about to scream.

Then it stopped without reason or warning, and a sudden and deafening silence took its place. It lingered for a time before a faint crackling began to creep into the space. It was peaceful, like the gentle flame of a campfire.

The blood-curdling scream of a young girl exploded around her.

It came from all directions, enveloping her. She sealed her non-existent eyes shut, but they were immediately forced open, and she found herself staring into the dead eyes of a Rabbethi, his mouth agape, his lifeless, colourless eyes piercing deep into her soul. Cara screamed, but no sound left her mouth. Her shapeless form ascended up and away from the body.

She was back in the bedchamber. It was dark. The torches were cold, and yet the room was bathed in an orange, flickering light that flooded through the tall, arched window. The sound of fires raged from outside as Cara stared down at the dead white-furred Rabbethi lying flat on his back. His white hooded robe was drenched with blood that poured from a deep wound in his abdomen.

Oh no... no, no, no. Not again... please...

Cara closed her eyes and willed herself to wake, begging her body to lurch out of bed and save her from this nightmare. She opened her eyes, but it was no good. Her eyes landed on a small trembling figure standing over the body, a jagged dagger in her tiny bloody paws. The young Cara stood wide-eyed as tears streamed down her cheeks. Her fur was matted and dirty, her dress caked with fresh blood. The door had been smashed open and now hung loose on its hinges. Half-eaten, half-rotten fruit stained the once pristine rug, and one corner of the room was smeared with what Cara had spent years trying to forget.

Luna lay trembling on the floor behind her. She stared at the young Cara in absolute horror, tears matting the fur on her cheeks, her golden circlet snapped in two at her side. 'You... you killed him,' she whispered, not taking her eyes off the back of Cara's head.

'I-I had to,' Cara stammered, the blood dripping from the dagger in a slow, methodic drip... drip... drip... 'He was a monster. A-And he was gonna take you away!'

There was a long silence. Luna said nothing. Cara spun to face her, blood flying off the dagger and splattering onto Luna's robe.

'I had to!' A fresh torrent of tears began pouring from her eyes, joined in equal measure by thick mucus from her nostrils. Luna scrambled backwards as fast as her tiny limbs would allow until she pressed up against the foot of the bed. The young Cara looked deep into her friend's terrified eyes, then down at the bloody dagger in her paw. She dropped to her knees and released the blade.

Tessina burst into the room, shrieking as she beheld the sight before her. Her once fine clothes hung loose about her bony frame, and what looked like dried blood was now matted to the fur around her snout. Two armoured soldiers flanked her, covered in scratches, dents, and dried blood. They panted as they reached the door.

'Cara! Are you okay?' Tessina called.

Cara jumped to her feet and ran into Tessina's arms. 'A monster came for Luna,' she cried through stifled sniffs. 'But I stopped him. I had to stop him!'

Tessina embraced her tighter and stroked the fur behind her head.

'Shh, shhh, shhh. It's okay. It's okay,' she breathed. 'The monsters are gone. My sister has gone.' Her eyes darted over to Luna, and her expression darkened. 'As for you!' She rose to her feet and signalled to the guards towards Luna. They marched towards the terrified cub, who shrank at their approach.

'What's going on?' Cara asked, holding onto Tessina's dress with one paw.

'We must send her away, far away. The city is not safe until she is gone.'

'No! Put me down! Cara!' cried the white cub as one of the guards scooped her up with one paw. She struggled and writhed in the guard's armoured arms, but he held tight.

'Leave her alone!' Cara screamed.

Tessina wrapped Cara up in her arms, restraining her. 'Shh, it's okay, it's okay,' she whispered. Tears streamed down Cara's and Luna's cheeks as they fought hard against their restraints.

'Be brave, Luna!' Cara yelled as the guard walked through the door frame. 'Be brave, like Silvana!'

And then they were gone, Luna's cries growing fainter and fainter until there was nothing but the roaring fires in the city beyond. Cara buried her face into Tessina's shoulder.

'She's gone,' Tessina whispered. 'She's gone...'

12

A Royal Breakfast

Asher stared out of the tall arched window at the sprawling city below, bored. It had been a few days since his arrival in Ignimarum, and there had been no correspondence with the queen since that first night. "I'm afraid she's seeing to internal affairs, Your Highness," was the most common response he had received.

He also hadn't seen Cara, and her lack of visits had left Asher feeling somewhat abandoned in this strange new kingdom. There were only so many meals he could have alone in his room before he began feeling more like a prisoner than an honoured guest. The floorboards thumped against his foot's impatient tapping as he watched the ships sailing in and out of the dock. He toyed with exploring the palace in search of Cara but decided against it. Unlike the burrow layout of the keep in White Cliffe City, this palace was unknown to him, and it would be all too easy to get lost wandering the many halls.

There was a knock at the door.

'Coming, Leylan,' Asher said, turning. 'I hope you're here to finally give me a guided tour of the palace. I'm starting to go a bit crazy cooped up in here...' He trailed off as he pulled the door open and saw Luce smiling broadly before him, eyes bubbling joyfully.

'The best people are, you know. Crazy, I mean.'

'I guess so,' he said with a smile he couldn't control. Her eyes glanced at his nose as it twitched excitedly. She giggled.

Get it together, for Folka's sake.

'I saw what you did the other night,' she continued. 'I liked how you ran into danger to save someone in trouble. It was obviously a trap, and you're an idiot for believing it.' She looked him up and down, a playful glint in her eyes. 'Though, I'm glad to see you're okay.'

Asher felt his cheeks blush under his white fur. The scent of freshly bloomed orchids wafted from her slender frame.

'I can teach you a few things, help you use a blade properly. If you like?'

'Y-yes!' Asher yelled, startled by his eagerness, his excitement overwhelming his control of volume. Luce giggled. Composing himself, he tried again. 'I would be most appreciative. Thank you, Domini Lucilla.'

Luce rolled her eyes. 'Eurgh, please don't call me that. I don't need reminding that I'm still a whole dom beneath Cara. I keep asking old Corvo to promote me, but apparently, I'm not "mature enough".' She accentuated Senator Corvo's words with a twisted face and finger quotes, earning an earnest chuckle from Asher. 'Never mind my mission success rate is the highest of all the other domini.' She winked. 'I'm also the prettiest.'

'Then Senator Corvo is a fool,' he said with a smile.

'Nah, he's okay really, grumpy at times, but okay.' She spun on the spot and began skipping away. 'I'll see you at daybreak for training then!'

Asher watched her leave until the tip of her bushy tail vanished from view before closing the door.

Wait, he thought. *Did she say daybreak?*

And so, Asher spent the next few days awaiting an audience with the queen by training his blade craft. Each morning, just as the Great Lighthouse's light dispersed the blackness of night, he and Luce sparred within one of the many courtyards of the palace, the other agents watching on. Luce seemed impressed by how fast he picked up many of the basic moves and techniques, his history as a boxer aiding him. As they spent those mornings together, sparring and talking, it hadn't gone unnoticed how her eyes drifted in his direction more than once and how his eyes floated to meet them. She was pretty, for sure, a positive beam of light, which Asher had very much needed after recent events. His heart fluttered at the thought of seeing her again.

But nothing could happen. He wouldn't let it.

Shangari had ravaged his city, his father was dead, and his brother taken. It was all too raw within him, a cyclone of emotions, wants, and fears. He didn't know whether he truly wanted Luce or whether his mind had yet to settle. Then there was Mia. Her death still weighed heavy on his heart. He had one more task to perform regarding her rest. Only then would he consider moving on.

***

BANG! BANG! BANG!

Asher shot out of bed, his heart pounding, nose twitching. He readied himself for a fight and scanned the room for an exit.

'Are they here? How did they find us?' he yelled through blurry eyes. The sound of chirping birds drifted through the tall, arched window as the warm glow of morning bathed the peaceful chamber. The room was still. After a brief moment of awkward quiet, a familiar voice sounded from the chamber door.

'The queen has requested your presence in the banquet hall for breakfast, Your Majesty,' Leylan said, ignoring Asher's outburst.

Asher rubbed the slumber sand from his eyes as consciousness fully returned to him. He looked down at where he had slept, spying the old stuffed hawk toy on the pillow.

He smiled. 'Good morning, little friend.'

'Good morning... Your Majesty,' Leylan's voice came again from behind the door.

'Ah, right, yes. Thank you, Leylan,' Asher stammered, now thoroughly embarrassed. 'I err... I'll be there shortly.'

'Very good, sir. I have taken the liberty of cleaning your clothes. I have laid them out on your table.'

'Oh, thank you, Leylan,' Asher said with surprise.

'Very good, Your Majesty.'

Uneasy that someone had been in the room whilst he slept, Asher made his way to the table and threw on his black trousers, long-sleeved dark green shirt and black boots. The intoxicating scent of lavender wafted from the fibres as they settled on his lean frame.

Finally, a meeting with the elusive queen, he thought as he tightened his thin brown belt. He left his old brown hood to one side, not thinking it regal enough for the palace of the Vulpen queen. After licking his paws and patting the fur around his cheeks, he brought his ears down and gave them the once-over to be sure. Happy with his look, he made for the door. He pulled it open and was startled to find Laylen already bowing deep, his one black ear flopping over the top of his head, the tip grazing the stone floor.

'This way, Your Majesty.' He rose sharply, turned on the spot, and began marching down the hall. The pair journeyed down the many hallways, proceeding past the immense golden doors of the throne terrace, down the corridor, and entered a grand dining hall.

Six thick stone columns supported the hall's lofty ceiling, three arranged on each side. Long banners of shining gold and fiery red hung from their height, featuring a symbol at their centre that Asher had seen before—a Vulpen head facing to the left, surrounded by a floral arrangement of Vulpen tails.

Just like Cara's iron sigil, he realised.

Long wooden tables with equally long benches ran parallel to each other along the floor. Hundreds of agents sat hunched over bowls of steaming oats, their black cloaks resting loose on a sea of wagging, bushy tails, a hushed murmur humming across the hall. Some glanced up to Asher before whispering to another, smirks growing across their snouts. Asher tried his best not to seem bothered. He turned his attention to a great fire roaring at the hall's centre from within a sizeable standing brazier of dark iron, its intensity ensuring the furthest corners of the hall were at a comfortable temperature.

'This way, Your Highness,' Leylan instructed as he turned left towards the far end of the hall. There, a large wooden table sat raised atop a wooden platform. It lay perpendicular to the other tables, so those who sat along its length watched over the entire hall.

'Morning, Ash,' came a familiar cheerful voice as Asher passed a nearby bench. Luce sat nestled between several much larger Vulpen agents who stared at Asher with utter contempt. She, however, smiled and waved. He returned a quick wave, hoping not to draw any more of the other agents' wrath.

'Ah, the guest of honour has arrived.' Queen Tessina smiled as Asher arrived at the raised table. The table was covered in a white cloth and featured an assortment of fine breakfast foods ranging from fruits and cheeses to various slices of cured meat. The queen sat at the table's centre, cutting with delicate strokes into a thick red steak. Next to her was Cara, who used a knife and fork in a manner far more polite and regal than Asher had seen from her on their journey here. 'Please, sit,' Tessina said, gesturing at the empty seat beside her. Asher bowed and approached.

A short, red-furred Vulpen in a white robe stared behind a set of large circular spectacles as Asher sat between him and the queen. 'This' – Queen Tessina gestured to the spectacled Vulpen – 'is Julius, my tome keeper. Expert on all things historical, mythological and everything in between.'

Asher turned and found the old Vulpen slumped back in his chair, head back and snoring like a Medvedian.

How old is this guy?

White flecks smothered the red across the aged Vulpen's snout. Long, bushy strands erupted from his eyebrows and within the depths of his pointed ears.

'Oh, for Thena's sake,' the queen exclaimed. 'Julius!'

'Huh, wha...?' Julius stirred, turning to Asher. His eyes went wide behind his spectacles, and he grabbed Asher's paw tight. 'Oh my yes, wonderful to meet ya, lad! I look forward to delving into the world of the ancients and the powers that be, or used to be, to your inquisitive little mind.' He shook Asher's paw with vigour as he spoke. Asher tried to pull away, but Julius held tight. 'Oh, and yes, of course, your royal blood! I wonder if you are able to approach the coffin or not. That is a test I would very much like to conduct, oh yes! But alas, I do not possess it, nor have I ever even seen it, so it was pointless to bring it up. But that's what we do, us scholars. We wonder and ponder and ask fruitless questions in the quest to acquire more. "More what?" you ask? Why, more knowledge, my lad! I bet you have many questions on many things. Come, come, we must go to my study. I will tell you everything you need to know about the holy relics and stones that power them. No time to waste!' He jumped off his chair, not letting go of Asher's paw and almost pulling him to the floor.

'Perhaps the young king would like to have some breakfast first, Julius?' came the stern, hard voice of Queen Tessina, not turning from her meal.

'Ah yes, deepest apologies, my queen.' He released Asher's paw and bowed deep, placing a finger onto his glasses to stop them from sliding off the end of his long snout. 'You must forgive me; I am only eager to expand the mind of one who knows so little. I shall retire to my study and await Your Highness's arrival.' With that, he hobbled his way from the table.

As he stumbled away, Asher noticed how short the old man was. He was about the height of an Otyren, which was most unusual for even an elderly Vulpen who only shrunk so far in old age. Julius carefully stepped down from the platform and headed towards one of the arches that lined the far wall. As he made his way towards the arch, Asher noticed that his hobble seemed more awkward than someone whose joints were just weak and faltering, as if he was catching himself with each stride.

Asher returned to the table and gazed upon the food before him in hunger. He picked an assortment of fruits and cheeses and placed them on his plate.

'I apologise for Julius,' said the queen as she cut into her thick, bloody steak. 'He can be quite enthusiastic when strangers visit, sometimes too enthusiastic. I've had to remind him of his manners on several occasions. I had thought the last time would have brought him down to size.' She placed a neatly cut cube of meat into her long mouth. The scent caught in Asher's nose, and he tried not to let his disgust show.

Glancing out over the hall, he found the recognisable face of Flora as she straddled one of the long benches near the fire, an empty plate beside her. She stared with intensity up at Cara. Based on their interaction the other night, Asher could no longer tell whether it was a stare of disdain, passionate intent, or even a bit of both.

'Now,' the queen said expectantly. 'Tell me what happened in your city, if it is not too upsetting for you, of course. Cara has given me her report, but I'd like to hear it from you.'

Asher's eyes drifted to his meal as he racked his mind for the right words to describe what had happened. It had been a nightmare, and he didn't know where to start. Cara leaned forwards from the queen's other side, awaiting Asher's retelling. He doubted the queen would be happy if the two accounts didn't align.

She continued eating her breakfast as Asher tried his best to describe the last several days, recalling as much detail as he could remember, though he had to force some details out through a clenched jaw and a heavy heart. Queen Tessina watched him closely, inspecting his reaction to his retelling. She occasionally raised a paw to ask a question, taking particular interest in Constance.

'Tell me about her,' she asked. Her demeanour was calm, but there was an eagerness in her eyes that was impatient for an answer.

'She wore a circlet on her head.' Asher glanced at the queen's crown and the clear gem mounted at its centre. It stared back at him like a giant crystal eye. 'Just like your crown, except...' He hesitated, unsure if what he experienced was real or a fever dream. 'The gem flashed when she gave orders. It felt... wrong.'

'I see you've experienced the power of the Judge's Bane.' She sighed.

'The Judge's Bane...,' Asher whispered to himself, attempting to recall any mention in his history lessons within the palace, but nothing came to mind.

'The Judge's Bane is the prize possession of the Vulpen, a relic of the ancients, passed down from queen to princess upon her ascension to the throne, a symbol of her right to rule. The power it holds can control one's will and force the truth from those under its effects, hence its name.' She reached to her lap and pulled a napkin to her mouth, patting away any loose food from her fur.

'Why does Constance have it?' Asher asked.

At this, the queen placed the napkin onto her empty plate and stared at it, deep in thought, her expression turning dark. 'She stole it and killed a lot of good Vulpen doing so.' There was a cold silence as the queen's eyes bored into her empty, bloody plate. She blinked, her eyes refocusing. 'Please, continue,' she said softly.

Sensing it best not to push, Asher continued retelling his journey to Ignimarum. He talked about meeting Cara, the attack in Saewic and their escape aboard *The Silvi*. He didn't mention Mia. The guilt he felt for her death still consumed him and was not something he was willing to share. Cara said nothing but stirred at her porridge as he spoke.

'... and then Domina Flora escorted us up the Royal Run, and here we are,' Asher finished, surprised that his mind had allowed him to retain so much information when his heart wanted nothing more than to forget it all.

'I see,' the queen said with a nod. 'Thank you, Your Highness. That was most helpful. I'm sorry you've endured so much. We will set it right. Now, I believe you have a meeting with Julius. You will learn a great deal from him.' Her smile then dropped as she turned to Cara. With a stern voice, she said, 'Cara, go with him. You could do with expanding your knowledge.'

Cara straightened and nodded in acknowledgement. 'Yes, my queen.' She rose from her seat and moved away from the table and her half-eaten breakfast. She quietly slid her chair beneath the table, then bowed deeply to the queen.

'Let's go, Asher,' she said, addressing Asher before turning and heading towards the archway Julius had hobbled through.

Asher jumped up. He hadn't realised they meant that very moment and was saddened to leave such delectable fruits and cheeses half-eaten on his plate, his belly half full. He stumbled around his chair and slid it under the table quickly, causing a deafening screech to echo across the hall. Asher winced and looked about to see if anyone noticed, only to find every set of eyes staring at him with utter contempt. He marched after Cara, head bowed in embarrassment. As he passed the queen's chair, he stopped, turned to face the queen and gave an awkward half bow, still unsure of the etiquette between one member of royalty and another. The queen gave a polite nod in return, and Asher continued.

He reached her just as she passed under the stone arch, and they descended a long corridor. It was much simpler in style than the ones Asher had previously walked down. There was no red carpet, and the stone walls were bare, save for the occasional torch fastened with iron rivets.

'She's too harsh on you,' Asher said, glancing at Cara. He didn't know why he had said it. It certainly wasn't his place to remark on a relationship he knew nothing about. Maybe it reminded him of how his father would criticise him despite Asher's best efforts or impressive accomplishments. Nothing was ever enough. There was always room for improvement. Seeing the same treatment befall someone else, someone he was coming to respect, irked him more than he cared to admit.

'Who?' Cara replied, not returning the glance.

'The queen. All I've heard so far is criticism.'

'You don't know what you're talking about,' Cara replied flatly, picking up her pace and creating a small distance between her and Asher. He matched it, returning to her side.

'What you did was incredible,' Asher continued. 'You saved my life and brought me here safely. I just don't think she treats you how you deserve.'

Cara shoved Asher into the stone wall, her paw firmly on his chest.

'Listen!' she said in a stern command. 'You don't know what you're talking about. If it weren't for her, I'd be nothing, or worse, dead.'

As she spoke, all the instincts in Asher's body screamed at him to flee, but he couldn't. Cara's strong black paw pinned him to the wall, a low snarl rumbling under her words. All Asher could do was shrink and wait for her mauling to cease.

'I owe her everything,' she continued. 'And I will spend my entire life making it up to her. Now, *drop it.*' She clenched her sharp canine teeth tight in her mouth.

'I-I'm sorry,' Asher stuttered. 'I didn't know.'

Cara's snarl lessened, and she stepped away, shifting her gaze to the stone floor. She sighed. 'She was the only one that didn't turn their back on me after I… after I lost my parents. I just need her to see that I was worth saving…'

'Cara…,' Asher breathed, reaching a paw towards her.

'It doesn't matter. This way.' She continued down the stone corridor, now marching with purpose. Asher followed in silence, a few paces behind.

The pair eventually reached the end of the corridor, where they came upon a narrow spiral staircase that wrapped around a central column within an alcove. Not breaking her stride, Cara began climbing. Asher followed close behind as he racked his brain for a suitable apology. They ascended only a short while before stepping out into a narrow corridor, at the end of which was a lone door, its iron plating far more reinforced than the others around it. Dark stains sprayed along the walls, floor and ceiling, creating a rather ominous shadow. It was as if darkness was leaking out from the chamber beyond. As they approached, the repetitive sound of a hammer strike rang out from the chamber beyond.

Cara reached for the iron handle and stopped. She placed an ear flat to the wood.

'What's wrong?' Asher asked.

'Listen,' she commanded, and Asher lifted one tall ear towards the door. He waited. The hammering had stopped, and in its place was a deep rumbling. A dazzling light shone brightly around the door's frame, illuminating the hallway. Both it and the rumbling were growing with intensity.

'Cara?' Asher asked, a rising worry creeping into his voice. He turned to her, and she returned his concerned expression.

The humming stopped, and Asher heard Julius's frail voice beyond. 'Oh, bugger it…'

BOOM!

Cara grabbed Asher and threw him to the ground as a deafening explosion filled the narrow hallway, the door blasting open. Thick black smoke ploughed from the doorway, hanging heavy in the air. Asher opened his eyes. He found himself on his back with Cara lying over him, shielding him with her body. If not for her, they would have been splattered against the wall, adding red to the already blackened stonework.

Great, he thought. *That's another debt I owe.*

The Vulpen agent stood, offering a paw to Asher, who kindly took it.

'You okay?' she asked, heaving Asher to his feet.

'I think so, but what was—'

The black smoke seared his throat, burning his lungs. He couldn't speak another word without choking on them. Cara buried her snout into the crease of her elbow and, with a muffled voice, instructed Asher to do the same. Asher lost sight of her as she passed through the splintered door frame, her shape disappearing into the thick smoke.

Whack!

'Ah, shit!' Asher exclaimed, walking straight into a low, solid table, his upper thigh bruising instantly. There was the sudden rattling of a chain somewhere in the room, and a hatch opened above, allowing a bright beam of light to pour into the stifled chamber and the smoke to rise through, though the stench of soot and ash remained.

When all was clear, Asher found he was standing in a large circular chamber, the walls covered in bookshelves filled with ancient tomes. Various desks and tables sat nestled between the bookshelves, covered with strange equipment he had never seen before. Sheets of old paper littered the wooden floor like a scholarly nest. Above, the ceiling climbed to a great height, reaching a point at its centre. Attached to the ceiling hatch's hinges was a metal chain that swayed side to side. Asher followed it down, where he saw Cara, her paw still grasped around metal links as she scanned the room.

Coughing and spluttering echoed again around the space, and she dashed towards an overturned table, pushing it aside. Julius lay sheltered and buried among countless books and pieces of paper, his white robe strewn about him. In his black paw, he squeezed the handle of a small hammer.

Something shiny caught Asher's eye from under Julius's robes. Asher felt rude but couldn't help but look as the gleam of two metallic objects reflected the fresh light pouring in from the ceiling. Asher gasped quietly as he saw two iron rods with large padded bases protruding from where the elderly Vulpen's legs should be. He quickly averted his gaze, feeling awkward for staring as long as he did. Julius righted himself and pulled his robes to the floor, Cara helping the old Vulpen to his artificial feet.

'Ah yes, thank you, dear.' The old Vulpen smiled before coughing.

'You need to be more careful, Julius,' Cara said, shaking her head.

'I'm perfectly capable of taking care of myself!' Julius said, wagging the hammer in Cara's face. 'Through extensive research and rigorous testing, I have discovered that eight hammer blows is one too many when attempting to ignite a contained quantity of black powder and recreate holy fire!'

'I can see that.' Cara chuckled. 'It's quite the mess you've made.' She gazed about the room. Julius joined her, his face becoming increasingly worried.

'Yes, the dusty substance was far more volatile than I had anticipated.' He snapped up to look at her, his magnified eyes wide.

'Y-you won't tell the queen about this, will you?' he asked, a genuine fear in his voice.

'I won't.' Cara smiled. 'But promise me you'll be more careful with... whatever this is.'

'Ah! You're one of the good ones.' Julius grinned.

Cara followed him as he hobbled over to the table. The table was thick and made of one solid piece of wood, its surface blackened and covered in thousands of chips, cuts and gashes. Asher's eyes drifted to the shallow, smouldering crater at the table's centre.

'Now, what do you and His Highness want? Hmm? I'm very busy,' Julius snapped, his eyes darting between Asher and Cara.

'You're supposed to tell us about these magic stones?' Cara reminded.

'Of course, of course!' he exclaimed, clapping his paws together. 'How much do you two know of the relics and the Shepherd Stones that power them?' He looked to Cara and then over to Asher expectantly, his eager stare magnified behind his thick spectacles.

'The relics were tools created by the ancients,' Cara said tediously, as if reciting old information, 'Imbued with with magic power and gifted to their followers. We've all heard the stories, Julius. The Medvedians supposedly have one, as do the Fenerathi.'

'Ah,' Julius said knowingly, 'But I bet you didn't know that they were powered by gems containing the power of a god, hmm? What we call "Shepherd Stones".' His eyes jumped between Cara and Asher, eagerness threatening to burst from within. When they didn't respond, he continued, 'After gifting the power to the ancients, the god mysteriously disappeared.' He narrowed his eyes, and remained silent for what could only be assumed was dramatic effect. 'Well,' the old

Vulpen said with a knowing grin. ‘What if I told you that the god *never* left?’

13

Making Father Proud

'You're saying the god is still around?' Asher asked, stunned.

'More importantly, what does it have to do with Constance?' Cara interjected.

Julius hobbled to one of the nearby desks and began rummaging through the various scrolls. 'Where is it? he mumbled under his breath. 'Ah, here we are! King Asher's father, King Hengist, gave me this on my last visit to his palace. Though I expect it to be a copy of the original, I still cherish it dearly.' He hobbled back to the table and unfurled the scroll. It opened before them, the dry paper crackling as it rolled down the table. It smelt ancient. The old Vulpen wiped away some of the dust and gave a final soft blow to disperse any lingering dirt. Asher gazed over the scroll, taking in the vivid scene depicted across its surface. The details and colour were still crisp and vivid as if painted just the day before.

The scroll showed four figures: a Rabbethi, a Vulpen, a Medvedian and a Fenrathi. The Fenrathi in this ancient painting had dark grey fur and a green hooded robe with golden chains dangling from under its upper lip, as was customary for their nobility. Beautiful gold plates covered the upper and lower jaws, ending under the intense predatorial eyes. Asher couldn't help but stare at the underside of the jaw where a sizable white gemstone sat embedded into the gold plating.

'Is that a...?' Asher began, pointing towards the image of the Fenrathi.

'A Shepherd Stone, yes,' Julius confirmed, a smile forming across his snout. 'That is Feargus, the first high king of the Fenrathi clans. It was said his howl could heal all but the dead. If you look at the others, you'll notice they all have stones.'

Asher's eyes moved to the figure beside the Fenrathi. An elegant red-furred Vulpen in a black dress pointed towards a grey rectangular object in the distance, a look of disdain across her regal face. Across her brow was a thin golden circlet, a large gem shining bright at its centre.

'That must be the Judge's Bane,' Asher said, gesturing to the Vulpen.

'Correct again,' Julius said with joy. 'That is our glorious mother, Thena, the first wielder of the Judge's Bane. Her just and noble actions united the Vulpen nobles and even brought the Shangari to heel.' At the Vulpen's feet were several smaller figures with thick pink tails and long snouts that ended with serrated teeth. Asher couldn't help but shudder at the sight of the Shangari, the ancient paint bringing to life the blood-soaked memories that now haunted his dreams.

'Here you see Loch, the first and mightiest of the Medvedian high kings,' Julius continued, pointing to the image of a tremendous Medvedian. His chest was bare, revealing thick brown fur and a muscular physique. Oversized plated trousers protected the titan's lower half as he stood roaring triumphantly, a huge gloved fist raised high. At the glove's centre shone another Shepherd Stone. 'And I imagine you know who that is?' the Vulpen scholar asked knowingly as his paw drifted to the last figure, a brown Rabbethi woman dressed in leather armour, a cobalt-blue cloak draped over her shoulders. She was kneeling before a grey object, eyes to the floor in what looked like grief. Asher knew who this was. He could see the unmistakable streak of darker fur running from her pink nose, between her eyes and over her head.

'That's Folka, the first of my people,' Asher said as he gazed at the scene, pride making him stand a little straighter. 'The first of my kind and…' His eyes drifted to something on the floor beside her, almost discarded, a short, simple bow. The light brown wood had an inwards curve in the middle. At its very centre was a shining Shepherd Stone.

'Ah, I see you've spotted it,' Julius exclaimed. He reached over as far as his short stature would allow and pointed a short black claw at the weapon, careful not to touch the scroll. '*That* is the key to victory over Constance. It was originally called the Bow of Folka, though it is now most commonly known as the King's Bow.'

Asher knew of the legendary bow, used by the Rabbethi rulers in times of battle, but he thought it was a legend told by the old to instil some sense of valour. He never thought it could be genuine, especially not a mighty weapon imbued with god's power.

'How?' Cara asked as Asher stared at the image of his ancestor.

'I'm not sure.' Julius shrugged. 'The queen, in her infinite wisdom, instructed me to teach you of the bow's existence. I was not privy to its application to your cause.'

Cara sighed and turned to Asher, frustration apparent across her face. 'What do you think, Asher?'

His thoughts were elsewhere, his eyes drifting across the artwork to the final shape on the scroll, a grey box standing taller than even the Medvedian high king. It most noticeably featured four circular holes on one side. Asher's eyes squinted as he focused on the object. 'It almost looks like the…' His mind raced back to the chamber under White

Cliffe, the old images painted across the walls, the glass orb, and the Silver Coffin within. 'No way...,' he breathed.

'What is all this?' Cara asked, inspecting the scroll closely.

'This, my dear, depicts the Divergence, a most turbulent time, where the ancients fought a god for dominance. Using the very tools and weapons gifted to them, our ancient ancestors defeated the Shepherd, sealing their essence away in a coffin of silver. You'll see here.' He gestured to the four circular shapes at the coffin's side. 'Four to seal the power, four to release the fury...'

Asher turned to Julius. 'That's what Constance said back in White Cliffe City, in front of the coffin.' He shuddered as his mind recalled the high priestess's passionate chanting, the poor Rabbethi noble burning before the foreboding Silver Coffin. 'What does "release the fury" mean? It doesn't sound good.'

The old Vulpen scholar nodded thoughtfully. 'It is a tale lost to ages, turned to myth. All across Tamuz, every lost record I've found has said the same thing: When the ancients rebelled, imprisoning the Shepherd's power in the Silver Coffin, the Shepherd swore terrible, holy vengeance.' He slowly turned to look Asher in the eye. 'So no, my young king, releasing the fury of a god would not be good.' There was a heavy silence as the weight of the consequences, should they fail to stop Constance, fell upon their shoulders.

'So,' Cara said, breaking the sombre tension. 'To release the Shepherd, someone would need the four Shepherd Stones.'

'Which are within the four relics crafted by the ancients,' Julius finished. 'One would also need four individuals with the strength to wield the stones and place them within the coffin, those with the ancient's fire burning within them.'

'Ancient-touched...' Asher breathed.

'So the church has been right all this time...' Cara said absentmindedly. 'Their god is real and destined to return?'

'I don't know why you're so surprised, my dear. It's what I've been telling you since you were a cub,' the old Vulpen said, cocking an eyebrow. 'Don't tell me you never believed me?'

'I... err...' Cara's eyes lowered to the floor. 'Sorry.'

'Yes, well...' He turned to Asher. 'How you would determine from the hundreds of families with royal blood who were ancient-touched is beyond me.'

A noblewoman's scream filled Asher's mind. It appeared Cara shared the same memory as they both went silent, gazing at the scene depicted on the scroll.

'Thank you, old friend,' Cara said, standing straight, snapping Asher from his thoughts. 'You've been most helpful.' With a smile, she patted Julius on the shoulder and marched around the table towards the open door. 'We will discuss with the queen how this can help us against Constance and the church.'

'Yes, thank you, Julius. This has been fascinating,' Asher added, surprised by Cara's swift departure.

'Anytime, my young friends,' Julius beamed. 'Always a pleasure...' As the pair passed out of sight, a faint cry echoed behind them. 'Oh! Could you send for Leylan, please? And tell him to bring a mop!'

***

The grand hall was empty when Asher and Cara entered. All plates and bowls had been tidied away, and the chamber was filled with a simmering quiet, the burning fire crackling at the hall's centre. The queen was nowhere to be seen.

'She must be taking counsel on the terrace,' Cara said, passing between the tables towards the opposite arch.

'What do you make of all this? The god and the stones, I mean,' Asher asked, following.

'I used to think he was just telling stories, keeping the children of the court entertained. I never thought he was telling the truth. The queen never spoke about such things, not even after I was full-grown or after my parents...' She trailed off, seeming to lose herself in her memories.

'Cara?' Asher asked as they passed into the lavish hallway.

'It's not important,' she dismissed. 'Just know that the stakes have gotten much, much bigger.'

Guards stood to attention as the pair reached the grand golden doors to the royal terrace. A crowd of voices murmured from the other side. Asher felt a knot form in his stomach. Some very important people were behind those golden doors, each with agendas and opinions already formed on the young king. He wasn't ready. That didn't stop the guards from grabbing the large golden rings and heaving the doors open.

The chamber beyond fell silent. Asher and Cara walked through and towards the fire burning at the centre of the ringed benches. They passed between the gap in the seating and stopped before the fire. Its heat was intense but not uncomfortable. The doors rumbled closed behind them, sealing shut with a resounding thud.

Asher looked up at the benches and found a cascading waterfall of predatory eyes staring at him, a mixture of harsh judgement and deep curiosity among them. Their owners were a wide array of well-dressed and regal-looking Vulpen, covered in an assortment of red, black and white fur. The members on the lowest row sat beneath Asher's eyeline and struggled to look down on him. They raised their snouts the highest to compensate, straining their necks. The age of the senate seemed to vary greatly, from fresh-faced nobles to grey-furred old patriarchs and matriarchs. The bushy tails of the elderly members were scraggy, their fur course and the tips of their ears had folded. Both young and old whispered in hushed voices as the quiet lingered.

Opposite the gap in the seating and high above the senate was the grand wooden throne. With a high back and large arms, the throne connected to the top ring and featured inlays of gold that threaded around the dark wood, making the throne appear ablaze. Sitting patiently on the throne was the queen.

The gold trimmings of the queen's red stola dress shimmered under the fire's blaze, and the palla shawl draped over her shoulder and around her waist was black as night. Her fiery red tail descended the throne beside her, the white tip twitching by her feet. After a time, she rose, raising a gentle paw to silence the room. All heads turned to face her, and Asher felt a sense of relief as eyes no longer weighed down upon him.

She spoke with a clarity and a regalness that demanded undivided attention. 'Fine members of the senate. This is King Asher.' She gestured a paw towards him, and all eyes returned to his direction, applying their oppressive weight once more. 'His kingdom and family have been taken by Constance and her savage legion of Shangari.' Disgruntled murmurs rumbled through the benches at the mention of Constance. The queen continued, 'Forced into exile, he has travelled far and into our protection in hopes that we may aid him in reclaiming his crown and freeing his people. Senator Corvo, how did this come to pass? What do your agents say?'

A middle-aged black-furred Vulpen stood to Asher's right, high on the benches. He wore clothing similar to Cara's, with dark leather armour and a flowing black cloak. However, his cloak featured a heavy plumage of black raven feathers around the neck and upper shoulders. Cuts and scratches covered his armour, and his face sported a heavy red scar that cut vertically over his left eye, partially hidden behind a circular grey eye patch. He bowed to the queen, who nodded in return before sitting.

'Your Majesty, the girls I sent to investigate the church in Rabbethia were killed whilst attempting to retreat. Only Domina Cara and Domini Lucilla managed to escape.' He gestured a paw towards Cara, standing a few paces behind Asher. The eyes in the room shifted from the black senator to Cara. 'Not only did she escape and provide us with invaluable information, but she also rescued the king. Her service to the crown has been exemplary, and I humbly request that she be rewarded.' Cara raised a fist to her chest and bowed. Senator Corvo gave a slight smile in return and a subtle wink, which looked more like a blink with his one good eye.

The queen's eyes never left Senator Corvo. 'The service she has performed is what the queendom has asked of her, nothing more. She will be provided with the benefits provided to all agents who return from a successful mission. Now, your report, please.'

The black Vulpen returned to face the queen and bowed again. 'Yes, Your Majesty. From the report provided by Domina Cara and the ravens received from across the Rabbethi Kingdom, it appears the capital was taken completely by surprise, and there has been no call to arms. There are rumours that the royal line has ended, and thus, the kingdom is leaderless, without hope. Without a king, the earls squabble among themselves, shoring up their own borders in the hope of fending off the imminent Shangari scourge. My agents continue to survey the situation and are attempting to penetrate the inner circle of the Rabbethi witan and the church itself.'

'Might I interject?' came a well-spoken voice from the opposite row of benches. Standing tall was a skinny, red-furred Vulpen wearing a fine purple shirt buttoned up to his jaw and slim black trousers that only exaggerated his weedy legs. His snout was long and narrow, and his sharp blue eyes looked not at Senator Corvo but towards the queen, whose attention he now had. She gave a permissive nod but said nothing.

'My gracious queen,' he continued. 'Although infiltrating the Rabbethi elite may provide useful titbits of information, *my* envoys and diplomats within the embassy have already managed to obtain invaluable information regarding the church and the fate of the remaining Rabbethi witan members. We have learned ownership of the kingdom is to be given to the five remaining noble families of White Cliffe, with more positions to be assigned. Your Highness, the kingdom is to become a church territory, with Constance as its head of state.' A fresh wave of murmurs echoed around the benches. The queen held up a paw, and silence fell. The skinny senator continued, 'Riders are to be sent to all corners of the kingdom, informing the earls of the news. There is hope for a swift transition of power.'

'The people would not stand for it,' Senator Corvo asserted. 'The church has long been viewed with mistrust and Constance even more so. Provide the people with a leader, and they will rise, I promise you.'

'And who is to lead them?' retorted the other senator, his head snapping towards him, eyes narrowing. 'This king you have brought before us? How do we know he is the true heir to the throne and not some farmer boy your agent picked up while fleeing?'

'You dare question my agents?' Senator Corvo exclaimed in disgust, dagger-like teeth becoming visible in his growling mouth.

'Enough!' yelled the queen, rising to her feet. Silence fell. She turned to the unknown senator. 'I trust in the information of our agents, Senator Sanna. To doubt them would be to doubt me. Are we clear?' Her eyes were hard as she bore down upon the red-furred Vulpen.

Senator Sanna bowed before her, his eyes falling to his feet.

'My deepest apologies, Your Highness,' he said calmly.

She nodded, then turned to the rest of the senate. 'I have spent time with the old king and his family. Though his son may not recognise me, I recognise him.' She gestured down towards Asher, who felt eyes upon him once more. 'This is the heir of Hengist, King of Rabbethia, and we will restore him to his throne, as a friend of the Rabbethi, as reparations for Constance, and as compensation for his people's treatment under our ancestors' rule.' Murmurs of approval washed over the senate, accompanied by a sea of nodding heads.

'My queen, if I may,' Senator Sanna said over the crowd. 'Although we *all* agree that he is the true heir, the people of Rabbethia will need... convincing. They would need proof, a sign that he is indeed of royal lineage and not just a puppet propped up by the Vulpen Queendom.'

'I'm afraid I have to agree with Senator Sanna, Your Grace,' agreed Senator Corvo. 'Many believe the royal line ended in the attack. Small bands are forming around local barons, but none have the pull to unite the kingdom under one banner.'

The queen raised a paw, and the benches fell silent. 'There is a symbol that, once wielded, will prove his royal blood, the Bow of Folka. It is a mighty weapon and sister to the Judge's Bane. Used by the Rabbethi kings of old, it has become known by another name, the King's Bow.' Murmurings rose again, and the queen raised a paw, silencing the benches. 'Wielding such a weapon will instil hope and fervour into the people of Rabbethia, uniting them. They will rally behind such an artefact and the one who wields it.'

It now made sense to Asher why she had Julius tell them about the bow and the significance of its power and history. The bow was on every flag, banner, and crest found within Rabbethia. If one were to wander the labyrinth of White Cliffe's keep, they would stumble upon the ancient portraits of Asher's ancestors wielding the bow, holding it aloft in glory.

'I have spoken with Jarl Vatn of Otyrheim,' the queen continued. 'Regrettably, he refuses to give the relic over.'

Asher's eyes went wide. The Otyren had his people's bow, and the Vulpen knew about it? Anger began to well up inside him. How long had they known? Why hadn't they told him about it? More and more, he felt like he and his people were mere pieces to be moved upon a political chessboard. He held his tongue, clenched his fists tight and waited to see what resolution this senate would come to. He willed his twitching nose to be still.

'Why do we not send agents into Otyrheim and claim the weapon under the cover of night?' one elderly senator asked aloud.

Senator Corvo shook his head. 'Their security has increased tenfold over recent years. The chances of getting inside the keep undetected are nearly impossible. Getting caught would be a diplomatic disaster.'

The once subtle murmurs of the senate rose into a cacophony of heated shouting, with ideas, insults and slurs thrown in all directions, teeth flashing from under curled lips as rumbling growls echoed around the fire. The queen remained silent, her predatory eyes scanning the heated senators below. The noise echoed all around Asher. Their shouts and curses vibrated in his head as the fire felt like it was roaring before him. He couldn't take it anymore. These people were deciding his fate and that of his people. He needed to take control, for his sake, for his kingdom's sake.

'I will go!' he yelled above the crowd, surprising himself. The uproar stopped at once. Bodies shifted as all turned to face the Rabbethi king. 'If there is a weapon that belongs to my people, I will claim it.' The queen raised an eyebrow. He continued, 'It is true that the Otyren are not fond of my family nor my people, but relations are stable, even prosperous. They will recognise my right to it. If not, I will remind them what Constance would do to get her paws on it.'

Hushed whispers trickled down from the benches at the mention of Constance, voices of concern and apprehension taking prominence.

'She needs it to take the power of a god.'

The whispers silenced, eyes slowly drifting up to the queen. She watched Asher unmoved.

He continued, 'If she succeeds, she'll have the power to take the one thing you hold dear, the one thing all of us hold sacred, our freedom. She'll cover the land in blood and death until she gets her peace and make sure no one is left to deny her.'

The silence lingered as Queen Tessina held his passionate stare.

Senator Corvo took a breath and broke the silence. 'Blood, death and gods aside, Your Highness, your confidence and willingness to undertake such a task for your people is admirable, but I fear the Otyren Allthing would simply have you thrown—'

'That's enough, Corvo,' snapped the queen.

Corvo snapped to Queen Tessina and bowed. 'Yes, Your Majesty.' He sat, as did the rest of the senators.

The queen leaned forwards on her throne and gazed down upon Asher. 'I believe that is a wise decision, Your Highness. Staking your claim as king would solidify your right to rule among one of your strongest neighbours, and if a deal is to be struck, then this would improve the fragile relations between your people. The Otyren are a reasonable people, and if what you say about Constance's plans is true, then it would appear retrieving the bow first is paramount for the safety of our world. Although, putting an end to her permanently will be another matter.'

Murmurs of approval echoed around, and Asher stood a little taller, confident in his decision.

'We will send an entourage with you to ensure your protection and voice our approval of your claim. Senator Corvo will begin the preparations for your journey.'

The black Vulpen nodded. 'Yes, Your Highness.'

'For now,' the queen said, rising from her throne. All members of the senate rose in unison. 'This meeting is adjourned.'

The Vulpen senators bowed as one, and the queen descended her throne, stepping behind and disappearing from view. The Vulpen nobility then descended the benches. Asher stepped aside, allowing the sea of short, pointed ears and bushy tails to pass. A few nodded towards him, mumbling 'Your Majesty' under their breaths, though most simply rushed through, either deep in conversation or avoiding Asher's existence. They dispersed throughout the terrace, forming new circles around the many smaller fire pits. Asher noticed Senator Corvo, the queen's spymaster and Cara's boss, still in his seat and staring down at him. He beckoned for Asher to approach. As Asher moved, he heard a quiet voice in his ear.

'You did well. You spoke like a leader.'

Asher turned, finding Cara beside him, an approving smile across her face.

'Thanks,' he said, embarrassed. 'But I don't think many of them see me as one.'

'They will,' she said, placing a comforting paw on his shoulder.

The pair approached the spymaster as he climbed down the benches to the lowest tier. He was taller than Asher, lean with slight shoulders but a muscular frame.

He bowed to Asher. 'Your Majesty, it's a pleasure to meet you.' He rose swiftly and said solemnly, 'Your father was a strong and noble man. I'm sorry for your loss.'

'Thank you, Senator Corvo.'

With a smile and a nod of acknowledgement, he turned to Cara. 'Now then,' he said, a broad smile growing across his snout. They reached out and clasped each other's forearms in a tight grip before pulling close and embracing. As they separated, Asher noticed something on the underside of Corvo's forearm, between the ties of his leather armguards. It was only a fraction of a second, but he saw a scar, the shape of which didn't quite seem accidental. Bare, pink skin traced a curved outline, ending in a sharp point at the base of the wrist. In its centre was a small circle. Before Asher could inspect it further, Corvo crossed his arms and looked upon Cara like a proud father.

'You did well out there. I'm sorry I couldn't convince your mother your deeds deserved more than a meagre allowance and some time off.'

'You know that's not why I do it, Corvo,' she said, shaking her head.

'Wait!' Asher exclaimed. 'The queen is your mother? Cara, are you a princess?'

Corvo and Cara looked at each other before erupting with laughter.

'No!' Cara chuckled. 'Queen Tessina took me in after my parents passed. I am of a noble house, but the throne would pass to many distant cousins before coming to me.'

'Thank Thena!' Corvo teased, slapping Cara on the back. He then turned to Asher, his demeanour becoming abruptly serious, eyes narrowing. 'So you say Constance is trying to free a god? Are you sure?'

Asher nodded.

'If that's true, then there's more riding on this mission than one kingdom. I'm afraid we're all in danger. Who knows the devastation she would unleash with such power.' There was a lingering silence as the three let the stakes settle upon their shoulders. 'Well, I best prepare you for the journey to Otyrheim and assign you a guard. I'm yet to decide who that may be, but for now, I can equip you with our finest gear. I've heard you already possess the bow of one of my girls. Keep it. In terms of protection...' He looked Asher up and down at his shirt and trousers. He smiled. 'We have something just right for you. I'll have it sent to your room right away.'

'That's much appreciated, thank you.' Asher nodded. 'Do you know when we'll be setting sail? It's just...' He paused, hesitating. 'I have something I'd like to attend to before leaving.'

Corvo raised the eyebrow above his one good eye. 'I see. Well, it'll likely be tomorrow afternoon once the preparations have been made. Where is it you mean to go? If you don't mind me asking?'

'There's a town in the mountains north of here called Petrosa. There's a family that lives there. I...' He paused again, a lump forming in his throat. 'I need to tell them their daughter is dead.'

Senator Corvo frowned. 'Oh, I'm... I'm sorry to hear. Petrosa is about a couple of hours' ride from here. I can set you up with a horse and a retinue of guards.'

'No, thank you, I'd rather go alone. I'd rather keep it private, and I can take care of myself.'

'I can't say I approve, but I won't argue with a king.' Corvo chuckled, turning to Cara. 'You should go with him, keep him safe.'

Cara nodded. 'Of course.'

'If you mean to leave soon, I'd suggest you head to your room and await the armour. I'll send for it right away. In the meantime, I need to talk with our friend Cara here. A debriefing, if you will. Ah, Leylan, just the man!'

Asher turned to see Leylan, a mop in one paw, the head blackened with filth and soot. In the other paw was a bucket of murky water. It sloshed as he stopped beside them.

'You called, sir?' he said with an unenthusiastic tone.

'Could you please fetch His Highness's armour?'

'Right away, sir.' He sped out of the room in an instant, the sound of sloshing water growing fainter as his one ear flopped out of view.

'Excellent, that should be waiting for you when you return to your chamber. When you're ready, head back to the main hall, and we'll get you on your way. Now, if you'll excuse us, Your Highness.' Corvo and Cara bowed towards Asher before departing for one of the smaller fires.

With no one left to pay him any mind, Asher left the terrace through the large double doors. He strolled slowly down the various carpeted corridors until he was back inside his quiet, lonely chamber. The warm golden rays of the Lighthouse shone through the tall windows, bathing him in a calming glow. It had been an intense morning, and Asher already wished to return to his freshly made bed.

Something in the corner of the room caught his eye. Leather armour stood mounted on a wooden armour stand, like a ghostly soldier standing vigil without a head. The condition was pristine. The chest piece's centre bore a circular emblem displaying the Rabbethi Kingdom's sigil, a golden bow with three golden arrows pointing up, set on a deep blue background. The cloak fastened to the shoulders was a fine, deep-blue linen. The craftsmanship was exquisite, and Asher spent time admiring the skill. The whole piece exuded regality.

Asher disrobed from his casual clothing and began donning the armour. First came the dark linen trousers and accompanying shirt, which lay beneath the tough leather chest piece and provided some protection within the creases. Simple greaves and bracers were next, granting protection to his limbs, and tall boots provided ample support for navigating rugged terrain. A thick belt sat across his waist on which numerous empty pouches hung, with several places daggers could be sheathed and accessed at a moment's notice. The blue cloak and hood fell from his shoulders and flowed over his round white tail. It all fitted perfectly.

'What is this armour?' Asher breathed, gazing down at his arms. He placed a paw on the emblem on his chest as a strange sense of pride began manifesting in his heart.

'It was made for you,' came a soft voice from the door.

Asher turned to see Queen Tessina. She stood in the doorway watching Asher, her paws clasped before her. She smiled at him, thoughtful, her eyes kind but mournful.

'Your Highness.' Asher bowed, mimicking what he had seen from the others.

'Your Highness,' she replied, nodding in return. 'That armour you wear was made for you, a gift for your coronation.'

'My coronation? My father wasn't dying or about to give up the throne.' Asher's father had always been in good health, even in his later years when he had locked himself away.

'Little do you know of your father's wishes,' the queen said softly. 'A month or so before the attack, he sent ravens to all the kingdoms announcing his abdication. We made this as a gift in hopes of maintaining our friendship with the new king.'

Asher looked down again at the emblem on his chest—the symbol of his kingdom, people, and family.

'I had no idea,' he breathed, almost to himself. 'What if I'm not ready? What if I'm not the leader my people need?'

'Your father thought you were, and you're the last hope your people have. I know you'll make your father proud when the time comes.'

Asher smiled, a sense of pride swelling within as he looked down at the emblem on his chest.

Make my father proud, his thoughts repeated.

'She's my sister, you know,' the queen said softly.

Asher looked up and found her eyes soft and forlorn. 'I'm sorry?'

'Constance was my sister.'

Asher was taken aback. Constance was Vulpen royalty? Having that level of power and influence before becoming the head of the church explained a lot but also raised many more questions. He tried not to let his utter surprise show.

The queen continued, 'She grew too close to the church, too zealous in her false idol. My mother realised the queendom would not be safe under Constance and so chose me to rule. Constance refused to accept it and ordered her acolytes to attack.' She paused for a moment, clenching her fists. 'Fortunately, they were no match for the palace guards. She fled, but not before taking the crown from our mother's brow and leaving her for dead. Many died that day, including my beloved.' She closed her eyes and sighed.

'I'm sorry for your loss,' Asher said, his heart sinking at her grief.

'Thank you. My husband, he... he was a good man.'

Asher looked back down at the emblem on his chest, this time guilt washing over him. It broke his heart to hear people had suffered because of Constance long before she attacked his kingdom. Asher looked up from the emblem towards the queen, but she was gone, and he was left staring at an empty doorway.

'Make my father proud,' he repeated. He picked up his bow, slung the quiver of arrows over his shoulder and placed the white ribbon dagger into one of the sheathes on his chest. He would stop Constance, save his brother and restore the Kingdom of Rabbethia. He inspected himself again in the mirror above the table and smiled.

'I'll make my people proud.'

14

The Next Right Thing

Filled with renewed confidence, Asher returned to the main hall, his new blue cloak floating behind him as he walked. He received many a bow as he strolled past the various staff and nobles who worked within the palace. 'Your Highness' was muttered by everyone. It was all so strange and, all of a sudden, very real. For the first time in his life, he felt respected, no longer the runaway thief, red apple in paw. Yes, he had been a prince back in White Cliffe, but since his mother's passing, he had spent more time outside the palace than in it. Even in the palace, he was only given respect by those paid to do so. Now, though, he was a king. He had the weight of an entire people upon his shoulders, the responsibility to do what was right by them. Every decision he made would affect so many lives, and everyone knew it.

Asher halted just before he entered the hall, his heart racing, nose twitching. *So many people.* He placed a paw on the wall to steady himself as he doubled over, his long ears flopping forwards. *They're all counting on me.* His ears began to radiate heat as his vision started to blur. His thoughts were racing. He could feel everyone's expectations growing heavy, becoming oppressive. It was suffocating. He had no idea how to rule, how to lead. Sure, he was decent in a fight and was charming in the right situation, but that wasn't enough to be king. Was it? He had always imagined his father would rule forever and that he could sit in his shadows, performing his princely tasks when required. *What if I fail? What if I make the wrong decision?* His chest tightened as nausea surged in waves throughout his body. The walls began to bear down upon him, and he desperately searched for his mother's necklace beneath the leather armour. He shut his eyes tight and tried to imagine her kind, loving smile. Her gentle voice echoed in his mind, and he imagined her warm arms wrapped around him, comforting him as she had so many times before. He could almost hear her slow, rhythmic breaths in his ears.

'It's okay to be afraid, my darling,' she used to say when Asher's courage had abandoned him. 'Being brave is doing the next right thing in the face of fear, and you are the bravest boy I know.'

He took a deep breath. 'The next right thing... the next right thing... the next right thing...' His breathing steadied, the manic thoughts coming to rest. The next right thing? The words always made his fears so digestible, so much easier to manage. Rather than the crippling weight of his biggest problem, he simply focused on what should be done next. He knew what it was. It filled him with a different kind of anxiety, not the type that would cripple him, but the type that filled him with dread for the pain he was about to cause. Telling Mia's family about her passing—that's what he would focus his racing thoughts on.

With his mind resolved and the troubles of his kingdom pushed to the back of his mind for now, the nausea subsided, and the walls ceased their relentless hounding. He stood tall as the tightness in his chest eased.

I'm okay, he breathed. *I'm okay.*

Order had been restored to his world, at least for now. Looking around, it didn't appear anyone had noticed his sudden episode, and he was thankful for the good fortune. *Not the best behaviour of a new king*. He took a deep breath and continued into the grand hall.

It was busier now, with many agents lining the wooden tables, feasting on all manner of food, from bread to dried meat, soup and cheese. Asher heard his stomach growl at the smell of the fresh-baked bread. He looked up to the royal table and saw no one sitting along its length and no food laid out. His heart sank. He walked, defeated, towards the double doors at the far end of the hall.

A firm white paw grabbed his arm, stopping him in his tracks. He looked down at the seated agent that had caught him. It was Flora. Without looking at him, she reached down to her plate, took a large piece of bread and gave it to him. Asher looked at it for a time before cautiously reaching out to take it.

'You look sick, Your Highness,' she said flatly before placing a piece of dried meat into her long snout. 'Eat.'

'That's very kind, thank you.'

'I'm not kind, but Cara seems to like you.'

'Right, well, thank you all the same, Flora.'

'Highness.' There was an awkward pause before Asher felt it best he continued, now with an exquisite-smelling piece of bread to chew on.

He reached the doors and, not seeing Cara, turned to look out across the hall. The warm bread was divine. As he watched the agents talking and laughing in a chorus of chattering voices, something tapped him on his shoulder. He turned, finding Luce looking him up and down.

'Well, don't you look grand,' she said with a coy smile.

Asher's cheeks grew warm. 'Thanks, I'm still getting used to it,' he said, bashful. 'But it does look pretty regal, doesn't it? Distinguished?'

'It sure does! Just remember your good friend Luce when you're sitting on your fancy throne, yeah? Maybe throw a castle or two my way?'

'I will,' Asher chuckled. Within the crowded grand hall, the fire roaring at its centre, the two shared a peaceful moment of laughter. It was the first time since his escape from White Cliffe that he had laughed. It felt good. The attack on his kingdom felt nothing more than a distant memory. A stab of guilt punctured his heart, and his laughter quickly faded.

'Is everything alright?' Luce asked, concern in her eyes.

'I'm okay. It's just... I shouldn't be laughing after what's happened.'

Luce reached out a soft paw and held Asher's cheek, taking him by surprise. 'Maybe that's the best time?' She smiled a caring smile with no sense of playfulness or mischief. 'Laughing heals wounds. Only then can you start to fix the broken things.'

Asher looked deep into her bright blue eyes and felt himself becoming lost within, enveloped by a blanket of calm and understanding.

'Thank you,' he breathed, savouring her gaze.

'You're welcome.' She removed her paw and quickly stepped back. 'Right, yes, well, I've got to get going and... Oh, look, there's Cara!'

Asher turned, but she was nowhere to be seen. He turned back and smiled. Luce had vanished.

After a time, Cara walked into the hall from the same arch Asher had prior. She scanned the hall, noticed the Rabbethi king and began making her way over. As she passed by Flora, she extended a black paw and grazed it over Flora's shoulder. They didn't look at each other, and Cara didn't break her stride, letting her paw fall from Flora's shoulder and sway as part of her natural stride. A coy smile formed in the corner of Flora's mouth.

Cara approached Asher with a smile. She appeared to have developed a more positive demeanour, almost becoming cheerful—far removed from the stern Vulpen he had come to know. Several evenings with Flora and reminiscing with Senator Corvo appeared to have done wonders for her mood. Asher had to tread carefully, lest he return Cara to her previously sour mood.

She inspected Asher in his new armour. 'It suits you.'

'Well, it was made for me.' He chuckled.

She patted him on the shoulder and continued, 'Shall we?' She grabbed the dark metal ring on one of the doors and heaved it open, a flood of daylight shining into the hall.

Asher followed, squinting in the bright light as he found himself within a large square courtyard. It was a hive of activity with many a Vulpen and the occasional Rabbethi hurrying about, carrying official documents or jingling pouches. Some wore fine linen, while others wore plain woollen tunics. Groups of organised soldiers marched in and out of the wide gatehouse at the far end, their dark armour appearing brighter and less intimidating in the midday light. One soldier stood tall to the side, barking orders to the others as they marched past obediently. His long crimson cape marked him as a captain, and his broad frame inspired respect. Small groups of agents dressed like Cara mingled about the courtyard. They spoke in hushed voices, likely sharing information from their last mission.

A magnificent statue of a Vulpen woman raised atop a tall plinth took centre stage in the courtyard. Her long robes and thick tail flowed behind in a proud stance frozen in stone. She faced out towards the gatehouse leading towards the sloping city, snout raised high as if judging all who entered the palace. To Asher's right stood a row of terraced buildings, each with heavy single doors at their base, reinforced with metal plating. Some were open and had well-dressed officials hurrying in and out. The courtyard floor was a smooth cobblestone. Various coloured bricks swirled across the expanse, representing a hundred raging magical fires. It would have been beautiful if not for the few piles of uncleaned horse droppings.

The stench of fresh manure and hay wafted from the stables to Asher's left. Rows of stalls housed horses that neighed and trotted over the hay covering the stone floor. Each beast was well-groomed and muscular, their beauty far overshadowing the stocky workhorses of Rabbethia.

Leylan approached from the stables, two sturdy horses led by their reins in tow. 'Here you are, Domina Cara, Your Highness.' He bowed towards Asher before passing one of the reins to Cara. 'This is Nox.' The horse was a black mare, her coat silky smooth and black as night. 'And this is Aurora,' Leylan said, passing the other rein to Asher, who took it cautiously. This one was a speckled grey stallion. Judging from his broad, muscular frame, he had once been a mighty war mount, but the years had demoted him to a more civilian role. 'Their packs have been filled with some light supplies for your journey. If there's nothing more, I have other duties to attend to.'

'That is all. Thank you, Leylan,' Cara said with a nod. Leyland bowed towards Asher before marching quickly towards one of the open doors, disappearing inside. Cara began inspecting the packs on Nox. 'Have you ridden before?' she asked, placing a foot into a stirrup and hoisting herself up. She swung the other leg over, easing into the saddle with ease.

Asher had ridden before, though nothing this impressive. Under his alias as Bill, he helped the local farmers with some of their work, and in return, they let him ride the workhorses awkwardly around the open fields. The Rabbethi were not known for their riding skills, preferring to rely on their own muscular legs rather than that of a beast.

'I have, but nothing this big,' Asher said as he placed a foot into one of the stirrups.

'You'll be fine. Aurora is a calm-natured creature when the war horns aren't sounding.'

That did little to calm Asher's nerves as he attempted to mimic Cara's mounting method. He lifted himself up and swung his leg around, and as he settled into the saddle, the horse unexpectedly trotted a few paces forwards. Asher's heart thumped in his chest, his nose beginning to twitch.

Cara chuckled to herself. 'See? You're fine.' She pulled on her reins, turning Nox on the spot, then kicked into the horse's flank and took off through the courtyard towards the gatehouse. Numerous guards and palace staff leapt out of the way, lest they be knocked over or trampled.

Asher followed suit, pulling on his reins and kicking Aurora's flanks. The muscular horse neighed in protest as it started at an alarming pace. Asher could feel the power beneath him as each gallop echoed against the stone floor, the heavy breaths of the stallion resonating within him. More folk leapt out of his path, leaving numerous curses in his wake. The red-furred Vulpen captain said nothing but glared through squinted eyes as Asher sped under the stone gatehouse.

'Sorry,' Asher mouthed as he passed.

He rounded a wide corner and began descending a long street at breakneck speed, his long ears and cape trailing wildly in the wind. On either side rose opulent manor houses, two stories tall and much wider than any house on the lower tiers. Their white stone shone in the light, contrasting against the windowsills and door frames, which were painted in a myriad of colours. Hundreds of flower beds passed by in a blur on either side. It was quiet compared to the lower tiers, save for the echoing of hooves and the heavy panting of Asher's horse. The occasional colourful clothes of a Vulpen noble flashed by as they stopped to stare at a horse galloping down the street.

Rising high above the houses to his left was the last and tallest cliff face, its jagged peaks looking like the teeth of a gigantic creature ready to consume the city. Green vegetation clung to its bare walls as rings of sea birds circled the rocky ledges, awaiting their turn to land and nest. Behind the row of grand homes to his right was a thick stone wall that ran parallel to the street, matching its sloping decline. Through the spaces between the luxurious abodes, Asher could see guards patrolling the wall's battlements. He didn't envy them. The effort of climbing the city's rising fortifications looked gruelling.

Cara waited ahead where the street curved and descended in the opposite direction. Asher pulled on the reins and slowed Aurora to a trot as he approached.

'How was he?' Cara asked. 'Did he behave himself?'

'He was fine,' Asher replied, panting. 'Though I don't think I was ready for such power!'

'I was talking to Aurora,' Cara joked with a chuckle. 'This way. It's best to keep to a slow pace through here. Security is tight between these tiers. You'll be surprised how many would risk punishment for a chance to break into the homes up here. One silver fork could feed a family for a month.'

The pair continued around the corner, their horses' hooves clopping against the stone at a steady walk. Asher gasped as a gargantuan structure rose before them, making his eyes grow wide. Splitting the tier in two and extending out over the next tier below was a massive stone wall, its face covered in hundreds of shallow arches. Asher's eyes scaled its height, noticing numerous precarious nests and hardy plants growing from cracks in the masonry. At its peak sat the palace's royal terrace. Several figures stood gazing down, but he couldn't make out much more than their silhouetted shapes. The houses lining both sides of the street were pressed right up to the wall, even appearing to merge into and partially climb the colossal stone, using it as added stability in the already cramped city. A gatehouse sat at the wall's base, its sturdy metal grate sealing the tunnel beyond, blocking the road. Several guards milled around on either side, some leaning against the wall while others sat around braziers, eating dried meat and bread.

Cara's horse trotted forwards, and Asher followed. A battle-scarred, black-furred guard pushed himself off the wall and limped onto the street, a tattered red cape trailing behind him. He raised a gloved paw towards the pair.

'Sigil, please, Domina Cara,' he asked gruffly.

Cara reached under her cloak and pulled out her iron sigil. She gave it to the guard. 'Here you are, Dario. How's the leg?'

Dario inspected the sigil before giving it back to Cara, who placed it under her cloak. 'It's fine, thank you, Domina Cara.' Saying no more, he turned towards the gatehouse and bellowed down the tunnel, 'Two to come through!' He then stepped aside to allow Asher and Cara to pass. With a heavy *ka-chunk*, heavy chains rattled from within the gatehouse, and the metal grate began lifting out of its trench. Peering down the tunnel, Asher could see the silhouetted shape of a second gate rising in unison.

He and Cara passed under the gatehouse and into the tunnel, where the temperature dropped. The warm glow of the many torches fastened to the rocky wall gave the illusion of warmth but did nothing to alleviate the chill. Asher pulled his cloak over his shoulders, gripping it tight. Cara, however, appeared unaffected by the sudden cold.

They trotted their horses down the length of the tunnel in silence, enjoying the echoes of the hooves and the crackling of the torches. As they approached the end of the tunnel, the bustling echoes of a crowd began to resonate around them, lively music drifting over a chorus of voices.

Asher squinted as he rode back into the light of the Lighthouse. Blurry shapes began solidifying around him, and he realised they were now standing at one end of a broad market plaza. Many colourful stands stood in the open space. Hundreds of Vulpen, Rabbethi and the occasional Otyren perused the various goods on sale, surrounded by tall buildings flanking the plaza. At the far end stood a grand gatehouse nestled within a gap in the curving cliff face that embraced the rear of the city. The cliffs on either side towered high above. At their peaks were two massive braziers, the fires roaring despite the midday light washing over the city. The gate was open, and beyond, Asher could see rolling fields dotted with rocky outcrops. A wide stone path curved away to his left, descending the cliff towards the tier below.

Asher and Cara continued into the market, following the wide gap between market stands that cut through its centre. Merchants called out, holding up items and produce while offering "fantastic deals". Cara ignored them and moved her horse through the crowd. Asher waved a polite paw to the merchants, profusely apologising that he wasn't interested. He was met with grumbles and glares as if he had performed terrible acts upon their daughters.

A sudden laughter and chorus of excited chatter erupted deeper in the plaza, accompanied by loud, upbeat music. The source of the uproar was a wooden stage to the left of the gatehouse, where a collection of colourfully dressed actors danced with dramatic flair, performing a show for a crowd of children and their parents. Asher smiled at the laughing children. It had been a while since he had seen so much joy and happiness, and that was a sad thought. Their horses stepped through and under the heavy iron gates hanging precariously above their heads, all tipped with thick spikes that aligned with holes in the stone floor. Before them were the wilds of Ignimarum. The hum of activity and the rhythmic beat of the music grew quiet as they followed the dirt road, becoming muffled. The vast plain of short, tough grass before them was broken up by large rocky outcrops like crumbs sprinkled over a plate.

The road was relatively easy-going. The lack of any recent rain had dried the land, and the horses kept trotting along the hard-packed dirt at a steady pace, dust clouds erupting beneath each hoof. Crickets chirped in the midday heat, and small birds whizzed overhead, catching the hordes of bugs swarmed above. Those not hunting sang songs within the dry branches of a few lone trees. Hardy-looking sheep with wool smothered in dirt and faeces grazed in packs on the short grass, moving from one patch to the next. As Asher and Cara passed, a couple would raise a head and give the pair a judgemental stare. Asher glared back in a strange game of intimidation. He usually won, the sheep losing interest and returning to its food. As they rounded a collection of scattered rocks, steep, craggy hills rose in the distance before them.

'That's our destination,' Cara said, pointing towards the bare hills. 'Several communities make a living there growing crops that favour the rocky land—olives and fruits, that sort of thing. They also have a fondness for goats and the cheese they make from their milk. Not a fan myself.' She furrowed her snout as she recalled the taste of an unpleasant memory.

'I like goat's cheese,' Asher said, thinking aloud. He hadn't expected a guided tour of the local produce, but Cara was in a chatty mood, and he didn't want to ruin it. 'Goat's cheese on a bed of rocket drizzled with thick honey.' His stomach growled.

Cara raised an eyebrow. 'There should be some food in the packs, but you'll need to eat and ride. We need to be back in the palace before dark.' She passed between two tall boulders flanking the path.

'Fine,' he sighed, disappointed at not having a short rest to ease his bruising inner thighs. He reached into the pack and pulled out a large carrot. It looked good, though he didn't appreciate the obvious stereotyping. Still, he crunched down upon it and enjoyed its crisp flavour.

***

It was late afternoon by the time the pair reached the rocky hills. The path split into several possible routes, each signposted, displaying their end location. To the west was the port town of Navitectum. To the east were the villages of Flumenca and Orisium. Asher found the one he was after, "Petrosa". The sign pointed north, deeper into the hills.

'This way,' he said, leading his horse down the much narrower trail, his heart growing anxious. The hills began to rise around them until they eventually came into a small clearing surrounded by steep rocky slopes. Several wooden cabins sat within the enclosed space. Goats with huge curved horns grazed on the sheer black slopes, defying gravity.

It was quiet, peaceful, and somewhat sheltered from the harsh world beyond its rocky walls. A tall, red-furred Vulpen man stood on the porch of one of the larger cabins. He was a broad man in a simple green shirt, a wide leather belt around his waist, and brown trousers. He hailed Asher and Cara, who steered their horses towards his home.

'Can I help you, stranger?' he asked, leaning his weight onto a shepherd's crook taller than him.

'Do you know Mia?' Asher replied with anxious expectation, almost hoping the man had never heard the name before.

'I do, sir,' he said, standing taller, his tail flicking to and fro. Worry rose in his voice, dismantling his stern exterior. 'She's my daughter.'

Asher dismounted and approached the older man hesitantly. 'Can we go inside? There's... something I need to tell you.'

15

Never Again

A large black pot hung above a fire that crackled with life within a stone hearth. The flames caressed its rotund base as a brown liquid bubbled inside. It was simple inside the wooden home. The scent of goat stew and boiled vegetables permeated the rafters, enticing Asher and Cara further inside. Against one wall lay a wide bed covered with soft goat fleeces, making it the comfiest, most inviting bed that Asher had ever seen, and in the middle of the room sat a long table surrounded by several three-legged stools.

Leaning forwards on one of these stools was a petite Vulpen woman, the sleeves of her brown woollen dress rolled up to her elbows. Her white apron was smattered with patches of dirt and food stains. She poured what appeared to be curdled milk from one wooden bucket into another, its opening covered with several layers of cloth. Movement behind Asher made him jump as Mia's father and a younger, angrier-looking Vulpen joined them. Mia's father closed the door, drawing the woman's attention, her bright blue eyes flickering with the glow of the fire. A look of nervous curiosity crossed her red-furred face. It was quickly replaced by a polite smile when she found the two Vulpen men entering behind Asher and Cara.

'Oh, hello...' she squeaked. Her eyes moved past the pair to the older man, who leaned his crook against the wall beside the bed. 'Vigo? Aren't you going to introduce me to your friends here?'

'This is my wife, Francesca,' Mia's father said, gesturing a rough, calloused paw to the woman. The woman smiled. He then gestured to the younger man standing guard, his arms crossed and brow furrowed in a failed attempt to look intimidating. 'And my son, Gaius.'

'I hear you have news of my sister? What is it? Who are you to her, patches?' Gaius snapped.

Cara moved, darting in front of the young Vulpen, catching him off-guard. 'Watch your tongue, boy, before I cut it from your mouth.'

Gaius's arms dropped, his eyes growing wide. Any attempt to look tough crumbled in an instant, his alarmed gaze flickering between Cara and his father.

'That'll teach ya for insulting the queen's agents, ya dung brain,' Vigo said with an unsympathetic huff. He then looked Asher up and down, raising an eyebrow. 'Though this is the first I've heard of a Rabbethi entering their ranks. What did you say your name was?'

'I'm Bill. I was a friend of your daughter's. And this is Cara, my... mentor.'

Cara stepped away from Gaius, who slumped to the floor. She turned and raised a fist to her chest, bowing to Vigo and then Francesca. They both dipped their heads in response.

Vigo returned to Asher. 'So you're Bill, eh? We've heard quite a lot about you from Mia's letters. If you beg my pardon, but what's a farm boy doing in Ignimarum attending an agent of the queen?'

Asher's chest tightened. His nose began twitching. This was it. This was the moment he would destroy these people's lives. A part of him wanted to leave, to say that Mia was fine and wouldn't be able to visit them ever again, and they just had to learn to live with that. No, they needed to know. With a heart the weight of solid lead, he met Vigo's confused stare.

'I think it best we all had a seat,' Asher said, moving towards the nearest stool. 'May I?'

Cara continued to stand, as did Gaius, who had pushed himself off the floor and quietly resumed his station by the door. Vigo took a seat next to his wife. The fire continued to crackle as the stew bubbled inside the pot. All along the way from Saewic, Asher had been thinking of what he would say, playing through different words, apologies, and excuses, but nothing ever sounded right. He just had to say it.

'Mia is dead,' he said abruptly.

Silence.

Asher's eyes looked from Vigo's to Francesca's, their faces marred with confusion as if Asher had just spoken in an unknown language.

'Wh-what?' Vigo stuttered.

'Shangari attacked her village. She-she didn't make it…' Asher's gaze lowered to the table, unable to look them in the eyes.

'I don't believe you.'

Asher looked up. Francesca was staring at him, tears forming at the corners of her eyes. She looked to Cara, who lowered her head as if to confirm.

'I'm so sorry,' Asher breathed.

'No! My baby girl. *No!*'

She began to weep deep, painful sobs. Her wails filled the cabin, heart-wrenching and full of the deepest sorrow any soul could bring forth. Vigo took her into his arms and held her tight, her moans muffled by his tunic, gentle tears trickling down his cheeks. He turned to Asher, a look of pure agony across his face.

'Why? Why did this happen to our little girl?'

'I... I don't know,' Asher lied, though he wasn't sure why. He didn't know if it was cowardice, but telling them her death could have been avoided if he hadn't walked into her pub was just too painful.

Gaius hurried from the door to his parents and wrapped his arms around them, burying his head into his father's shoulder.

'I think you better leave,' Vigo whispered, holding his family tight.

'Of course,' Asher said solemnly, rising from the table, the great chains of guilt returning once more to pull him back down. He paused for a moment, looking at the broken family, at their heartbreak, before turning towards the door.

Cara bowed to the huddled family. 'I'm sorry for your loss. May her fire be welcomed into the library of Thena,' she said softly.

Vigo nodded in thanks, and Cara turned to follow Asher. As he opened the door, Asher turned back and saw a broken man, his eyes red with the tears that trailed down his face.

'You were a good friend to Mia. Thank you,' he said with a forced smile.

Asher nodded, though he wholeheartedly disagreed. He hadn't been a good friend, and every fibre of his being wanted to break down and cry, to confess that she had died because of him. He closed the door, and the cool evening breeze brushed against his face.

Muffled footsteps echoed in the twilight, rushing towards them. A young, dark-furred Vulpen woman appeared from the shadows. In her arms, she cradled a young cub with red fur, beautifully speckled with patches of black. 'I heard crying,' she said in panicked breaths. 'What happened?'

'You best go inside,' Cara said gently. 'You should be with the others.'

Confusion and worry twisted on her face, and she rushed into the cabin, pulling the door shut behind her. It wasn't long before a fresh chorus of woeful cries and painful sorrow echoed out of the open window.

Asher and Cara untied their horses and climbed into their saddles, not saying a word as they did. Asher's heart had sunk deep into the pit of his stomach. Tears crept down his soft cheeks. As they moved away from the homestead, a deep, mournful song began to flow from within, joined soon after by others until it was a symphony of harmonious sorrow.

'We need to go,' Cara whispered.

Asher said nothing but kicked into Aurora's flank, trotting at a pace towards the road.

'Asher?' Cara asked with growing concern. She caught up to his side, but he didn't look to greet her. His eyes were focused on the road ahead, tears no longer falling down his cheeks.

Anger had taken hold.

'Never again,' he breathed. Never again would someone die because of him. Never again would he run from his problems, from his responsibilities. Never again would people suffer at the paws of those who call *him* enemy. The fire he felt aboard *The Silvi* was now raging in his heart, fuelled by a broken family's grief, and Asher stared at the road ahead. He thought of his city, his kingdom and the bitch that took it from him.

Never again.

***

A chilling breeze coursed through Asher's fur as they followed the path. He and Cara remained silent despite her best attempts to initiate a conversation or inquire about his well-being. The anger within him had subsided but still smouldered, ready to be rekindled at a moment's notice. He gripped the reins tight as he rode.

The light was beginning to fade, and it would be night by the time they reached the city gate. There was no sign of any roaming sheep, and the birds above had flown home to roost, resting their voices for the morning to come. All that was left was the song of the crickets that chirped louder now that theirs was the only music.

Something caught Asher's eye as they drew near a cluster of rocky outcrops. Torches flickered off the bare rock as dark shapes huddled around two smaller forms on the ground. He and Cara slowed their horses, stopping not far from the figures. With their backs turned, the strangers didn't detect their presence.

Asher and Cara dismounted and drew closer, remaining silent, and the strangers' details started to become clear. Asher paused as he recognised the uniforms of the queen's agents, their distinctive black hoods pulled tight over their heads. There were five in total, all of equal size and build, save for one that was much shorter, their cloak tattered and off-colour to the others. Two of the taller agents held torches, illuminating more figures on the ground that they loomed over. Cowering in the dirt was a woman—a Rabbethi with sandy-brown fur—and a child whose fur matched the woman's.

'Wait here,' Cara whispered, drawing her blade. Asher let Cara move ahead, taking hold of her horse's reins.

'Please, don't hurt us!' cried the woman, holding her child in her arms. 'We don't have anything!' Her eyes darted around the group of agents.

'Oh, but you do,' one of the agents sneered, his voice carrying a lick of malicious intent.

'What's going on here?' Cara demanded, stepping out from the shadows.

The agents froze as if remaining perfectly still would deter Cara's probing. Hushed mutterings began murmuring between them as they quickly realised that wouldn't work. After a short time, the two taller agents turned to address her, chests puffed out. They were both red-furred Vulpen. One had blood trickling down his chin from a cut on his lip, staining the white fur under his jaw.

'Nothing to see here,' he called as he reached for his belt, pulling out an iron sigil. 'Just some riff-raff attempting to smuggle illicit goods into the city.' He held the sigil up and pointed it towards Cara. Shining under the torchlight was the familiar head of a Vulpen woman resting on several tails arranged in a flower pattern and facing to the right. Something wasn't right.

They're not agents, just more scum preying on the weak. He reached for his bow, not waiting to see if Cara had reached the same conclusion.

'See? Official queen's business.' The imposter agent smirked as the woman on the floor started to weep. 'Now, if there's nothing else, we'll get on with our busin—'

A whistle cut through the air, and the agent dropped the sigil to the floor, eyes wide, mouth hanging in stunned silence. Protruding from his chest was an arrow shaft, the base slick with his blood. His companion stared on in stunned horror.

'What the fu—'

Another whistle and an arrow materialised in the second agent's chest with a solid *thud*. Blood spewed from his mouth as he cried out in pain. Another whistle, another thud, and both imposter agents collapsed to the road, small puffs of dirt erupting beneath them. Asher stepped out from the shadows, bow raised, the string still vibrating by his cheek.

'So much for subtlety,' Cara said, eyeing the others.

The three remaining agents spun. One was a black-furred Rabbethi, another a white-furred Vulpen, both wielding rusted shortswords and black leather chest pieces across their torso. The unmistakable black eyes of an Otyren peered out from the hood of the shorter bandit. Unlike their companions, the Otyren had clearly scrounged his gear from the streets and back alleys of the city, wearing a training leather chest piece designed for children and a bed sheet used as a cloak. What he did have was a nasty-looking trident, which he thrust with angry strikes in Cara's general direction.

'Impersonating an agent of the queen is a crime,' she growled, her fangs revealed beneath her curling lips. 'Prepare to be punished.'

With panicked cries, the Rabbethi and Otyren charged. Cara readied herself, bending her knees and gripping her sword's handle with two paws.

The last bandit—the Vulpen—took off low for Asher, who released an arrow straight towards the attacker's chest. With a swift swipe of his blade, the Vulpen deflected the arrow, snapping it in two as it clattered to the ground. Asher dropped the bow and pulled the white ribbon knife from his chest, gripping it tight in his paw. The bandit lunged. He stabbed his blade directly towards Asher's face. Asher ducked away with ease, flipping his knife into a backwards grip, and brought his right fist square into the Vulpen's jaw. The blade cut deep across his snout as Asher leaned his weight into the punch. Blood splattered onto the ribbon of the knife as it trailed behind, becoming speckled with crimson. The Vulpen roared in pain. He stumbled away, turning his head with the hit to avoid losing his entire snout. A thick trail of blood dripped from the tip of Asher's knife down the stained ribbon and onto the dirt at his feet.

A fire had erupted in Asher's heart, feeding off his adrenaline and the anger in his mind. He raised his fists and bounced from one foot to the other, thinking back to his days in the boxing rings of White Cliffe and his training with Luce in the palace. Her advice echoed in his mind like a mantra: *Stay calm. Fists high, elbows low. Move your head. Don't lean back, and don't take your eyes off your opponent*. He took a deep breath, planted a foot and accelerated. The Vulpen had but a moment to react. He chopped down at Asher, who drifted left and brought his fist hard into the Vulpen's ribs.

Crack.

Another roar of pain, and the Vulpen flashed his sharp canine teeth. He sliced with wild abandon across his body, aiming to take Asher's head clean off. Asher ducked again, the rusty blade barely missing his tall ears, and he brought the knife across the Vulpen's inner thigh. It cut deep, slicing through the thin black trousers. Heavy drops of blood began falling onto the ground as Asher spun away, ready to lead another assault.

He was done with always being on the back foot, done with always running. It was time to attack, to take down his enemies rather than avoid confrontation. The ribbon flowing from the knife was now more red than white as it absorbed more and more blood with each cut. He stared at the Vulpen with nothing but pure hatred. The Vulpen panted, exhausted, his free paw holding onto his cracked ribs. A bloody gash scarred his snout, and his leg was wobbling, blood trickling from the wound.

The sound of swords clashing caught Asher's attention. He glanced at Cara. She was fending off an Otyren frothing at the mouth, the small man stabbing at her with his trident. At the same time, the Rabbethi slashed at her with uncoordinated swings of his sword. She ducked and weaved with finesse, avoiding the heavy swings of the blade and deflecting each stab of the trident with her scimitar. Asher watched in amazement as neither bandit could get close to landing a blow. The Otyren overreached, and Cara grabbed the shaft before he could pull the trident back. She pulled hard, dragging the Otyren screaming towards her. With a spinning swipe of her scimitar, she took his head clean off, and blood poured from the stump like a fountain. The tiny head fell to the floor, rolling to the feet of the Rabbethi. The Otyren's headless body slumped to the ground, blood coating the dirt path. The Rabbethi no longer looked as confident as he once had.

A memory of Luce's voice yelled within Asher's head, *Don't take your eyes off your opponent!* He snapped to the Vulpen and dodged just as a blade streaked past his face. The sword sliced deep across his right cheek. The fire inside roared once more, and he planted a foot, leaned into the bandit with all his might and brought his knee as hard as he could into the Vulpen's abdomen. He felt his knee embed into the armour, the leather tearing on impact. The Vulpen bandit hurtled backwards in a blur, tumbling along the dirt before slamming hard into one of the boulders lining the path. He cried in pain as the impact forced the air from his lungs, his sword sent clattering from his paw.

Asher wasn't done. The fire inside raged like an inferno, desperate to break free and consume everything in its path. He ran after the battered Vulpen and leapt onto him, straddling and pinning him to the floor. Trembling, ears radiating heat, he held the red ribbon knife to the Vulpen's throat. He wanted to do it. He needed to do it, to make sure the road would be safe from scum like this, but something was holding him back, some last trace of empathy clinging to his heart for dear life. The Vulpen growled, bared his vicious teeth and snapped at Asher in a desperate attempt to maim.

Asher didn't flinch. He simply stared into the Vulpen's rageful eyes. He found fear, the same fear he had seen in Henric's eyes, in Mia's. His mind flashed to that moment, to Mia's kind blue eyes as they cried, afraid. He remembered the fear in her strained voice, the bolt protruding from her throat.

'I'll kill you!' spat the man beneath the blade, blood splattering against Asher's white fur.

Asher gripped the knife tighter and pressed it harder against his throat.

'Never again,' he growled.

'Wha-what?' A flash of confusion crossed the man's eyes before Asher ripped the knife across his throat. Blood sprayed from the wound, painting the rock beside them. The Vulpen clutched at his throat, his eyes bulging. He tried to scream, but that merely quickened his death, his cries forcing the blood through the gushing wound. His gurgles began to diminish as the flow of blood weakened, his frantic grasping becoming sluggish. His panicked eyes closed, and he was dead.

Asher stood, remaining over the body, feeling nothing. Not sadness that he had just taken a life, nor happiness that he survived. He supposed he felt... content, content that there was one less bastard in the world, one less creature that could harm good people, good, innocent people like Mia. The ribbon around the knife was now a deep crimson as blood trickled down the blade's length. The dark crimson dripped from the tip to form a pool at Asher's feet.

'Never again.'

16

A King's Promise

Asher stared at the corpse, at the lifeless face of the man he had just killed without mercy, without remorse. The fire inside still burned. This man was dead, but Asher still hated him for everything he represented. Those who hurt others for profit or pleasure didn't deserve to breathe the same air as good people. Images of Mia flashed before him, her kind face and warm smile. It felt like he had done right by her, and the rage inside crackled with contentment.

'I will find the one who killed you,' he promised as the visions of her face faded from his mind.

He turned his attention to Cara's ongoing battle. She panted lightly, her scimitar held tight in her left paw, a short, jagged trident in the other, a decapitated Otyren in a bloody pool by her feet. The remaining bandit's face had become twisted with fear and anger. He shifted anxiously, adjusting the grip on his rusty shortsword.

'Bah! A curse on you!' he spat, and he dropped his blade, taking off from the path towards a cluster of hardy trees, his powerful Rabbethi legs carrying him with lightning speed. Quick as a flash, Cara dropped her scimitar and passed the trident to her other paw. She held it high and steadied her breathing. With a heavy step, she planted a foot, leaned her weight forwards and launched the trident as hard as she could towards the fleeing bandit. The Rabbethi glanced over his shoulder, expecting to see Cara chasing behind, but she wasn't there.

Asher could almost see a sly smirk before the trident collided with the centre of the bandit's spine, snapping him backwards like a twig. He skidded along the dirt face first, the trident shaft standing like a bloody flagpole from his spine.

Cara placed a paw on her shoulder, shifting it in circular motions, wincing at an unseen wound. Asher approached, collecting his bow and slinging it over his shoulder.

'I've never seen bandits impersonating agents before,' Cara said as she wiped the blood from her blade onto the sheet around the Otyren's stump. 'They're getting bold, creative even.' A concerned look crossed her face.

Asher moved without a word to the body of the Vulpen leader and began searching for the "agent's" sigil. He shifted the body aside, finding what he was after. He stood and inspected it in his bloody paws, brushing the dirt from its surface. A presence appeared over his shoulder as a curious Cara peered over, trying to see what he was looking at. Asher passed the iron sigil over.

'The head's pointing the wrong way,' he said, pointing to the Vulpen head as Cara took the heavy iron slate.

'That's new,' she said, inspecting the metal. 'They either made it themselves or paid for a cheap knockoff. Either way, it cost them their lives.'

'Preying on the innocent cost them their lives,' Asher replied with a bite. 'They don't deserve our pity.'

Cara clasped a paw onto his shoulder as he rose. She spoke calmly, but there was worry in her voice. 'You fought well today, but don't let that rage burn you out. You should fight for the right reasons, to protect those needing protection, and to defend yourself. Yes, these bandits needed taking care of, but I saw your eyes. They were hateful.'

So what if I hated them? Asher thought. He had won, and there was one less shit in the world. The result was a good deed done, and Asher held on to that. 'Fine. I won't hate criminals as much,' he said flatly.

Asher tried to break free, but Cara's grip tightened. His head snapped round, ready to scorn her, but as their eyes met, he was frozen by the sadness that gazed back at him.

'I mean it, Asher,' she said softly. 'I've seen where this path leads, the pain you'll cause yourself in the name of vengeance or justice. Sooner or later, innocent people will get hurt.' She paused, closing her eyes. 'A blind fury cannot see who it hurts.'

She released his shoulder. Her words felt like she had drawn them from a deep well of truth, and they doused the flames in his heart. Asher breathed, allowing his old self to return. Like a sheet removed from his vision, he saw the world as he used to.

'I'm sorry,' he whispered, resting his head on her shoulder. They stood together in the silence of the evening, resting in the tranquil quiet. 'The woman!' Asher spun to where the Rabbethi woman was lying, but the harassed mother and her child were gone.

'Must have made a run for it,' Cara surmised, walking back to Nox and Aurora. As warhorses, they were completely unfazed by the battle that had raged before them and spent the entire time grazing on the tough grass of the wilds.

Aurora approached Asher and nuzzled his head into Asher's shoulder. 'Hey, I hope that wasn't too scary for you.' The speckled warhorse nibbled at his blue cloak. Asher chuckled and pulled the blue cloth from the horse's mouth. 'That's not for you!'

Cara smiled as she mounted Nox with ease.

'Should we do something about the bodies? Tell the city guards or something?' Asher asked.

'No need. They'll be gone by the morning, taken by the meat grinders,' Cara replied with a shrug. 'They never let fresh meat go to waste.'

'Meat grinders?'

'Scavengers. They roam the battlefields and slave markets, searching for fresh folk-meat to sell to the highest bidder.'

'I thought it was illegal?' Asher asked, concern starting to creep into his mind about his temporary home.

'It is. The queendom halted all consumption of folk-meat when your people gained independence.'

'So why are the grinders here?'

'We invited them. We let them into the city, sell them dead prisoners, and they leave. Sometimes, they linger, waiting for more to drop dead, but no one gets hurt. I think they have a camp not too far from here.'

Asher didn't know what to think. Sure, no one was getting hurt, but knowing there were markets full of folk-meat, the flesh of people, made him shiver, and a wave of nausea washed over him.

'Look,' Cara said, sensing Asher's unease. 'If we shut down all the folk-meat black markets, those who consume it would resort to kidnapping and murdering innocents to get what they want. If we quietly keep the markets open and provide the meat using... expired prisoners, we can keep the peace and prevent psychopaths from invading civilised society. It's the lesser of two evils, I'm afraid.'

Asher nodded slowly, though her words did little to ease his mind. He mounted his horse, and they continued along the dirt path towards the city's growing lights, avoiding the bodies now littering the dirt, blood mixing with the cold soil.

Asher and Cara eventually passed under the city gate and into the market square. The joyful music had ceased, and the market stands were gone, yet a large crowd had gathered, forming a wide semicircle around the gate, trapping Asher and Cara within. Countless Vulpen, Rabbethi, and Otyren citizens stared at them as they entered, a look of wonder in many of their eyes and mistrust in others. Asher and Cara dismounted and stepped forwards, scanning the crowd with growing concern. The crowd didn't stir.

Cara projected her voice across the sea of faces. 'Good people! What business do you have for halting our progress?' An eerie silence descended upon the stone plaza as the last murmurings of the crowd ebbed away.

A sandy-furred Rabbethi woman stepped forwards, tears building in the corners of her eyes, a young kit cowering behind her legs as they approached. She walked straight towards Asher, who recognised her as the poor Rabbethi from the road.

'Are you hur—' he started before the woman threw her arms over his shoulders and squeezed him tight.

'Thank you. Thank you so much,' she cried. Her tears seeped into his cheeks, and he winced as they soaked the cut he received from the bandit's blade.

'Mummy?' called the little boy, tugging on his mother's dress, worry upon his tiny round face. The woman pulled away from Asher and picked up the kit, holding him on her hip.

'It's okay. This nice man saved us.'

'Who is he?' whispered the little boy.

The mother turned to Asher, expectant.

'I'm... well, you see, I'm...' Asher's voice began to trail off as voices from the crowd grew.

'Is that the Rabbethia sigil on his cloak?'

'It is!'

'Look at the patch on his eye!'

'He must be the lost prince.'

'Don't you mean king?'

'I thought he was dead?'

Asher looked about him. The whole crowd was murmuring in a chorus of speculations and theories. They pointed and nodded to each other, with some averting their eyes when Asher met them. Others stared intently, their motives unknown. Asher's heart thumped in his chest, his nose twitching anxiously. He was on the brink of turning and bolting away, back into the cold wilds. At least out there, the weight of the world wouldn't press down so heavily upon his shoulders.

'Are you really a king?' came a little voice, bringing focus back to his mind.

He looked down and saw a wide-eyed little boy staring up at him, a big grin across his face, two big front teeth descending out of his mouth. Within the wide-eyed gaze of this hopeful child, Asher's worries melted away. If simply being king was enough to bring hope and wonder, then that would have to do for now, and he would learn the rest in time. Asher smiled and patted the child on his head.

'I am,' he whispered, giving the boy a wink.

The boy shook with excitement as his grin grew into a full beam. He turned to his mother. She smiled back, bringing her nose to his and rubbing it gently.

'Our king saved us,' she whispered to her giggling son. 'Isn't that amazing?'

The child nodded and threw his arms around his mother in a tight embrace. They reminded Asher of himself and his mother a long, long time ago. With the confidence of this one small child urging him on, he raised his chest and looked out over the crowd. All fell silent in expectation.

'I am King Asher of Rabbethia! And I have come to Ignimarum for help in taking back our land from the church. Rabbethi are being slaughtered in their homes by vicious Shangari!' He scanned the crowd, praying to Folka he was doing a good job. Their eyes were wide, some with mouths agape. None made a sound. He continued. 'I promise you, Rabbethia will be free once more!' He raised a clenched fist into the air, and the crowd erupted with a torrent of cheers and clapping. The adrenaline was incredible. Asher watched as people chanted his name and punched their fists into the air. He honestly hadn't expected so many of the Rabbethi living here to feel this strongly about their ancestral homeland, and it swelled his heart to see such pride in his people. Even some of the Vulpen began cheering.

A paw clasped him on the shoulder. 'That was good.' Cara smiled as she pulled away and made for her horse. Asher smiled, following.

They mounted and directed their horses towards the tunnel gates leading to the higher tier. The crowd parted like waves before a ship, the Vulpen and Rabbethi cheering as they passed. Among them, many of the Rabbethi stood with a fist on their chest, another raised high, pride exuding from their large, hopeful eyes. Asher could feel their hopes and dreams pouring from them, and he nodded to each one he could.

The guards at the gate formed a defensive line behind them as they entered the tunnel and began their ascent. The cheers started to quiet, and the adrenaline began to seep from Asher's body. He sighed, slumping in his saddle, exhaustion beginning to take hold.

'You surprised me down there,' Cara said, the orange flicker of the torches bathing her red-and-white fur.

'I surprised myself.' Asher chuckled. 'I hope being a king isn't always that intense.'

'I wouldn't know, but from the senate meetings I've been in, it doesn't get any less hectic.'

Asher smiled, as did Cara.

'Thank you... for everything,' he said with full sincerity. 'I know this has been a difficult... assignment for you.'

'It is no trouble,' Cara dismissed. 'I will admit, though, there's more to you than a royal upbringing, Your Highness. You're a good person, and I think you could do some real good for your people. I'd like to make sure you get a chance to do so.'

'I'd like that too.' Asher smiled.

They spent the rest of the journey up to the palace in relative quiet, slowly enjoying the silence the upper tiers brought after nightfall, though the faint hum of the lower tiers still rose from below.

The palace square was empty when they arrived, except for a few patrolling guards and a pawful of agents carrying documents between buildings. The statue of Thena watched judgingly as Asher and Cara trotted inside, her upturned snout filling Asher with an unwelcome sense of disapproval. A young stable boy led Nox and Aurora back to their stables, and the pair walked tired to the large double doors that marked the entrance to the grand hall.

Unlike the exterior, the inside of the grand hall was a hive of activity. The large fire at the centre was roaring, and every table was full of agents excitedly chatting as they ate their dinner. Strips of meat with roasted vegetables covered each plate, the aroma filling Asher's nostrils. He scanned the sea of Vulpen heads, hoping to catch the eye of a particular, highly skilled and excitable friend, but there was no sign of her. A pang in his shoulder made him wince, and it was only now that he realised how much his body ached. It felt as if a rampaging Medvedian had beaten him with a chair leg.

'I think I'm going to go to bed,' Asher said, tapping Cara on the shoulder.

'You should eat something,' she said as more of a command than a friendly suggestion.

'I know, but I think I may collapse at any second. Today has been... eventful.'

Cara nodded. 'I'll get Leylan to bring you a plate of something. You'll need it.'

'Thank you,' Asher said with a smile, appreciating the kind concern behind the command.

'You're welcome. Now, if you'll excuse me, my queen doesn't look too happy.'

Asher looked up to the royal table where there was a wide spread of sumptuous food. Court nobles enjoying their dinner packed the seats. Senator Corvo chewed the last scraps of meat from a long bone as Senator Sanna, the thin-nosed diplomat, was deep in conversation with the queen. However, the queen stared directly towards Asher and Cara, her brow furrowing.

'Good luck,' Asher said as he hurried out of the hall before an agitated queen could summon him. He strolled tiredly down the opulent corridors, eventually arriving at his chamber door. Candles illuminated the room in a comforting glow as Asher moved to the mirror and inspected the blood splattering his clothes. He now sported a nasty scar across his right cheek.

'Lucky that wasn't my eye,' he whispered as he removed his cloak and armour, placing them back onto the stand until he was dressed in only the dark linen shirt and trousers that complemented the armour.

He examined the blood staining his white fur and the cuts and bruises that decorated his skin.

Movement from the shadows made him spin.

'Who's there? Show yourself!' he commanded, the confidence of the plaza still coursing through his veins.

'Look at you,' sang a playful voice. 'King of the Rabbethi and killing bandits in foreign lands.' From the corner of the chamber stepped a beautiful, slender Vulpen. Her red fur glowed in the candlelight as she clasped her paws behind her back, a coy smile crossing her soft face.

'Luce...' Asher breathed, his body relaxing, the aches returning. His heart continued to thump inside his chest, sounding like a war drum in his ears. 'It's good to see you,' he whispered, as if their meeting was a secret rendezvous.

'You too, Ash,' she beamed. She leapt onto the bed, scattering the decorative pillows in all directions. With legs crossed, she patted the bed beside her. He looked to the spot, then back to her, hesitating just in case he misunderstood. She nodded, and he crawled onto the bed to lie awkwardly beside her, his heart ready to leap out of his chest. She joined him, lying down.

'How do you know about the bandits?' he asked, trying not to think about how much the candlelight made her fur shine with the radiance of a raging fire or how her eyes sparkled like a day-kissed ocean.

'Everyone knows. You've made quite a name for yourself with your kingly speech,' she teased. 'I just wish I could have been there. I would have brought my lute and played your triumphant return into the city!'

'You play the lute?' Asher asked, curious how many talents this deadly agent of the Vulpen Queendom was hiding.

'A little. Cara taught me. She's much better than me, though.' She leaned in with a grin and whispered, 'But I'm a better fighter.'

'I promise not to tell her you said that.' Asher chuckled, though his twitching nose betrayed his faux confidence.

He received a hard fist to the shoulder. 'You better not! Remember, I know where you sleep.'

The pair spoke and laughed for hours, Asher pushing aside his desperate need for rest to spend as much time with Luce as possible. The morning seemed like a world away, and anything outside his chamber's four walls ceased to exist. She asked him about his upbringing, about his mother and father. The solemn change in Asher's tone caused the atmosphere to become melancholy, and on more than one occasion, she placed a gentle paw on his leg.

'They would be so proud of you,' she said with a comforting smile, her eyes soft and kind.

'Thank you,' he replied sincerely as fond memories of his parents entered his mind. Asher wondered whether his father would be proud of him, of what he had become, far removed from the runaway prince, the apple thief, the farm boy. He didn't know the answer.

The weight of exhaustion grew too heavy for Asher's weary eyes. Though he fought it with all his might, the darkness of sleep descended over him, and as his eyes closed and consciousness drifted out of reach, soft fingers began intertwining with his own. They gripped his paw tight, resolute not to let him go.

17

Setting Sail

The scent of freshly baked goods filled the room, drawing Asher from deep sleep. The midday light shone through the tall windows above the bed, warming the chamber as seagulls squawked beyond, a hive of activity resonating outside and inside the palace walls. Asher rolled over, expecting to find a beautiful Vulpen sleeping peacefully beside him. Luce had gone, leaving barely a trace that she was ever there. He wondered whether it had all been a dream, smiling as the faint but distinct scent of orchids rose from the pillow beside him.

He crawled out of bed blurry-eyed, eager for a good breakfast and cleansing wash. A silver plate sat on the table against the wall, covered in delicious-looking pastries of different sizes and culinary styles. Beside it was a large silver bowl with thick plumes of rising steam, a soft cloth folded beside it. The pastries didn't last long, and Asher filled his empty belly, leaving an avalanche of flakes around his mouth and on the floor. He wiped his mouth with his forearm and stepped before the hot water, the steam rising and warming his face. It had been a while since he had properly washed, and he longed to feel clean again. Scooping a pool into his paw, he splashed his face and scrubbed his cheeks. Red-soaked water dripped into the bowl as a sting throbbed on his left cheek. He looked into the mirror and saw the red cut from the bandit's blade.

'That'll leave a scar.'

He collected another pool of water in his paws and leaned closer to the bowl. Pulling down a tall white ear, he ran the hot water along its length, repeating this for the other ear until he was happy they were clean and presentable. The long ears of the Rabbethi had to be maintained and cleaned regularly. Having dirty or damaged ears was unthinkable within the upper circles of the Rabbethi nobility, though Asher was never of the same stuffy mindset as the upper elite. Still, he enjoyed the care and attention that came from a good wash. He pressed the folded cloth to his face. It was warm, and the heat seeped into his fur and skin, soothing his entire body. He stood there for a time, letting his aching muscles relax and wishing he could just live the rest of his life smothered by the embrace of a hot towel.

Knock. Knock. Knock.

Asher pulled the towel from his face and turned to the door. It was open, and standing in the door frame was Cara, eyebrow raised.

'Sorry. I didn't mean to disturb you from your morning...,' she said, looking Asher up and down, 'ritual.'

With a sudden realisation, he made for the armour, aware he was standing before Cara in nothing but his undergarments.

'I'm to escort you to the queen and Senator Corvo,' Cara said as Asher pulled items off the armour rack, put them on, and fastened the straps with surprising speed. 'They'd like to brief us before we set sail.'

As he donned each piece, Asher noticed the distinct lack of blood and dirt coating the smooth surfaces. Someone had cleaned his armour, and he wasn't sure he liked how easy it was to sneak into his room unnoticed.

'We?' he repeated as he pulled the cloak over his shoulders.

'Senator Corvo has chosen me to accompany you to Otyrheim as your guard. After he heard about last night's encounter, he was impressed, said we made a good team. I didn't disagree.'

Flashes of last night raced through Asher's mind—the blood, the anger. It still felt raw to him, like a tender nerve just below the skin's surface. The fire inside started to burn as he reflected on the bandits and the woman they attacked.

'Asher?'

He snapped back to the room and looked towards Cara, who was looking at him with concern.

'Are you all right?'

The visions of the fight faded from his mind, and the fire within eased to an ember. He strapped the quiver of arrows across his back and slung his bow over his shoulder.

'I'm okay,' he said with a reassuring smile as he stepped towards her.

'It'll be a long journey to Otyrheim,' she said, seemingly unconvinced. 'They've picked a captain and boat for us, something quick.'

'Hopefully, it'll have more space than *The Silvi*,' Asher jested, thinking back to the single-room cabin and its many levers and pulleys.

The two left the room and approached the doors leading to the royal terrace, where armoured palace guards halted their progress. Beyond them, deep in conversation, were the queen and Senator Corvo. They spoke in hushed voices as the queen caressed the spymaster's arm, her vibrant red fur contrasting against his black, feathered armour. The queen wore a simple purple stola trimmed with dazzling gold threads, and she smiled at Senator Corvo as they spoke.

'I'm sorry, Your Highness,' apologised one of the burly guards, raising his palm towards Asher. 'This path is closed until the queen has concluded her business.'

At this, the queen took notice, and her smile dropped. She removed her paw from Senator Corvo's arm and became rigid, clasping her paws behind her back and raising her snout. Senator Corvo's smile didn't fade, and as he turned to the pair, he raised both paws towards them with welcoming motions. The guards parted, and Asher and Cara approached.

'Ah, here they are!' Corvo declared. 'The heroes of the north road, King Asher and his faithful warrior.'

Cara bowed to the queen, then to Corvo. 'Your Highness. Senator.'

'Despite my... misgivings about your recent excursion northward,' the queen said with a weary tone, 'it appears you've managed to create a name for yourselves. Many are talking about the return of the Rabbethi king and what I will be doing to aid him. This is good for you.' She nodded to Asher. She then turned to Cara and stared daggers. 'Less so for an agent of the queen whose main objective is to remain *hidden* and *silent*.'

Cara's eyes dropped to the floor, her tail lowering under her cloak. 'I'm sorry, my queen, it won't happen again.'

'She saved my life,' Asher said abruptly. 'If it weren't for Cara's actions, I would have been killed many times over. I owe her a great deal, as do you.' Stunned silence. 'With respect, Your Majesty,' he ended as he began to regret his outburst.

The queen tilted her head in his direction, her eyes devoid of emotion.

Senator Corvo clasped Asher on the shoulder and chuckled. 'Wonderful! A leader should support their retinue. You will make a strong king yet, I'm sure of it!' He beamed down at Asher, who smiled back, thankful for the break in tension.

'Yes, well,' the queen interjected. 'Senator Corvo has convinced me that Cara would be best suited to guard your person and represent our interests within the Otyren Republic.'

'What about Agent Luce?' Asher asked. He knew it was a long shot, but if he could get Luce to travel with them, he'd enjoy the journey far more. He desperately wanted to spend more time with her, and her tendency to disappear made that very difficult. At least on a ship in the middle of the ocean, there weren't many places she could vanish to.

The queen's eye twitched as she again repressed a brewing storm.

'Domini Lucilla has other duties, I'm afraid, Your Highness,' Corvo said with a respectful nod. 'She will be remaining in Ignimarum. However, I will inform her you were asking for her.'

'Thank you,' Asher replied, polite but disappointed.

'If there's nothing else to keep me from my duties,' Queen Tessina said sharply. 'I will leave you in Senator Corvo's capable paws. You may use the Queen's Passage down to the docks.' And with that, she turned and marched with dignity down the corridor towards the great hall, her palace guards following obediently behind.

After she was out of earshot, Senator Corvo began chuckling, his friendly demeanour returning. 'That was excellent to watch. Thank you, Your Highness.'

'I hope I didn't offend her,' Asher queried, worried at what repercussions he may have set into motion.

'Not at all. You're a king, after all! Sometimes, Tessy needs reminding that she isn't the queen of everyone, not yet anyway.' His chuckle began again in earnest, and Asher forced an awkward laugh to remain polite. 'Right, well, I best see you to your ship and captain. This way, Your

Highness.' He set off down the corridor towards the wooden box that hung precariously over the Queen's Run.

The metal gates were open when they arrived, and the wooden box swayed loosely by its chain, creaking as they entered. Standing between Cara and Corvo, Asher felt like they were escorting him from the premises or to a cell in the darkest, dankest dungeon. The chains started to rattle, and the sound of groaning wood and shifting metal echoed around the cold shaft as the box began its descent, a chilling breeze rising between the gaps in the wood. Asher looked to Senator Corvo and then to Cara, both standing silently, watching the rock pass by.

'So, who is our captain?' he eventually asked.

Senator Corvo looked down at Asher, seemingly surprised that anyone would break such a pleasant quiet. 'He's an information runner with a small vessel. It's swift and will get you to Otyrheim faster than any other ship we can provide. Speed is key here. We need to get you that bow before the church takes full control of your kingdom. As this is a mission of political importance, and you are a high-value individual, we'll send a small security force to follow. They'll keep you safe once you reach Otyrheim, but you will arrive before them. Cara here will keep you safe in the meantime. She's the best agent I've got.'

Asher nodded, and the box continued its descent of the stone shaft. The torch fastened on the inside danced as cold gusts continued to pass between the box and the stone wall. Asher felt his eyes drift around the quiet space, aimlessly searching for something of interest to latch onto and distract him from darker thoughts threatening to plague his mind. His head lowered, his eyes floating to Corvo's side and over to the underside of the spymaster's forearm. The scarred flesh was still visible between the straps of Corvo's armguards.

'I was young and stupid once,' the Vulpen said.

Asher snapped his attention forwards in a failed attempt to hide his curiosity. 'I'm sorry?' he said in fake surprise.

Corvo chuckled, raising his forearm to inspect the scar. 'I was in a gang once. "The Daggers". Stupid name looking back, but we were stupid. All new initiates had to carve a curved dagger into their flesh to show loyalty. Of course, I did, no question, but there isn't a day I don't regret it.' He inspected the arm, deep in thought. 'Now I try to help people before they get roped into the stupid decisions of the young. I guide them to nobler pursuits.'

Asher nodded and smiled, unsure how to respond to this sudden dive into the spymaster's history. He should have felt honoured, but he knew the skilled Vulpen didn't get where he was by telling the whole truth.

More light began to glow from below as they aligned with another set of metal gates. Asher readied himself for an abrupt stop, but it didn't come. Instead, the box descended further, and although relieved not to make the arduous trek through the entire city, he couldn't help but imagine all he was missing—a city full of life, basking in the midday light, the day markets full of music and laughter roaring all around, folk shouting in angry voices and the thrill of a brawl—all things he loved and missed dearly. He thought back to the familiar streets and plazas of his home, and a longing filled his heart. It was quickly replaced with anger as the thought of Shangari swarming the streets flashed before his mind.

'You've been through a lot, and there's still a lot more to go,' Corvo said with sudden gentleness. 'We'll get you to your throne soon.' He patted Asher on the shoulder before returning to the rising rock wall.

Asher turned to Cara, who smiled down at him. If she trusted the black Vulpen, so did he.

The three descended in relative silence the rest of the way, watching the rock rise before them. Light began to creep through the gap at Asher's feet, and with great relief, metal gates rose before them. The box shuddered to a stop as it halted its descent. Two guards approached the gates and opened them outwards, standing to attention as the three stepped out of the box and into a long hallway. It was identical to the one Asher had walked down when first entering the Queen's Run, except the scent of salt hung heavy in the air here, carried upon a cool breeze. It filled Asher's nostrils, and he breathed deep as they walked down the passage, led by the hum of the city beyond.

Asher winced as the heavy iron gate opened onto the corner of the bottom tier, the light blinding as he stepped out of the darkness. The street was thrumming with activity. The familiar sound of a blacksmith's hammer rang out, blending with the chorus of laughter and chattering as people entered a multitude of shops and taverns. Before him, the road reached out towards the docks, merging with a grand plaza filled with all manner of folk going about their daily business. Numerous jetties pointed out towards the bay like thick fingers cooling in the cold waters, each crawling with hundreds of traders, sailors and fisherfolk keeping to their own business.

At the centre of it all stood another stone statue of the ancient Vulpen, Thena, made with equal skill and attention to the one in the palace courtyard. Unlike her cold, guarded look in the palace, this depiction was one of warmth and affection. She stood with arms open wide, a broad smile across her long face, welcoming all into the heart of the Vulpen capital.

The three pushed through the crowd, moving past citizens of all classes and races. There was a more respectable atmosphere than the seedy ongoings of the night, with characters Asher would have expected to find in the top tiers socialising around the market stands and various cafes, formerly rowdy taverns. The owners had cleansed last night's clientele from the premises.

One corner of the plaza, however, was unlike the others. Where elsewhere stood colourful market stands and respectable businesses, makeshift tents covered this section, crammed with Rabbethi, young and old, wealthy and poor. The fine clothes of the richer-looking folk were in tatters, and they stared dead-eyed as if in sheer shock that something like this would ever happen to someone like them. All sat before tents, defeated and broken, a contingent of Vulpen guards surrounding them.

'They began flooding in not long after you, Your Highness,' Senator Corvo said solemnly. 'We've been trying to set them up in the less populated areas of the island, give them jobs to keep them busy, but more keep coming.' He sighed as he shook his head. 'We're doing our best, but, well, this is why speed is key.'

Asher nodded in understanding, ever thankful for his host's hospitality. Gathering up the broken and lost, keeping them well fed and together: it was the sign of a great land and a true friend to his people.

They headed left at the water's edge towards a large stone arch built into one of the two-storey buildings flanking the plaza. Guards stood rigid on either side, and numerous more were marching in and out of the area beyond, each led by a captain with a red cape. The guards began making motions towards Asher and Cara, but a swift flick of the paw from Corvo sent them scurrying back to their posts, and the three passed through without issue. They entered a wide military square filled with soldiers marching and training in strict, regimented exercises. Soldiers marched in tight formations as archers shot at hay bales mounted on wooden legs. Others practised vicious strikes with their curved swords against dummies made of straw. The air was far more serious here, and Asher's whole body tensed up as if one wrong step would bring the entire place down upon him. His nose twitched with nervous anxiety.

Idiot, he told himself. *Stop trying to act so innocent. You haven't done anything wrong.*

Countless military vessels lined a series of stone jetties to their right, each made of a dark red wood trimmed black. Most were sleek and elegant, with only a modest crew needed to sail, but there was one that took Asher's breath away. Sat lazily in the water, on a jetty all to itself, was a monstrous Tail o' War, its many sails rolled up to reveal the maze of ropes that kept the titan together. Its deep hull was enough to hold a small army. Aboard its hulking mass, hundreds of sailors and soldiers hurried about tying ropes, washing the deck and making general preparations for what looked like a soon-to-be voyage.

Asher's eyes returned to the square and wandered up to a wooden balcony where a large, lean, white-furred Vulpen woman with vibrant red eyes surveyed the soldiers. Her curved, plated armour was thick and black, the points of the plating seemingly sharper than that of the other captains Asher had seen. With pupilless eyes, she gazed down at the soldiers beneath her, watching them all like a hawk, a stern expression across her face. Her eyes suddenly snapped to Asher, and she stared at him, expressionless and unflinching.

'Who is that?' Asher asked, not taking his eyes off the captain.

Cara looked to where Asher was staring and instantly looked down to avoid eye contact. 'That's Imperatrix Fira, captain of the Royal Guard,' she whispered. 'Flora's mother.'

Asher snapped his head to Cara. 'That's Flora's mother?'

'Quiet! Unless you want to be diving for oysters in full armour!'

Asher tightened his lips and slowly turned back to the balcony, but Imperatrix Fira was gone. He prayed to the ancients that his wandering eyes hadn't gotten him into any more trouble.

'You know your task, Your Highness?' Corvo asked as he led Asher and Cara towards the behemoth Tail o' War. He turned to the pair, clapping his paws together.

Asher nodded.

Corvo then turned to Cara, his smile dropping. 'And you know yours.'

Cara nodded, and Asher couldn't help but feel the seriousness in his words. Without speaking, Corvo and Cara clasped each other's forearms and raised their free paws to their chest.

'Your captain should be around here somewhere,' he continued. 'He was given instructions to meet you at midday. It's now midday, so I will take my leave. Good luck.' He bowed low towards Asher before disappearing into the crowd of marching soldiers. He vanished in a blink of an eye, his sizeable black cloak and feathery plumage nowhere to be seen.

'He's good,' Asher said, impressed.

'That's why he's my boss,' Cara agreed.

They both gazed up at the monstrous Tail o' War. Thousands of arrow slits peppered the hull like a colossal sieve, and its five titanic masts were larger than any tree Asher had ever seen. A beautifully carved figurehead depicting a Vulpen maiden hung beneath its prow. She wielded a round shield and thrust a spear out towards the sea, rage and malicious intent across her carved, snarling face.

'Could we not take this to Otyrheim? It would certainly be quite an entrance,' Asher joked.

'I'd rather not risk open war on my first visit to Otyrheim by sailing a warship up the Flood Road.' Cara chuckled.

'Oh, for Thena's sake,' came an exacerbated voice from behind.

They both turned and saw a tailless Vulpen man with black fur carrying a scroll bearing the queen's royal seal in one paw and, in the other, a bottle of wine. His amber eyes looked at Asher and Cara with utter defeat.

'Hey, Marius.' Asher smiled.

18

The Brotherhood

The Great Lighthouse shone brightly as *The Silvi* skimmed across the sloping waves. The ocean sparkled under the deep sky as fluffy clouds floated high overhead, creating islands of shade on the water's surface. Asher pulled a little tighter on his blue cloak as the nimble vessel darted through a patch of shadow.

They had been sailing for a day or so, travelling southwest across the Cinder Sea from Ignimarum. It had been a wondrous sight, sailing between the tremendous sea doors of the Blazing Gates under the light of the Great Lighthouse. It was just as busy as the night Asher had first arrived on *The Silvi*, with hundreds of vessels of contrasting sizes transporting goods and people in and out of the Vulpen capital. It was only fitting that *The Silvi* should carry him away.

It hadn't taken long for the ship's captain, Marius, to lose his grumpy demeanour and return to his playful and sarcastic self. He had not been happy about transporting Asher and Cara once more across the sea, stating that the escape from Saewic and the murderous church still haunted his dreams.

'They gave me compensation for having my ship hijacked, then offered me a job,' he explained whilst he and Asher ate lunch within the gentle rocking of *The Silvi*'s cabin. 'How could I refuse? Especially when they threaten to take my ship away.' He chuckled, but there was frustration in his voice.

'They can't do that, can they?' Asher asked, taking a large bite out of a chunk of bread.

'The queen can do whatever she wants,' Marius said, moving a chunk of cheese around his plate with a fork. 'But!' he exclaimed, stabbing the cheese and placing it in his long mouth. 'She offered a large sum of money for my troubles, so I accepted, and here we are.' He gestured his knife to Asher, holding it loose between his long fingers. 'Didn't expect it to be you two disrupters of the peace. What business do you two have with the Otyren?'

'Well, we're—'

'You were told not to ask questions,' Cara's voice came as she appeared in the cabin's open door, her eyes glued on Marius with a disapproving glare. She turned to Asher as she approached. 'And *you* are not to answer any.' She reached down to Marius's plate and picked up the last chunk of cheese, dropping it into her mouth. Marius squinted his eyes in a playful sneer, and she returned one in kind before turning for the door, her bushy tail whipping into Marius's face. He pushed it away, spluttering and pulling red strands from his mouth.

It was strange not being able to tell Marius about their mission to reclaim the King's Bow, the level of secrecy and security between Vulpen institutions providing something of a mystery to Asher. Maybe Marius was a spy for the church, and Cara was waiting for the right time to take him out. He dismissed the thought as childish imagination. Whatever the case, Cara had told him not to say anything, and Asher had come to trust her without question.

The rest of the day passed by with ease. Marius showed Asher how to work *The Silvi* from inside the cabin and out on the deck, taking the eager Rabbethi through each pulley and lever and showing him where ropes connected within the cabin. Asher learned how to raise and lower the sails and which direction to turn them depending on the wind. Most excitingly, he learned how to steer using the wheel. Asher loved it. In another life, he imagined himself as a member of the navy on a large warship or even as a simple fisherfolk on a small raft, heading out to kelp farms and dragging up the harvest in his overalls.

That wasn't his life, though.

His life was full of responsibility and pain. So many depended on him, and he had a duty to do right by them. 'When all this is done,' he breathed, gazing out from the ship's bow, 'maybe I'll let my children take the throne, and I can sail the Cinder Sea for the rest of my days.'

The Great Lighthouse eventually turned, and the air grew cold. Asher sat and watched as the horizon turned from bright blue to orange, then to shades of lavender, then a deep purple. Finally, it was black, and Asher leaned back against the mast and stared up at the night sky. He hadn't lit the lantern above—Cara's idea to avoid unwanted attention from roaming pirates—and the ship remained in utter darkness. The upside was that Asher could gaze upon a plethora of dazzling stars. It was beautiful, and he wondered whether his mother and father were gazing down from the brightest stars. Asher wasn't religious or superstitious, but he enjoyed the idea of loved ones protecting him, forever present, even if he couldn't reach them. With that reassuring thought, he wrapped himself up in his blue cloak and closed his eyes, the gentle lapping of the waves against the hull lulling him to sleep.

***

Asher awoke to a sudden sound, a faint scratching echoing beneath him. His ears stood to attention, twitching and turning to pinpoint the sounds. This was different from your average noise made by waves against wood. It was sharp, strange and altogether unwelcome. Asher surveyed the darkened deck, searching for Cara and Marius. Marius was up at the wheel, peering into the darkness beyond, the warm glow of a lit pipe illuminating the end of his snout. It grew brighter as he sucked in the smoke, which poured from the side of his snout in wisping plumes of grey clouds. His black fur almost made him invisible against the night sky.

Cara was nowhere to be seen. She was likely resting in the cabin, taking ownership of *The Silvi*'s only bed. The scratching stopped, replaced by the soft padding of footsteps moving beneath him. The gentle sounds move towards the grated cargo hole at the ship's centre. Asher turned and stared at the wooden grate in silence, waiting for something or someone to show themselves.

Nothing happened. The waves continued to lap against the ship. A cold sea wind surged through Asher's fur, chilling him. As thoughts of doubt started to creep into his mind, several long fingers reached through the holes and grasped at the wood. Each finger ended with dagger-like claws curved into sharp hooks. Asher quickly and quietly rose to his feet. He reached to his chest and pulled the dagger from its sheath, holding it in a reverse grip as Luce had taught him. The fingers hoisted up the grate and slid it to one side. They clasped the edge and heaved up a small, hooded figure, their face covered in darkness. The stranger landed on the deck and crouched low, placing its front paws down and lowering its head to the wood. It sniffed short, erratic sniffs as it assessed its surroundings.

It's hunting, he thought as panic began to take hold.

All of a sudden, its head snapped straight towards Asher. Two glowing yellow eyes stared at him within the shadows of the hood, narrow black slits cutting vertically through each. Before Asher could react, the black slits grew wide, and the figure pounced. It bounded towards Asher on all fours, sprinting at a speed he hadn't seen before. With a paw outstretched, it leapt, claws flying right for Asher's throat. He stumbled back, narrowly avoiding a deadly swipe that slashed past his throat and connected with the thick wooden mast. Splinters exploded across the deck as the attacker wrenched its claws free. It hissed. Slowly standing, it raised both paws, revealing sharp, hooked claws that glinted in the starlight.

Asher raised his fists.

'Hel—!' he started to call, but the moment the word left his mouth, the figure attacked, swiping once more for his throat. Asher stepped back again just as a second swipe rose from below. He stepped to the left, extending his fist towards the hungry orange eyes.

He missed, and a sudden wave of pain raked his side, followed by a warm sensation creeping down his leg. The stranger crouched low, paw extended, a thick trail of blood dripping from the claws. Asher looked down and found he had been cut deep across his side, right under a slight gap in his leather armour. He winced as the wound started to burn, pain throbbing across his entire flank. The clawed attacker stood, and Asher watched as its bloody paw disappeared into the shadow of its hood, the sound of a licking tongue emanating from within.

'Ahemnfik nenti dwe?' the stranger uttered with a thick accent. It was a male voice, but Asher had no idea of what race the owner belonged to.

'Wh-what do you want?' he asked, wincing at the pain in his side.

The figure crouched low and bared its claws again. 'Heidn eidk Mia, milne?' The stranger let slip a deep, rumbling chuckle.

Asher didn't know what they had said, but he could feel the mocking behind the words. Worse, he recognised Mia's name.

He tightened his grip around his knife's handle, gritting his teeth. The fire inside him roared as questions began to circle in his mind. Who was this attacker? How did he know Mia? And what did he want with him? Before Asher could consider the answers, his attacker moved.

Asher planted a foot and darted right. The figure pivoted and moved to a defensive stance. Asher made a sharp change in direction and charged into the stranger's flank, extending a hard right hook, blade in paw. Sensing the figure drop and expecting another claw to the side, Asher pulled his punch, spun around the incoming swipe and sliced the blade down between the shoulder blades of his assailant. Luce would have been proud.

A cry of pain as the blade tore through cloth and deep into flesh. The attacker stumbled forwards, spinning and hissing. It pounced again, more savage this time with wild swipes that forced Asher to dodge in frantic movements across the deck. With each attack, the stranger pushed him closer and closer to the ship's bow. Once cornered, Asher was done for.

Then Asher felt it, the press of wood against his lower back. He was at the end of the ship with nowhere else to go. He looked to the stranger, whose eyes widened within the shadows of their hood. They crouched low, swaying ever so slightly. They then exploded straight towards Asher, paws extended. This was it. With nowhere to go, his body growing weak from the wound in his side, Asher raised his blade.

But the stranger never got to him. Instead, he dropped to the deck with a sudden thud, hissing and scratching at the wood, a look of wild ferocity in his orange eyes. Asher looked up and saw Cara straining, trying to hold on to something long and thick emerging from under the back of the stranger's cloak.

'Cara!' Asher called, never before being so thankful to see her in his life.

'Run!' she yelled, trying to keep the lashing stranger from reaching Asher's ankles. You can't win this. Run!' Without question, he leapt onto the railing and ran along its edge, balancing along the narrow wood like he used to along the rooftops of White Cliffe. Once out of reach, he landed back on the deck by Cara.

'What is this thing?' Asher asked, panting.

'It's a Brotherhood assassin.' She released the assassin's tail and drew her sword. 'I'm afraid you've been marked.'

The assassin stopped thrashing and slowly rose to his feet, pulling back his hood to reveal short, pointed ears and dense fur covering his body. It turned. His nose was short and had thick whiskers extending on either side. Large fangs protruded down from his upper lips, and his orange eyes seemed to glow in the darkness—a Muuraki.

The wide black circles within his eyes darted from Asher to Cara and back again. He was clearly enjoying the tension, the suspense before the fight. A sickening grin stretched across its feline face as it raised a clawed finger towards Asher and licked its lips.

'You taste good, little one. You are fast prey. You make good hunting. It is shame Constance want you alive. I would enjoy your meat very much.' It then turned to Cara, and its smile dropped. 'Stay out of way. You are not prey. You need not die this day.'

'Tough shit,' she spat. 'He's with me.'

'So be it.' He sprinted towards Cara at lightning speed, reaching for her neck with an outstretched paw, hooked claws ready to rip out her throat. Cara slashed down at the assassin. She was quick and strong enough to split the mightiest warrior in two, but the assassin was quicker. He dropped, spinning away from the blade and raising a paw towards her gut, the claws puncturing her leather armour like hot knives through butter.

Asher moved.

Without hesitation, he planted a foot into the assassin's side and sent him soaring across the deck. The Muuraki crashed into the wooden railing. The wood dented, and the whole ship rocked sideways as hefty splinters cascaded across the deck and into the racing sea. The assassin slumped to the floor, struggling for breath. Asher lowered his foot to the deck.

'She's with me.'

Cara's eyes were wide, her mouth agape.

Asher placed a paw onto her shoulder and gave a slight shake. 'Cara! Cara, are you okay?' he shouted, attempting to bring her back to reality.

She blinked and shook her head. 'Y-yes,' she stuttered, raising a paw to her stomach. She looked to Asher. 'Thank you, Asher.'

Asher smiled. 'Don't mention it. We've got each other's back, okay?'

She nodded. 'Okay.'

A wheezing cough made them turn. The assassin was pulling himself to his feet, blood dripping from his mouth. 'That... was surprise, little one. I know now to watch you.' He pulled the cloak from his shoulders, revealing simple leather armour with no distinguishable features that could catch the light, his muscular physique visible in the dim light.

The three readied themselves, waiting for someone to make a move. All went quiet, save for the gentle breeze that rushed through their fur as *The Silvi* continued along its course. The ship lurched as it dropped over a small wave, and the assassin pounced, heading straight for Asher.

Asher stepped to the left as a claw slashed at his chest, scoring the leather armour. Asher brought his fist down in response, connecting with the assassin's cheek. The assassin rolled with the punch, minimising the damage, and came at the Rabbethi with a backwards swipe from their other paw. Before they could connect, Cara thrust her sword towards the assassin's chest, and he ducked, the blade cutting deep against his ear. He spun away, remaining low, a trail of blood trickling down his forehead and between his eyes.

Cara pressed the attack, slashing down. The assassin once again flowed to the side but was met by Asher, who stabbed his dagger into the assassin's stomach. It connected, but the assassin latched onto Asher's forearm, preventing the blade from penetrating too deep. With a menacing grin, the assassin started to squeeze, his claws stabbing through Asher's armguard and into the soft flesh beneath. Asher cried out in pain as the assassin's vice grip tightened. Blood dripped from the armguard onto the wood below as the Muuraki grinned a toothy grin, his dagger-like teeth inches away from Asher's face. Despite the blood trickling from his stomach, the assassin opened his mouth wide, ready to take a bite out of Asher's face.

There was a sudden swish, followed by a horrific scream, and Asher crashed backwards to the floor. He opened his eyes and looked down at his forearm. The assassin's claws were still gripped tight onto him, but no assassin was attached to the claws. He looked up. Cara stood before him, panting, her sword embedded into the deck at his feet. Next to her, the assassin was on his knees, wailing in pain and cursing in a language Asher couldn't understand, blood pouring from two red stumps at the end of his arms. Cara pulled her sword from the wood and pointed it at the assassin. His cries began to fade as the blood loss took its toll. He slumped, his head swaying and drooping as life drifted from his body. He looked up at Cara, grinning weakly.

'It was good fight, no?' he breathed.

She forced her blade through the assassin's chest. Ribs cracked as the sword erupted from his back, and a fresh spout of blood sputtered from his mouth. He convulsed but didn't take his hungry eyes off Cara. They grew wide as his mouth twisted in a sickening grin. Cara ripped the blade from their chest, and the assassin slumped to the floor with a thud. Blood poured from the hole left behind, collecting around Cara's feet and seeping into the sea-soaked wood. She stared down at the corpse, a look of utter defiance in her eyes.

'No,' Cara replied, cold. 'It wasn't.'

19

Good Food and Fine Wine

It was early morning by the time Asher and Cara had finished scrubbing the blood from the deck. Even then, visible stains still coated the wood, with a sizable dark splotch now painting where the Brotherhood assassin had fallen. Marius eventually crawled out of the hidden compartment within the cabin and stepped out to survey the damage. His eyes went wide with an unspoken fury as he found the blood, the dented railing and the marks where Cara had embedded her sword. Asher swore he could hear the black Vulpen's teeth grinding, but the tailless information runner never shouted nor flew into a rage. He just stayed at the wheel and said, 'You're never coming on my boat again,' over and over in a cold, flat tone.

After Asher had mopped up the worst of the blood, he removed his armguard and inspected his forearm. Blood still trickled from the claw holes when he tensed, and it stung worse than anything he had ever felt. Cara disappeared into the cabin, emerging moments later with a bottle. She pulled the cork out with her mouth, spat it over the side and poured the purple liquid over Asher's arm. She then took a long, deep swig.

Asher was wrong. *That* was the worst pain he had ever felt.

It stung like fire as the wine filled the holes in his arms, and he recoiled as the excess liquid splashed to the floor. A great weight bore down on him as he felt eyes turning in his direction. It was Marius.

He glared down at them from the wheel, one eye twitching as his stare jumped between the bottle and the wasted wine soaking into the deck. Asher looked away, feeling a pang of guilt as Cara wrapped his arm in loose cloth. She fastened the armguard to secure it.

She then collected the assassin's paws and carefully removed the claws from each finger, using a pair of pliers to wrench the daggers free and placing them into a small pouch at her side.

'These will go for a decent price to the right buyer,' she said as Asher watched with a sick curiosity. 'Or they'll make a good trophy. Few can say they went up against a Muuraki assassin and lived to tell the tale.'

'I know of someone,' Asher lamented, thinking back to Harold, his father's grizzled old captain of the guard. He thought about the stories Harold used to tell him, of his adventures and battles with mighty foes. Asher hoped he was okay, but the memory of him slumped against the stone wall of the inner keep, unmoving, did little to comfort him.

'Well, I hope to meet this person one day,' Cara said, straining as she pulled free the last claw.

'Me too,' Asher said, almost to himself. He looked to Marius. 'Maybe we should give him some of the claws. Might help pay for some repairs and a fresh coat of paint?'

'The queendom is already paying him handsomely for this job,' Cara said, not looking as she placed the last claw into her pouch.

'It's the right thing to do after we made a mess of his ship. You know how much he loves *The Silvi*, and it's not like the assassin was after him.'

Cara looked about the ship. With a reluctant sigh, she turned to Asher. 'Fine.'

She chucked the declawed paws overboard, and they fell to the water with a splash. The body was next. Asher could get a better look at his attacker in the morning light. He was definitely Muuraki—there was no mistaking the feline face. It continued to grin a wicked smile in a defiant last act. It was also easier to see the thick grey fur covered in much darker stripes. It was beautiful and well-maintained.

Asher had never seen a Muuraki before, and for good reason. Hired assassins that rarely ventured from their mountainous northern domain, seeing one usually meant you were prey or made a horrible turn on your way to the Fenrathi capital. Asher took a moment to stare at the Muuraki in defiance of whoever said such a thing. He had stared into the orange eyes of death and lived.

It required both Asher and Cara to heave the body up and unceremoniously over the side. The assassin was short but dense with muscle, making him much heavier than he looked. Death's stun had crept in, making the body rigid but easier to lift, and they watched as it splashed into the ocean. Cara then reached for the black cloak discarded during the fight, a jagged hole scarring the cloth down the middle. Just as she went to throw it into the water, something glinted in the light, catching Asher's eye.

'Wait!' he called out, startling Cara.

She frantically grabbed the cloak as it left her fingers. 'What?'

'What's that pinned to the front?' he asked, taking the cloak and pulling the metallic object from the cloth. He held it in his paw for Cara to see. It was a clasp of simple design, fashioned into a ring and featuring one thin piece of metal that ran vertically through its centre.

Asher recognised it in an instant.

'The one that killed Mia was wearing this exact sigil,' he exclaimed wide-eyed. 'Do you... Do you think we just killed him?'

Cara inspected the sigil. 'I doubt it. She stepped away and threw the cloak into the sea. 'That's the sigil of the Brotherhood. Every assassin wears one.'

The idea that Mia's killer still breathed enraged Asher, but a tiny part of him was thankful he might yet have the chance to kill them himself, to stare them in the eyes and make them fear death, as Mia had.

Cara spent the rest of the morning inspecting the cargo hold for intruders. She didn't find anyone else but did discover a collection of sealed ceramic pots with cork lids fragranced with lavender. Cara brought them on deck and immediately chucked them overboard.

'What were those?' Asher asked, looking up from his mop.

'You don't want to know.'

***

The air grew warmer as *The Silvi* sailed southeast towards Otyrheim. The calm sea breeze carried an ocean spray over the deck, cooling Asher in the midday heat. It all seemed too calm. With Cara and Marius relaxing again, it would be a perfect time to attack them. The longer nothing happened, the more Asher flinched at any sudden sound, a wave thudding against the hull, a small crate falling over. Even a sneeze from Marius caused Asher to go for his knife. As he leaned against the upper deck railing beside Marius, his eyes remained fixed on the cargo hatch at the ship's centre.

'Why don't you go for a nap? It's your turn anyway,' Marius said, gazing out over the endless blue from behind the wheel. After Cara had offered *The Silvi*'s captain half of the Muuraki claws, he slowly began behaving like his old self. He now treated Asher and Cara with a pleasant politeness, and Asher was thankful for it. He hadn't realised how much he missed the chipper, sarcastic demeanour of the black Vulpen sailor.

'I'm okay.' Asher yawned. 'Not sure I'd be able to sleep anyway. Might wake up with claws wrapped around my throat.' He chuckled, though the fear was genuine.

'You're safer here than in Otyrheim,' Marius replied with a smirk. 'Otyren don't take too kindly to Rabbethi.'

'What do you mean? I've met plenty of Otyren, and they've all been good to me.'

'Yes, but I bet you were a customer. I'm afraid, outside Otyrheim, you're something of a monster used to scare little Otyren children.'

The Otyren-Rabbethi wars were a widely known part of history, but Asher thought most considered it just that, ancient history. It's not like his ancestors didn't have a good reason to attack. Their numbers were growing too great. Disease and famine killed thousands, and the Otyren refused to help. The Otyren Republic preferred to let Rabbethi families starve and perish from disease. Still, that was a long, long time ago.

'All I'm saying is don't expect a warm welcome,' Marius continued, looking over. 'And keep that agent close. You'll need her.'

Asher looked to the base of the mast where Cara sat, her back pressed against it. She appeared to be asleep, her bushy red tail wrapped around and under her cloak.

'I will,' he said, smiling.

Despite Asher's paranoia and surety that something terrible would happen at any moment, the rest of the day's sailing went smoothly, the Lighthouse continuing to turn, *The Silvi* continuing its course, skimming along the calm waters. Asher gave in to his body's needs and was able to nap as the light began to fade, the sky shifting from a light blue to a deep purple. It was a restless sleep. Flashes of the Muuraki assassin filled his mind, along with bodies back in White Cliffe, Mia and Henric.

The touch of a paw against his arm startled him awake. Cara recoiled, jumping back as Asher shot up, breathing heavily.

'I'm sorry,' she whispered. 'You were having a nightmare. I wasn't sure whether to wake you or let you sleep. Are you okay?'

Asher rested his head on the pillow and stared at the wooden planks that made up the cabin's ceiling. 'I'm okay,' he breathed, his mind still racing.

Cara nodded and made for the door. Before stepping through, she paused and glanced at Asher with an awkward smile. 'Marius is cooking dinner if you want to join us. I won't blame you if you don't. It smells like a wet Shangari and looks like crow shit.'

'Thanks,' Asher chuckled.

She nodded and stepped through the door onto the deck.

The smell of Marius's cooking flowed into the cabin on the chilled evening breeze. It smelt *worse* than a wet Shangari. Asher wiped the slumber sand from his eyes. Judging from the lack of light, he had been asleep longer than expected, and a pang of guilt hit his stomach when he realised he'd missed his shift steering the ship. He crawled out of bed and stepped out onto the deck.

The wind coursed through his fur. The evening sky was a beautiful shade of deep purple, and the air had a refreshing chill. Asher breathed deeply and immediately wanted to vomit. The stench of wet Shangari was thick and now more akin to a dead Shangari. Covering his mouth, Asher searched for the source. At the base of the mast, facing the door to shield the flame from the wind, was a small metal stove, its flames licking the bottom of a large round pot that rested heavily on three tall legs.

'Ah! Here he comes. Come, have a seat. I made this just for you,' Marius said, grinning like a schoolboy. He leaned over the pot, a ladle in one paw and a bowl in the other.

Cara sat with her back to the mast, facing the railing, an empty bowl on the floor beside her. She stared at Asher wide-eyed, subtly shaking her head in a silent warning.

'It... err... smells... err... what is it?' Asher asked, approaching cautiously.

Marius dipped his ladle deep into the bubbling liquid and scooped a spoonful of murky brown fluid. He slopped it into the bowl and passed it to Asher. Blackish-green lumps floated around the surface. It looked like it had already passed through someone's digestion.

'It's kelp soup,' Marius said with pride. 'I know you Rabbethi don't eat meat, and you've been missing your home, so I wanted to make something just for you.' He looked to the bowl and back to Asher, expectant.

'Thank you, Marius,' Asher said with a smile. 'You really shouldn't have.'

He meant it.

He lifted the bowl to his lips and took in some of the foul soup, a piece of overcooked kelp slapping against his lips. It was vile, but Asher swallowed it down all the same. This was one of the nicest things someone had done for him in a long while, and he wasn't about to insult its maker.

'Mmm,' he said as convincing as he could.

Satisfied, Marius dropped the ladle to the floor with a clatter and moved to the steps that rose to the wheel, sitting himself on the bottom step. He pulled a small pouch from his belt, opened it, and began placing small chunks of what looked like salted pork into his mouth. He chewed with a broad smile across his face.

'Aren't you going to have any?' Asher asked, confused.

'Thena no,' Marius scoffed. 'It's old wine and mouldy cabbage. Hurt my Silvana again, and I'll feed you something worse.' The black Vulpen started chuckling to himself as he chewed his salted snack.

Asher didn't know what to think. Marius had blown his kind act to the wind, and Asher was left disappointed, a rotten taste in his mouth. Then he heard something he had never heard before.

It was Cara, and she was... laughing.

A loud, bellowing laugh echoed around *The Silvi*, floating for miles on the evening breeze. Before Asher knew it, he found himself smiling, the contagious laughter of his friend creeping into his spirit. His smile erupted into a laugh, harder and more joyous than he had experienced in a long, long time. His pains, worries, and responsibilities seemed like a distant memory, and the hardships yet to come, a faraway worry not yet worth his time.

The three laughed well into the night, enjoying each other's company, eating good food, and drinking fine wine from Marius's stores.

They paid no mind to the dark clouds that hung on the horizon.

20

Otyrheim

Asher was miserable.

Heavy rain thudded against the deck as strong winds bloated the sails, hurtling *The Silvi* over the climbing waves. Plumes of white spray exploded from the ship's bow as it crested a frothing peak before descending the other side, the salty water cascading down onto a sodden Asher. His tall ears were tucked inside his blue hood, and his cloak clung to his drenched fur. He held on tight, bracing himself on the upper deck, hunched over the steering wheel. In his arms, he could feel the pull of unseen currents working hard to steer *The Silvi* astray. His bandaged forearm burned with the fresh application of salty brine.

'Why did it have to be my turn?' Asher mumbled to the storm. The weather had been drizzly at best when he had taken the helm—no cause for concern for Marius, who took the opportunity to rest and enjoy Asher's misery from the warmth of the cabin. Cara had initially joined Asher to keep him company, but as the rain grew more intense, she thought it pointless for both of them to catch a cold, so she went inside and took the stove with her. Asher hated her for it, but he would have done the same.

The Silvi dropped down the back of another large wave, landing with a splash before ascending the next. They were growing. Crates shifted within the cabin beneath him, and empty bottles smashed as they dropped from their shelves. He looked at the steps to the lower deck and debated whether to wake Marius and let him take over. It was his ship, after all, and despite the lessons Asher had received, Marius hadn't taught him how to handle waves of this magnitude. He returned his eyes to the bow, deciding it best not to leave the wheel. All he could do was hope the next landing would wake his Vulpen captain. As the ship crested another summit, Asher peered through the wall of rain towards the horizon. He had seen nothing but darkness for hours and did not expect that to change, but desperation for the journey to end compelled him to look again.

The faint glow of dawn was beginning to creep across the ocean, and to his delight, shapes began to form, illuminated by the growing morning light. The outline of distant mountains created a jagged horizon like a broken saw. As the light grew, vast swathes of flat forested land emerged between the mountains and shore from the amorphous shadows, countless rivers ebbing and flowing through the trees, spilling into the sea. It was all he could see for miles and miles in either direction.

Despite the rain hammering down upon the deck, the view before him filled him with a calming inner peace. It was beautiful, and he found himself becoming strangely reflective. So much had happened, so much heartache and pain that had forced him to grow up and stop running from his responsibilities. He just wished his father was there to see him grow.

Asher's face twisted slightly at the thought of his father getting what he wanted. He loved the man but loathed what he had tried to force Asher to be. Henric had always been the apple of his father's eye, and Asher often suspected his father would have preferred Henric to be his heir. However, the Rabbethi laws forbade the youngest from ruling. So his father was stuck with him, the rebellious thief, spoilt and ungrateful, devoid of any will to take on responsibility.

Oh, if he could only see me now, Asher thought, sniffling under his blue hood.

His thoughts turned to Henric, and he smiled. If Henric was alive, Asher was sure he'd be causing chaos for whoever held him captive. He'd attempt to escape at every opportunity, fighting and screaming until he had nothing left. He had a fiery heart, a rambunctious youthfulness. Asher imagined his father had seen much of himself in the young Henric. They even looked alike, unlike Asher, who had none of his father in him. No, he was his mother's child, both in appearance—save for the off-colour patch covering his eye—and in nature, free-spirited yet content. She was the one he truly wished could see him now. He felt the necklace around his neck shifting under his leather armour. A sudden truth pulled at Asher's heart: Henric was the only family he had left.

The Silvi lurched forwards, coming to a thunderous splash at the base of a massive wave. More cargo crashed to the floor, followed by a heavier thud.

'Agh, for Thena's sake!' a voice yelled from the cabin beneath Asher's feet.

'Well, hopefully, you'll come and help me now.' He smirked, recognising Marius's disgruntled cry. At the peak of the next wave, he took in the horizon once more.

Among the thousands of rivers streaming from the wall of trees, one appeared much wider and was flanked by two imposing circular stone towers. Fiery beacons shone from the tower peaks, sheltered beneath a flat, wooden roof. Long banners of a deep green hung across the tower's front. Taking pride and place at their centre was a singular silver trident.

'That must be it,' Asher said, thankful the end was within sight.

In his relief, he loosened his grip on the wheel. It slipped from his grasp, violently spinning until it slammed to a stop with a loud *bang*. The ship started to drift. With a quick turn, it began descending the backside of a wave sideways. Asher desperately tried to turn the wheel and correct the ship's alignment. It was useless. The pull of the water beneath was too strong.

His eyes widened as the base of the wave approached with rapid eagerness to meet them. If they remained at that angle, the whole ship would smash into the water, exploding into nothing more than driftwood, and Asher *knew* Marius would have something to say about that. He pulled as hard as he could once more.

This time, the wheel began to turn.

Glancing to his side, he saw Cara and Marius straining and soaking wet, with paws gripped tight on the wheel's handles. They heaved. Just as *The Silvi* was about to slam sideways into the ocean below, the wheel shifted, and *The Silvi* straightened. A humongous splash echoed among the rain, and a torrent of water poured onto the decks, drenching the already wet trio. The water cascaded back into the sea through small holes in the railings, and they all released their long-held breaths.

'Thanks,' Asher said through heavy breaths as he stepped aside, allowing Marius to take control of the wheel. 'And sorry. I should have come and got you.'

'Don't worry about it,' he replied, equally out of breath. 'I shouldn't have left you alone in that.' His black fur was matted around his reassuring smile.

'I'm going back inside.' Cara sniffed as she marched down the steps, her once bushy tail dragging along the sodden wood. She stepped into the cabin below and slammed the door behind her.

The sea began to calm as the waves lost their zeal, their once great might now bobbing *The Silvi* up and down in gentle motions. The commotion had drawn seagulls towards the ship and now circled high above, squawking expectantly for whatever catch they believed *The Silvi* possessed. The rain had begun to lessen but still patted against the deck in a constant light patter. Marius left and returned with his own cloak. Now, only his snout and glowing orange eyes were visible from within the shadow of his black hood. Asher remained with Marius by the wheel, not wanting Marius to suffer the same loneliness he had earlier.

'Is that it?' Asher asked, pointing a wet finger to the towers before them.

'Sure is. Those towers mark the entrance to the Flod Vegr—or Flood Road if you're sensible,' Marius replied. 'From there, we need to travel inland until we reach the capital of Holtbjarg. It's easy sailing when you're in the Otyren's good books. Get into their bad books, though, and they'll drain the river, leaving you high and dry.'

'Wouldn't the sea just flood in?' Asher asked.

'From what Erik has told me, they can raise a metal chain to keep ships from leaving. Then they raise a wall between the two towers, keeping the sea out. Pipes then drain the water elsewhere.'

'How?'

Marius gave a sideways glance to Asher before returning to the water before them, shifting awkwardly. 'It's all very complicated,' he said with a dismissive headshake. 'I couldn't begin to explain it to you.'

'Right...,' Asher replied, dubious. He was surprised, though. He hadn't thought about Jarl Erik for a long while and wouldn't have expected him to know anything about engineering, even if he was from Otyrheim.

'So please,' Marius continued. 'While we're there, don't do anything to piss them off? I'd rather not be stuck while they refill the riverways after hauling you off to the dungeon.' His tone seemed half-joking, half-not.

'No promises,' Asher chuckled. Marius scoffed though his eyes remained fixed on the towers.

It wasn't long before *The Silvi* reached the mouth of the river. Clouds lingered overhead, covering the sky in a blanket of grey as the pitter-patter of the rain continued to fall upon the deck. It would have been peaceful without the uncertainty plaguing Asher's mind. This was not enemy territory, but it was a maze of waterways surrounded by thick forests and patrolled by people who generally regarded Rabbethi as unwelcome.

The Silvi passed by a similar-sized vessel sailing between the two looming towers. The Otyren sailors aboard were dressed in leather overalls and were moving large cages from the deck to a cargo hold below. Each had a pouch dangling from their hip that varied in size from sailor to sailor, undeniably containing their Oathstone. They didn't pay much mind to *The Silvi* until one noticed Asher. The short Otyren sailor pointed and called out to the rest of his crew, who all turned and stared in a mixture of surprise and distrust that made Asher uneasy.

Not a great start, Asher thought as he shifted to avoid eye contact.

Before him was the Flod Vegr, a vast, straight river stretching as far as the eye could see. The stone banks were expertly cut, with steep, smooth sides and flanked by a thick tree line, broken every so often by a pair of towers on either side. Their lit beacons guided a straight path down the river towards a large mass rising in the distance. It looked like a castle of some kind, though Asher couldn't make out the details.

'I thought this was supposed to be a maze of waterways?' Asher queried.

'It is. On either side of the Flood Path is a labyrinth of trees and rivers with only narrow walkways to lead you through—not that the Otyren use those. They prefer the water itself. If you can figure them out, the paths will take you to several small villages and, eventually, the Medvedian Kingdom to the northwest and the Rabbethi Kingdom to the southeast.'

Asher peered into the dense forest wall as golden rays poured through a sudden break in the clouds, creating brilliant pillars of light that descended onto the river and surrounding forests. The blanket of deep green became highlighted with a golden shimmer.

'It's beautiful,' Asher breathed.

'Yeah,' Marius said softly, smiling. 'I suppose it is.'

Splashes caught Asher's attention, quickly followed by several heavy thuds from the deck below. He raced to the railing and peered over. Standing to attention around the mast were seven Otyren soldiers, their bodies dripping water to the deck. They stood shoulder to shoulder facing the upper deck and carried gleaming tridents in webbed paws. Their shimmering armour was made of what looked like many interlocking golden scales that curved and bent with the shape of their bodies, encasing their thick, powerful tails. Their helmets featured a nose guard and two cheek guards that spiralled to a point just before their mouths. The whole headpiece flowed into a sharp point behind their heads. One of the soldiers stepped forwards. His armour was coloured every so often with emerald-green scales that shone brilliantly, and as *The Silvi* sailed through a ray of light, his armour reflected a mosaic of dazzling light upon the deck.

'Who are they?' Asher whispered to Marius.

'Palace guards. It seems the Allthing are aware of our arrival,' he replied in a hushed voice. 'Must have seen us coming out of that storm. They're miserable bastards, all work and no play. Best keep quiet, mind. Those tridents are for more than just fishing.'

Asher nodded and gazed down at their new guests, expecting the leader to ask for the king of the Rabbethi to show himself at any moment.

I hope the other ships will be okay through that storm, Asher thought. The extra vessels and soldiers would have provided just the boost he needed to confront these impressive-looking soldiers with confidence. Still, he had a job to do.

'I am—'

'Cara of the Vulpen Queendom,' the leader barked in a commanding voice, cutting Asher off. 'We are here to escort you to Holtbjarg. The Allthing is expecting you.' There was a brief pause before footsteps echoed from within the cabin. Cara emerged and stepped onto the deck, her hood around her shoulders.

She bowed, and the captain returned the courtesy. 'Thank you,' she said, stern but politely. 'I shall instruct our captain to follow your instructions.'

'Very good.'

The captain looked to where Asher and Marius were watching, his eyes landing on Marius. 'Carry on sailing through the gates. They will remain open to you. Once we enter the city, follow the river left until I say so.'

Marius gave a silent, obedient nod and returned to the wheel. The captain's eyes landed on Asher with an intense, unemotional stare that instantly made Asher uneasy. Then, without acknowledgement, he turned and passed through his soldiers. He stopped at the ship's bow as the other soldiers remained like statues. Without a word, Cara returned to the cabin.

'These guys aren't messing around,' Marius breathed. 'Remember what I said? This escort is to keep you safe through the city. Otherwise, I can't imagine you'd make it far outside one of the docks.'

'I didn't realise it was that bad,' Asher said, peeling his eyes away from the Otyren captain.

'This city is likely one of the only in Tamuz where you won't find Rabbethi, and that's not because they don't have much in the way of roasted cauliflower.' Marius turned, his eyes serious. 'If someone offers you something called River Jade, *don't* take it.'

'Why?' Asher asked, concern growing.

'It's a lot of fun for the Otyren but not so much for the likes of Rabbethi. For some reason, your people just don't react too well to it.'

'Right, well, I'll be sure to avoid it.' He had never heard of River Jade, and it sounded like bad news, judging by the seriousness in Marius's tone.

The Silvi sailed further down the broad river, the rain falling gently against the soldiers' scaled armour, sounding like a chorus of tiny bells. Numerous vessels sailed by, each full of Otyren sailors who cried out a chorus of patriotic yelps and squeaks. The captain raised his trident in return as if a returning triumphant hero.

They eventually approached two circular stone towers, much taller and broader than the others. These had several banners draped around the outer rim and featured massive fires that burned with intensity at their peaks. Stationed around the flames were many soldiers, with more patrolling the paths that led deep into the forest. Emerging out of the tower's base, just above the waterline, was a thick, heavy metal chain that disappeared under the water. There was the same at the base of the opposite tower.

'A chain gate,' Asher said with a realisation. There hadn't been any solid gates to bar their passage, and the river had, up to that point, been entirely open to them.

'It's a good thing the captain's here,' Marius said. 'Without him, we'd have to stop at each of these gates, process all the documentation, and maybe even pay a toll. With a simple raise of his fancy little fork, we have free sailing all the way to the city.'

Asher gazed at the river before them and noticed more chain gates standing tall and proud, evenly spaced along the water's edge. He, too, became thankful for the captain's "fancy fork".

The rest of the journey crawled by tediously but without issue, and the captain raised his silver trident several times as *The Silvi* sailed through the remaining chain gates. The riverbanks slowly became populated with small, unassuming wooden shacks, each with its own dock, some of which had sailboats and dinghies anchored to them. Other docks were empty but featured elderly Otyren fishing with worn fishing poles. They watched *The Silvi* pass with weary frowns while absentmindedly moving simple smooth stones in their off-paw. Even from *The Silvi*'s upper deck, Asher couldn't help but marvel at the grace and finesse with which they passed the pebbles between their webbed fingers, a display of skill only achievable with years of practice.

As *The Silvi* passed between more and more gates, the poorly constructed huts transitioned into well-built wooden houses with stone garden walls, and the docks became filled with sturdier vessels. The land between the forest and the water's edge became wider and wider until the space was several houses thick. The dirt path that ran parallel became full of activity. Otyren travelled up and down, carrying goods to and from the city further upstream. Children ran through the crowds, squeaking and pointing at *The Silvi* as their parents discussed the morning's goings-on. It was starting to feel like a city, which eased Asher's tension—cities he could handle.

The large structure he had previously seen rising from the river was becoming clearer. Between the last stone towers, a towering island split the river in two, the base of which was surrounded by a high stone wall and dotted every so often with thick circular towers, each draped with the green banner of the Otyren Republic. Growing tall from the island into the clouded sky was a huge bare cliff, a sheer wall that fronted the strait of water. On top of that cliff stood an immense keep, surrounded by many thin circular towers that grew in size and grandeur as *The Silvi* sailed ever closer.

The towers of the final chain gates were the largest of the journey, extending into tall walls that grew outwards, cutting into the forest and disappearing from view. Asher gasped as they sailed through and entered the arms of the city within. It was enormous, a cyclone of activity. A sea of coloured sails coursed up and down the two rivers that split left and right before them. Hundreds of boats rested by wooden docks lining the river's outer banks. They were a hive of Otyren, Vulpen and Medvedians, all hurrying about their daily lives within this river capital. Numerous stairs led up from the docks to the higher banks, and Asher could see a dense row of simple stone houses, one or two stories tall, though he couldn't tell from the water how far back they went. He imagined the city extended deep before meeting the city walls.

He turned his attention forwards and gazed up at the central island and the thick stone walls circling its base. Beyond them rose the sheer cliff face, the multi-towered keep standing tall and vigilant at its peak. It was enough to make Asher forget about the rain sprinkling his face.

Marius pulled on *The Silvi*'s wheel, and the ship steered left, carefully avoiding the chaotic bustle as the vessel drifted around the centre island. They passed under a wide stone bridge connecting the centre island with the outer banks, the long arch disappearing deep among the buildings.

The river eventually began to curve right to connect with its sister, where a dockyard of stone extended out from the centre island. Anchored to the dock's arms were several large vessels, each made of a dark wood that matched the surrounding forests and trimmed with varying shades of green. Their sails were furled, but Asher recognised the emerald green as the same as the tower banners. They sat proud in the water as Otyren soldiers carried large wooden crates over narrow planks onto the decks, disappearing below.

The Silvi came to rest at an available space at the dock, signalled by a soldier standing to attention, a silver trident held high. The rain began to ease as soldiers tied ropes to the ship and extended wooden planks onto the deck. The escorting soldiers onboard disembarked first, followed by the captain, who marched down the stone jetty, where he turned and stood once more to attention.

'Let's go,' Cara called as she stepped across one of the wooden planks, fastening her sheathed sword to her waist.

Asher turned to Marius. 'You'll still be here when we're done, right?'

'That entirely depends on how long you are and how much paperwork I need to fill out,' he replied, tightening a knot around a wooden post on the railing. He looked to Asher, seemingly aware of the disappointment the answer provided. Patting him on the shoulder, he smiled. 'I'll see you soon, Your Highness.'

Asher smiled.

After grabbing his bow and quiver from the cabin, he crossed the wooden planks. As he walked, he glanced at a regiment of soldiers on one of the Otyren vessels as they heaved heavy-looking wooden boxes onto the deck. Asher cringed as he noticed a dark stain coating a corner of one of the boxes. It looked like blood, though he assumed it was likely a shipment of meat hunted from within the forest depths. His stomach churned as countless soldiers carried more and more boxes aboard. Just as he was about to turn away, out stepped from the cabin a red-furred Vulpen woman dressed in the gear of a queen's agent. She held in her paw several ruffled documents and was in deep discussion with an Otyren captain.

Huh.

'Asher!' came a cry from down the jetty. It was Cara. She stood in front of a large collection of soldiers, her face cold and stern. She looked like a giant, standing among the Otyren, who barely came up to her waist. Asher jogged after, not wanting to provoke a telling-off.

'This way,' the captain commanded, turning and moving through the soldiers that parted before him. Cara followed, with Asher keeping pace by her side. The soldiers closed ranks behind them and marched in unison, their harmonious steps echoing around the stone jetty. Before them was a large gatehouse, its spiked metal gate hanging precariously within the entrance.

With the soldiers marching close behind him, the walled interior of the island before him, and the weight of eyes bearing down on him, a pit began to grow in Asher's stomach. He turned to Cara for reassurance.

'This will work, right?' he asked, desperate for reassurance.

Cara's eyes glanced down before returning forwards. She didn't turn to him, and her face remained cold. She picked up the pace, marching to the captain's side before speaking with him in a hushed voice. Asher's spirits dropped. Not since their first meeting had she looked so callous; even then, she never outright ignored him.

Something was very wrong.

21

The Allthing of the Great Tree

The sense of unease grew within Asher as the party walked through the stone gatehouse and into the inner castle. A stone path lay before them, rising towards the foreboding stronghold, the immense structure growing tall from the summit. Its narrow towers climbed high into the sky, all of differing heights.

It's very regal for a republic, Asher thought as he climbed the steep slope behind his escort. He looked up and noticed the path crested halfway up the hill, the tops of brightly coloured market stalls peeking over the ridge. The thrum of vendors selling their wares emanated beyond. Cara was still marching ahead with the captain, leaving Asher with soldiers at his back alone. Worried thoughts began to swirl in his mind. His wrists began to itch as imaginary restraints tightened against his fur, and he willed his twitching nose to calm.

Glancing either side of the main road, Asher found smaller paths leading to many stone houses, each with slated roofs and the sound of life coming from their large decorated windows. Expansive lawns surrounded each house, and streams of crystal-clear water flowed within narrow channels that descended the hill, passing through the base of the island's thick stone walls.

Well-dressed Otyren stopped and smiled at the captain and Cara as they passed. Their faces dropped when their eyes landed upon Asher, twisting into a mixture of disdain and disbelief. More and more began crowding around the path. A sea of brown fur, black eyes and fine linen tunics squeaked all around, though they made sure not to block the procession. Whispers and murmurs hummed beneath the squeaks as hundreds of eyes were fixed upon Asher, some in tight scowls and glares, others wide in shock.

A clacking sound permeated the squeaks as many in the crowd moved their Oathstone about their webbed paws. Most of the pebbles were simple and smooth, but some had patterns painted over the surface, which created flashes of colour among the crowd. Some of the children even had small pebbles of their own. They were adorable. With adult Otyren only just taller than Asher's waist, their children made it to about his knees. They stood or sat near their parents, concentrating hard as they desperately tried to move the tiny rocks with fluidity. It was a strange custom to Asher, but he supposed it was no different to the Rabbethi's love for jumping or the Medvedian's love of fishing or wrestling.

Small pockets of Vulpen and Medvedians stood tall among the gathered crowd. They, too, were dressed in fine clothing and looked at Asher, not with any malicious intent or mistrust but with the general curiosity that came from the gathering of so many people. The Otyren children who weren't concentrating on their pebbles clung to their parents' legs, their tiny black eyes darting from Asher to their parents, confused.

'Why hasn't he got bad man bracelets on, Mummy?' asked a young Otyren to her mother.

'Hush now,' the mother replied. 'Just be happy they got him.'

Got him? Asher repeated in his head, his heart skipping. He was sure Cara wouldn't let anything happen to him, but the expressions of relief surrounding him caused his stomach to knot. He reached out and pulled at Cara's arm to get her attention. She yanked it back and glared over her shoulder.

'Don't,' she snapped. Cara's eyes were hard, her voice sharp.

Asher hesitated, not knowing what to do with himself.

Her expression softened as she scanned the uncertainty in his eyes. 'Everything will be fine,' she whispered, but before Asher could reply, she returned to the path ahead.

He followed in silence, feeling his ears growing warmer. It was more humid here than Ignimarum and certainly more than White Cliffe, where, although the light shined bright, there was always a coolness in the breeze. There was no cool breeze here. It was midday, and the air was hot and damp. The Great Lighthouse loomed taller and broader than Asher was used to, and he wondered whether Otyren found White Cliffe freezing in comparison.

They'd probably turn to ice the moment they stepped a single webbed foot onto the Outer Rim.

The slope flattened into a wide stone plaza as they reached halfway up the hill. Taking pride of place at its centre was a large, circular fountain. On the far left and right of the plaza were two large gatehouses. They were detached from any wall, but beyond were bridges that stretched out from the hill, leaping over the island's walls and rivers and into the outer city. The bridges themselves were filled with well-dressed citizens crossing to and from the rest of the city.

The procession didn't stop and began navigating around the fountain. Asher looked about the market around him. As was the usual sight when entering a city plaza, many stands were positioned around the edge, all manned by well-groomed Otyren that oozed charm and expressed an air of showmanship. They enticed the wealthy to peruse their wares, primarily beautiful jewellery encrusted with precious stones.

One trader, however, wasn't selling jewellery or any other expensive item a member of the elite would typically be after. He attempted to sell delicious-smelling soup served with a chunk of thick, soft bread, the scent of nuts and other herbs cutting through the floral perfume, warming Asher's being. It was too humid for hot soup, but this smelt so good he would have eaten it in any weather. Unfortunately, he appeared to be the only one who thought so, as not a single passerby had been tempted by the delectable scent. With his huge, bushy red tail the size of his body, mouse-like face, and tall, pointed ears, the Ruadrae trader was undeterred and waved at citizens with a broad smile across his face. Asher had never seen a Ruadrae before. He had been told of their cheerful nature by the Otyren traders back home in White Cliffe.

The red-furred trader stopped as he met Asher's eye, his nose twitching in an oddly familiar way. The trader then began waving with increased enthusiasm, a massive grin across his face. Asher couldn't help but smile in return and raised a polite paw in recognition. The Ruadrae beamed before resuming his unsuccessful attempts to entice shoppers to his stand.

He's a long way from Kilruad, Asher thought, recalling what he had learned from his tutors in his youth. The treetop kingdom of the Ruadrae existed as a Fenrathi subject state and was nestled near the hostile border with the Medvedians. The subjugation of the Ruadrae had occurred hundreds of years ago and had been a peaceful affair, the Ruadrae seeking protection from Cozati raiders and Medvedian marauders. The Fenrathi stationed a garrison in their capital and expanded their borders to include the vast forest realm. In return, all the

Fenrathi asked for was an annual protection tax and mandatory service in their army for a few years. Asher looked to the trader.

He's a deserter.

The war between the Fenrathi and Medvedians had claimed many lives, including young Ruadrae serving their mandatory service. Asher had heard stories of the Medvedian War Brigades, of the bloodthirsty berserkers that could tear a full-grown Fenrathi in half. He didn't blame this Ruadrae for running.

His gaze wandered to the fountain as they passed. A tall marble Otyren in elaborate scaled armour stood triumphant, a webbed foot on a wet, rugged rock as water cascaded from the tip of a trident raised high. He didn't recognise the Otyren carved into stone but assumed it was the ancient Otyren founder. Strangely, he couldn't recall the name.

He became uneasy as he looked at the statue's plinth. In small but exquisite detail was a series of much smaller figures, their naked forms doubled over, straining to hold the statue up above with their backs in a brutal display of servitude. They were all Rabbethi. Asher averted his eyes, pretending not to notice as the worry in his gut grew deeper and heavier.

Ahead, the hill climbed towards the imposing castle. The path's sloping stone slabs gave way to tiny steps, forcing Asher and Cara to step awkwardly over several at a time. Larger homes covered the upper half of the sloping rock, undoubtedly the stately homes of the jarls, or at least those with the deepest pockets. The castle loomed through the weakening rain. The many towers rose high into the sky, circular and thin, each with pointed slate roofs and surrounding a vast square building with curved corners.

The vista from the top of the hill took Asher's breath away—though that was likely due to the steep climb. From the path behind him, he could see the roofs of the inner city, the plaza and fountain and the crowd following from further down the steps. He saw the rivers circling the island and the hundreds of vessels sailing its waters. The outer city sprawled out before him on the two riverbanks on either side of the water, the city walls encircling them, breaking where the river flowed through the city. Beyond that, a vast, dense forest stretched for miles and miles in all directions. It was no wonder the city was said to be impenetrable. Marching organised soldiers through the maze of walkways and tangles of swamped bush would be impossible. On the horizon rose the Rimwall Mountains, which encircled the world, their jagged shape reminding Asher of a great beast's lower teeth.

He turned, realising Cara and the captain had moved on, and followed through a lush garden towards the castle's grand wooden doors. The scent was intoxicating. Green lawns and flower beds surrounded the castle, covering every inch of free space, the scent of flowers floating heavy on the wind. Asher felt lightheaded as he took in the sweet aroma.

At the base of the great square keep stood tall double doors studded with heavy iron rivets—far more extensive than any Otyren would have need for. The captain of the escort knocked on the solid wood, and a much smaller door creaked open, revealing an old Otyren servant dressed in a well-trimmed black tunic laced with green embroidery that swirled around like vines on a tree.

'Ah y-yes, welcome, Domina Cara,' he said with a bow. 'Th-the Allthing is expecting you. Please follow me.' He turned and disappeared into the dark interior.

Cara nodded and followed through the small door, ducking low. The captain waited to one side, his eyes watching Asher like a hawk. Asher hesitantly followed, ducking through the door frame, his ears grazing against the wood. The captain then stepped through and locked the door.

The air inside was cold and still. It was so quiet that Asher could hear his heart's worried thumping. The vast hall was slick with white marble, its tall ceiling vanishing high into the shadows above. Thick columns rose on either side of the hall, supporting expansive stone balconies, and Asher could see a multitude of wooden doors that opened onto them. Where they led was anyone's guess. At the far end of the hall were two sets of stairs, divided in the middle by a balcony overlooking the hall and a black marble sculpture carved into the floor. The design was a beautiful scale model of the entire area, including the city, trees and outlying towns, all frozen in time. Water flowed throughout the model in tiny grooves that mimicked the rivers, cutting through the floor towards the walls of the grand hall and disappearing into small metal grates. It was exquisitely detailed.

Footsteps drew Asher's attention from the sculpted art. Cara and the servant were making their way around the model towards the stairs on the far side. He followed as they climbed the steps, the Otyren captain close on his heels. Long benches lined the wall at the top, separated by potted plants with large, flat leaves, and embedded into the black marble floor was a trident made of emerald green, the sigil of Otyrheim. Grand double doors of gold stood shut on the far wall, engraved with triumphant Otyren holding tridents high as huge waves crashed around them. The craftsmanship was extraordinary, and the details were intricate.

'Are you ready, Domina Cara?' came a hushed voice, his voice carrying in the stillness and bouncing off the marble floors. The words resonated in Asher's ears as if spoken directly into them. Secrets could not be so easily kept here, it seemed.

Asher approached in silence as Cara nodded to the servant. The echo of Asher's boots and the pitter-patter of the captain's feet behind him caught the old Otyren's attention.

He gave Asher a dismissive glance before addressing Cara again. 'When inside, please do not address the jarls unless spoken to.'

Cara nodded. 'Understood.'

He gestured to the captain behind Asher. 'Please give your weapons to Captain Grotsvik here.'

None of this sat right with Asher. The dirty looks he received walking through the city, the comments from the citizens, and Cara's cold attitude. Now, they were asking, no, demanding him to give over the last thing that made him feel safe. He said nothing, but his eyes pleaded with Cara.

'Do as he says,' she said softly but sternly.

Asher hesitated. His instincts were screaming at him to run, to get far away from the city and run deep into the forest, never looking back.

I'm okay, he thought. *Everything will be okay.*

He unslung his bow from his shoulder and passed it to the captain. The captain took the bow with one paw and snapped his fingers with the other. Out of nowhere, two Otyren soldiers in gold-scaled armour appeared, not making a sound as they approached. Had they been there the entire time? How many more were there? Asher wasn't sure he wanted to know the answer.

The captain gave the bow to one of the soldiers, who took it and slung it over his shoulder, the bottom scraping against the marble floor. Asher then removed the quiver of arrows and passed them to the soldier, who took it and held it under his arm, not once making eye contact. Asher unsheathed the red ribbon blade from his chest and, with a sigh, passed the knife over. The soldier took it and slid it into the quiver. It disappeared into the bundle of arrows, sliding to a thud as it hit the bottom. Cara unstrapped her curved sword from her belt and passed it to the other soldier, along with several smaller daggers. He watched as she pulled them from hidden pockets within her armour.

'They will be returned to you when you leave,' the captain said as she passed over the last dagger. He snapped his fingers again, and the soldiers turned, descending the steps and disappearing from view.

'Very good,' the elderly servant said. He knocked once on the golden double doors.

There was a brief pause before one of the doors groaned open, its immense weight gliding inwards just enough to allow entrance. Voices echoed from within. The servant entered with Cara following, her tail disappearing from view behind the golden door.

Asher paused.

This was it. Here, he would declare himself as king of the Rabbethi and, as king, humbly request, no, demand the return of his people's relic. Surely they would want to maintain friendly relations with their neighbour? And with the support of the Vulpen Queendom, how could they refuse? Of course, he would offer something in return and expected much negotiation. He stood straight and marched through the golden doors of the Allthing chamber.

He took in the expansive, cylindrical room. Thick stone columns rose high along the walls, supporting a tall, domed ceiling. The columns were decorated with long banners of various colours and emblems, likely representing the sigils of each jarl's house. Some featured images of fish and nets, others of creatures like deer and boar, hounds and horses, but all with at least one image of a silver trident. Between the columns of the opposing wall were tall arches of glass, which commanded a stunning view. Far below, the river stretched straight as an arrow towards the ocean, flanked by thick forests. Tiny vessels dotted the shimmering water as they sailed up and down its length.

Rays of golden light shone through the windows as the clouds parted, bathing the chamber in a warming glow. In the centre of the chamber, and taking up an unreasonable amount of space, was a large circular table seemingly made from one solid piece of wood. Its varnished surface even featured rings one would expect within the trunk of a great tree. Asher looked to the base and found roots disappearing beneath the black marble floor. This was no table but the actual trunk of a colossal tree.

It must have been enormous.

A tree this size would have once towered over Otyrheim, visible from as far away as the Rimwall Mountains, its branches providing shade for miles around. It saddened Asher to think of how the Otyren had destroyed such an impressive feat of nature, replaced with cold, hard stone.

The Otyren jarls were in attendance around the table and dressed in tunics embroidered with swirls of silver thread, the colours matching the banners they sat under. There were old, hunched Otyren with speckled white fur and younger Otyren sitting straight with an air of arrogance. Some were skinny with sharp angular features, whilst others were fat with puffy cheeks and rotund bellies. Many had woollen cloaks over their shoulders, and the women seemed to be covered in more gold finery than the men. They all sat in tall, grand thrones that rose behind them. Each throne was carved with images of leaves and winding branches.

The familiar sound of pebbles clacking together echoed faintly within the chamber, and Asher's eyes moved to the Allthing members' paws. His eyes widened. Never before had he seen such beautiful stones, smoothly shaped and shining in radiance. Stones of all shapes and sizes danced before him, stones of dazzling white, radiant red, deep greens and obsidian black. Asher almost mistook them for Shepherd Stones with how they shimmered in the fading light. Patterns of sparkling light reflected against the table and the owners' clothing, yet none were blinded. Each jarl shifted their pebble, or pebbles, from one paw to the other with such finesse that they reflected all light away from the eyeline of those around them. These Otyren knew their stones well.

'We humbly request you relinquish the relic in the name of the Shepherd,' spoke a calm yet exasperated voice. 'The high priestess does not wish for any further... bloodshed.'

All jarls stared with stern expressions into the centre of a table where a white-robed figure stood within a hollow circle cut into the grand wood. Some of the closer members angled their stones to reflect the light directly into the eyes of the speaker, who flinched with annoyance yet did not protest.

'Do not come here with threats of violence, sir! You shall not have it, and that is final!' erupted a plump Otyren as spittle sprayed onto the table before him. He wore a deep-green tunic covered in swirling patterns of silver thread. His brown fur was speckled with grey, and the white fur under his chin was stained red with what looked like wine. It was Jarl Vatn, the head of the most influential family in Otyrheim. His pebble was not in his paw but resting idly on a velvet pillow on the table before him. The stone was a tremendous spherical mass of white that glinted all the colours of the rainbow. It was the size of Asher's fist and utterly beautiful.

'It is not a threat, my lord,' replied the figure, maintaining his calm demeanour. 'It is a promise. No one will stand in the way of Her Radiance and the righteous path she leads towards everlasting peace.'

Asher's fists clenched into tight balls as his eyes narrowed on the hooded figure. It seemed Constance knew the Otyren had a Shepherd Stone. He would have to act fast.

Jarl Vatn slammed his webbed paws onto the table and rose from his chair. 'Your witch should cease whatever plans she has involving the bow and Otyrheim! It will not end well for her, and *that* is a threat!' He lowered himself back into his seat as deep chuntering resonated from his chest, the wood creaking as his great weight settled. 'Tell your mistress we approve of the royal family's removal of White Cliffe and the witan's instalment. We will open trade negotiations with her once she has dealt with the unrest.' He leaned to one side, looking past the acolyte and acknowledged the elderly servant. 'It appears I have other matters to attend to. We will meet again to discuss how you learned of our possession of the bow. It seems we have not been as secure with this information as we had liked, and I demand to know who is responsible. Now, please leave.'

Asher couldn't believe what he had heard. The Otyren Allthing approved of Constance's attack and the killing of his family? He wasn't safe. The plan wouldn't work, and he needed to get out of there. He shuffled up to Cara's side.

'Cara?' he whispered through gritted teeth as he gazed upon the hooded figure.

'What?' she replied, not looking at him.

'I don't think they're going to give us the bow.'

'I know.'

Asher's head snapped to Cara, concern twisting his face, his eyes wide. Quick as a flash, she grabbed his paws and twisted them behind his back.

'What are you doing?' he cried as he struggled against her tight grip.

'I'm sorry,' she whispered. 'It was the only way.'

She shoved Asher forwards, leading him towards the table's centre and passing the church acolyte—a frustrated red Vulpen man. As his eyes met Asher's, he paused, eyes widening. It was clear from his surprise that he was not expecting to find Asher, of all people, here. After taking a brief moment to collect himself, he marched towards the golden doors as if a whip was cracking at his back, disappearing between the narrow gap. The doors slammed shut, and Asher was trapped. Cara pushed him through the opening in the wood and into the central cutout, where beady black eyes stared at him with a smug curiosity.

'Ah, yes... I recognise this one,' Jarl Vatn said, resting his webbed paws over his rotund belly. He turned to Cara and smiled, content.

'Queen Tessina wishes this gift mends any offence,' Cara said with a bow, not lessening her grip on Asher.

'What's going on? Cara!' Asher cried, panic coursing through his veins, his eyes darting around the room.

Jarl Vatn clicked his fingers, and soldiers appeared from hidden spaces behind the pillars. They entered the table, pushed Cara aside and clasped heavy iron shackles around Asher's wrists. A thick, dirty rag was wrapped around his mouth, muffling his pleas and heightened breaths.

'A very gracious gift,' Jarl Vatn said with a curt nod. 'You will have to explain your queen's sudden change of heart, perhaps over a glass of wine?' A slimy smile crawled across his face.

Cara lowered her eyes with a polite smile, leaving a heavy silence to sit upon the chamber.

The fat Otyren's smile dropped as the quiet lingered longer than was comfortable. He cleared his throat with a forced cough. 'Yes, well, as a gesture of goodwill, you are permitted to stay within the castle grounds as a guest of the Allthing until you are rested. On top of that, your queen will receive a double shipment next month!'

The guards turned Asher and shoved him through the gap in the table. Cara's eyes met his with nothing but emptiness, cold and void of emotion. There was no sadness, no regret, nothing. He called to her, but nothing but muffled cries left his mouth, the rag stifling any attempt to plead with his friend. The fire within him burned with rage at the betrayal. Asher felt it, let it course through him, and became enraged alongside it. He lashed out, slamming a boot into the chest of one of the soldiers, sending him flying through the air and skidding across the floor. He turned to face the others, ready to take on as many as possible.

Whack!

And everything went black.

22

The Warden King

Asher slowly came to consciousness face down on a cold, hard floor, a scattering of straw beneath him, a splitting headache emanating from the back of his skull. He raised his head and let out an arduous breath. Pushing off the floor, he eased himself up, crossing his legs. The pain in his head throbbed, and he brought a paw around to the source, wincing at the touch, his fingertips now painted with sticky blood. He groaned as he looked about his new surroundings.

The cell was dark, damp, and cold. It was small, with three stone walls, a low ceiling, and a set of heavy iron bars where a fourth wall would be. Water dripped through cracks in the bricks above, echoing as they splashed against the hard floor. To one side was a bundle of loose rags, and it was then that Asher realised he was completely naked.

'Bastards,' he murmured, pulling the loose cloth towards him. There was a simple beige tunic—which appeared to be just a sack with holes cut into it—and black woollen trousers. He draped the tunic over, then tore a small hole in the trousers for his tail before pulling them up, tying the rope cord around his waist. A stench like an old cesspit wafted from a full bucket in one of the corners. He retched and scrambled to the opposite corner, resting his back against the cold stone.

Then he realised something.

'Oh no...' he said with a sudden urgency. 'No, no, no, no!' He began patting around his neck and chest with frantic taps, worry in his heart growing deeper as he found nothing. He searched the floor, scattering the thin strands of straw that made up his bed. His nose began to twitch as his chest became tight. The walls started to close around him, smothering him in his dread. His mother's necklace was gone, taken.

'The next right thing...'

He shut his eyes tight. *I'm okay. I'm okay.*

'The next right thing... The next right thing... The next right thing...'

It wasn't working. There was no "next right thing".

Tears welled as he leaned back against the damp wall, resting his shoulder on the cold iron bars. Shivers cascaded down his spine, but he didn't care. His whole world had come crashing down around him in an instant. Those he trusted had gifted him like a slave to satisfy a quarrel between two leaders; all the while, his people were being ravaged by Shangari. On top of that, one of the very few people he trusted, whom he could call a friend, betrayed him like he meant nothing to her. Was there no one he could trust? How far did this betrayal go? Queen Tessina certainly gave the order, but what about Luce? Asher's heart twisted at the thought. There was no way she could know about this. She was just an agent. She wouldn't have been privy to the plots and plans of the queen and her spymaster. Luce wouldn't send him to Otyrheim, knowing he'd be thrown in the dungeon to rot, not after their time together.

Would she?

Was what they had together even real? It had certainly felt it, whatever *it* was. It felt like his heart had been torn out three times over. His people had lost their only ally, he had lost his only friend, and he had lost Luce. It was too much to bear. He put his paws to his face and sobbed into the darkness. The sound of Asher's faint cries trickled from his cell and into the rest of the dungeon. What few torches there were crackled in the passageway beyond. A sudden shuffle came from the shadows of the cell opposite, and Asher's ears stood to attention.

'It's okay,' came a gentle feminine voice. 'Breathe.'

Asher wiped the tears from his cheeks. He gazed out through the iron bars and into the dimly lit space beyond. Flickering torches lit a wide passage that ran left and right before meeting junctions at either end. Many more cells lined the walls. Shapes moved within, some pacing back and forth, others slumped motionless against the damp walls and metal bars. He turned to the cell opposite, where the kind words had echoed from. There was movement in the shadows, hay scattering as a figure shifted its weight.

'Where did they grab you from?' the voice asked.

'G-grab me?' Asher replied, peering into the darkness.

'Yeah. Which part of the border? Orneford? Elmstead? Folkingham?'

'I don't know what you're talking about,' he said with abrupt harshness. He usually wouldn't be so cutting, but his emotions were a maelstrom of sorrow and frustration, betrayal and dismay. He was in no mood to be interrogated by a fellow inmate, no matter how kindly the words may be. His chest tightened as a seed of guilt took root.

'What's your name?' the voice continued, unfettered by Asher's sharpness.

'Asher,' he replied bluntly.

'Oh, like the prince?'

'Yeah, like the prince.'

'I've heard of him. I heard he was dead.'

'I'm sure he's alive somewhere,' he scoffed.

'I hope so. It's the only thing keeping the people down here going, knowing their king is out there somewhere. Some of them even hope he'll save them, though I doubt he has any idea what's happening here.'

'What do you mean?' Asher asked, suddenly curious as concern and unease began to seep into his mind. 'What *is* going on here?'

'They're—'

A door slammed from somewhere in the dungeon, and the voice became silent. A few moments passed as Asher stepped away from the bars, holding his breath. Heavy footsteps echoed nearby, each one followed by a jangle of metal. It grew louder until a tremendous shape emerged from beyond the bars. It stopped in front of Asher's cell. It was a colossal Otyren, twice the height of the two walking at its side and twice as wide. It wore black leather armour, gloves, boots and a white apron splattered with blood. Around its belt hung many rings, each holding a multitude of keys. They rattled as he shifted his great weight, the behemoth gazing into Asher's cell with beady black eyes.

'Welcome, Your Highness, to the Under Kitchen,' he sniggered, his deep voice overflowing with malicious intent. 'I am the warden of this realm, the king under the castle. Down here, my word is law, and my law will be enforced. Break any of my laws, and you will be punished severely. Behave yourself, and I will be... rewarded.' His wide mouth grew into a sickening grin. 'Do you fight?'

Asher said nothing but stared at the hulking figure.

'Well, if you don't, you best learn fast. Winners survive down here. Losers do not.' Without looking, he pulled a single key from the metal horde on his belt and unlocked the cell door. Two guards squeezed past and entered. 'Now, don't go making any inconveniences for us, or that will count as an instant defeat. That would not be good for you.'

The two guards shoved Asher out of the cell into the passageway. He looked up at the giant Otyren, at the black eyes and obnoxious grin across his broad face. The stench was terrible. It was a horrific mixture of blood, and what Asher could only guess were voided bowels.

'Leave him alone!' cried the voice from the shadows opposite Asher's cell. 'He's just got here. Give him time to rest!'

The warden slammed a colossal fist into the bars, denting them and sending a deafening wave of crashing metal echoing around the passage. 'Shut it, thief! You're lucky we're not in the habit of killing unborn cubs, or you'd be fighting, too. Now, one more word, and you'll spend the night in the guards' quarters!' Silence hung in the air, a silence only broken by the crackle of torches and the metallic echoes fading out of existence. 'That's what I thought,' he said, returning his paw to his side. 'Now, Your Highness, after you.' He gestured for Asher to walk.

The guards didn't give Asher much of a chance as one shoved him forwards. Stumbling, he began trudging down the passageway, the sound of heavy footsteps and jangling keys following close behind. He could feel the titanic Otyren's hot breath on his neck from several paces away, smelling like rotten meat and stale blood.

Asher peered into the cells he passed and found Rabbethi, only Rabbethi, all battered and beaten. His kind wasn't welcome in the city, so they couldn't be criminals.

'They're slaves,' he breathed.

'Livestock,' corrected the warden. 'Took them from right under your father's tiny nose. He should have paid more attention to his borders and the poor little bunnies that lived there. The forest can be a dangerous place.' He chuckled a deep and sinister belly laugh, and it took everything within Asher not to rise to it. The fire inside burned with fury, but he clenched his fists tight and pushed it down.

A frail, skittish voice floated over the ruckus from one of the cells. 'P-please, sir. Is th-there any more? I-I've been good and won my fights, haven't I? Please, sir, please...'

Asher looked into the cell and found a scraggly old Rabbethi, his white face pressed up to the bars, one eye black and bruised. His gaze was fixed on the warden, a look of desperation deep across his broken face.

'Shut it,' the warden ordered. 'You'll get more when you win. Now back with you!'

The Rabbethi jumped away from the bars and scurried into the shadows.

'What are you giving them?' Asher asked, not taking his eyes off the figure.

'River Jade. Those above get a little kick out of it, but it sure does make you bunnies go nuts.' He snorted as if remembering a funny joke and shoved Asher towards another dark, damp passage.

More cells flanked the entire length. These contained more beaten and bruised Rabbethi, though some appeared more muscular than others, their ears tied together in the traditional topknot of warriors.

Soldiers, Asher realised.

One stood close to the bars of his cell, head bowed, his light brown fur shining in the torchlight. As the escort passed, the warrior snapped an arm through the bar with incredible speed and clasped a guard by the throat. He pulled the Otyren into the bars with a thunderous clang, knocking him out. The other guard charged forwards, thrusting a trident through the bars. The prisoner stepped to the side, grabbed the shaft of the trident and kicked the guard through the bars directly in the face. There was a sickening crack as the Otyren's head snapped around further than it should have. Blood and teeth sprayed everywhere, coating Asher's tunic. The guard dropped to the floor dead. The prisoner slowly brought his leg back through the bars and placed it on the ground with precise control, gripping his newly acquired trident tight in one paw, the butt resting against the stone floor.

The warden let out a deep sigh. 'That's the fourth guard this month, Osgar,' he said, unimpressed. Then, with the tone of a disappointed father, 'Give me back the trident.'

'Come and get it,' Osgar sneered, glaring back at the warden, his hazel eyes willing the warden to try.

Osgar, Asher repeated in his mind, the name so familiar to him.

All of a sudden, a large webbed paw wrapped around Asher's skull, and before he knew it, he was yanked backwards into the arms of the warden. 'Give back the trident, or I'll crush your king's head.' He began to squeeze.

Asher grunted in pain as he felt the warden's colossal strength bear down on his skull.

Osgar looked at Asher, and his eyes went wide. 'No...,' he breathed. 'It can't be...'

'Tell him, little king,' the warden ordered, tightening his grip. 'Tell him who you are before I turn your head into carrot soup.'

'My name is Asher!' Asher screamed as quickly as his lips could. 'My father was King Hengist, and my mother was Queen Aethel!'

'You see?' the warden said, looking at Osgar. 'Just look at that *beautiful* patch of fur.'

Osgar looked at Asher in disbelief, then down to the trident in his paw. Asher screamed again as the warden's claws broke the skin around his head, and Osgar tossed the trident through the metal bars. It fell to the stone floor with a clatter. With a wicked grin, the huge Otyren released Asher's skull from his grip. Asher dropped to his knees and grasped at his head, begging the throbbing pain to stop.

'See? That wasn't so hard, was it?' the warden said as he slung the dead guard over one shoulder and the unconscious guard over the other. 'Now, I'm going to take His Highness to see the champion. Throw him in at the deep end, so to speak.'

'No!' Osgar cried. 'He—'

'Don't worry,' the warden interrupted in a condescending tone. 'If he's anything like his old man, he'll be fine.' He lifted Asher to his feet and shoved him forwards. 'I'll deal with you later, Osgar.'

They continued down the passageway, leaving the wide-eyed and dumbfounded Osgar behind. Heavy footsteps and jangling keys were ever-present behind Asher, as was the hot breeze on the back of his neck. Whispers and murmurs began to echo from the other cells. Their hushed voices bounced off the walls, audible over the rattling keys and crackling torches that flickered in the darkness.

'It's the king...'

'I thought he was dead?'

'What's he doing here?'

'Is he going to save us?'

'There's still hope.'

'But he's been captured.'

'If he loses, all hope is lost.'

'He'll get eaten for sure.'

Those last words stuck in Asher's mind. Eaten? Have the Otyren been kidnapping people to *eat* them? The idea terrified him. The Otyren people have only ever been interested in fish and vegetables. So who? Before he could ponder these questions further, he was face to face with a large iron door, from which emanated a chorus of cheering squeaks and curses.

'I've got a little secret.' The warden grinned. 'Just don't tell anybody upstairs, yeah?'

Asher nodded cautiously, not turning from the door. A huge fist glided past his ears and pushed the door open.

'I like to watch you bunnies fight.'

Inside was a wide square chamber devoid of decorations but full of Otyren guards. They all shouted and jeered towards the centre of the room, where two taller figures circled each other in frantic steps, throwing limbs at one another in hopes of landing a blow. It was a sight Asher was very familiar with, back in the boxing rings of White Cliffe, although he was used to far fewer Otyren. A simple door lay on the opposite wall, beside which stood a hooded figure. They were taller than the guards around but without any other discernible features that Asher could see. It appeared to be watching the centre of the room, where guards were crowding and throwing both words of hatred and encouragement. Asher's first thought was that they were another Muuraki assassin, come to drag him back to Constance. No, their bearing was wrong. Whoever this was, it was something else entirely.

The crowd grew quiet, parting as the warden pushed Asher forwards towards a circle of sand. Asher gazed down at the scowling faces. Some began pointing and exchanging what looked like gold coins. Others joined in, and before long, a whole cacophony of bets were being squeaked towards a few individuals, who did everything in their power to keep track of the gold shoved into their tiny webbed paws. They scribbled notes on small pieces of parchment and gave them to nearby individuals.

Within the ring were two Rabbethi in ragged beige tunics splattered with dirt and blood. One was tall and lean with brown fur, the other shorter and stockier with black fur speckled grey. They were both exhausted and caked in blood, neither one able to admit defeat, knowing what was on the line. The stocky one charged, wrapping his arms around his opponent's waist and slamming him to the ground. The taller one thrashed but to no avail. Too late did he see the fist descending towards his face, and with a mighty thump, he was unconscious, blood trickling from his still nose to the sand beneath. The winner scrambled away and stared at the unconscious Rabbethi. Tears began crawling down his cheeks as he placed his face into his bloody paws.

'I'm sorry,' he sobbed as two guards approached. They dragged him to his feet and pushed him through the crowd towards Asher and the warden. A mixture of cheers and boos echoed all around as gold moved between paws.

'Well done, Byrnstan!' The warden laughed. 'You get to live another day. And what a fight! You'll get an extra chunk of bread tonight. I'll even throw in some River Jade. You've earned it.'

The Rabbethi said nothing but stared at the floor as he was led out of the chamber, a solemn trail of apologies haunting his steps.

The warden turned his attention to the unconscious Rabbethi in the ring. 'Get him to my table before he wakes up. He'll be in the next shipment.' Three guards approached the Rabbethi and carried him through the crowd towards the door on the opposite wall. With two heavy thuds, the warden dropped the guards from his shoulders to the floor. 'Now then!' he proclaimed, addressing the room. 'It is time for our newest guest to earn his right to live!'

A cheer erupted from the sea of guards.

'I give you our honoured guest, King Asher of Rabbethia!'

With that, he shoved Asher into the ring. Asher stumbled forwards, sand spraying around his feet. Looking out over the sea of black eyes staring back at him, he found nothing but scowls, with some spitting at the ground when they made eye contact.

The warden continued, 'And as a royal welcome, he will fight our fabled champion!'

At this, the hooded figure pushed himself from the wall and marched towards the ring, shoving aside any guard that didn't move in time. The warden leaned close, placed a heavy webbed paw onto Asher's shoulder and spoke directly into one of his ears. Asher held his breath against the putrid hot air.

'We picked this one up near the Outer Rim, trying to sneak through the border, a fugitive from a mine in Irohell. Cruelly taken from his family as a child, he's had a certain... resentment for the royal family. Have fun...' He chuckled as he stepped away, backing out of the ring.

The mysterious figure stepped into the ring and faced Asher, raising two muscular black paws to his hood and pulling it down onto his broad shoulders. Two long ears sprung upright as the hood settled. He was a Rabbethi, fur filthy and wiry, piercing blue eyes full of violent intensity, hatred and malice. Two large jagged teeth protruded down from the upper lip, purposefully chipped to give them a serrated edge. Asher winced as he looked at them, instinctively touching his tongue to his own teeth. Then he noticed markings on the Rabbethi's forehead—three vertical lines burned into the flesh, leaving behind pink scars on the skin where fur no longer grew.

'A Third Son...,' Asher breathed.

'Yes,' the warden confirmed. 'And he wants justice.'

23

Flowers and Death

Asher fell to the floor, his cheek split from the Third Son's fist. He spat blood into the sand as he pushed himself to his knees.

'Get up, you royal prick!' the Third Son yelled, his voice bubbling with hatred.

The troubled Rabbethi was faster than Asher had anticipated. His hesitation after seeing the man's scars across his forehead slowed his reactions, dulling the fight in his heart. He slowly brought himself to his feet and wiped the blood from his cheek, crimson red staining the white fur on his forearm. The Third Son paced back and forth like a caged boar, not taking his eyes off Asher.

'I'm sorry about what you've been through,' Asher said with genuine sympathy. 'But I can't die here. There's more at stake than your vengeance.' He raised his fists and began bouncing on the balls of his feet, remembering his days in the fighting ring and his training sessions with Luce.

Luce.

The fear that her closeness to him had all been a ploy to earn his trust filled his very being with dread, numbing his will to survive. His mind urged him to keep going, screamed at him to keep fighting. He had to win—for the sake of his kingdom, for his people suffering under the Shangari scourge, Mia's memory.

But there was something else holding him back. He had no real desire to fight this man. He felt sorry for him, for the life he was forced to live, all because his family had one child too many. It wasn't fair, and Asher knew it. It also wasn't fair, however, that *he* was the target of this man's rage despite not having a single say in the kingdom's laws. He looked into the Third Son's hateful eyes.

The fight refused to rise in his heart, the familiar fire refusing to burn, no matter how much he willed it.

'Typical royal shit,' the Third Son spat. 'You don't give a shit about us, the forgotten, the stolen. You just... don't... care!' He charged, unleashing a flurry of reckless attacks at Asher's face and gut.

Asher was ready, ducking, weaving away from the blows, and blocking those he couldn't dodge. One fist hurtled at his left cheek, and he managed to grasp onto the forearm, pulling the Third Son close. He headbutted the raging Rabbethi square between the eyes. Luce had taught him that. The impact shook his skull, and spots danced in his vision. It quickly cleared, and he saw the Third Son stumbling backwards, dazed as he brought his paw to his forehead. A small stream of blood trickled down his nose.

Asher pressed the attack.

He leapt forwards and brought his fist down into the side of the Rabbethi's temple, sending him spinning to the floor. A spray of sand and the Third Son rolled across the floor, popping back onto his feet. Squeaks and squeals of approval erupted around the Otyren guards as Asher raised his fists and moved in, carefully analysing the Third Son for any signs of weakness.

He noticed something strange.

The Third Son's breaths were becoming shorter and sharper as the fight progressed. Thick wads of saliva started to froth from the corners of his snarling mouth. Asher stared, worried about what was becoming of the crazed Rabbethi. The cheering guards seemed unaware or unfazed, their cries for blood unrelenting. Asher glanced back over his shoulder at the warden, who did nothing but smile, a smug, knowing look in his beady black eyes.

Rushing footsteps made Asher turn just in time to see a pair of large, jagged teeth hurtling straight for his face. He narrowly stepped to the side as the Third Son collided with an unfortunate guard standing on the edge of the ring. The Otyren's eyes went wide as the teeth punctured deep into his throat. The guard's gurgled scream was cut short as the rabid Rabbethi ripped his teeth free, blood spraying in all directions, coating those nearby as they scrambled away, screaming.

He then turned to Asher.

There was something new in his eyes, something wild. They no longer stared at Asher with just hatred but were now filled with a manic craze devoid of any semblance of rational thinking. He had become a wild beast, relentless in his quest for blood and death, and his eyes were set on Asher.

'Oh shit...,' Asher breathed, backing away.

The Third Son dropped the Otyren. The body crumpled into a pool of its own blood with a heavy splash. The crazed Rabbethi then began taking slow, heavy steps towards Asher, blood dripping from his teeth, foam frothing from his mouth. Seeing the red around his mouth—a Rabbethi's mouth—was unnatural, sickening even, and Asher's stomach churned like a storm at the sight. The Third Son's eyes were unblinking, unmoving, never losing focus on Asher, his prey. His head twitched sporadically. It was as if each jerk was caused by a caged animal smashing itself against the bars of his mind. He re-entered the ring, and Asher prepared himself for whatever came next.

The rabid Rabbethi leapt forwards, covering the distance of the ring in a fraction of a second. His fist raced towards Asher's face. Asher just managed to bring his forearms together to block it, and a terrible pain pulsed throughout his arms. He skidded backwards, his large feet burning as the sand became hot beneath him. Guards pushed and prodded at his back, demanding he fight, their high-pitched squeaks piercing his ears.

His crazed opponent was on him again, reaching for his chest with an open paw. Asher stepped aside and watched as the outstretched fingers connected with one of the guards poking at Asher's back. Terror consumed the Otyren as he was pulled into the ring and immediately thrown out of it, sailing over the crowd and landing with an echoing clatter and chorus of angry squeaks. The Third Son turned. The foam within his mouth had turned a dark red, and his breaths were now heavy and lumbering. One eye began to sag. The other was focused on Asher, rage still burning within.

'By Folka...,' Asher breathed. The fire in his chest remained a simmering ember, unwilling to rage against a man with so much injustice in his life. Asher was now responsible for him, responsible for all those like him, brandished as unwanted, sent away to a life of gruelling hardship. Despite the pain and death this Rabbethi had likely caused, Asher could only feel sorry for him.

The Third Son lunged with a sudden flash of speed, grabbing Asher by the tunic and throwing him hard to the ground. The wind left Asher's lungs as his back thudded against the compacted sand. Before he could think, the Third Son was on him, straddling him and raining down a storm of fists. Asher blocked and dodged the best he could, landing a few of his own against the Rabbethi's chest and face, but it did little to deter the savage assault. Jagged front teeth dripped with blood, ready to puncture Asher's throat. He closed his eyes as he strained against the hatred pressing down upon him, drawing closer and closer.

'I'm sorry,' he breathed as the crowd grew quiet.

The force against him eased.

Wet and sticky droplets patted Asher's face, and he opened his eyes. The manic Rabbethi was frozen, a rasping, bloody statue with droplets of his foaming mouth dripping onto Asher's face. Both eyes wandered around their sockets with no sense of direction or purpose, the anger behind them having vanished. What was left was an emptiness. The Third Son released one final lingering breath and collapsed to Asher's side, the foam in his mouth black and thick as mud. The crowd remained silent, their eyes fixed on the Third Son.

He was dead.

Exhausted, Asher pushed himself to his feet and looked down at the body, at the pain in the Rabbethi's wide eyes and the three lines seared into his forehead.

Did they all feel this way, so full of hatred? Asher couldn't imagine a world in which they wouldn't, and he was disappointed in himself for only now realising how much pain his ignorance had caused. Staring down at the body of this nameless Rabbethi, he promised he would fix it. Crouching down, he closed the Third Son's eyes.

'I'm sorry.'

Lumbering footsteps echoed behind him, and he soon felt an overbearing presence at his back. 'I told that little shit to go easy on the Jade,' the warden said with a disgruntled huff. 'He was only supposed to rough you up. Upstairs would not have been pleased if you had bitten it on your first day.' He then grabbed Asher's bloody paw and yanked it high into the air, parading around the ring in a broad circle. 'We have our winner!' he boomed. 'Our champion is no more, and the young king survives his first day!'

An explosion of cheers, boos and high-pitched squeaks erupted around the chamber as individuals gave out webbed paws full of gold. The warden dropped Asher's paw and shoved him out of the ring. They headed towards the door they had entered from, the crowd of chattering guards parting as they approached.

'Take the body to my table. He'll probably taste rotten, so he'll go in with the cheaper cuts,' the titanic Otyren ordered the crowd.

Asher said nothing. Physically drained and emotionally exhausted, all he could do was walk, the hot breath of the warden at his back once more. They passed through into the passages lined with endless prison cells. Whispers and murmurs echoed from the shadows, tracking their movement.

'He survived! He beat the champion.'

'Maybe he will save us?'

'Don't be stupid. He's trapped in here like the rest of us.'

'Who do you think he'll fight next?'

'Shut it!' roared the warden, and the voices instantly ceased, the passage falling into utter silence, save for the crackle of torches.

They reached Osgar's cell and stopped. The warden leaned over, resting a massive forearm against the metal bars. 'Your men did well today, Osgar. Well, one of them did.' A wicked grin grew across his face. Hay shifted from the corner of the cell. 'I'm rewarding him with a special treat tonight. Make sure he doesn't eat it all in one go, will you?' Some time passed without a response before the warden stepped back, sighing. 'If he turns rabid, that's on you.' He then placed a huge webbed paw against Asher's back and shoved him onwards.

Asher's cell was open when they arrived. He stepped inside before the warden could throw him in, and the great Otyren slammed the door shut. Asher was caged once more.

'Well done out there, Your Highness,' the warden mocked as he returned the keys to his belt.

Asher didn't turn. He didn't want to give him the satisfaction of an acknowledgement.

'Didn't think you had it in you. I've given you a little present, a prize for beating our champion. Rest up now.' He chuckled as he returned down the passage, disappearing from sight.

Asher waited for the last echoes of rattling keys to fade before turning to the new items in his cell, a collection of beautiful flowers strewn about the hay pile. They were tulip-shaped and featured a tall yellow pistil emerging from an array of deep green petals, reminding Asher of a precious stone.

Jade.

He limped to the flowers. His muscles were starting to ache, the numbing adrenaline of the fight rapidly leaving his body. With a wince of pain, he scooped up the flowers and inspected the petals. They were beautiful, the smell hypnotic and strangely familiar.

A flash of memories rushed into his mind, a vision of a grand library seen through an ornate keyhole. He saw his father at a desk, tired and frustrated, hunched over a scattering of scrolls and surrounded by towers of old books. The old king moved the papers aside with agitated huffs and mumbling slurs. In one corner, haphazardly placed as if dropped from the high ceiling, was a wide unmade bed, beside which were strewn more dusty scrolls. On the floor at the foot of the bed stood a decorated ceramic pot full of delicately arranged green flowers—flowers gifted by the high priestess.

'That bitch...,' he breathed in disbelief. 'That conniving little witch!'

He stormed over to the bucket in the corner of his cell and threw the flowers into the sludgy liquid. They landed with a splat before sinking beneath the thick brown surface. Asher watched as they disappeared, a fresh wave of hatred taking hold. Who knows how much of this could have been avoided if Constance hadn't poisoned his father's mind with lies and concoctions. He closed his eyes and breathed deeply, knowing his rage would do him no good until he could leave this place.

'I'm glad you survived,' a soft voice said from the cell opposite.

He opened his eyes, turning. He stepped from the shadows and leaned against the bars.

'You're hurt,' the stranger said in a worried tone.

'I'm okay,' Asher lied, thankful someone seemed to care for his well-being.

'Did you kill him? That psycho Rabbethi?'

'He wasn't a psycho,' Asher snapped, surprising himself. 'He was just... mistreated. And no, I didn't kill him. He just... dropped dead.'

'Well, at least you don't have his blood on your paws,' the voice said solemnly.

'Yeah...,' Asher breathed.

But he did have blood on his paws. He had the blood of all those children taken from their families. He could have stood up for them and persuaded his father to do something about the laws, but he always pushed the thoughts aside, convincing himself that it was a necessary evil, that running the kingdom wasn't his concern. What he saw in the Rabbethi's eyes told him otherwise—the anger, the rage, the lengths he went through to get vengeance. Asher now knew how much these people were suffering. He slumped to the floor, resting his back against the cold metal bars. It wasn't fair.

'Maybe Constance is right,' he whispered. 'Maybe peace is better than freedom.'

'Did you say Constance?' the stranger asked, her curiosity piqued.

'Do you know her?' Asher asked, surprised at how good her hearing was.

'You could say that...'

Asher rose to his feet and turned to her cell. 'So you know about her plans? About the relics and the coffin beneath White Cliffe?'

The stranger sighed. 'I know about all of it. It's kind of why I'm in this lovely cell. I learned that one of the relics was here in Otyrheim. I asked one too many questions, and they threw me down here.'

'Are you one of her acolytes? A spy or something?' Asher asked, unable to hide the mistrust creeping into his voice.

'No,' the voice said thoughtfully. 'I'm much worse. You don't have to worry, though. I'm not working for her or anything.' She paused as her breaths became shorter, the signs of agitation rising in her voice. 'I can't let the relic fall into that woman's awful paws. If she gains the Shepherd's power... none of us will be free ever again.'

There was a long silence as both prisoners contemplated the severity of their shared mission.

'How do *you* know about all this?' the stranger asked. 'And who even are you? Your name's Asher, and I heard the warden call you "Your Highness," but that's a joke, right?'

Asher hesitated for a moment, unsure whether he could trust this disembodied voice. The fact that she was locked up like him meant she was no friend of the Otyren, and they wouldn't throw an acolyte in jail, lest they invoke Constance's wrath.

With a tired sigh, he said, 'I *am* Prince Asher—well, king now. I need the bow to take my kingdom back from Constance and the church. It's mine by birthright.' He realised this was the first time he had said the plan aloud.

It sounded ridiculous.

'Oh,' the woman said, surprised. 'If that's true, shouldn't you be raising your army or something? How did you end up here?'

'How long have you got?' Asher scoffed, a slight smile forming across his bruised face.

'I think I'll be here long enough for a story.'

Asher lowered himself back to the floor and began recounting his journey, pausing briefly when thoughts and visions of those close to him crossed his mind.

'Cara sounds like a formidable warrior,' the woman said at Asher's retelling of the battle with the knight.

'She is,' Asher replied, a pit growing in his stomach.

The voice grew silent when Asher mentioned Marius and described their voyage to Ignimarum aboard the nimble *Silvi*.

'Are you there?' he asked, thinking she might have nodded off or lost interest.

'Yeah. It's just... I've always wanted to go to Ignimarum. I've heard it's beautiful.'

'It is.' Asher smiled, thinking back to the tiered city and the beautiful chaos of its many sloping streets.

'I'm sorry your friend did that,' the voice said after Asher described his capture within the Allthing chamber. 'I'm sure she had her reasons.'

'I hope so,' he replied, struggling to think of any. 'It was a stupid plan to start with. There was no way they would just give me the bow.'

'It really wasn't a great plan,' she said with a chuckle.

Asher winced as his bruised cheeks crinkled into a smile. 'I'm sorry, I haven't asked your name,' he said with a sudden realisation. 'And what *are* you to Constance?'

Hay rustled against the stone floor as the stranger's shape rose and stepped towards the metal bars. Out of the shadows walked a beautiful white-furred Vulpen. Her face was kind and soft, and her bushy white tail flowed gracefully behind her. From beneath her dirty beige dress, Asher could see the unmistakable bump of an unborn cub. The mysterious woman smiled and met his eyes with a light green gaze.

'My name is Silvana, and Constance is my mother.'

24

A Thief in Red

'I think I'll give that a miss,' Cara dismissed as she neatly laid a beautiful red stola dress over the chair by the dresser. The chain of her new necklace rubbed against her neck as she moved. She hated necklaces. They were just tools for strangling, thoughtfully provided by the victim before the kill.

After Asher's arrest, she had been granted a modest chamber within the Delegations Tower, one of the smaller towers of the castle. Marius had remained onboard *The Silvi*, waiting for further orders. She didn't feel too guilty leaving the Vulpen captain aboard the cramped quarters of his precious vessel, as he quickly made friends with the Otyren dock workers, with whom he now spent the day drinking and playing Foxtail's Bluff. Like most games, Cara had no idea how to play. She had left them to it, gathered her belongings and climbed the many steps of the narrow tower to her designated room, where a heavily perfumed ball invitation was waiting for her, placed on a luxurious double bed. Beside it lay a beautiful long-sleeved red dress.

She ignored the invitation and spent the next few days exploring areas of the castle, searching for any sign of Folka's Bow and pretending to be lost if guards grew suspicious of her. With no luck inside the castle, she turned her attention to outside the keep. She wandered among the people of the inner walls, eavesdropping on conversations while attempting to seem inconspicuous, which was difficult considering she stood a good couple of feet taller than most around her. The Ruadrae that had waved so enthusiastically at Asher was gone, and a generic jewellery stand identical to the others around it had replaced his homely-scented soup stall.

I'm so sorry, Asher, she thought as she made for one of the shops. Rehearsed apologies swirled around her mind like a tempest of guilt. No matter how many she manifested, they couldn't dislodge Asher's face from her thoughts, the look of utter betrayal crossing his confused, innocent face. She had done as ordered by her queen.

She had no choice.

After flashing her iron sigil, a well-dressed Vulpen trader pointed Cara to a black tower standing tall among the buildings of the outer banks.

'Th-that's where the scholars live, miss. Best ask them about old things. Though they might n-not be so kind as to give you answers.' The trader then hurried back to his wares, waiting for the intimidating agent to leave him alone.

Cara looked down towards the structure. A black tower with a considerable fire burning at its height in a blatant imitation of the Great Lighthouse.

She thanked the trader and made her way through the open gatehouse, crossing the wide bridge over the castle walls towards the northern outer bank. The arched bridge rose high above the curving river and had only a short stone wall to prevent anyone from plummeting into the busy waterway. Many Otyren citizens passed by, gracing Cara with the briefest of glances, uninterested in yet another Vulpen agent in their city.

The water below heaved with vessels, fighting for a space along the wooden docks lining the outer riverbanks. Hordes of sailors loaded and unloaded crates from docked vessels into wagons while the captains perused the market stands, resupplying their ships for the next voyage. From such a height, they looked as small as ants. As Cara descended towards the opposing gatehouse, their faces became clearer and excited squeaks began to fill her pointed ears.

She passed through the gatehouse and entered a bustling cobble street humming with activity. Horses and cattle pulled wagons full of produce and unhappy livestock in all directions, the angry cries of chickens and pigs mixing with a cacophony of hurried citizens. The scent of the beast's excrement assaulted Cara's nostrils, though she preferred it to the scented concoctions those within the castle applied to their bodies. It was as busy a city as she had ever seen, more so than even Ignimarum.

She found the tower rising above the rooftops and began navigating through the dense crowd, careful to avoid the lumbering wheels of carts while also steering clear of what she assumed was horse manure. The fire at the tower's summit peeked over the rooftops, guiding her like a lighthouse.

She eventually entered a wide grassy plaza after passing down narrow street after narrow street. The cobblestone path wrapped around the border and continued at each corner, disappearing back into the winding maze of tall city buildings. At the plaza's centre stood a tall cylindrical stone tower. It rose above the surrounding city and featured no visible windows up its smooth black walls. A single path led to a small wooden door at its base. Numerous elderly Otyren, each garbed in deep-blue robes trimmed with gold thread, conversed among themselves by the open door, unaware of the approaching Vulpen agent.

'Excuse me,' Cara said in her most polite voice.

'Ah, what? No!' exclaimed one of the Otyren scholars with a squeak. The others escaped through the door, shutting it behind him. Realising he was trapped, the remaining scholar turned to Cara with a nervous smile. 'Erm... can I help you?'

'I'd like to look inside your tower, if I may?' Cara asked with as friendly a smile as she could muster. 'I've been sent here on behalf of Jarl Vatn as part of an information exchange with the Vulpen Queendom.'

The elderly Otyren eyed her up and down with his beady black eyes, confidence manifesting in his posture at the mention of the jarl. 'If this is some cheap trick, you can forget it!' he exclaimed as he reached for the door. 'Your feminine charm won't sway me, no, no!'

'Wait!' Cara exclaimed, chasing after. 'Please, the queendom would greatly appreciate any information about the relics. Folka's Bow, for example. It is a subject of great scholarly interest to Her Highness.'

The shuffling scholar opened the miniature door without acknowledging Cara's pleas and scurried through. Just as the door was about to close, his small round head poked through the gap, whiskers brushing against the wood. His face was twisted in a pompous scowl.

'Tell Jarl Vatn he'll have the bow by the young master's party as promised,' he declared, now under the protection of the wooden door. 'Not before so he can show off to one of his... female companions. Sending pretty hussies like you will do nothing to speed the process!'

There was a brief pause as Cara considered this.

'You think I'm pretty?' she asked with an alluring smile—something she detested doing. Sometimes, though, the job called for it.

The old Otyren's cheeks blushed noticeably beneath his grey-speckled fur before slamming the door.

'Dammit,' Cara sighed. She turned and began making her way back towards the castle. 'I guess I'm going to a party.'

***

Cara shifted uncomfortably in the castle's entrance hall among a sea of wealthy, aristocratic Otyren, listening to the drivel of Jarlskona Hafdal. Her fifth son, as it turns out, had just married the second eldest daughter of the Grotsvik family. Cara pulled against the tightness of her long sleeves as she raised a glass of wine to her lips. There was no doubt in her mind that a certain round jarl had carefully selected her deep-red dress to accentuate her feminine features. However, it was clear that breathing was not the seamstress's top priority. A narrow gap in the lower back allowed her long, bushy tail to flow free behind, and it followed her like a red-and-white shadow. She did feel pretty, but the lustful looks she received from the more senior members of the party made her skin crawl and her fur bristle with unease.

They wouldn't be so brazen if I had my blade, she lamented, feeling the emptiness at her hip where her long curved blade usually rested. Her invitation had stated in elegant gold ink that no weapons were permitted at Jarl E. Vatn Jr.'s Birthday Ball. Although she had reluctantly obliged the request, she was able to sneak in a concealed dagger strapped tight to her inner thigh. It eased the parting of her sword but didn't stop the longing for her leather armour and the cold embrace of the shadows.

Jarlskona Hafdal spoke with exuberance as she waved a webbed paw in dramatic motions, clearly attempting to show off her new gold band that dangled loose around her forearm. The band was thick and encrusted with many emeralds around its rim.

She's going to knock somebody out with that thing if she's not careful, Cara thought as she smiled down at the middle-aged Otyren. She raised her glass to her lips once more, her two silver rings clattering against the stem of the glass as her dress strained against her back's toned muscles.

After what seemed like an age, Jarlskona Hafdal excused herself from the conversation. Cara took the opportunity to escape, moving briskly to the balcony overlooking the model city before anyone else could boast about one of their unimpressive offspring. She leaned against the stone railing and looked down at the sea of Otyren nobility mingling among the miniature buildings of the marble city. No pebbles were out on display tonight. Cara had learned it was considered uncouth to flash one's pebbles at a formal gathering. Jewellery so hefty it could kill a Medvedian was fine, but a shiny stone? Absolutely not. Even having their pouches dangling at their side at these events was considered risqué by the more elderly nobles.

What a ridiculous people, Cara thought as she scanned the spoilt crowd before her. This was not her usual type of assignment. She longed for the more straightforward task of assassinating a Medvedian chieftain. It would have been easier and much more enjoyable.

'You look like you're up for some fun,' came a voice that slithered into her ear like a worm.

Rolling her eyes at the exchange about to happen, she turned to see a handsome white-furred Vulpen man dressed in fine black clothes trimmed with delicate red thread. He had a slimy smirk across his canine face. Perfume oozed from him like a noxious gas, threatening to knock Cara unconscious, and as her eyes met his, he winked.

'You're not my type,' she said, unimpressed, turning back to face the crowd below.

'Oh, I beg to differ,' the young man said, undeterred. 'I could treat you to a passionate night of pleasure and treat you like a princess afterwards. I'm one of the nice guys, you see. I could keep you safe from the assholes out there.' He gestured to the crowd below before shuffling closer. Cara stifled a gag at the obnoxious scent. 'What is your type anyway? Red fur? Black f—'

Cara placed her glass on the railing, then, quick as a flash, she clamped a paw over his member and squeezed. The man's yelp was cut short as her other paw wrapped around his snout.

'This is *not* my type,' she spat through gritted teeth, leaning towards his ear. 'Good guys with small pricks are not my type.' She squeezed a little harder. The man whimpered, his eyes staring at Cara in fear and regret. Cara stared back. 'The women you "protect" aren't as helpless as you think. Understood?'

The Vulpen man nodded as far as Cara's paws allowed.

She smirked. 'Good. Now, *back off*.'

She released her grip around his snout and removed her paw from his crotch. The man fought hard not to double over before staggering away, his once proud tail tucked firmly between his legs. Cara watched him descend the stairs, a smirk across her snout as he rejoined his friends, who seemed to have enjoyed his failed attempt at seduction.

With a heavy groan, the giant golden doors behind her heaved open. All eyes fell upon the rotund figure of Jarl Vatn standing proud between the open doors.

'Honoured guests!' he bellowed. 'It is with great pleasure that I welcome you to my son Erik's birthday ball!' The crowd cheered and squeaked as they raised their glasses in approval. Jarl Vatn raised his webbed paws to quieten the crowd. 'Now, as some of you may know, my son is an eager reveller, and so he has... begun the festivities early. Please place any gifts you may have for him in front of his chair, and we will ensure he is made aware of who has gifted what. Thank you.'

Hushed murmurs and a chorus of stifled laughter floated over the crowd.

Jarl Vatn scanned the hall, a smirk growing across his face. 'As an additional treat for you, our most loyal guests, we have brought a most holy relic out of the vaults for one night only.'

Cara's ears pricked up at this, as did most of the people around her, who were unaware of such an addition to the night.

'When the Rabbethi scourge robbed us of our land and slaughtered our people, we took from them a mighty weapon. A weapon so powerful, it cannot be wielded by mere mortals!' He gazed upon the crowd, smiling with smug amusement at the air of wonder and amazement he had created. The jarl stepped aside and gestured to the centre of the Allthing chamber beyond. 'I present to you the Bow of Folka!'

All present surged towards the golden doors, eager to see the fabled artefact. Cara joined the torrent of short, squeaking nobles and was swept inside.

'Ah!' Jarl Vatn exclaimed as he tiptoed through the guests. 'I must warn you all to keep your distance. The weapon contains some kind of internal heating system that'll burn the flesh right off your paws!' He let out an awkward chuckle to keep the mood light, but his tense demeanour implied he was not joking.

As Cara entered, gasps and whispers replaced the chorus of excited squeaks. A bow was in the centre of the wide tree stump table, positioned within the circular opening and placed upon a grand wooden stand. This, however, was not just any bow. This bow was exquisitely crafted with an inwards curve at its centre and made of polished oak that looked as if it was newly crafted despite its supposed age. What caught Cara's eye, however, was the clear gemstone at the bow's centre. It appeared lifeless and unassuming, but she knew the significance of it. It was a Shepherd Stone—a fragment of god's power. An expensive green cloth had been draped over the pedestal beneath it, looking like a waterfall of delicate moss.

Now, how do I get it?

Mingling resumed once most of the party had filtered through. Chattering voices echoed off the stone pillars as business deals were struck and the gossip of the wealthy was passed around the inner circles like children in a school field. A sophisticated melody poured from musicians stationed at one end of the chamber. The stench of over-applied perfumes assaulted her sensitive nose as Cara strolled around the table, avoiding eye contact with any who would attempt to spark a conversation. She glanced at the chamber's walls, noting the guard positions and possible doors she could slip through unnoticed.

An evening light bathed the chamber in a deep orange glow through the enormous arched windows. Beyond and far below, the river stretched away, falling into darkness as the forest's shadows grew long. An annoying itch began to scratch at her mind as she found the towers lining the river hadn't lit their beacons despite the growing darkness. They should have been lit. Not wanting to draw attention to the oddity and with it herself, she made a mental note and returned to the party.

A massive stack of linen-wrapped gifts sat tall on the table before Jarl Vatn's chair. As Cara deviated to escape an incoming conversation with Jarlskona Sundr, trumpeting snores from Jarl Vatn's chair caught her by surprise.

Well, let's have a look at you, birthday boy, she thought as she pushed aside a few of the gifts to get a better look at the future Jarl Vatn.

'No way,' she breathed.

Sat slumped in the grand chair was an unconscious young Otyren noble, his polished boots resting lazily on the table, an empty bottle in a brown-gloved paw. His shirt was a fine turquoise, and his trousers a pearly white. On his shirt, embroidered with fine yellow linen, was the image of a clam under which were two tridents crossed at the shaft. The clothes were new, but she recognised the face in an instant. It was Jarl Erik, *their* Jarl Erik, who had sailed with her and Asher from Rabbethia to Terravulpa.

'Happy birthday,' she said with a smile.

The rest of the evening was filled with wine, music and heated debates between jarls and foreign dignitaries. As the festivities drew to a close, guests bid farewell to Jarl Vatn and his unconscious son. Cara had spent much of her evening avoiding the verbal attacks of Jarlskona Hafdal—her emerald-encrusted band shining like a beacon to be avoided—all the while edging towards one of the chamber's side doors. Finally spotting a gap in the guard's patrol, she opened the door and slipped inside.

The room was small and lit by a single torch fastened to the wall. Tall shadows clung to the walls as stacks of wooden crates blocked the flickering light. It was a storage room and, by the smell of it, likely held refreshments for guests of a more carnivorous nature. It was perfect. She would hide within the shadows, wait for all the guests to leave and emerge in the dead of night. They wouldn't return the bow to the scholar's tower so late, so she'd have till morning to finish her task, and if she got caught, she'd feign drunkenness, an old but reliable trick made all the more potent by her beautiful but tight dress.

The sound of something wet caught her attention. She grabbed the torch off the wall, slowly reached under her dress and pulled the dagger from her thigh. Cautiously, she approached the sounds.

'Who's there?' she asked, raising the torch. The sounds stopped as she rounded a stack of crates. The young Vulpen man who had attempted to seduce her stood with his back to her, lauding over a smaller shape. He was unsteady, likely due to consuming too much of Jarl Vatn's private reserves. Cara sighed, her hiding spot now blown.

'Could you two not have picked a better…' Cara's words drifted as she looked past the drunk Vulpen towards the smaller shape.

Something long and thick was slumped on the floor around their feet, twitching and splashing in a pool of something crimson. She raised her torch, and her eyes went wide. There was another Vulpen, a young woman lying on the floor, eyes wide, not moving. She and the stone floor were soaked with blood. Cara's eyes snapped up to find bulging red eyes staring back at her over the Vulpen's shoulder. She raised her knife just as the Vulpen man crumpled to the floor in a sickening heap, blood oozing from a shredded wound in his neck. The figure lunged at Cara with claws outstretched as gnarled teeth raced towards her throat.

The pair burst through the door and slid across the marble floor. Cara collided with the grand table, her back slamming into one of the thick wooden roots. A sickening screech filled the room as her attacker halted their momentum, claws scratching against the smooth floor. The chamber fell silent after a chorus of gasps, the remaining guests staring in absolute horror. Nobody dared move. The guards around the chamber's edge shifted uncomfortably as they tightened the grips on their tridents. Under the Allthing chamber's flickering torchlight, the ragged figure rose to its feet, a Shangari in white acolyte robes drenched in Vulpen blood. It swayed as its bulging red eyes pierced Cara's very being, blood dripping from its long, blistered mouth. Its eyes darted to the bow behind Cara and back to her. She knew what it was after. It had the same plan as her but was rudely interrupted by Cara as it was having a late dinner. Where it had come from, though, was a mystery.

Bells suddenly began ringing across the city beyond the tall windows. One or two at first, and then at once, hundreds rang out in unison across the rooftops, followed by muted screams that murmured into the chamber through the glass. Cara looked to the Shangari. It stared back knowingly, a vicious grin growing across its face. Not taking her eyes off the gnarled creature, she bent down, brought the knife to the bottom of her dress and tore up the side, creating a slit that ran up her long muscular leg. The Shangari watched her every movement with eagerness, enjoying the tension before the plunge into battle. Cara stood straight and raised the blade towards her opponent, the unease continuing to fester as the bells and muffled cries echoed around them.

An Otyren soldier burst into the chamber through the open golden doors. She was panting heavily, her trusted trident gripped tight in one paw, dripping fresh blood. More was smeared across her golden-scaled armour.

'Shangari! They've come through the sewers!' She froze as she took in the scene before her.

Cara and the Shangari remained locked onto each other while the others stared at the soldier wide-eyed.

'Sh-Shangari! Shangari in the chamb—' Her cry was cut short as a serrated sword exploded from her chest. A spray of blood splattered to the floor before her as she gasped short, painful breaths, her eyes falling to the vicious blade. The Otyren guard dropped her trident to the floor with a clatter as the life left her body.

A low, sickening chuckle echoed around the chamber as the sword was wrenched free. A torrent of blood flowed from the open wound in the guard's chest, and she crumpled to the floor, dead. Emerging from the open door was the hulking, rotten shape of an enormous Shangari, his wiry black fur splattered red. Two long, serrated teeth dripped with blood from his upper jaw as his one red eye scanned the terrified nobles before him. The sound of clattering bones echoed in the chamber as he lumbered forwards.

Nin-Kilim, high chieftain of the Blood Tooths, had entered the castle.

Behind him, a host of Shangari warriors waited, blood dripping from their mouths, jagged weapons clenched tight in their long, bony fingers. Nin-Kilim's great weight pressed down upon the Otyren guard's skull, crushing it inside its helm. The sound made Cara's stomach churn. Nin-Kilim's bulging red eye landed on the bow before shifting to Cara. He chuckled again, the smile across his wretched face growing darker and more sinister. The Shangari joined with their master's laughter. The one opposing Cara turned to face her once more, his confidence renewed.

There was a sudden whistling sound as something travelled with great speed through the air. As the Shangari's red eyes locked onto Cara, its head snapped violently backwards, sending it flailing to the ground, Cara's dagger embedded right between its bulging red eyes. Without a second thought, Cara turned, leapt onto the table and made for the bow, her dress now torn around her muscular shoulders. Nin-Kilim released an ear-piercing screech, and the Shangari horde at his back surged into the room. The remaining guards dropped their tridents and ran for the doors lining the chamber, the panicked nobles following their lead. Some managed to make it through, but others were not so lucky.

With one swift movement, Cara leapt for the bow, grabbing it and the cloth as she flew across the table. An agonising, burning pain erupted between her paw and the relic. She cried out as she rolled awkwardly on the other side of the table, sliding off the edge to the floor in a heap. The smell of burnt flesh rose from her palm, but there was no time to stop. She wrapped the bow in the green cloth and made for a wooden door in the far corner. Nin-Kilim shrieked, and the entire room of Shangari converged on her, bounding at her on all fours with ferocious speed. She was a step ahead of them and threw open the door, leaping inside and slamming it behind her. A chorus of thuds echoed from beyond the thick wood. She could hear horrific screeches and cries as the Shangari scratched and hacked with all their might. It wouldn't be long before they realised it was a pull-only door. She sprinted down the stone stairwell before her, descending into the darkness beneath the castle.

'I'm coming,' she whispered through heavy breaths. 'I'm coming.'

25

Blood and Fire

Within the cold depths of the warden's realm, Asher was finding it increasingly difficult to determine the passage of time. Based on how often he had slept and been given bowls of slop, he assumed it had been a few days since his bout with the Third Son. An eruption of squeaks resonated down the passageways. Another fight for life or death had begun in the fighting ring. The echoes bounced off the stone floor, reverberating above the few crackling torches that lit the shadows beyond his cell. He was thankful the warden hadn't called on him to fight again.

He probably wants me rested and fighting at my best.

Asher's eyes drifted to his bucket in the corner, where a fresh batch of River Jade protruded from the muck like a grotesque bouquet. He shivered as his mind returned to the Third Son's empty eyes and frothing rage. He then thought about the other Rabbethi in the dungeon, those taken from the border and fed the green flowers to remain obedient or used for meat if they fell in the fighting ring. More captives had been brought in since Asher's arrival, their defeated forms shuffling by his cell as they marched deeper into the dingy depths. Their wide eyes, twitching noses and lack of trained physical fitness marked them as ordinary folk rather than warriors. Asher never saw them return. Not all captives were given a chance to fight, it seemed, and in a sick twist of fate, he was one of the lucky ones. It was heart-wrenching.

That night, or what Asher assumed was night, he awoke to faint whimpers and soft murmurs coming from Silvana's cell. He lifted his head from the straw and strained to listen. Her voice was soft as her whispers echoed off the walls.

He had been stunned after her declaration that she was Constance's daughter. He didn't know what to say. A stab of paranoia had sunk into his heart at the revelation, and he regretted everything he had told her about his journey and mission. She spoke of her journey to the Great Lighthouse and her confrontation with her mother at its peak, promising at the end that she had no love for Constance, no allegiance towards her. She had been just a small cub when she arrived at her home in the cold Outer Rim, with no memory of Constance or her life before. Looking around at the miserable place they found themselves in, Asher had found himself believing her.

She bolted upright. 'You killed him!' Her heavy panting permeated through the shadows.

Asher couldn't see her, but he heard hay rustling as she fully came to consciousness. He said nothing but listened to her rhythmic breathing. Eventually, she exhaled deeply and settled down on the loose hay. She was a good woman, Asher decided as he closed his eyes once more, given a rotten start in life but trying her best anyway. He couldn't help but wonder what nightmares haunted his Vulpen companion. A pit grew in his stomach. He knew there were likely more nightmares to come.

***

'Good morning, Your Highness!'

Asher awoke to an enormous shadow looming before his cell. It was the warden, his keys jangling as he shifted his gigantic weight. Asher peered with blurry vision at the huge Otyren and his two much smaller, fresh-faced guards. The warden grinned.

'Or is it evening? I guess that's the fun of my realm. You never know.' A low, rumbling chuckle emanated from his veiny throat.

Asher wiped the slumber sand from his eyes and propped himself up against the wall, not saying a word but staring blank-faced towards the huge Otyren.

'I have good news!' the warden exclaimed. 'I've arranged a fight, just for you, later today. Our dear friend Osgar and you will fight.' He threw into the cell a fresh bouquet of River Jades. They scattered across the floor of Asher's cell. 'You'll need these.' Without another word, the warden turned and began walking down the passageway, banging a heavy fist against each cell as he passed and waking every citizen of his domain.

Why do I recognise that name? Asher thought with growing frustration.

He looked at the flowers. Their beautiful green petals were a stark contrast to the filthy cell he currently called home. He gathered them up and marched to the bucket of foul-smelling sludge, the half-decayed stems of previous bouquets climbing from the liquid like rotten fingers, thin and wilting. He threw the fresh flowers deep into the muck.

'You might have needed those,' came Silvana's voice from her cell.

Asher turned and saw her leaning against her cell bars, eyeing the fresh bouquet in the bucket.

'I've heard Osgar is a mighty warrior.' Her green eyes rose to meet Asher's. 'Unless something happens, you best prepare yourself for the fight of your life. I know he'll... be...' Her voice trailed off as she slowly tilted her head to one side, her pointed ears twitching. 'Can you hear bells?'

Asher tilted his head and raised his tall ears. He *could* hear bells, a whole cacophony of them, faintly ringing somewhere above.

'I wonder what's happening,' he asked, curious. He guessed there was a festival or some Otyren noble had just gotten married.

A door swung open from somewhere deep within the dungeon. It was then quickly slammed shut with a metallic thud that echoed among the passageways. Asher and Silvana instinctively backed away from their bars, retreating to the shadows of their cells. There was shouting, a voice ordering somebody to halt. It was quickly replaced with the sounds of a struggle, followed by a couple of heavy thuds.

A few tense moments passed.

The pitter-patter of webbed feet raced towards Asher's cell, and a small figure appeared before him. It spun, breathing heavily. He was an Otyren guard, eyes wide and staring down the passage at something or someone Asher couldn't see.

'Get back!' he cried as he slowly edged backwards, raising his trident. 'I'm warning you, bitch!' As the last word left his mouth, he was set upon by a blur of red.

Was that a dress?

Quicker than Asher could follow, the blur assailed the guard, ducking under the wildly thrust trident and slamming several lightning-fast fists into the Otyren's small circular face. He crumpled to the floor, his nose a bloody mess. The figure stood from the body and began peering into the cells around them.

'Asher?' the stranger whispered. 'Have any of you seen a white Rabbethi called Asher? Patch over one eye?'

He couldn't believe it. It was Cara, the last person he expected to see coming to his rescue. A wave of relief and joy overtook him, and he ran from the shadows to the cell bars.

'Cara!' he cried.

'Oh, thank Thena,' Cara exclaimed, the sternness in her face melting to relief as she ran to his cell. They reached through the bars and embraced, the cold metal chilling Asher's fur against his cheek.

'I thought you left me,' he said, pulling away, tears welling in his eyes.

'I'm so sorry,' she said, a faint, almost imperceivable whimper in her voice. 'It was the only way to earn their trust and get us inside. I should have told you, but I was ordered not to. I'm so sorry.' She looked at him with an expectant stare, waiting for his judgement.

Asher stared deep into her eyes. What he found in her gaze was a genuine regret, an overwhelming sense of guilt and heartbreak that seemed to reflect his own. It was as if she, too, had felt the sting of her betrayal. Asher stared hard at his former companion. He could feel her stuttered breaths as she held at bay her true emotions, emotions that must have been truly overpowering to make the stern agent lose her composure.

She's telling the truth, Asher thought, a wave of guilt and relief washing over him. He suddenly felt tired as the pain he held—the crippling betrayal and loss—eased from his heart, the bitterness no longer fuelling him. A part of him even understood why she had done it, though the act of it still hurt. She was just following orders, orders from a woman she held dear. Queen Tessina. He may have forgiven Cara, but there was something about Tessina that Asher couldn't let go, a sense of masters and pawns creeping into his mind as it had back in the senate meeting.

Then there was Luce. Asher released a long-held sigh, closing his eyes.

Maybe there is something there after all, he thought with a hopeful smile.

'It's okay,' he said with a sincere smile. 'You're here now.'

With a broad smile, relief washed over her stern Vulpen face. 'I've got something for you.' She reached up to her neck and lifted a thin chain from under the neckline of her red dress. Asher instantly recognised the tarnished metallic bow that dangled loosely from the scuffed links, and his heart fluttered with relief and joy.

'I thought it was gone forever,' he breathed, reaching a paw through the bars.

Cara lifted the necklace over her head and placed it into Asher's open paw. 'I knew it meant a lot to you, so I told the jarls I wanted it as a trophy. It was tarnished and old, so they didn't seem to care.'

Asher inspected the miniature bow in his paw. He lifted the chain over his tall ears and down his neck, letting it sit upon its usual spot. Its weight pulled ever so slightly down his chest. It was an old comfort, and he hadn't realised how much it calmed him until it was gone.

'You have to get us out of here,' he said with sudden urgency, his thoughts returning to the dungeon.

'Us?' Cara repeated.

'Yes, *us*. I can't leave these people here. Do you know what they're doing to Rabbethi? They're chopping us up and sending the parts away to be eaten! *Eaten*, Cara! Do you understand?' The anger he had felt when he first learned the truth returned in force, bubbling over and erupting before her.

'One problem at a time,' Cara said with a deep breath as she placed an object wrapped in a luxurious green cloth on the floor. She then pulled two small metal rods from the sleeve of her dress and crouched before the cell door. She inserted the rods into the keyhole and asked, 'Who are they selling the meat to? Meat grinders?' She moved the pieces of metal, fiddling them into position before they jolted into place. The cell door swung open.

'I don't know,' Asher said, stepping quickly into the passageway. 'But we need to get everyone out of here.' His eyes landed on the object on the floor and paused. 'Is that what I think it is?' A great heaviness settled in his chest as he gazed down at the object. It was as if it had a force bending the air towards it, drawing him in. The fire in his chest crackled softly, longingly. Asher was drawn to this thing, but the fire *longed* to be near it.

Cara smiled and carefully removed the green cloth, revealing a bow. 'Sure is.'

Asher gasped as he stared at the expert craftsmanship, the wood polished as if new. It was so simple and yet beautiful. It was as if it had been designed for his interpretation of beauty. Then there was the crystal-clear gem at the centre—the Shepherd Stone. It hummed as he drew close, a fragment of god's power contained in such a small thing. Without thinking, he lifted the bow and grasped it firmly in one paw. It was warm despite the frigid air of the dungeon.

'Just be careful,' Cara said, raising her paw to reveal a blistered palm. 'It gave me quite the burn when I grabbed it.'

'How does it work?' he asked, wincing at the wound.

'I don't know, but we can figure it out when we're back aboard *The Silvi*. Right now, we need to move. You don't want to know what's chasing me.'

'Did you say *The Silvi*?' asked a soft voice from the shadows of the opposite cell.

Cara turned. 'I did. What's it to y—'

She froze. Her eyes widened as she stared at the white-furred Vulpen cautiously approaching the cell bars, the orange torchlight revealing Silvana. Cara's words began to tumble in a convoluted string of intangible nonsense, her mouth hanging in complete disbelief. She approached the cell.

'Are... are you alright?' Silvana asked, concern crossing her face as Cara drew closer.

'I don't believe it,' Cara breathed. 'After all this time, you're alive.'

Silvana took a step back, placing a protective paw over her belly. She looked past Cara to Asher, who just shrugged.

'I'm sorry,' she said with a reassuring but awkward smile. 'Do I know you?'

'I've missed you so much, Luna,' Cara said with trembling words.

Silvana's smile dropped, replaced with a severe look of confusion, her eyes narrowing as she scanned Cara's face. It was as if her mind was wrestling with itself, desperately trying to remember why that name meant something to her.

'This is Silvana,' Asher called out, attempting to break the tension.

'Like the hero,' Cara said softly, not taking her eyes off Silvana. 'I know who she is. We grew up together. She was... my best friend...'

Silence descended. All that could be heard was the faint ringing of the bells and the rumbling of what sounded like thunder far in the distance.

'I know you...' Silvana said, unsure, her green eyes gazing at the features of Cara's face.

Cara nodded, smiling.

'Shouldn't we be getting out of here?' Asher called, not wanting to disturb the reunion but growing ever more concerned by the rumbling thunder growing louder and louder from the shadows.

Cara snapped to the present. 'Right, yes.' She quickly picked the lock of Silvana's cell, and the white Vulpen stepped out, still cautious of the emotional Cara. Cara smiled, then turned to Asher. 'Where are the keys? There's not enough time for me to pick every lock here.'

'You mean these keys?' boomed a voice from the end of the passage.

Asher and Cara turned to see the great mass of the warden, his long white apron splattered with fresh blood, his huge cleaver dripping in his webbed paw. The keys fastened to his belt jangled like a musical instrument as he shook his waist. 'You'll have to take them off my cold dead body!' he bellowed, and he took off towards them, his thunderous stomps shaking the stone.

Cara raised her fists and spread her feet. Asher stared dead-eyed at the gigantic beast, the fire in his heart crackling to life at the sight of his bloody captor. So many innocent Rabbethi had been killed by this man, and for what? To be diced up and shipped to who knows where. To be eaten like common game. It made Asher's blood boil, made his heart ache for vengeance, for justice. The bow in his paw began to tingle as if reacting to his pain, and the clear gem at its centre started to hum with energy. Asher glanced down at the relic and pulled lightly at the bowstring, testing its strength. As the string twanged, a surge of energy pulsated around his fingertips, crackles of white light sparking around his knuckles. He couldn't explain it, but somehow, he knew what to do. It was as if he had always known.

'Okay, you bastard,' he breathed, raising his eyes to the charging Otyren, bringing the bow forwards. The bow vibrated with increased fervour as if aware of his intent, shooting tremors up his arm and into his chest. An overwhelming strength filled Asher as he pulled back the bowstring, the gem shining bright from beneath his fingers with a warming radiance. An arrow of blinding white intensity materialised from the wood, growing longer as he pulled the bowstring to his cheek. He felt heat rise through his chest, through his very being and into his eyes. The rush was incredible, the power, the warmth. He wished it could've lasted forever, but the roaring Otyren told him he had to put that energy to use. He closed one eye and focused on the rampaging warden.

Just as the warden was about to reach Silvana and bring his mighty cleaver thundering down, Asher let loose the arrow, imbuing it with all the rage and anguish he felt for his people, all the vengeance they deserved. The bowstring twanged, and the wild, crackling energy left his fingers at explosive speed, hurtling towards the Otyren's massive shoulder. It hit its mark, and the dungeon fell silent as if the walls themselves were holding their breaths.

BOOM!

A tremendous explosion filled the narrow passageway, engulfing the warden in an inferno and hurtling him into the nearby cell, taking the metal bars with him. The inferno surged towards Asher and Cara. They dropped to the hard stone, shielding themselves as best they could.

Then there was a scream, a painful, terrible scream.

'Luna!' Cara yelled, dashing into the smog as the fire dissipated.

Asher rose to his feet, his fur now singed from the blast. His lungs burned as he drew arduous hot breaths, the power of the relic ebbing from his body, leaving him drained. The hum of the gem eased as quiet descended. The ringing faded from Asher's ears until all that remained was the sound of crumbling stone and a gentle sobbing. Asher searched for the source, finding Cara on her knees. He staggered over, stepping over the broken stone and bent metal bars now strewn across the floor. What he saw made his heart sink. Cradled in Cara's arms was Silvana, sobbing, her once beautiful white fur blackened across her back, large holes in her rags revealing the raw, red skin in a dreadful display of what could only be unbearable pain. What made his heart tighten was the blackened remains of what used to be a beautiful long tail. It was all but gone, the only remnant a thin, scorched stump protruding from under the darkened rag.

He had done this. In his fury and anger, he had hurt someone undeserving of it. He hadn't cared who got in his way as long as that Otyren bastard got what was coming to him. He had been a monster.

'Get the keys,' Cara breathed, sensing his approach.

'Cara, I—'

'The keys!'

Asher hesitated, then backed away without a word. He walked to the shadowy cell where the warden had landed, the scent of burning flesh growing intense as he entered. A hulking mass bulged from one corner, completely shrouded in darkness, unmoving and sizzling. The cell was heavy with shadow, as if the sheer presence of the warden's great weight extinguished all that was good and hopeful. Asher found the keys by the opposite wall. He snatched them up and made his way out of the cell, keeping an eye on the dark corner where the warden lay, just in case. Without disturbing Cara, who was helping Silvana to her feet, Asher began unlocking the cells that had not been blown open, releasing the terrified prisoners. Each thanked him profusely, raising a fist to their chest in a weakened salute.

'We need to move,' Cara said with a calm sternness.

Asher nodded, unable to make eye contact with either Vulpen.

After a brief stumble, Silvana was able to support herself, and they moved quickly down the passageway, a small group of Rabbethi prisoners following closely behind. Asher unlocked Osgar's cell and the cells of those around him, and they joined the escape. They burst into the fighting ring chamber, expecting to find a small hoard of Otyren guards. It was empty, save for the circle of sand in the centre of the room, clumps of dried blood scattered throughout.

'They must have been called up to defend the city,' Asher said, inspecting the circle.

'Either that, or they fled like the cowards they are,' spat Osgar as he knelt beside the bloodstains. He closed his eyes, placed a gentle paw onto the sand, and whispered a prayer to Folka.

'Over here,' Cara called as she reached the wooden door on the far side of the chamber. The group approached, and as she pulled it open, Asher was hit with the most foul-smelling air he had ever experienced. Everything in his body screamed at him to run.

Cara and Silvana stepped inside, and Asher hardened his nerves, following the Vulpen women, who seemed less affected by the putrid stench. The air was hot and rich with the metallic tang of blood. An assortment of tools and instruments littered the workbenches of a narrow chamber, each designed for carving and cutting into flesh and bone, each covered in dried blood. Even the torchlight was stained a dull red. Piles of clothes littered the damp corners, tunics and shoes separated into discordant heaps. On one of the workbenches lining the walls, a crate of simple jewellery glimmered in the blood-soaked light. Some glinted brightly, while most appeared dull and rusted, the most expensive pieces likely already sold to the citizens that resided above, unaware or uncaring of their previous owners.

Osgar clocked the crate and dashed towards it. He didn't seem to take in the horrors that lay about him but was focused on one thing and one thing only. He rummaged through the box of metallic trinkets, desperately searching, for what, Asher couldn't tell—a favourite ring, perhaps? Or a family heirloom? With a sigh of relief, he pulled a chain from the pile of clanging metal and held it tight in a clenched paw. He then draped it over his head and onto his neck, a small pendant sinking beneath his rags to rest by his heart. He closed his eyes, smiling.

Asher turned his attention to the largest wall. Hung from hooks embedded high into the stonework was a sizable rectangular banner. It was black, except for a wide red circle. In the centre was the silhouette of a curved dagger pointing down. At the base of where the blade met the handle was a clear-cut circle, which allowed the red to bleed through. It certainly wasn't tied to any of the Otyren houses or other noble families of Tamuz. Still, it had an overwhelming sense of foreboding that added to the unease of the bloodstained room.

Asher's stomach turned as his eyes drifted to what lay beneath the banner. On a large, chipped wooden workbench was the torso of a poor Rabbethi man, his limbs hacked away and his entrails strewn about the table. It took everything in his power to force the vomit back into his stomach. The Rabbethi's head was placed atop a stack of blood-crusted books, a candle mockingly stuck between the ears.

'This is awful,' Cara breathed.

'Let's just get out of here,' Asher replied, averting his eyes towards a door on the far side, the fire in his heart burning, willing him to go back and ensure the warden was well and truly dead. But there was no time. Behind him, he could hear the freed prisoners wretch and gasp in shock as they entered the room, some vomiting.

'Herewulf! *No!*' cried one of the prisoners, who slumped to the floor by the mangled corpse, a mess of bottomless wailing. The others picked the howling Rabbethi up, speaking softly to him, urging him to continue. There would be time to mourn later.

Some Rabbethi began picking up discarded daggers and bows from a heap in the corner as Asher ran to the opposite door. He heaved it open with an arduous shove, releasing a cold wind from a long, dark stone hallway. His fur blew gently against the cool air, carrying with it the faintest sound of a city in panic.

'I don't see anything. Who knows where this goes,' Asher warned, peering into the blackness.

'It's better than what's behind us,' Cara said, keeping an eye on the open door they came from.

'You mean the warden?'

Before Cara could reply, an almighty crash echoed deep within the dungeon. The sound resonated through the fighting ring and into the bloodstained room. A symphony of screeches and wails followed, sounding like a stampede of angry boars rampaging through the passageways, heading straight for them.

The sound grew louder and louder as the stone beneath began to quake. They all steadied themselves and peered through the doorway leading back into the fighting ring. No one spoke.

Asher turned to Cara, keeping his voice low. 'What is i—'

A tsunami of Shangari poured around the corner in an unstoppable wave of bulging red eyes, serrated dagger-like teeth and rusty blades. They scurried along the walls and ceiling, all scrambling over one another in a bloodthirsty craze, their painful and rageful shrieks piercing into Asher's mind.

'*Run!*' Cara yelled, and the group bolted into the dark corridor, praying it would lead to safety.

Their panicked footsteps echoed against the cold, wet stone. Cara led the way, her beautiful red dress flowing elegantly behind her, her sensitive nose and keen instincts guiding the way. Silvana followed closely behind, then Asher, with Osgar and the freed Rabbethi prisoners taking up the rear, the shrieks and cries of their bloodthirsty pursuers growing louder behind them. Asher peered over his shoulder, and his eyes went wide. Hundreds of shapes writhed and flailed in the murky blackness, a sea of monstrous red eyes reflecting what little light permeated the shadows.

One of the older Rabbethi by Asher's side tripped and stumbled to the ground. Asher slowed to help but immediately felt a tug on his tunic, dragging him onward.

'We can't do anything for him!' cried Osgar with sorrowful but determined eyes.

Asher nodded as a blood-curdling scream filled the passageway, the mass of Shangari swarming over the fallen Rabbethi, devouring him in seconds. The sound pierced Asher's heart, but he knew Osgar was right.

Falling was death.

As the group bounced off a corner, a faint light beckoned them in the distance, silhouetted by the shape of a door.

'Keep running. We're almost there!' Cara yelled.

They were halfway down the corridor when a mighty crash sounded behind them. The horde rounded the corner, slamming into the stone wall, shaking the foundations of whatever lay above. That did little to slow them, and the mass of gnarled flesh and jagged teeth continued its relentless rampage towards the group. Cara reached the door first with a slam, her shoulder shaking the wood. She reached for the handle and pulled.

Locked.

'Shit!' she yelled. 'Shit! Shit! Shit!'

The stampeding horde was fast approaching, their bloodthirsty shrieks growing louder and louder. Cara looked at Silvana, fear consuming her face. Silvana looked to the floor, her eyes wide.

'Move!' Asher yelled, approaching the door and raising his knee high. Before he kicked, he felt a presence by his side. It was Osgar, mimicking his stance. With a nod, they both kicked as hard as they could, and with an explosion of splinters, the door flew off its hinges.

It hurtled through the open air beyond and skidded along a white stone floor, coming to rest beside a large Otyren ship. The group raced through the doorway and found themselves standing on the stone docks of the inner city. The sound of death and chaos was deafening. Asher could see nothing but blood and fire, the darkening sky glowing a warm orange as thousands of homes were ablaze. The entire outer banks were burning. Bells from hundreds of watchtowers rang out in terrible unison, and the squeals and screams of the dying floated along the wind. The evening breeze carried the all too familiar metallic stench of blood, and he could see the signs of hard fighting on the docks. Blood coated the white stone, and half-eaten Otyren soldiers lay about them, their eyes wide, their mouths open forever in permanent screams.

'There!' Cara yelled, pointing to *The Silvi*, bobbing lightly in the water. She sprinted towards it, followed closely by the rest of the group.

'Marius!' Asher cried, waving his arms frantically. 'Marius! Get the boat ready!' The small square porthole in the back of the ship swung open, and out popped the head of their captain, panting, his face shrouded in fear.

'C'mon! This place has gone to shit!' His eyes widened as he looked past the group. 'What is *that*?'

From the open doorway, a torrent of screaming Shangari surged onto the docks, blood dripping from their mouths, all rampaging towards the moored *Silvi*. Marius disappeared from view, and within seconds, the ropes holding the ship to the docks fell away in a chorus of loud snaps, splashing into the water below. Asher and the others reached the gangway and bounded across the thin wood just before it tumbled into the water below.

The Silvi slowly veered away from the docks. Asher raced to the top deck and drew back the string of his bow, feeling the crackling energy course through his fingertips and up his arms, the burning in his eyes returning in full force. An arrow of pure white manifested from the glowing stone at the bow's centre. He lined up the shot. The first of the Shangari leapt high into the air, attempting to land on the deck of *The Silvi*.

And Asher couldn't release the bow string.

Silvana's burnt back flashed into his mind. Her cries flooded his ears, and the guilt he felt weighed down upon him like a lead blanket. He couldn't do it. He couldn't risk the power at his fingertips getting out of control.

The bloodthirsty Shangari soared through the air, its rabid shape sailing ever closer to the back of *The Silvi*. A twang echoed across the ship, and the Shangari dropped from the air, splashing into the water below, an arrow placed between its hungry red eyes. Many more Shangari came flying after the first but splashed into the water with cries of anger as *The Silvi* sailed out of reach.

'Asher!' Cara yelled as she ran up the steps to the top deck, a simple bow gripped tight in her black paw. The rest of the horde came to a screeching halt at the jetty's edge, gnashing their teeth and screeching angrily at their escaping prey. *The Silvi*'s sails unfurled, and the ship was off, gliding around the island of the inner city and under the bridge connected to the outer banks.

They sailed in silence through the burning city. Asher scanned the scene as Cara and Silvana stood in silent horror beside him. Countless bodies floated in the water. Raging fires consumed buildings and nearby vessels. Despite the hatred he had been shown, the distrust and cruelty, not even the Otyren deserved this. Flashbacks of his own city raced into his mind.

'Hold on, everyone!' Marius cried from *The Silvi*'s cabin as the ship entered the broad straight to the sea. With a heavy *ca-chunk*, the rest of the ship's sail unfurled, and *The Silvi* sped off, skimming across the water's surface.

They sped down the river, racing past other vessels attempting to flee the burning city, Asher's tall ears trailing in the wind behind him. The buildings lining the riverbanks burned in an inferno as dark shapes skulked among the destroyed homes, terrible screams audible over the roaring fires. The river grew dark as the last remnants of civilisation were left behind, the waning light of the Great Lighthouse providing little illumination on the path before them. The towers dotting either side of the river were not lit.

Asher turned to Cara. 'Why haven't the chains been raised? Or the water drained?'

'The guards must have all been killed,' Cara replied as she held on to the wooden railing, her eyes squinting as sprays of river water splashed into her face. Silvana stood beside Cara, eyes closed, one paw placed on her stomach. They passed by more and more towers, fires unlit with no sign of life.

The entrance to the waterways eventually came into view, the great towers on either side standing tall, their beacons ablaze. As they drew near, a horn blew from one of the towers, and hundreds of shadowy figures began swarming in and around the base.

'That's not good,' Asher said over the buffeting wind. He leaned over the stern and gazed into the open porthole of the cabin. 'Marius! They're raising the chain!'

'She can't go any faster!' came a frustrated reply.

It was then that Asher noticed something strange in the water, keeping pace and following close behind the ship. The water was swelling as if a great mass waited just beneath the surface. Asher stared at it, trying to determine its shape.

His eyes went wide.

With a mighty splash, the hulking, scorched mass of the warden exploded from the water, his body a half-mangled mess of burnt flesh. Bones protruded at awkward angles from his shoulder, and the fur around one side of his face was all but gone. Muscular sinew stretched between his skull and jaw, barely keeping it together and allowing Asher to see deep into his bloody throat. An empty hole stared at Asher with a groaning blackness from where an eye had melted away. The remaining eye was hysterical with rage. Sharp canine teeth were clenched tight in a painful grimace, and with a mighty swipe, the warden brought his giant cleaver down upon the startled Asher, narrowly missing the Rabbethi's throat.

'You motherfu—!' he screamed with a forced strain before plummeting back into the water in a humongous crash.

'What now?' screamed a panicking Marius from the cabin.

'Just keep going!' Asher shouted back, watching the water behind swell again as the warden continued his pursuit.

We can make it.

Something heavy began to rattle from the towers before them. The heavy chains at their base had started to move. Before long, they would be in position, barring any vessel from escaping. It would be close, *very* close. Everyone held their breath as *The Silvi* drew ever closer, the chain beginning to rise from the water's surface. Asher glanced at the water behind them and found the bulging shape of the warden nearing once more.

C'mon... C'mon...

The warden leapt from the water just as *The Silvi* soared between the last two towers. With a thunderous crash, the metal chain scraped across the bottom of *The Silvi*'s hull, sending splinters erupting in all directions. At the same time, the warden's cleaver came slicing down towards Asher's skull.

Crunch!

The upper deck was washed in a torrent of steaming hot blood. Asher, Cara and Silvana turned and stared, their mouths agape. Hanging from the thick metal chain was the colossal Otyren body of the warden, the metal chain embedded deep into his skull and neck. Blood poured from the mangled head like a sickening waterfall into the mouth of the river. It was a grotesque sight, horrible beyond belief, and yet the fire inside Asher crackled joyfully at the justice served this day. With the warden dead, the Rabbethi people were now free from slaughter, free from being cut up and sold as meat. The Shangari at the towers shouted and screeched in anger as their prey sailed away into the open ocean. Asher closed his eyes and breathed deeply.

He had the King's Bow, and he was free.

26

A Threat Returned

Constance watched the city below burn. The glow of a thousand fires shimmered in the still water of the river, illuminating the night sky. Most of the ships were ablaze, drifting along the gentle water, aimless, like blessed lanterns caught in the breeze. The incessant bells had finally ceased, the bellringers having fled or been consumed by one of her ravenous Shangari prowling the streets. Screams still floated faintly on the wind like a choir of repenting sinners.

It was a glorious, burning offering to the Shepherd.

Of all the exalted races that inhabited Tamuz, the Otyren were the most heretical and needed divine correction. The Rabbethi worship Folka, the Medvedians, Loch. Even the Cozati on their poxy island of Cozat worshipped the bloodthirsty Lenkor. They were not gods, however. No, they were merely the first of their kind, the chosen of the Shepherd, blessed with the Shepherd's fire and given life anew. The Otyren, however, followed no one. Their ancient founder fell into disgrace long before the dreadful sealing, abandoning their people to live a life of cold, unguided lawlessness. Those who follow the ancients were misguided children, but the Otyren were little more than the mice that scurry in the undergrowth, vermin to be cleansed.

'Godless insects,' she sneered, wrapping her fingers around an oversized white rock. They'd all be brought to heel once she succeeded in her holy mission. With the divine power of the Shepherd, she would bring everlasting peace to Tamuz, whether it wanted it or not. So what if a few sacrifices had to be made, a few weeds pulled from the Shepherd's garden?

She observed the heavy stone in her paw. Its smoothness was pleasant against her palm, but it was nothing but a cheap imitation of the divinity residing in the circlet upon her brow.

'Worthless,' she breathed, letting the sparkling stone fall from her fingers. It dropped, landing with a crack as it hit the marble floor. She looked down and smiled, noticing a sizable fissure splitting the stone in twain. Inside was nothing but unimpressive grey rock.

A faint whimper pulled her attention from the rock, and she turned to face the vast Allthing chamber of the castle. It was a mess. Blood stained the beautiful stone floor, seeping into the giant dead stump at the chamber's centre. Then there were the bodies. Countless Otyren corpses littered the floor, each with chunks of flesh ripped from their person or missing various limbs. They were a mixture of nobles in garish party attire and weak soldiers who had fruitlessly tried to defend themselves against the savagery of the Shangari onslaught.

When Constance had ordered the attack from the drowned forest, she hadn't expected the city to fall so quickly or so easily. Numerous Shangari tribes were already living within White Cliffe's sewers when she had attacked, and most of her acolytes had remained hidden in the city after the crazed king had banished her from his keep. She didn't have acolytes within *this* city, however, and no sewers to hide the Shangari. Thankfully, the surety of the city's guards that no coordinated army would ever attempt to march through the drowned forest had made them lazy and unperceptive. Quickly and quietly, a small party of her Shangari clambered over the outer city walls and vanished into the streets, moving within the shadows until they could reach the gatehouse. There, they opened the city for the horde. Most of the city's guards were butchered before they could even raise their tridents. Others simply dropped their weapons and ran like godless cowards. Their beautiful screams filled the evening air like a serenade as Constance and her new companion rode through the open gates.

Those who had survived the attack on the castle were now on their knees before her, their webbed paws bound behind them. Their fine clothes were torn and stained, and what jewellery they owned had been stripped by her loyal acolytes. They reeked of fear and voided bowels. Constance especially disliked the fat one that had rebuked her messenger, the insufferable Jarl Vatn, whose eyes were now glued to the marble floor, a dark stain running down his inner thigh.

Threaten me, will you? Well, look at you now, you snivelling little shit, she thought, maintaining her raised snout as she strolled to him. He raised his head as Constance neared, a bleeding cut across his cheek. Fear poured from him, the scent intoxicating.

Constance smiled. 'I hope you've learned a lesson,' she said as if scolding a disobedient child. 'You see what happens when you refuse the will of the Shepherd? When you refuse *my* will?'

Jarl Vatn said nothing but continued to stare with the same miserable expression across his face. Constance hated it, hated the weakness in him. He had the power of the land, had the means to make changes, and what did he do with it? *Nothing.* Nothing but sit in his oversized chair around his oversized table, throwing parties and getting... oversized. She could feel the anger growing inside her, the fire in her chest burning, fanned by his hubris. She would show him what happened to those who defied her.

She looked to her allies in the chamber. A small band of Shangari surrounded the kneeling Otyren while others gorged themselves on the flesh of the dead. Constance could hear the crunching of bones and slurping of wet, bloody meat as it slid down their gullets. She shuddered internally. She would command them to stop if she wasn't so wary of their wavering loyalty. It was best not to deny them the spoils of war. The more meat they ate, the happier they were, and Constance wanted to keep them that way. Besides, the noises seemed to bother the fat jarl more, who couldn't help but glance at a nearby Shangari chewing on the arm of an Otyren noble. Around the severed wrist dangled a gold band encrusted with emeralds. The Shangari had wrapped its lips around where the bone had been snapped from the torso and was sucking out the marrow with deep, dreadful slurps.

'Friend of yours, was she? Or one of your many mistresses?' Constance mocked, enjoying the horror in his eyes.

The terrified jarl looked away. 'A... a friend,' he stammered through quaking lips.

Definitely a mistress.

A wicked grin formed across Constance's face. 'I see.'

Her eyes moved up and past the row of survivors towards the titanic Shangari chieftain, Nin-Kilim. In his gnarled paws were two more Otyren nobles, a young man and an older woman of similar age to cowardly jarl. Constance nodded, and Nin-Kilim stepped forwards, throwing the two to the floor. They tumbled to Constance's feet, groaning as they pushed themselves to their knees. The woman was skinny, unhealthily so, and had about her body all manner of gold jewellery that rattled as she shifted uncomfortably on the floor. Upon her chest was a golden brooch of a large clam with two tridents crossed beneath it. Constance recognised it as the mark of the Vatn family. The young man wore a turquoise shirt and white trousers, now covered in blood, the same sigil embroidered with fine yellow linen on his shirt.

'Ah, the birthday boy himself!' Constance mocked with a smile.

Jarl Erik Vatn Jr. stared back at the high priestess, not in fear but with utter contempt. Something made Constance pause. Through those beady black eyes, deep within the hatred, was something she recognised, something that piqued her interest—a spark, a fire, young but burning bright.

'Fascinating,' she breathed.

I'll have to watch this one.

She studied him for a time before returning to his whimpering father. Deciding what type of punishment to inflict upon the senior Vatn was difficult. It had to be harsh enough that he'd never think about crossing her again, yet sapping all his will so he didn't have the strength to rise up, all while promising further, worse pain in the future. An idea sprung into her mind, a wicked idea that made her smile.

'I think this lesson needs to be personal,' she said, turning to Nin-Kilim. 'Smash the window, please.'

With a guttural grunt, the giant Shangari lumbered over to one of the tall arched windows and slammed a mighty fist into the glass, smashing it into a thousand tiny pieces. Jagged shards rained to the marble floor as a gust of hot air rushed through, the sounds of a city ablaze becoming sharp, filling the chamber. Blood dripped from Nin-Kilim's black fist, where pieces of glass were now embedded deep into his knuckles. He trudged back to his Shangari horde, picking at the glass and dropping it to the floor as he walked.

'Choose,' Constance commanded, not taking her eyes off Jarl Vatn, her white-and-gold robe buffeting in the warm wind.

Jarl Vatn blinked. 'Wha… what?' he asked.

'Darling, I need to make sure you'll remember this day when you think about defying me again. Now choose. Who is going to die?'

Jarl Vatn's eyes went wide. Whatever colour remained in his petrified little face drained away as tears began to stream from the corners of his tiny black eyes. Constance couldn't help but grin at this overprivileged noble squirming, forced to give up something he didn't want to.

'Please...' he whispered, glancing at his wife and son, their eyes meeting his in desperate pleas.

'Choose one, or they both die,' Constance repeated, her patience growing thin.

A moment passed as Jarl Vatn's eyes glanced from his wife to his son and back again. Constance's smile faded as frustration took hold. Who did this Otyren think he was, keeping her from conducting important ceremonial tasks? She had places to be, princes to catch and a bow to reclaim.

She was done waiting.

'Fine,' she said with no patience left. She stood straight and turned to the fat jarl's wife, summoning the power of the Judge's Bane. She felt the stone at its centre begin to hum and resonate into her mind, felt the fire in her chest draw the power down and into her being. Like a gentle stream, the energy seeped into her skull and down into her throat. Her eyes burned with a radiant fire, but there was no pain, only power. She spoke and felt the force surge from her snout, carrying each word like a breath of fire that coursed over the kneeling Otyren.

'Stand,' she commanded, and the power of the Judge's Bane took hold immediately. White flames ignited in the black eyes of the two kneeling Otyren nobles. Their fear and anger faded, their faces void of emotion. They stood obediently, and Constance turned once more to Jarl Vatn.

Without breaking eye contact with the fat little Otyren, she said, 'Jump out of the window.'

No sooner had the words left her lips than Jarl Vatn Jr. and his mother began walking towards the smashed window. The pair ambled side by side, their webbed paws tied behind their backs. Shards of glass crunched underfoot with each dreadful step towards the shattered window, fragments catching in their thick tails as they dragged along the marble, leaving faint bloody streaks behind them. Jarl Vatn's mouth trembled as his eyes darted from his family and back to Constance. She did not care if these godless river vermin lived or died. The great Shepherd had not gifted their kind a Stone and thus were not worthy of her love. What she saw behind the young one's eyes, however, gave her pause, and, for the first time in years, doubt crept into her mind. She would have to consult the old texts upon her return to the Lighthouse as soon as she had punished herself for such heretical thoughts.

Jarl Vatn's eyes met hers, and he took a sharp breath.

'Stop!' Constance commanded, and the pair at the window halted, the tips of their shoes hanging precariously over the window's edge.

'Please...,' started Jarl Vatn through trembling breaths. 'Spare my son.'

Good choice, she thought, mildly relieved she wouldn't have to find an excuse to spare Vatn Jr.

Constance turned to the Vatn family with a smile. They swayed on the window's edge, jagged rocks and burning ships hundreds of feet below.

'Come here, boy,' she commanded.

Jarl Vatn Jr. turned and stepped back into the chamber, stopping by Constance's side. 'Good,' she said in a condescending tone. 'Now, sleep.'

The young Otyren noble collapsed to the floor in a heap, unconscious, the fire behind his eyes fading beneath closing eyelids. Jarl Vatn stared at his son and released a long-held breath, a look of relief washing across his short snout.

Constance hated it.

'Jarlskona Vatn.'

Jarl Vatn's head snapped to Constance and then to his wife, who remained teetering over the edge, silhouetted by the raging fires that burned below.

'Jump.'

'No!' Jarl Vatn screamed, but it was too late.

Jarlskona Vatn leapt forwards and dropped out of sight. The chamber fell silent. Moments later, a faint, terrified scream rolled in through the open window before being cut short. Jarl Vatn began to sob into his webbed paws, and Constance felt the power leave her throat and the fire fade from her eyes. The hum of the stone grew softer until it was still once more.

'Thank you for your power, my Shepherd,' she whispered in prayer, closing her eyes. She briefly blessed the Shepherd with her thoughts before slowly opening her eyes.

'Now then, darling,' she said cheerfully, addressing the broken Jarl Vatn Sr. 'My friends and I must be leaving. We have a rebellion to put down, and I need you to clean up this mess.'

She nodded to the Shangari standing behind the surviving Otyren nobles. One by one, they reached down and raked their sharp claws across their fluffy throats, blood spraying across the marble floor. A chorus of gargling screams filled the chamber, their eyes rolled backwards, and they thudded heavily to the floor, large pools growing around their lifeless bodies. Jarl Vatn stared in horror, his mouth agape.

'You and you alone are in charge now, just like you always wanted,' Constance said as she strolled past the traumatised jarl. 'In return for this wonderful gift, you will make contributions to our cause, and I expect weekly ravens at the Lighthouse.' A deep grunt sounded from Nin-Kilim at the mention of contributions. Constance sighed. 'And, of course, all meat deliveries are now to be sent to the Lighthouse.' There was another grunt from Nin-Kilim, this one seemingly of approval.

Jarl Vatn said nothing as he stared at the lifeless bodies of his fellow jarls. Constance continued around the tree stump table, stepping over the many bodies that lined the floor as the congregation of Shangari parted before her. Nin-Kilim and the others fell in behind her as she passed.

She glanced at the centre of the table, at the wooden stand where she was told her prize should have been, and remembered the fear in the old Otyren's eyes as he stood before his poxy tower in the outer bank. He hadn't lied to her; he couldn't, not while under her control. Her focus returned to the chamber and the empty pedestal. She clenched her jaw at the thought of being so close, only to have it taken by her sister's lowly agent and that cowardly prince.

As she reached the grand golden doors to the chamber, she turned to her new companion, who had watched the whole affair from afar.

'Ensure the young Vatn is still breathing,' Constance commanded in her most pleasant voice. She had grown fond of this young man. His rebellious nature had initially amused her but had quickly grown tiresome. After she had broken him, he became quiet, which she found a comforting change from the arse-kissing she was used to from her other followers. The young man stared blankly at the broken window from the shadow of his white acolyte hood.

'Henric!' Constance snapped, losing her patience.

Henric jumped and turned to Constance, blinking himself back to reality. 'Oh, sorry, mistress. I'll collect him right away.' He took off around the large table towards the unconscious Jarl Vatn Jr. Constance watched him closely. He would need another session with the Judge's Bane to ensure her grip on him remained secure. She turned to the golden doors and walked through.

'We sail for White Cliffe,' she said over her shoulder to Nin-Kilim, who she could feel breathing down her neck. 'Ready your men, but leave those you trust here. Ensure our new friend doesn't get any ideas.'

There was a grunt of acknowledgement, and he was gone, the clatter of skulls across his belt growing quieter as he pushed past his minions.

Constance marched through the long entrance hall of the castle, turning towards an acolyte keeping pace by her side, a Vulpen snout poking out from the hood's shadow.

'Send ravens to the mines and labour camps in the east,' Constance commanded.

'Of course, mistress. What should the message say?'

Constance smiled. 'Tell the Third Sons to come home.'

27

The Banished

A light breeze propelled *The Silvi* silently across the gentle waves under a blanket of stars. Travelling east, it hugged the forested coast of Otyrheim as sprays of salty water splashed onto the deck, coating it in a briny layer and partly washing away the thick pools of blood and brain matter. Cara and Osgar had agreed it was best to move quickly and quietly, ordering those on board to extinguish all torches and remain silent. So, in shadow, *The Silvi* sailed, its crew not making a sound. The drowned forest passed by in a blur off its starboard side.

Asher stood with his eyes closed, a smile across his face, droplets of seawater streaking across his brow and down his cheeks. He was exhausted and longed for nothing more than to sleep and never wake. But he couldn't, not now that he was as free as a raven. He didn't want to miss a second of it. From the ship's bow, the wind coursed through his fur, his ears flapping wildly behind him. He shifted his weight, feeling the pull of the legendary bow slung over his shoulder. He still couldn't believe he had it, the power of a god at his fingertips. It was the symbol of his people, of his right to rule. Its power had been revealed when he shot the warden and left him for dead, scorched and smouldering. He unslung the bow and gripped it tightly in his filthy paw, the bow humming with energy as familiar tremors vibrated his arm. They travelled up and down into his chest, and his heart fluttered at the power. It felt amazing. He felt like he could swim all the way back to White Cliffe City faster than even *The Silvi*.

Staring at the stone embedded within the wood, Asher watched with wide eyes as it emitted a subtle glow, faintly illuminating the shadows of the deck. A swirling mass of white light shifted gently inside, and he somehow felt connected to it, like a kindred spirit or long-lost sibling. It was beautiful.

Creaking wood made Asher's head snap up, and he turned. All around him were dark shapes, crouching low to the deck, remaining silent. He held up the bow and let the light wash over them, revealing tall ears flopped forwards over lowered heads, the tips grazing the wooden floor. Asher gazed over the now free Rabbethi, not knowing what to say or do. He had seen people kneel to a king before when his father held court, but he had never been knelt to himself. These freed Rabbethi hadn't been riled up into a state of excessive patriotism by a fancy speech like in Ignimarum. They saw Asher, saw the bow, and that was enough.

'You don't have to kneel,' Asher said, uneasy, lowering the bow.

The man at the front rose to his feet. It was Osgar, who smiled as their eyes met.

'They want to kneel, Your Highness. You are their king, and you saved them from certain death.'

Now that they weren't all fleeing for their lives through an Otyren dungeon, Asher could finally get a good look at Osgar. He was taller than Asher and lean with muscle. Specks of grey were nestled among the fading oak fur, and judging from the many nicks and scars across his arms, he had seen plenty of action. His ears were bound into the style of a warrior, with a loose thread keeping the tall, scarred ears together.

The veteran's hazel eyes looked him up and down. He reminded Asher of his father but with kinder eyes and a gentler air about him.

Cara's voice carried over from the upper deck. 'Okay, we're all clear! You can light them up!'

The other Rabbethi all rose, and the glow of torches began to bathe the deck. Asher lowered the bow and rested it against the side of a barrel. He turned back to Osgar, who he found staring. He was smiling, a sense of what looked like pride in his eyes, but there was also a sadness.

'You look just like your mother,' Osgar eventually said softly, almost as a whisper.

Asher eyed the old Rabbethi with growing wariness. 'You knew my mother?'

Osgar blinked away distant memories and took a deep breath, his smile fading. 'You don't know who I am, do you? You probably didn't even know I existed. I'm not surprised. I dishonoured my family and position.' His eyes dropped to the floor. He had the look of someone running through painful memories in his mind, his face awash with shame.

Asher stared at the man for a short time, desperately trying to figure out who he was or where this feeling of familiarity was coming from. The idea, the memory, was so close, but he couldn't quite grasp it.

'Who *are* you?' he eventually asked, the feeling of not knowing becoming unbearable.

'I suppose you should know,' Osgar said with a sigh. He eyed the deck, glancing at the Rabbethi around them as they made themselves busy. 'You should all know, and I am sorry I have kept this from you all this time.' He took a deep breath and stood straight, almost to attention. His posture grew into something exuding strength and nobility. 'I am not Osgar. I am Horsa, older brother to King Hengist.'

Asher froze in stunned silence, as did all the other Rabbethi who were no longer pretending they weren't eavesdropping. He stepped back until the wooden railing pressed against him, and he slumped to the floor. His mouth hung open as he stared at the older Rabbethi. It was a lie—it had to be. Horsa was gone, dead by all accounts. Asher didn't know how or why, but his parents had all but confirmed it.

'I—' Asher began, not finding the words.

'It's a lot to take in,' Horsa said as a soft smile formed across his rugged face. 'You've grown so much.' A shadow fell upon the veteran, and his smile faded. 'I heard about your mother. She was a... wonderful woman. I'm sorry. I heard her burial at the North Barrows was beautiful. Lots of white lilies, I was told. Your mother loved those white lilies...' Horsa's voice trailed off as he became lost once more in thought.

Most people thought his mother's favourite flowers were the blue hydrangea that grew throughout the palace gardens. Only a select few, very close to her, knew the truth of it. Asher watched the old soldier in his silent mourning.

'What happened? Why are you out here?' Asher asked as the truth began to sink in.

Horsa shook his head. 'That's not important anymore.' He sighed. 'I'm sorry we had to meet like this. It isn't how I imagined it would go.'

Asher thought for a while, studying Horsa's face. Slowly, his blurred memories of his uncle began to clear, Horsa's features filling the gaps in his mind. It fit so well. It had to be true. Other than Henric, this man was the only family he had left, and Asher was going to make sure he wouldn't lose him, too. He rose to his feet, pushed himself away from the railing, and stepped towards the old Rabbethi. He reached an outstretched paw towards his uncle.

'My name is Asher. It's nice to meet you,' he said with a warm smile.

Horsa looked at Asher's paws and smiled. He reached out his own and held Asher's forearm tightly.

'It's a pleasure to meet you, Asher.'

A roar of approval erupted around them as the others clapped and cheered, causing the ship to rock from side to side.

'Steady!' Came a cry from Cara as she leaned over the front railing of the upper deck. 'I don't know what you're cheering about, but knock it off!'

Asher and Horsa chuckled, gently squeezing each other's forearms before letting go. The energy of the Rabbethi around eventually subdued, and they all went back to talking in hushed voices or resting against the wood of the ship, staring out at the calm waters rushing by. Horsa and Asher stared out over the ship's bow, the water racing beneath them.

'So this is the Bow of Folka? The King's Bow?' he asked, reaching for the relic. As his paw clasped around the wood, the sound of sizzling flesh penetrated the night air. Horsa recoiled. 'Agh! That hurt!' he yelled, shaking his paw, the smell of burnt flesh wafting from the singed paw.

'It doesn't hurt me,' Asher said, confused, as he picked up the bow without issue.

'Amazing,' Horsa breathed. 'All the more reason for these men to follow you. It's been a long time since a king wielded that bow. You'll do great things, I'm sure of it.'

'I hope so,' Asher said thoughtfully, the weight of his people resting on his shoulders once more.

***

The forest eventually thinned as the land rose, the wall of trees giving way to rocky cliffs and short, tough grass. The shadows of the towering rock face loomed in the darkness over the tiny ship. Waves gently lapped against its vertical face. The Silvi rounded a rocky outcrop and drifted into a broad cove, where a narrow sandy beach hugged the base of the tall cliff. The beach was widest at the cove's centre, and *The Silvi* came to a gentle stop a short way from the gentle lapping of waves against the shore. Chains rattled beneath the deck, and a mighty splash erupted beside the small vessel as a heavy iron anchor sank into the shallow water. There were no rowboats, so all on board had little option but to climb down the ladder, descend into the frigid water and swim the short distance ashore.

Once ashore, and with shivering urgency, they began gathering what little driftwood they could find. Campfires ignited along the beach, bathing the white sandy shore in a welcoming glow. Asher, Cara and Silvana remained aboard, ensuring everyone had disembarked safely. They also ensured no unpleasant stowaways were hiding within the cargo hold.

Silvana drew Asher aside with a gentle pull of his arm. Not having said a word to each other since the explosion in the dungeon, Asher followed her anxiously, wanting nothing more than to pour his heart out in remorse. He held his tongue and followed, the scabby flesh along her back and charred stump of a tail reminding him of what he had done—what his anger had done. She reached the bow of the ship and stopped.

'I'm so sorry,' Asher erupted, unable to keep the guilt behind the wall of patience he was attempting to build. 'I promise I won't use it again. It's too dangerous, and I can't control it, and I'll just end up hurting more people and…' Tears began to well up in the corners of his eyes, the guilt toppling his foundations.

Silvana turned, her emerald eyes meeting him with a soft understanding. 'It's okay,' she said with a gentle smile. 'It wasn't your fault.'

The words were like honey tea for Asher: sweet, warm and just what he needed. The tears built further as a wave of relief washed over him.

Silvana sighed. 'Though Cara is right. You need to control your emotions. You can't let the things that hurt you cloud your mind and force you out of focus.' She reached out and grasped Asher's paws in hers. 'Love and kindness will always shine brighter than anger. You, my dear Rabbethi king, have an ample amount of both. Use them to protect people, not hurt them.' With a squeeze, she released his paws.

Asher smiled in return. He would not forget her words, her kindness or her forgiveness.

Marius hadn't left the cabin for the entire journey, refusing to open the door until he deemed it safe. Amazingly, he had sailed *The Silvi* all the way from the burning docks of the castle to the safety of the cove, all within the cramped confines of his aquatic home. A frustrated Cara now thumped on the cabin door.

'Open the door, for Thena's sake!' she yelled, pounding a fist against the solid wood. 'I need to get out of this damn dress!' She looked quite beautiful, but Asher understood why she'd be desperate to escape it. It had no practical applications for fighting, and it didn't seem like her style.

'Noooooope!' came Marius's disgruntled voice from beyond the door. 'If you would kindly leave my ship and never bring danger this way ever again, that would be most appreciated!'

Cara snarled, bearing her sharp canine fangs. 'Marius, I swear to Thena! If you don't let me grab my stuff, I will burn this dinghy with you in it!'

There was a long pause as the ship captain seemingly contemplated this new proposal.

'Piss off!'

Cara continued her assault on the door, harder now, a fresh wave of anger fuelling her strikes. Silvana stepped forwards before Cara could do any serious damage to the fine wood or her fist. The white Vulpen raised a gentle paw, and Cara stopped, her rage dissipating in an instant. Silvana then approached the door and knocked twice.

'Marius?' she asked softly. 'It's me, Silvi. I... see you named your ship after me. That was... nice of you.'

There was a sudden movement within the cabin. Hurried footsteps rushed to the door, quickly followed by the sound of many metal locks turning and bolts sliding. The door swung open, and standing in the door frame was the dishevelled and wide-eyed Marius, his black-and-silver fur an unusually scruffy mess.

Silvana smiled. 'Hey, Mar—'

Marius wrapped his arms around her. Silvana winced as the black Vulpen's arms pressed against the wounds at her back. It wasn't long before she smiled and put her arms around him, closing her eyes.

'It's good to see you,' she whispered.

'I never thought I'd see you again,' he breathed. His black paws searched Silvana's back, feeling the holes and bare blistering skin. They parted, and he looked deep into her eyes, nothing but concern emanating from within. 'What happened? Who did this to you?'

Asher tensed, a fresh pang of guilt stabbing at his heart.

'It's okay, Mar. It was an accident.' She placed a paw against his cheek and held it there, letting him take in her scent. He closed his eyes and nodded.

'Can I get my things now, *Mar*?' Cara asked abruptly.

Marius's eyes snapped open. 'Ah yeah, sorry about that, can't be too careful, you know?' She shoved past him, slamming the door behind her.

'Marius...' Silvana said softly, grabbing his black paw and bringing it down to her stomach.

'Yeah—' He stopped as his paw reached the small bump, and his eyes grew wide. They remained fixed on his paw for a while before rising and finding her tender gaze, a burning question clearly lingering behind his amber stare. She smiled and nodded. A boyish grin exploded across his face, and he wrapped her up in his arms again, gentler this time but with no less joy and even a little relief.

Asher shifted awkwardly by their side.

'We... err... we need some time to talk,' Marius said with a polite smile, sensing Asher's lingering presence.

'Y-yeah, of course.' Asher smiled. 'Congratulations.'

Marius and Silvana smiled their thanks before running up onto the top deck, Marius helping her up the steps despite her playful objections.

'These are some interesting friends you keep.' Horsa chuckled, appearing from within the depths of *The Silvi*'s cargo hold.

'Tell me about it.' Asher nodded.

The cabin door opened to reveal Cara in her usual dark armour and black cloak. She looked far more comfortable, and Asher could see it on her face.

'That's better,' she breathed with a smile. She turned to Asher. 'There's something in there for you. Something I was able to pick up during my stay in the castle. Don't ask how.' She shivered, a look of disgust crossing her face. Before Asher could even think about what that could imply, she was gone, diving over the ship's side, barely making a splash.

Asher shook his head. 'Show off.'

He and Horsa stepped into *The Silvi*'s dimly lit cabin. Broken boxes and bottles littered the floor, countless sheets of scribbled parchment strewn all over like a ransacked library.

'Now that is a wondrous thing,' Horsa said, eyeing something on the bed.

Asher stepped beside him, and the smile on his face grew. Neatly laid before him was the armour gifted by Queen Tessina. The sigil of Rabbethia shone bright on the chest piece. Without a second thought, he removed his beige prison tunic and donned the armour, temporarily forgetting his lack of any other clothing and that he was with company. He fastened the leather straps until it fit just as it had before.

'Now *there* is a worthy king,' Horsa said with pride, inspecting Asher in his royal armour.

Asher felt it. There was never a time he felt more like he belonged than when he was in that armour. The sigil on his chest filled him with pride.

'We should probably join the others on the beach,' Asher said, turning towards the cabin door.

As he reached the door frame, he felt something grip tight around his forearm, pulling him back into the cabin. Horsa had the look of someone with a burning question, a question he could no longer keep buried. Asher shifted nervously, preparing himself for something uncomfortable.

Horsa tightened his grip. 'Before we continue, I need to know. What happened to my brother to make you king?'

Asher let out a deep sigh. He had expected this question at some point but dreaded it all the same. He wasn't even sure he was ready to answer it. Still, Horsa had a right to know. Within *The Silvi*'s cabin, the war veteran listened intently to all that had happened, watching Asher with dismayed eyes, nodding occasionally when appropriate. A smirk crept across his face when he heard of Hengist's courageous last moments at the claws of the Shangari horde.

'He was a mighty warrior, always had been,' Horsa said with admiration. 'Better than I, but I suppose old age dulled his senses in the end. Oh, how I wish I could have mocked him for it.'

An ache grew in Asher's heart at the sight of his uncle's longing. Of all the loss that Asher had suffered, Horsa had lost too. It created an almost kindred bond between them and, despite the pain, provided a moment of reassurance in this dark moment of dower reflection.

To Asher's surprise, Horsa questioned him about his upbringing, whether he had had a happy life, and whether his father had been good to him. It was only natural, Asher supposed, for his uncle to want to know about his family and how they had been after all this time. He never once asked about Henric, and any time Asher mentioned his younger brother, Horsa quickly dismissed it with another question about what Asher was like.

Then there was Asher's mother. There were so many questions about his mother.

'She gave me this just before she passed,' Asher said as he pulled his silver bow necklace from under his leather chest piece, the tarnished metal glinting softly under the dim orange glow of candlelight. Horsa's eyes widened when he saw it, and he exhaled in awe and disbelief.

'That—' he said with a stutter. He collected himself, forcing a smile. 'That is a fine gift, Asher. Make sure you treasure it.'

'You sound like my mother.' Asher chuckled as he placed the necklace back into the confines of his armour. 'Though I don't know where the other part is. The arrow, I mean. I honestly don't remember it being there when she gave it to me, but I know it's supposed to be there.'

Horsa's smile faded, his restored posture faltering slightly. 'I'm not sure about that, I'm afraid.' He gave Asher a firm pat on the shoulder and smiled before making for the door. 'I, uh, I need some time. This is a lot to take in.' With that, he quietly left the cabin and slowly made his way to the ship's bow, where he spent the night staring up at the night sky, watching the stars above with a sombre reverence.

I have to know what happened to him, Asher thought as he bedded down on the soft sand that night, happy to have family with him once more, sorrowful that the warrior had suffered as much, if not more, than he.

28

A Debt Repaid

The morning's warmth softly caressed Asher's face as sand shifted beneath his back. Waves gently lapped across the shore before retreating once more. Asher opened his eyes, rising gradually as his makeshift pillow unravelled behind him, his cloak returning to its intended place at his back. Rubbing the slumber sand from his eyes, Asher let out a deep yawn, his two large front teeth glinting in the morning light. Out to sea and high into the sky, the light of the Great Lighthouse shone down upon the camp, illuminating the clear blue sky without a single cloud to disrupt it. He took in his surroundings, now revealed under the Lighthouse's gaze.

The beach was relatively narrow, with sand rising quickly into sloping dunes, which shielded the cove from outside view. A small stream nearby cut through a section of the sand dunes, providing access to the land beyond. The clear water trickled across the beach and snaked into the sea. It branched like a tree, searching for the quickest route to the waves.

Must be the tail end of the Aver River, Asher thought, thinking about how close they still were to the Otyrheim border. Voices brought Asher's attention back to the shore. The others were up and eating breakfast, chatting with high spirits, huddled around several campfires along the sandy beach. Each held wooden bowls full of a steaming liquid. Asher jumped to his feet, suddenly aware of his tardiness and hoping no one had noticed his laziness.

'Sit yourself back down,' came a voice behind him.

He turned and found Horsa squatting beside a campfire, stirring a bubbling broth of oats and milk with a long-handled ladle.

I'm glad he's speaking again, Asher thought. From the large iron pot before him, plumes of steam rose, carrying the heavenly scent of cinnamon. There was a sudden pain in his stomach as it growled expectantly. The veteran warrior smiled and picked up a wooden bowl from the sand, scooped a ladle full of porridge and slopped it into the bowl before passing it to Asher.

'Here. You'll need your energy for what lies ahead.'

Asher took the bowl with a polite smile, lowered himself back to the sand, and with ravenous energy, he spooned the porridge into his mouth. It was exquisite compared to his meals within the warden's dungeon. It was also blisteringly hot.

'Thanks,' he said, opening his mouth to allow heat to escape. Steam billowed into the morning air, and he remembered the times he and Henric would pretend to be fire-breathing monsters around the dinner table as scalding hot soup sloshed within their open mouths. He ate the rest of the oats cautiously. 'Where's Cara?' he asked, placing the empty bowl onto the sand.

Horsa nodded towards *The Silvi*, its sleek frame gently bobbing in the still water of the cove, the dark red wood splattered with darker stains of blood.

'She went aboard soon after dawn,' Horsa said with mild disdain. 'Been talking with the other Vulpen all morning.' He leaned close, his voice becoming low. 'I know she's your friend, but I don't trust anyone *that* close to the Vulpen queen.' He returned to the pot and stirred before passing a bowlful to a waiting man.

'I trust her with my life,' Asher asserted, a mild offence taken on behalf of his companion and friend.

Horsa met Asher's determined stare with his own, seemingly judging the resolve in Asher's eyes.

Eventually, he sighed and pushed himself to his feet. 'If you trust her, then so do I. Just... be careful.' He offered a paw to Asher, who took it and was hoisted to his feet. 'We should head out soon. We have a long way to travel and a lot of towns to visit along the way. Some of the folk from the dungeon have already made for home, but they've assured me they'll return, and with their lord's forces no less.' He kicked sand over the remaining embers of the campfire.

'We need to wait for Cara,' Asher said, nodding as he scanned the beach, noting that there weren't as many Rabbethi as when they first set up camp.

Horsa grunted begrudgingly. It was clear he still had reservations about Cara, but he was unlikely to raise them again, at least not with Asher.

'You're finally awake,' a familiar voice said from over Asher's shoulder.

He turned and found Cara emerging from the shallows with a smile, her fur and armour dripping wet, matting against her body.

'And fed,' Horsa added gruffly.

'That's good. We should head out soon,' Cara said. She shook her body, coating Asher and Horsa in a spray of salty water.

'Bah!' Horsa said, jumping back. Asher chuckled.

Cara smiled as her fur immediately puffed up, and she went about patting it back down, stroking her head, arms and tail gently until it had returned to its regular smoothness.

Asher wiped the water from his face and nodded towards *The Silvi*, two Vulpen speaking upon the deck. 'What are they planning to do now?'

Cara turned to the ship. 'Because of the cub Luna—' She paused, a slight smile growing across her snout. 'I mean, Silvana, carries in her belly, they're going to lie low in one of Marius's hideaways on the Northern Continent.'

'Did you talk to her? About your past? About her past?' Asher asked, curious.

'We talked for a time. She told me she doesn't remember much before she arrived in the Outer Rim. Apparently, she was taken in by a tundra hunter who used to be a queen's guard in the Vulpen court. I don't know why he was chosen, but he raised her as his own, and she stopped believing she ever had a life before.'

The Silvi bobbed gently in the shallow cove, Marius and Silvana talking to one another on the deck, smiles across their faces.

'She told me some memories came to her in her dreams, memories of our time together, playing in the palace. But she just dismissed them as dreams.' She breathed a deep, satisfying sigh. 'You have no idea how good it was to see her again, Asher. To see her alive and well. It makes it all worth it.'

Asher smiled and nodded. He had never seen Cara with such hope in her eyes, such contentment.

She continued, 'When this is all over, I'm going to visit them. I'll tell her all about what we got up to as cubs, the games we used to play, the trouble we'd get ourselves into. I'll make sure she remembers everything.'

Asher couldn't help but feel a smile grow across his face, his friend's hope proving impossibly infectious. 'I'll miss them,' he said, an ache growing in his chest. He watched Marius and Silvana return to the ship's cabin, smiling and holding paws as they slowly closed the door behind them. A longing to see them again already began to eat at him.

'Me too,' Cara said, placing a gentle paw on his shoulder. 'Well, we best make our way to the nearest port—see if we can get passage back to Ignimarum.'

'No,' Asher said with an authority he was still getting used to.

'What do you mean?' Cara asked, confused. 'We have the bow. Constance can't open the Silver Coffin without it.'

'I know that.'

'So we need to get it to a safe place. The royal vaults in Ignimarum are impenetrable and the city itself unbreachable.'

That's what the Otyren used to think about Holtbjarg, Asher thought, images flashing into his mind—blood, fire, screams.

'I can't let Constance live,' he finally said with conviction. 'I can't let her Shangari run free across my kingdom, slaughtering and devouring my people as they please.'

The confusion across Cara's face began to soften. Horsa remained silent, nodding as Asher spoke.

'If I can take her out, the Shangari won't have anyone to lead them. They'll flee to the caves and sewers they crawled out from.' He wasn't sure if that was entirely true, but it was a gamble he was willing to make. He had to do something. His people still needed him, and this seemed like the most logical plan.

'What about Nin-Kilim?' Cara said thoughtfully.

'Nin-Kilim is nothing more than a blunt instrument,' Horsa said, stepping forwards. 'Constance is the one giving the orders. Nin-Kilim's grip on the clans will deteriorate without her until only the most loyal remain. He'll return to the Medvedian lands and hunt the roads as before.'

'Look around, Cara.' Asher raised a paw, gesturing to the beach and the Rabbethi prisoners enjoying their newfound freedom. 'Look at the people we've already helped. There's a whole kingdom that needs us, my kingdom. With the bow, we can finally help them.' He stared deep into Cara's eyes, pride and resolution pouring from his own. Deep within his chest, the flame within his heart burned with approval.

Cara eventually sighed. 'Well, who am I to refuse a king?' An exasperated smile grew across her face. 'Let's get your kingdom back.'

***

Asher's ears drooped under the early afternoon heat as they pulsed with heat. It had been a long day of walking under the cloudless sky, the intense light of the Lighthouse blazing down upon the Rabbethi band and their Vulpen companion. The heat didn't seem to bother the others, however. Their beige tunics hung loose on their shoulders, providing a pleasant circulation of air with each gust of wind. They hiked with smiles on their faces, taking in everything around them and enjoying their newfound freedom. It filled Asher with pride. He had helped these people, his people, in their time of need.

The path they trod was not often used, indicated by the thin grass covering the trail as it led through rough shrubbery and heather. The land was flat and had little in the way of shade, save for a few clusters of trees. In the distance before them, the imposing jagged outline of the Rimwall Mountains rose on the horizon, their snow-covered tops disappearing into a thick layer of cloud.

That snow would be a welcome change, Asher thought, not caring that the tips of his long ears would turn to icicles.

In the distance to his right, a line of thick-rooted trees marked the southern border of Otyrheim. It stretched southwest as it raced towards the base of the mountains. It was a peaceful scene despite the forest's presence reminding him of the death and destruction they had just escaped from. Small birds chirped overhead, and wild ponies grazed on the thorny foliage. They raised their heads to glance at the Rabbethi band as they strolled by, unthreatened and uncaring.

Eventually, the group crossed the Onne River via a rickety wooden bridge and joined the main dirt road as it curved east, the harsh vegetation and wild landscape giving way to fields of tilled soil and fences of stone and wood. Some fields had tall stalks of corn, while others had short leafy cabbages, cauliflower and other ground-based vegetables that were staples in a Rabbethi's diet.

In the distance, a cluster of gentle hills rose from the land like the burial mounds of ancient titans, their tombs overgrown and long forgotten. Following the path between the walled fields, it didn't take long for the company to reach the foot of the hills, only stopping occasionally to "borrow" a few potatoes. There wasn't much chance of being scorned by the local farmers, as all the fields were strangely empty. An eerie quiet hung in the air, and even the birds had quieted their joyful songs. The path climbed the side of a grassy hill, and as the group neared the summit, a choking, burning scent suddenly grew thick in the air. Asher, Horsa, and Cara shared a worried look and raced to the summit.

'Oh Folka...,' Horsa breathed.

Before them, a town burned. Huge plumes of black smoke rose high into the air from many thatched roofs, all ablaze. Screams sailed above the crackling fire as dark figures scurried around the small buildings and wide dirt roads.

'We have to go. Now!' Asher yelled, sprinting down the hill towards the inferno.

Horsa and Cara followed closely behind, with the rest of the Rabbethi racing after. Cara unsheathed her curved scimitar, and Asher drew the dagger from his chest.

As they reached the bottom of the hill, they were met by a terrified young Rabbethi woman fleeing towards them, her simple dress torn and drenched in blood from an unseen wound. Behind her was a Shangari, drooling at the maw, hunger in its eyes. The woman stopped and stared wide-eyed at the charging group.

An arrow hissed towards her, soaring inches past her white-furred face and embedding itself deep between the bulging red eyes of the Shangari. The vicious assailant dropped and skidded through the dirt, coming to a stop at the heels of the terrified woman, twitching.

'Are you okay?' Asher asked, coming to a sliding halt.

Her eyes were fixed on the dead Shangari by her feet. She slowly nodded before turning to meet Asher's gaze.

He smiled. 'Get to safety. Everything will be alright.' With that, he raced into the burning town.

Cara and Horsa followed behind, the string of Horsa's bow still humming in his paw.

Asher rushed into a wide town square where villagers usually held markets and festivals. Today, there was only fire and slaughter. Numerous streets disappeared in different directions, flanked by small thatched cottages and larger shops, many of which had collapsed and were now nothing more than burning rubble. Bodies littered the dirt, their blood mixing with the drying mud. Screams echoed from all directions as choking black smoke rose high into the sky, the metallic scent of death thick in the air.

Asher peered through the smoke and found Cara, Horsa and all the freed Rabbethi engaged with Shangari. Cara fought efficiently against multiple foes with the finesse and swordsmanship of a trained dancer, whilst Horsa had his fists raised like an experienced boxer, dodging the reckless slashes of a Shangari's serrated dagger, his bow on the floor by his feet. He returned an attack with his flurry of blows, ending with a solid kick to the Shangari's chest, his foot embedding itself deep into his opponent's bare torso. Bones cracked as blood exploded from the Shangari's mouth, and the rabid creature flew through the air, colliding with burning rubble with a solid thud. The Shangari collapsed to the floor, dead. Another lunged at Horsa, and he expertly stepped to the side, returning to his boxing stance, ready for another bout.

Happy that the veteran warriors could handle themselves, Asher turned his attention to the freed Rabbethi of his group. They were not doing so well. Two had already been slain and were now being feasted upon by their attackers. Asher lunged forwards and stabbed his dagger with surgical precision into the voracious Shangari's chest, narrowly avoiding the serrated front teeth. Its eyes went wide as it screeched in agony, and Asher removed the blade with a sickening slurp. It dropped to the floor, twitching as thick blood began to ooze from the small wound.

He barely had any time before another was on him. It slammed into his flank, throwing him to the ground and sending the King's Bow free of his shoulder. No sooner had his back hit the dirt than his assailant was on him, straddling him with thick black legs. Large red eyes glared down at Asher with an insatiable hunger as a thick wad of blood-soaked saliva dripped from its snout. The stench was putrid, like a latrine full of corpses.

The Shangari brought its teeth down. Asher moved his head at the last second, the long, lacerated snout slamming into the ground in a plume of dust. As the Shangari pulled back for another strike, Asher wrapped his arm around its thick, muscular neck and brought it down, pinning its face in the dirt. It lashed out with razor-sharp claws that tore through Asher's regal blue cloak and left deep grooves into the sides of his leather armour, muffled screeches and wails resonating from its throat. With a swift movement of his free paw, Asher plunged his dagger deep into the Shangari's temple. There was a sudden screech of pain, and the Shangari's body went limp, collapsing with its full weight onto Asher's chest.

'Get off, you rancid bastard,' Asher grunted as he heaved the dead Shangari off, rolling it onto its back. Breathing heavily, he gripped the handle of the dagger still embedded in the Shangari's skull and pulled. With a spurt of blood and a spasm of the Shangari's limbs, the knife was out. Asher breathed heavily, already exhausted—thanks in part to the day's hiking—and wiped his dagger on the Shangari's rags.

I think I've made it dirtier, he thought, studying the stains covering the Shangari's patchwork clothing.

His ears twitched as footsteps approached steadily from one of the burning buildings before him. They were cautiously faint, barely audible over the blazing fires as if the owner weighed next to nothing. Asher looked up, and his eyes went wide. Striding towards him with the calculated grace and nimbleness of a trained assassin was not a Shangari but a cloaked figure, their face hidden beneath the shadow of a black hood, dark brown leather armour upon their chest. Keeping the cloak tight was a circular metal clasp, a vertical piece running through its centre flickering in the firelight. Asher recognised it in an instant. What made his heart truly sink, however, was what the stranger held at their side.

A sinister black crossbow.

Fresh images of Mia's lifeless body flashed into Asher's mind, the black crossbow bolt protruding from her neck, the blood dripping from her mouth. The fire within him raged with a white-hot fury.

'*You!*' he screamed.

'Me,' the figure returned with a low hiss, raising its crossbow with two thick paws. Asher and the figure watched each other in tense silence, fires raging as Shangari and Rabbethi fought for their lives among the rubble. Asher's eyes narrowed on the stranger's paws, focusing on their gloved finger resting on the trigger. He could hear the blood coursing through his body, could feel his soul burning like an inferno.

The assassin's finger twitched, and Asher moved.

He grabbed the Shangari's body beneath him and hoisted it up just as the tip of a black crossbow bolt exploded through its chest. It stopped inches from Asher's nose and sprayed him with fresh, hot blood. He threw the body to the floor, planted a large, booted foot into the earth and propelled himself forwards at lightning speed. If there was a time to be fast, it was now. The figure dropped the crossbow with a heavy thud and threw their black gloves to the ground, revealing two grey paws lined with long, hooked claws.

Asher stepped forwards, swiping his dagger across the assassin's body, but they dodged left and brought their claws down on Asher's shoulder. Asher pulled back, landing a hard punch into his opponent's right cheek. They stumbled back with a grunt of pain, their hood falling from their head. Revealed were the familiar features of a Muuraki assassin, but with feminine features more slender than that of the previous—but no less terrifying or ferocious. Her fur was a dark grey and speckled with darker fur around her eyes and neck. Her orange eyes stared daggers at Asher as she moved her jaw left and right, feeling the impact of his fist.

'I look forward to killing you, little bunny,' she hissed with an excited grin.

'You'll pay for what you did to Mia,' Asher spat through gritted teeth.

'Who?' the Muuraki grinned. 'Oh, you mean the Vulpen woman, yes? In the tavern? She was just... in my way.'

Asher's heart was beating like a war drum, his teeth grinding in his skull. He had a fury in him that he had never felt before. 'Never again will you bring pain to innocent people. *Never again!*'

The Muuraki laughed, exposing her long feline fangs.

Then she pounced.

She came at Asher with erratic movements, darting left then right as she closed the distance. Asher watched as close as he could as the blur of black fur and claws raced towards him. In the end, all he could do was guess which direction she would strike. He stepped to the left as five hooked claws flew into the space where his face had just been. He quickly stepped back again, ducking as another five claws swiped across his throat.

An opening.

Stepping forwards into the Muuraki's space, he brought a knee square into her stomach, lifting her off the ground and sending her tumbling backwards into the dirt. Coughing and heaving, she pushed herself to her feet, blood dripping from her mouth.

'Very good, little bunny. I have underestimated you.' She grinned, panting. 'For that, you've earned the right to know who will be killing you this day.' Standing straight, she wiped the blood from her chin and closed her eyes. With a low bow, she said, 'You should feel pride in your death, knowing you landed a strike against the daughter of the Aguu Ni, leader of my order. My name is Erdene.' Her eyes flashed open, and the vertical slits in her eyes widened to fat black circles. She sprinted towards Asher at a speed he had never seen before, faster than even Cara or Luce. The Muuraki assassin was a blur he couldn't follow. There was no way to tell from which direction she would strike.

He had to guess.

He stepped to his right, and a burning sensation raked up his left shoulder. He screamed. Staring down at his shoulder, he found strips of torn leather were now stained red as pools of blood gushed from within.

Pain, horrific and unbearable pain.

He fell to his knees as blood continued to pour from the five deep gashes on his shoulder. His vision began to blur as he swayed to and fro, the corners of his vision growing dark, the fire in his heart losing its ferocity. The Muuraki assassin stood before him, and he cumbersomely looked up to meet her gaze, a vicious grin across her feline face.

'That was a good fight, no? I think I will remember you.' She raised a claw into the air, and her smile widened. 'Unlike that tavern whore.'

Mia...

Asher's soul erupted within his chest, an immense surge of unyielding fury suddenly coursing through his veins, fuelled by the fire in his chest. His vision was filled with a burning clarity. All the pain faded into background noise. If he were to die here, he would be damned sure this bitch would never hurt anyone again.

He slammed a fist hard into the Muuraki's kneecap, and with a sickening crack, her leg snapped backwards. She howled in pain, crumpling to the floor, grasping her obliterated knee. Asher jumped to his feet, raised his foot above the assassin's head and, with all his might, slammed it down onto the skull of the writhing Muuraki. With a final hiss of rage and pain, the Muuraki's head exploded in a spray of blood and bone. Asher's foot embedded into the ground, the earth trembling at the impact. The assassin's body writhed for a few seconds before slowly becoming still.

A wave of relief washed over Asher as darkness descended over his eyes, the pain in his shoulder returning with horrific speed. The fire inside fled from his muscles and eyes. It was now just a dying ember, breathing its last breaths before the cold night. He collapsed to the ground beside the Muuraki. As he drifted out of consciousness, he heard voices approaching from a distance.

'Asher!' a woman screamed.

'Where's the bow?' a panicked voice asked.

'Over here!' cried a distant fourth.

'How did he do that?'

The voices continued but gradually became dull and muffled, eventually fading from all hearing. He floated in a void, with nothing to see nor hear, no pain nor happiness.

A calm resolve washed over him as he floated in darkness. He hadn't saved his people from the Shangari, but at least Constance didn't have the bow. Most importantly, he had avenged Mia's death. Should his people survive long enough to tell stories of this dark time, he prayed to Folka that they would speak fondly of their short-lived king.

29

Touched by the Ancients

Asher's eyes burst open, his breaths short and fast, his nose twitching wildly. He instinctively reached to his shoulder where the assassin had ripped her claws and found the wound still there, still raw. Thick, sticky blood coated his fingers as he touched the tears in his leather armour, the pain throbbing as he pulled away. He searched for Cara, Horsa, or anyone he recognised.

The sound of chirping birds caught his attention first, and he quickly realised he was no longer in the burning village. Instead, he was standing waist-deep among a sea of tall green grass, surrounded by a dense wall of thick trees. A bright light shone into the clearing, filling it with a vibrant green.

I must be dead, he thought, slightly relieved that there was indeed an afterlife but perturbed the pain from his wound had followed him here.

A strong breeze rolled through the woods, and the tall grass swayed like an ocean tide around him. Trees rustled as the wind surged with intensity before slowly dying, becoming calm. Asher closed his eyes to feel the refreshing chill of the midday breeze. But he couldn't feel it, nor the warmth of the light upon his face. The only sensation plaguing him was the burning in his shoulder.

Yep, definitely dead.

Above, he saw the burning fire of the Great Lighthouse towering before him, floating in the haze of a bright blue sky. It was close, but there was something about it that seemed... off. It didn't take long for Asher to realise the tower was not standing atop a great cliff as it should be but was surrounded by vast swathes of lush trees. The wind died once more, and the forest became deathly still.

The Cinder Sea was nowhere to be seen.

A voice echoed around him. It was a slow, peaceful voice with no apparent owner, and it filled Asher's chest with a comforting warmth like a parent telling a child they are loved. A force within him compelled him forwards, and without thinking, his feet began to move through the tall grass towards a large, fallen tree. The once mighty giant lay half-rotten, its branches long void of greenery, its roots rising high from where they had been ripped from the soil. The tall grass around Asher fell away as he drew closer, growing short as large patches of bare soil began to litter the forest clearing. Loose dirt clung to the roots of the fallen titan, which exploded outwards in all directions, a vast array of insects creeping and slithering around the dead wood. The voice was louder now but muffled, as if Asher was listening from deep underwater.

The warmth in his chest drew him ever closer to the trunk and around the eruption of roots. He stepped past and stopped. A figure sat with its back to the dead tree, a green cloak wrapped around its body, shielding its face and covering its arms.

'H-hello?' Asher said cautiously.

The hooded figure snapped up and began scanning the treeline, his movements panicked and worried.

Asher waited. After a short while, the figure eased, lowering itself and returning its gaze to something hiding in the grass—a creature of some kind that Asher couldn't quite make out.

'I don't think you can hear me,' Asher whispered, defeated. He was now firmly in the belief that he was, in fact, a spirit doomed to wander the world. Marius would be the first he haunted.

The figure then spoke. The voice passed through him like a soothing wave, the soft, muffled words drifting from the shadows of the stranger's hood. Asher's chest once again filled with an overwhelming warmth and sense of inner peace.

'Who are you?' he asked, thinking aloud. Movement caught Asher's attention, and he turned to see a tiny creature appear from the grass. 'And what is *that*?' he breathed, taken aback at the strange little beast.

A small brown-furred animal hopped out of the foliage on four short legs. It had long ears and a nose that twitched. Its fur was a light brown except for a streak of much darker fur running from its nose to its forehead. Its large round eyes sat on either side of its tiny head, and out of its rear protruded a round, fluffy tail. Asher watched in amazement as large hind legs pushed the creature towards the hooded figure in short, controlled leaps. He had never seen such a creature before, yet the adorable little thing had features that he found disturbingly familiar.

As it reached the stranger, it sniffed at their black boots, its small nose twitching curiously. The hooded stranger began to hum as a bright light shone within their cloak, the glow basking the soil beneath their feet. They reached in and pulled out a brilliant white fire, its crackling flames permeating through the stillness of the forest clearing. The pull in Asher's chest intensified once more, and it took all Asher's strength to keep himself from lunging forwards. The figure lowered the fire towards the small creature. It reared onto its hind legs, unafraid of the intense flames that swirled furiously around the stranger's peculiar furless paws.

As the creature's inquisitive nose made contact, a blinding flash exploded from the flame, enveloping Asher in an endless white. He shut his eyes tight, turning away as the stranger's voice echoed in his mind, a single word spoken softly with love.

'Folka...'

***

An upbeat tune began to grow around Asher, breaking the deafening silence. It filled his ears with a melody of rhythmic drums and bouncing stringed instruments. He opened his eyes and found himself standing in the middle of a broad, cobbled street. On either side, buildings of white stone rose high and were lined with trims of gold and silver paint. Flowering vines climbed the structures, and a multitude of trees and beds of vibrant orchids bordered the street as it led away, ending at a monumental building. Asher gasped as his eyes followed the edifice skyward.

'The Great Lighthouse,' he breathed.

Its massive frame filled his entire view as it faded into the deep-blue haze above. This was the closest he had ever been to the Lighthouse, and its immensity was breathtaking. Its sleek black walls streaked upward, creating sharp, oppressive edges.

'What is happening?' Asher exclaimed aloud, beginning to doubt that he was merely dead.

Behind the black monolith, way up high in the sky, sat a perfectly circular shadow, like a spot of blackish blue just hanging in the air, with nothing beneath it to keep it there. Asher knew in a heartbeat what it was—the Wanderer, the mysterious dark spot that only appeared in the eastern sky, worshipped by Medvedians and Fenrathi alike. He couldn't believe he was finally able to see it—so much mystery and divinity, core pillars of eastern beliefs. It didn't seem to move; if it did, it was exceptionally slow. As he stared at the shape, a coldness began to wash over him, as if he was slowly being submerged in icy water, the cold filling his lungs, unable to breathe.

He shivered, his eyes returning to the street, and he watched the people bustling around him. There was every kind of person imaginable. Rabbethi and Vulpen walked side by side while perusing market stands run by much shorter Otyren merchants. Horse-drawn carts filled with goods were led up and down the street as the clang of hammers rang out from smithies, the Medvedian smiths pounding metal into tools. Two Muuraki men enjoyed flagons of beer outside one of the many noisy taverns where bouncing music emanated. They banged their flagons together and laughed joyously whilst other patrons attempted to push past to gain entry. Children laughed high above, and as Asher looked up at the rooftops, he found Ruadrae and Cozati children clambering and scampering across the vines, merrily playing some form of keep-away. He gasped as he saw the pointed black-and-white striped faces of the stocky Shadri conversing with Fenrathi on the many stone balconies. They spoke with eccentric paw gestures as they hung wet clothes on long laundry lines.

I thought the Shadri were all dead, he thought with bewilderment as his history lessons came flooding back to him. *They were all culled during one of the church's early crusades thousands of years ago. There's only supposed to be a pawful of wanderers left.*

A commotion made him turn. A huge procession was walking towards him, a host of all folk parading towards the Great Lighthouse. Asher recognised the pack's leader as the hooded figure from before, their shape still covered by a long green cloak, their face hidden within their hood's shadow. The stranger seemed different this time, hobbling forwards with a hunched back, a long walking stick aiding each step. They raised a trembling naked paw to the crowd in humble acknowledgement, their pink skin seemingly glowing under the midday light.

Keeping the cheering crowd at bay were a few well-armoured, well-dressed individuals. One was a red Vulpen woman, tall, elegant, and strolling with grace and regality. She raised her snout as she regarded the crowd in disdain. Upon her slender frame was a black dress, and she held her paws clasped before her as she glided along the cobbled street. Asher stared in stunned recognition at the item that sat perfectly atop her well-groomed head, a thin golden circlet with a large clear gem at its centre.

'The Judge's Bane,' Asher breathed as they approached, not believing his eyes.

He looked at the others guiding the procession. Towards the back of the initial group was a huge Medvedian man, bare-chested and towering over the rest. His brown fur was thick, as were his muscles and frame. Despite his intimidating size, his face was kind and docile, and he looked around at the people with a joyous grin. The titan waved at the crowd with a massive gloved paw, enjoying the words of rejoice and affection shouted his way. The glove was strange, covered with some kind of dark metallic material as black as the Great Lighthouse itself. Asher gasped as his eyes locked onto something at the centre of the glove—a beautiful clear-cut gem.

'No way...,' he marvelled, taking in the object's significance. But as soon as he had noticed it, the Medvedian lowered his paw, and it disappeared behind his hulking mass.

Heavy sniffing drew Asher's eyes in front of the Medvedian, where a hunched hooded figure patrolled, the fluffy grey tail of a Fenrathi trailing behind and swaying as they walked. A black hood covered their torso and face, but a recognisable long canine snout protruded from the hood's shadows, sniffing the air as if hunting. Gold chains dangled from the lower jaw, looping under the upper lips. It was a beautiful piece of jewellery. Wrapped in golden chains and fixed to the lower jaw was another Shepherd Stone. Asher couldn't believe it. He was in the presence of not one but three relics of the ancients, the power of the Shepherd—god. His mind raced through his memories, through lessons and books, desperate to figure out where he could be and what it all meant.

A sharp rasping made Asher turn. A Shangari erupted from the shadows of a nearby alley and sprinted towards the hooded leader of the procession. Cries and gasps coursed over the crowd as the creature raced ever closer, his ragged brown tunic fluttering in a cloud of dust. The figure calmly raised a paw from within their green cloak, and the procession halted. The crowd behind ceased their chatter. The music in the tavern stopped, and the street became silent as all present held their collective breaths. The Shangari screeched sharp, chattering sounds that grated in Asher's ears and wrenched all sense of well-being from his heart.

A Rabbethi woman leapt between the stranger and the charging Shangari. She was short, covered in light brown fur and wore dark leather armour, a deep-blue cloak clasped at the shoulders. At her side was a long sword, and slung over her shoulder, Asher could just make out the sturdy string of a bow. He couldn't help but stare, the flare of recognition burning away in the back of his mind like a rash. A strange pull in his chest heaved him in her direction, and he took a heavy step towards her.

'What keeps doing this?' he said, frustrated at his body, worried that something within was attempting to break out.

As the Shangari reached the Rabbethi woman, it drew a rusty dagger and thrust for her abdomen. The woman's eyes burst into flames, and with a speed faster than Asher had ever seen, she slammed her fist down across the Shangari's long, snouted face. Blood sprayed across the stone street, and the Shangari crumpled to the floor. Asher looked at the Rabbethi woman, at her bloody fist, then back to her face. The fire in his chest began to burn. He recognised her markings, the streak of much darker fur that ran from her nose, between her eyes, to the top of her head.

'The creature from the forest,' he breathed as his eyes widened. The force in his chest surged forwards with a renewed intensity. He let the surge take him. Whatever was doing it, it clearly had somewhere it desperately wanted to take him. With a burst of sudden acceleration, he flew towards the woman.

All sight and sound vanished instantly, and Asher was engulfed in a black void. Much to his annoyance, however, the pain in his shoulder still burned with a stinging fury. He peered into the darkness around him. The city and all its people were gone. There was no music, no hooded figure or great crowd of people, no bloodied Shangari lying in the street. His feet were still firmly placed on what felt like solid ground, but looking down, he saw nothing.

Well, now what?

A ball of raging white fire suddenly burst from his chest. Asher stumbled back, shielding his eyes from the sudden light, wincing at the fiery heat. He patted at his chest, but there were no scorch marks to be seen. The fire stopped just out of reach, and he stared in bewildered wonder at the flame now floating in the emptiness before him.

Footsteps began to echo in the darkness, and Asher searched the void, desperate for the source, desperate for anyone other than him. He looked beyond the flame and found the Rabbethi woman from the street approaching, her eyes fixed on Asher. No longer were they ablaze like before. Instead, they watched Asher with a look of joyous relief and pride, like a parent gazing upon a returning child. They looked wet.

She's crying.

'You...,' Asher began, watching the woman, unable to move away. He thought hard about what he was about to say, about how crazy it sounded in his mind. 'You were the creature in the forest.' It sounded crazier, but something in his bones told him it was true.

She nodded. 'Yes.' Her voice was soft and trembling as if holding back a torrent of emotions.

Another thought crossed Asher's mind. The idea warmed his heart, and without permission, his mouth spoke. 'You're Folka...'

She nodded again, a broad smile growing across her face. 'Yes.'

Asher smiled as a great weight ascended from his chest. He couldn't explain it. This was Folka—*the* Folka—the founder of his people, his long-lost ancestor. Whether he was dead or in a near-death fever dream, Asher didn't care. Being face to face with her was like reuniting with a long-dead loved one, like finding a part of himself he had lost long ago. Tears began to well in the corners of his eyes as he chuckled with joy.

'My dear, brave Asher,' Folka said, stepping forwards. 'I'm so proud of you.'

He rubbed his eyes dry. 'But I failed. Constance doesn't have the bow, but my people, our people, are still in danger.' He sighed. 'I've failed them.'

Folka shook her head. 'That's not what I'm proud of. I'm proud of all the times that you struggled, you carried on. I'm proud of you for never giving up, never backing down. Even in your darkest moments of despair, you always got back up because people needed you. You might not tell others around you. You might hide your pain behind a mask of smiles, but I see your pain. I know you've struggled, and I am oh so very, very proud of you.' She smiled softly at him. 'It's okay not to be okay.'

Asher stared at her, unable to speak. All his life, he had put on a smile, hidden his pain the best he could because there was someone else who needed him to be strong. His pain had gone by hidden, stashed away in the back of his mind where only he knew it was there. But she had been there, through every brave face, through every forced smile. Folka had felt the pain with him, understanding him, knowing him.

Tears began to fall down Asher's cheeks, a lifetime of troubles releasing at once. It felt good, so very, very good. Folka crouched beside him with a sincere smile, the ball of white fire in the palm of her paw.

Asher sniffed, nodding to the fire as the last of his tears trickled down. 'What is it? It came from me. I-I don't understand.'

'It's you, and it's me. We're the same.'

Asher nodded in understanding. The fire that had once belonged to Folka, her gift from the Shepherd, now resided in him. She had always been there whenever his emotions got the better of him, whenever a fight began, and his senses became sharper, his muscles stronger. It was her fire that allowed him to wield the King's Bow, her fire that kept him safe before the Silver Coffin under White Cliffe. It all made sense now.

Folka took the fire and placed it firmly against Asher's chest. Without even a sizzle and no sense of heat or pain, it merged into his chest, disappearing beneath the scratched leather armour. 'I share your burdens. I feel your joys. I lend my strength to you, but know that you are the one with the heart to wield it.'

Asher closed his eyes, embracing the familiar warmth.

***

He bolted upright, panting heavily. His eyes raced around the unfamiliar space. Soft linen caressed the inside of his clenched fists, and the thin sheet that covered him was bunched under his tight grip. Eventually, the sleep haze passed from his mind, and he opened his fists, letting the thin white sheet fall over his legs.

He ached horribly.

Every attempt to move was met with stiff resistance. It was as if he had been turned to stone, with every twitch of his muscles causing a fresh wave of pain to quake through his rigid body. His shoulder hurt the most, the stiffness working in unison with the searing pain of his wound to ensure Asher was the most uncomfortable he could be. He looked down and found bandages wrapped across his torso. They appeared fresh, with little to no staining where the Muuraki assassin had cut him.

Someone's been taking care of me.

He settled back against his pillow and remembered his dream, remembered the white fire seeping into his chest.

Her strength is mine, he thought, repeating her words. As if called to action, a warmth began to pulse from his chest, seeping into his arms and legs and easing his aching muscles.

'Thank you,' he whispered, and Folka's fire warmed in his chest. There were no words, but Asher could feel her meaning. "You're welcome."

He looked around the room as he shifted in the bed. It was a small space, dimly lit by an assortment of candles placed inside plastered white nooks in the wall. There were no windows to speak of. A thick root emerged from the plaster in one corner of the room before looping up and disappearing into the ceiling.

I must be in an underground burrow, he realised, the closed walls and earthy scent breathing comfort into his mind.

Beside the bed sat a simple wooden table and chair. On it, bloody rags spilt over the rim of a clay bowl. Asher strained to see inside, and he saw the water within was a dark crimson.

'I must have lost a lot of blood,' he mused, feeling a fresh sting in his shoulder as if someone had poked it.

'You did,' came a quiet voice from the far corner. 'Almost didn't make it.'

Someone was sitting in a chair, their figure masked in shadow. They stood and stepped towards the bed, becoming fully bathed by the candlelight, two silver rings reflecting the flickering flames. Cara looked down at Asher, a soft smile illuminated in a yellow glow across her face.

'I'm glad you're alright,' she breathed, visibly relieved.

Asher smiled, happy to see his friend still alive. 'You too.'

'You had us worried for a while,' Cara continued, walking closer. 'Five days you've been asleep. We thought if the blood loss didn't kill you, the infection would.' She reached the end of the bed and sat, her feet firm on the wooden floorboards, her eyes inspecting Asher's bandaged shoulder.

'Five days?' Asher breathed. That was too long, too much time wasted while Shangari ravaged the land, too much time given to Constance in her search for the other Shepherd Stones or those capable of wielding them.

'Do you remember what happened that night? When you killed the Muuraki?' Cara asked, staring into his eyes, searching them for something, though Asher couldn't tell what.

He looked away, not having thought about it till now. The last he remembered, blood was pouring from his shoulder, his eyes closing. Then blackness. 'No,' he replied, feeling the sting in his shoulder re-emerge. 'I saw her claws, and then... nothing.'

'You moved faster than I had seen any Rabbethi move before,' Cara said, watching Asher closely. 'And your eyes... they were on fire.'

He thought about that for a while, recalling Constance and the Judge's Bane, how her eyes burst into flames as the stone hummed to life. 'It must have been the bow,' he said with a dismissive shake.

'You weren't holding the bow,' Cara said flatly. 'Whatever that was, it came from inside you.'

'Inside me?' Asher said, surprised, and then in a hushed whisper, 'Folka...'

'Folka?'

'It's a long story,' he dismissed with a reassuring smile. 'Just know that everything's okay. I'm okay.' He meant it this time. There were no lies, no masking to ease the worry of others. His troubles and resilience had been noticed, his fears and pain validated. He was truly okay.

Cara nodded with a smile before rising from the bed. 'Come on. There's a lot of people waiting for you.'

Asher didn't move. A question still plagued his mind, a question whose answer he wasn't sure he wanted to know. He trusted Cara completely, yet no amount of trust could stop the nagging in his mind, the venomous thoughts whispering paranoia.

What if you're wrong? What if she lies again?

He met the Vulpen's eyes and steadied his nerves. 'Why didn't you tell me about the plan?' He was unable to keep the sting of betrayal out of his voice. 'Don't you trust me?'

Cara eased herself back onto the bed, her smile fading. The look in her eyes shifted to one of guilt and sorrow. 'I do trust you, Asher, but I had orders not to get you involved.' She edged closer. 'Corvo and Tessina told me it would be more believable if you didn't know.'

'Were there even any ships following us to Otyrheim?' Asher asked, knowing the answer already.

She shook her head. 'It was just us. I was supposed to get you in and out with as little attention as possible. Some agents were already in the city if I needed them, but I don't think they made it out when Constance attacked.'

'I thought you abandoned me,' Asher said as he looked down at the bed sheets, a pit growing in his stomach. 'I nearly died down there, you know, and you would have never found me. I didn't think I—' He suddenly felt arms wrap around his shoulders, Cara's head resting on his.

'I would *never* abandon you,' she said softly. 'You're my friend.'

Asher wrapped his arms around the Vulpen and rested his head on her shoulder. He believed her—he had to, for his sake. 'I don't have many friends left,' he breathed as tears gathered in the corners of his eyes.

They held each other for a short while within the dimly lit room of the underground burrow, the candles flickering in their earth and plaster nooks, the scent of soil and root hanging faintly in the air. Wrapped in Cara's lean but muscular arms, Asher released a long, calming sigh.

For the first time in a long while, he felt safe.

30

On the King's Orders

Cara paced within the small room. 'You spoke to her? You spoke to Folka?' She shook her head in disbelief. 'But she's been dead for thousands of years.'

'I know it sounds crazy,' Asher replied, attempting to make sense of it all himself. 'But her fire, her essence, lives in me. It's why I can use the King's Bow and others can't, why I could get close to the Silver Coffin. I don't know if my ancestors had her fire before me, but it would make sense if they were able to wield the bow, too.'

Cara stopped, turning to Asher with a frown. 'Does that mean Constance has Thena's fire in her?'

'I guess it must do,' Asher replied.

'Damn. The first of my people, trapped inside that mad woman.' A snarl arose from the depths of Cara's throat. 'Well, did you ask Folka anything? Is the Shepherd's power really in that Silver Coffin? Why did the ancients fight the Shepherd in the first place?'

Asher shook his head. 'I didn't get a chance. Before I knew it, she was gone, and I woke up. We can't talk, but I can... *feel* her, if that makes sense?' On cue, Asher's chest warmed with Folka's presence. He smiled, satisfied.

Cara sighed. 'I guess we'll have to figure things out the old-fashioned way.' She smiled, meeting Asher's eyes. 'Get dressed. We have a lot of work to do.' With that, she exited the room through a wooden door opposite the bed.

Asher's leather armour was draped over a chair in the corner, cleaned of all blood but still bearing gnarled tears across the left shoulder. With a wince of pain, he rolled out of the bed and heaved the armour over his shoulders. He strapped himself in, fastening the buckles around his waist, groaning as his body refused to bend, but thankful the red-ribboned blade was still safely sheathed within the chest piece. The blue cloak clasped into place on both shoulders, bearing tears where the Shangari had raked its sharp claws across its blue threads. Asher didn't mind. It made him feel battle-hardened, and a part of him hoped it would gain a certain level of respect among the veterans.

Once his armour was on and complete, he took a deep breath, feeling safer, less vulnerable, and more like a king. Confidence began to seep into his very being, and he stepped through the wooden door. On the other side, a long, winding corridor of dimly lit earthen walls and wooden floorboards stretched away before him, every so often branching in a new direction that vanished around a corner. Asher followed the lit candles around several bends and up a steep slope before coming to a small wooden door. He pushed it open.

Cara leaned over an iron pot hanging from a chain that dangled from the thatched ceiling. It hovered above a small fire close to one corner, a bubbling pool of porridge steaming from within, filling the room with the scent of hot oats and milk. Rays of light shone through cracks in a boarded-up window. Specs of dust drifted lazily in the warm space, dancing in the golden spotlight. The white plaster walls were covered in all manner of farming tools and dried produce tied together with frayed string.

Cara sniffed at the porridge, a grimace crossing her snout. Asher chuckled, and she looked up, smiling. 'Shall we?' she asked, rising to her feet and gesturing to a sturdier door. 'No time for breakfast, I'm afraid.'

After a deep breath, Asher nodded. Cara passed a long table and over to the wooden door, pulling it open and letting the bright light of day pour inside. Asher shielded his eyes as Cara stepped out, disappearing into the whiteness.

A chorus of noises hummed from beyond, a cacophony of shouting and movement. For a moment, he thought he was still dreaming, that the door would whisk him away to some far-off land. It couldn't possibly be the sleepy, half-burned village he had been in previously. He stepped through, and his eyes went wide.

The village was overflowing with activity. An ocean of Rabbethi hurried about him, carrying materials, weapons and food. Many wore the armour of a noble house and carried sturdy, well-kept weapons, while others wore simple, muddy tunics and wielded scythes, pitchforks, and other farming tools. Senior soldiers barked orders, pointing in different directions and sending soldiers and resources where they needed to go. One of the soldiers stopped and stared, his mouth agape. With a start, his training abruptly returned, and he lowered his head, raising a fist to his chest in salute.

'Y-Your Highness,' he said in surprise.

Others took notice, and the orchestra of motion suddenly stilled, the street becoming eerily silent. Asher gazed over the sea of floppy ears as hundreds of Rabbethi up and down the street stared in awe. They then slowly began bowing their heads, their fists thumping into their chests.

'They've been arriving since the attack on the village,' Cara said with a smile, sensing Asher's disbelief. 'Word about your return spread across the kingdom, about how *you* rescued your people from the Otyren dungeon and reclaimed the King's Bow.'

'But that was all *you*,' Asher replied, his eyes wandering over the multitude of different coloured ears flopped in his direction, many tied in the traditional warrior's bun.

'True, but they don't need to know that,' she whispered, giving Asher a nudge in the ribs. 'Let's get you to Horsa and the war witan. They'll tell you more.'

'War witan?' Asher blinked, but Cara was already moving.

The Rabbethi army parted as Cara led Asher through the crowded streets. He smiled at as many friendly faces as he could, giving a nod of thanks or acknowledgement despite his aching muscles. In each Rabbethi's eye was something Asher hadn't seen in a long time, something that had the strength to carry them to the ends of the world.

Hope.

The street climbed a slight incline, and as the pair walked, the sounds of organised chaos returned behind them. On either side of the street were more homes similar to the one Asher had recovered in, though most of the thatched roofing had turned black or been reduced to ashes. People were moving in and out of the more intact structures, using them as abodes or bases of operations. Others were destroyed entirely, smoke rising where faint embers still burned. A thicker plume of black smoke rose in the distance as the remains of the Shangari attackers were piled high and burning, their filth removed from the sanctity of the world. The smoke that rose from their corpses seemed almost darker than regular smoke.

Asher and Cara passed a group of kneeling villagers praying around one of the many red stains that coated the white walls. An elderly woman dressed in black wept as she pressed a brown paw to the dried blood. Asher's stomach knotted at their grief, their sorrow. The mourners didn't notice as those around stopped and bowed to Asher.

'Never again,' he breathed, the words echoing in his mind. He felt the fire in his chest burn with a sudden intensity before dying once more, Folka's fire flaring in agreement.

As they neared the hill's summit, a long thatched building came into view, a column of smoke rising through a large hole in the centre of its sloped roof. It stretched to the left and right and was much taller than the homes and shops surrounding it. The wooden frames and supportive beams were engraved with Rabbethi toiling away in fields, images of grain, corn and vegetables swirling around the figures like a whirlwind of countryside culture. It was an impressive building, not awe-inspiring like the keep at White Cliffe or the grand palace of Ignimarum, but the level of craft and love that went into its construction couldn't be denied. It was clear the people living within the town cared deeply for it.

The area around the hall was a hive of activity. A sea of tents flapped in the gentle breeze, all of varying colours and all with carts close by, full of equipment and supplies. The powerful scent of horse manure lumbered in the wind as high-ranking soldiers marched in and around the tents, barking orders and directing the lower-ranking soldiers in their daily chores. Closer to the halls, large open doors—where Asher imagined a market would usually be—were much more extensive and decorated tents with squires meticulously maintaining weapons and armour around larger campfires. As Asher walked through the makeshift camp, he marvelled at the intricacies etched into the armour and the decorations adorned to the weapons being sharpened.

These must be officer tents.

There was even a pop-up blacksmith working in one corner of the dirt plaza from the back of a large cart, the familiar sound of hammers clanging against iron and steel echoing over the barrage of voices. They all stopped when Asher passed, bowing their heads and raising clenched fists to their chests. Asher and Cara calmly walked through the parting crowd, Asher smiling and nodding if any soldiers peeked a glance from their deep bow. The thick open doors of the hall were guarded on either side by two tall Rabbethi soldiers, both with intricate helmets that pulled their ears down behind their backs, protecting them. They kept their sharp glaives pointed up as they bowed.

The inside was dimly lit, save for the soft morning light leaking from the open doors and the large square hole in the thatched roof where a column of gold poured into the space below. A small fire crackled beneath the hole, surrounded by a ring of low wooden benches. The flames did little to illuminate the shadows created by the bright daylight.

More high-ranking soldiers sat around the fire, sharing flagons of what Asher assumed was some kind of apple cider, judging from the sweet scent. Spanning the width of the hall on either side of the fire were rows of long tables and benches full of soldiers who ate and drank in a tense quiet. The air was warm and had a halted calm about it as if on the eve of a great storm. This was where vital decisions were made, and the mood certainly reflected it.

Beyond the fire was a heavy square table raised upon a wooden stage with steps leading up on either side. Several men and women surrounded the table, their tall ears flopping forwards as they gazed down at a large scroll. They were all dressed in leather and plated armour, each embellished with different colours and iconography.

They're all the earls of the kingdom, Asher thought as he followed Cara around the fire.

My kingdom. My earls.

He recognised a couple of them from when his father held court, but that was many years ago. The earls rarely came to the palace in person after his mother's death, sending representatives in their place to formalise decisions within the realm. He didn't know whether his father had expected this method of running the kingdom to continue when Asher was king, but he quietly wished his father had spent at least some time introducing him to the earls and less time pouring through old books. Asher looked up at the table before him, at the most powerful people in his land, trepidation in his steps. Cara patted him on the shoulder. She said nothing, but after a smile and a nod, Asher's confidence rose, the agent's unspoken support giving him what he needed to continue.

As they reached the top of the stairs and their footsteps echoed on the floorboards of the stage, one of the men at the table turned. Unlike the others, this man's oak-coloured ears were tied together in the style of a traditional warrior, his fur covered with specks of grey. This Rabbethi Asher knew very well. Out of his dirty prison tunic and now in worn leather armour was Horsa. His eyes widened at the pair, and he hurried over, a broad grin growing across his aged face. Before Asher realised what was happening, the war veteran wrapped his arms around him and embraced him tightly.

'Thank Folka, you're okay,' Horsa said with relief.

It felt nice, feeling the embrace of someone pleased to see him, and Asher wrapped his arms around him in return. The two parted after a short time, and Horsa turned to Cara.

'Thank you for staying by him all that time. You're a... you're a true friend.'

'Of course,' she replied with a nod.

Horsa slapped Asher on the shoulder. 'Come, Your Highness! I'd like you to meet your earls. When news reached them of your return, they immediately assembled their forces and marched here, slaying any Shangari in their path.' He stood a little taller as he spoke, a prideful shine in his eyes. 'All the lands west of the Avon River have been cleared of the vile creatures.'

Asher turned to Cara, smiling as they followed Horsa towards the large rectangular table.

'What?' she said, returning his gaze.

'Nothing. Just... thank you for taking care of me.'

'You're welcome,' she said gently, returning the smile.

As they walked across the stage, Asher noticed a grand, intricately designed chair deeper into the stage, with swirling patterns carved into its frame – an earl's chair. At its centre was the image of a horse rearing on its hind legs.

A large map of Rabbethia covered the table, the Rimwall Mountains curving around its eastern border, under the southern border and disappearing to the west. Otyrheim formed an impenetrable barrier along the western side, and the Cinder Sea separated Rabbethia from the Northern Continent and Terravulpa, the Vulpen Queendom. To the northwest stood the all-powerful Great Lighthouse. Beyond that were the warring kingdoms of Fenrath and Medvekov and the home of the mysterious dark shape known as the Wanderer.

Asher looked up from the table and found himself staring into the eyes of several men and women patiently waiting for his attention. They bowed deep at his gaze, soft thumps sounding as their fists padded against their chests. Asher smiled at each, nodding. Horsa gestured to each Rabbethi as he introduced them.

'This is Edgar, Earl of Ironsire and lord of the iron-rich hills to the south,' he said, gesturing to a short, stocky individual with black fur and dull, heavy-plated armour clasped with a black cape.

'My hardened men are at your disposal, Your Highness,' the muscular man said, smiling a toothless grin at Asher as he bowed once more, his voice a deep rumble. 'Our iron fortitude will bear down on this witch and crush her into dust! Just like we squashed that little Third Son uprising a few years back.' He chuckled as he tapped the head of a two-pawed hammer resting against the table beside him, its thick head simple and covered in old nicks and scratches.

Asher's mind raced back to Otyrheim, to the Third Son he fought within the bowels of the Under Kitchen. He remembered the hatred in the rabid Rabbethi's eyes, the acid in his words. A solemn ache filled his chest. He would have words with this earl about their treatment after this war was all said and done. He nodded his thanks to the short man, who grinned broadly.

Horsa then gestured to a white-furred woman, who gave a courteous nod. She was dressed in brown leather armour, clasped with a cape of sky blue, and Asher was taken in by the intricate details engraved into the chest piece, designed in such a way as to imitate fish scales.

'This is Eawynn, Earl of Saecasire, lady of the rugged coast,' Horsa said as the woman stood straight. She was taller than Asher, with a long face and tall ears that remained rigid despite their great height. Bright red eyes watched him with curiosity. He had never seen a Rabbethi with the Blood Eyes before, though he knew they existed throughout the kingdom. They were shunned by most common folk, who believed them to be cursed or bringers of ill tidings. To see one as an earl, a representative for a whole region, was incredible.

'I'm sure you're wondering how I became earl, Your Highness,' Eawynn said, aware of Asher's inquisitive stare.

He averted his eyes. 'My apologies.'

'Not to worry, Your Grace,' she said with a smile. 'Although some see my condition as a curse, all see my strength of will. No one questions my ability to lead, but that is a tale for another time.'

'There are none more skilled with the glaive than those that call the white cliffs and rocky shores of Saecasire home,' Horsa continued.

'Prince Horsa is too kind,' Eawynn said with a nod of appreciation. 'His absence from the kingdom has been sorely missed. Having both of you returned to us is truly fortuitous.'

'Please, Wyn,' Horsa said, raising a paw. 'I am no prince. I... forfeited that title long ago.'

Wyn? That's very familiar, Asher thought as he watched the earl's eyes shift to Horsa, her expression softening as she lingered there.

Her smile lessened, and she nodded.

'Thank you,' Asher said with a smile, breaking the silence. 'I'll do my best to be worthy of your strength of will.'

Eawynn's smile returned as she bowed to Asher.

Horsa next gestured to a man whose fur was a dark, woody brown. His ears were shorter than the others, and the fur under his sharp hazel eyes was black and matted. The man's gaze as he stared at Asher was intense. His leather armour was clasped with a cloak of deep green, and the armour itself had engraved on its front vines and leaves wrapping around the Rabbethi's chest and sides. Asher let slip an exhale as he marvelled at the beautiful leatherworking.

'This is Cedric,' Horsa said. 'Earl of Valwoodsire and lord of the woodland valley that follows the Avon River south to the Rimwall Mountains—best archers in the kingdom.'

Cedric said nothing but maintained his concentrated stare. All Asher could think to do was smile and nod.

Horsa lastly turned to a man standing proudly as Horsa's paw pointed in his direction. 'And this is Athelbad,' Horsa said with a tone that did not mask a slight exasperation. 'It was his town of Highguard you saved and whose hall you now stand in.'

He was an average-sized Rabbethi with light brown fur and long ears that drooped on either side of his head. His leather armour was simple and engraved with a stallion rearing on its hind legs, a powerful image for a distinctly average-looking individual. It also appeared to be in perfect condition. Clasped at the shoulders was a cloak of crimson red.

'He is Earl of Guardsire, lord of the horse riders that roam the great plains this side of the river.' As soon as Horsa had finished the introduction, the young Athelbad marched around the table, grinning from ear to ear. Cara shifted.

'It's alright,' Asher whispered.

Seemingly unaware, Athelbad continued his approach with one paw raised forwards in greeting. Asher raised his paw instinctively, and they clasped each other's forearms in a solid embrace.

'Thank you so much, Your Highness,' Athelbad beamed, shaking Asher's forearm with excessive vigour. 'If you hadn't shown up, that would have been it for my people and me!' He released Asher's forearm and stepped away, his nose twitching excitedly.

'Don't mention it,' Asher replied, smiling. 'Your armour is beautiful, by the way. Is it new?'

'No,' Athelbad replied quickly. 'I've had it for years. Saved my life in many a scrap, I can tell you, fighting with bandits and the like.' A scoff from Edgar made Athelbad snap his head in his direction. 'Got something to say, little man?' he spat, an explosive change in the young earl's tone. Edgar just smiled a knowing smile and shook his head. 'That's what I thought.' Athelbad turned back to Asher, and his smile returned. 'If there's anything you need, Guardsire and her horses are at your disposal.' He bowed a deep and prolonged bow before backing away to his spot at the table.

Horsa placed his paws on the table and eyed each earl. Asher could feel the atmosphere become tense, growing heavy like a prelude to a brewing storm.

The pleasantries were over.

'Now to business,' Horsa said, his voice dark. 'Earl Goda of Westersire has refused the call. He assures the church would never breach his defences, and we should all flee to his inner stronghold of Dunburh for protection.' Horsa pointed to the far southwest of the map, at the image of a castle nestled among some trees near the border.

Edgar spat a thick glob of saliva onto the wooden floor in disgust. 'Coward.'

Horsa nodded in agreement and pointed at another castle east of the Avon River, which split the kingdom in two. 'We've had no word from Earl Theodora of Wealdasire, and I fear the worst. The Shangari forces that attacked here were likely a large scouting or hunting party, part of a larger force. Oakenhall has likely fallen.' A sombre silence fell upon the table.

'My sister is tough,' Earl Eawynne said with a quiet resolve. 'She's alive.'

'What of Earl Cuthred of Eastingsire?' Athelbad asked, pointing to the image of a castle nestled within the mountains on the far east of the map. 'Could he not rally the mines to fight for us?'

Horsa shook his head. 'This morning, I received a raven from the steward of Bourneburh Castle informing me that the castle had fallen. Cuthred is dead, as are his family. Sending this message was likely the last thing the steward ever did. I'll make sure his family is compensated handsomely.'

Even in times of war, Asher thought, watching Horsa. *He's thinking about others, ensuring their hard work does not go unrewarded, even in death.*

'Bloody Third Son,' Edgar breathed, spite biting into each word.

Horsa continued, 'The city is now under the control of the mine workers. They have sided with Constance and have sent men to bolster her forces. She has likely promised them their freedom, though whether she intends to keep that promise remains to be seen.'

'We let them keep their miserable lives, and this is how they repay us?' Edgar bellowed, slamming a fist down upon the table and denting the wood beneath his clenched paw. 'These Third Sons will pay for their treason!'

'Agreed,' Horsa continued, glancing around at the other earls. 'But without the aid of Goda, Cuthred or Theodora, our forces are not strong enough to take on Constance and her army of acolytes, Shangari and now Third Sons.'

The table fell silent as all around delved into deep thought.

'My queen will provide aid,' Cara said, stepping forwards. 'She has aided Asher in his fight thus far. She would not abandon him now.'

The others looked at each other with mistrustful eyes, not saying a word.

'I have already sent ravens to Ignimarum. They will come.'

'You did what?' snapped Earl Eawynne, her crimson eyes growing wide as she locked onto Cara.

'I did what was best for *your* kingdom, for Asher.' Cara met Eawynn's stare, and the two began to fight an intense battle of will and fortitude.

'I'm sorry, Domina Cara,' Horsa eventually said as the atmosphere became too tense to bear. 'We cannot rely on the word of a foreign queen. We must look to bolster our own forces from within.'

'You question the word of my queen?' Her irritated gaze snapped to Horsa as she stepped towards him, her upper lip curling to reveal sharp canine teeth.

Horsa remained still, unaffected by the predator before him, and it felt as though a single spark could ignite the hall in flames.

'What say you, Your Highness?' came Athelbad's voice from across the table, a few paces further back.

Asher blinked, pulling himself away from the confrontation, and looked towards the young Rabbethi earl.

He took a deep breath, choosing his words carefully.

'I trust Cara, and if she trusts her queen, so do I. Queen Tessina will come.'

No one spoke, but it was clear upon the earl's faces that they disapproved. Asher pointed to a coastal region on the map, just south of White Cliffe City. 'Queen Tessina's forces should land there. After we discover what has happened in Earl Theodora's land, we will march to that location and await her arrival.'

Silence.

After what felt like an age, each earl raised their fist to their chest and bowed. Asher released a long-held breath, feeling Folka's fire warm his chest, a sense of pride coursing through his veins.

Horsa dipped his head. 'The king has spoken.'

31

Death and Thunder

Earl Theodora's body swayed gently in the gathering wind. A frayed rope had been tied around her long brown ears, pulling them tight and suspending her corpse from a winding branch of a huge oak tree. Dark, cavernous holes stared down at Asher from where crows had feasted upon her eyes. Her fur was blackened, charred from the fire she likely died upon. The remains of a pyre smouldered beneath her, thin wisps of smoke rising to catch the wind like grasping spectres.

Asher retched, the taste of bile filling his mouth, making his eyes water. He raised a paw to his mouth and swallowed, feeling the contents of his breakfast return to his stomach. His gaze moved to the others in the tree. There were hundreds of them, ranging from the very young to the very old, many missing limbs, the white of their bones stained red and revealed to the world. Asher tightened the grip on his horse's reins, the fire in his chest surging and crackling. His eyes landed on the lifeless face of a young kit, still holding a stuffed toy mouse in a bloody paw. He clenched his jaw, turning his horse.

The air was heavy as dark clouds drifted encumbered overhead, threatening to unload their great weight upon the city of Oakenhall. Horsa, Cara and the earls were all mounted and staring up at the tree with the same look of horror and disgust across their faces. Behind them, the combined military might of the earls shifted uneasily, some staring up at the tree, others looking down at the muddy street underfoot. They whispered private prayers as their boots sank into a mixture of blood and mud, their words rolling mournfully beneath the heavy quiet. Asher looked at their faces. A mix of fear and frustration flowed through them in equal measure.

The sea of Rabbethi filed into the lower half of the city's market square, where the giant oak tree of Oakenhall's namesake grew tall, thick and weary. The soldiers stood in regimented units, each man and woman keeping close to others of the same earl, their glaives standing tall like a forest of blades. The rest filled the winding streets like snakes back to the main gate. Those at the back received whispered words of the gruesome tree passed down along the ranks.

The main gate had been wide open upon their arrival, the thick wooden walls scorched in some areas and covered in thousands of deep scratch marks in others. Shangari bodies lay strewn about the walls, rotting where they died. Hopes had been high at the lack of Rabbethi defenders, soldiers or civilians, with most expecting to find streets filled with slain innocents. Hope continued to climb as they found the road leading to the central plaza devoid of anything other than blood and Shangari. That changed upon seeing the corpse tree. All hope had been ripped from the hearts of those foolish enough to believe the city had survived, Asher included.

Beyond the tree stood the earl's hall, standing tall before the remains of its citizens. It was similar in style to Earl Athelbad's hall but on a much grander scale. Several gaps marked the thatched roof, indicating the presence of more than one great hearth fire within, though no smoke rose through them. Outside, the lower walls were splattered with drying blood. What bodies were not hanging from the tree like sadistic harvest decorations were dumped unceremoniously before the hall. They, too, were half-mangled, half-eaten, chunks of flesh ripped from their bodies. Flies buzzed relentlessly as decay wafted in the wind and up Asher's nose.

'It's a warning,' Horsa said through gritted teeth as he read the words scrawled in blood upon the tunic of a large, decapitated blacksmith.

"*More will die.*"

'It's a disgrace,' Edgar grunted. 'There's no honour in it. War shouldn't be fought like this. Never like this...' He trailed off as his eyes scanned the tree once more.

'They must have slaughtered the town and fallen back to White Cliffe,' Cara said, peering down the empty streets, ever cautious of hidden threats.

'I'm sorry for your loss, Eawynne,' Athelbad said softly beside the tall earl. 'I know you two were close.'

'She was a good sister,' Eawynne whispered, not taking her eyes off the body of Earl Theodora. 'She would have fought to the very last to save her people. She was an honourable woman.'

She wiped a tear from her cheek and turned her horse to face the army, taking a deep breath. 'They will be avenged!' she boomed, drawing the attention of all. 'We will march upon the capital, slay the witch Constance and slaughter all Shangari that lay in our path!' A roar of approval erupted from the soldiers, cascading like a waterfall through the ranks. Feet stomped, and glaives clanged together, creating a deafening sympathy fuelled by anger and vengeance. The sound echoed across the city.

Horsa pulled his horse close to Asher's. 'It is good to see them with such a strong fighting spirit,' he said, nodding to the soldiers.

'The price was too high.'

'Aye,' Horsa agreed solemnly, resting a gentle paw on Asher's shoulder. 'We should move out. It does not do well to dwell on the dead.'

Asher closed his eyes and nodded. Horsa turned his gaze to a senior soldier standing at the front of the column and nodded. The soldier raised a horn to his lips. An echoing trumpet resonated around the haunted market, and every soldier obediently shifted to attention. Another blow on the horn, and they were all moving forwards, following Asher and the earls as they made their way out the eastern side. Asher looked up at the tree one last time as they passed, making sure to remember each and every one of the faces hanging there. Behind him, hundreds of hushed prayers were whispered as the rest of the soldiers marched by. Asher hoped they, too, would not forget the faces of the dead.

***

Bolts of lightning crashed onto the horizon to the west, illuminating the base of the Great Lighthouse and the turbulent seas that raged before it.

'... ten, eleven, twelve, thirteen, fou—'

Thunder rumbled across the sky, resonating deep in Asher's chest as he huddled over a campfire, an empty bowl by his stool and his royal blue cloak wrapped around his shoulders. Horses snorted and stomped nervously nearby.

'It's getting closer.' He sighed as he fiddled with the necklace around his neck, the metal chain sliding through his fingers. He looked up from the fire. Hundreds of other campfires burned and crackled in the darkness around him, illuminating a sea of white tents and a few huddled figures. It was quiet, save for the patrolling guards and the quiet chatter of those who couldn't sleep, like Asher. He enjoyed the quiet. The march north towards White Cliffe had been full of shouting and chest-thumping songs designed to keep the morale high and the fighting spirit burning. Their pass through the city of Oakenhall had ignited a fire within most but sent some into despair, and the marching songs had done well raising morale.

It was peaceful now, and Asher was thankful for it.

Upon arriving close to White Cliffe, Horsa had sent scouts to find a suitable site to set up camp and await the Vulpen reinforcements. They returned with details of a wide-open field shielded by a low hill, out of sight of the city. To the east lay King's Wood. A torrent of memories flooded Asher's mind—his and Cara's escape from White Cliffe, her fight with the Medvedian knight, and their travels to Saewic, of Mia.

'Why does my mind always come back to Mia?' Asher asked into the wind. He closed his eyes, sighing deeply.

'It's not your fault,' came a voice from one of the tents encircling the campfire. Cara emerged, fully armoured, and approached Asher with a soft smile. She sat on a nearby stool and wrapped her cloak around her shoulders, bracing herself against the chilling wind.

'Couldn't sleep?' Asher asked, returning her smile.

'I always get up this early,' Cara replied, poking the fire with a long stick. 'The question is, why are you up?'

The embers crackled with new life. Asher stared into them, watching the flames dance in the wind. 'Is it morning already?' He looked towards the Great Lighthouse at the black clouds approaching from across the churning waves.

'You won't be able to kill Constance sleeping on your horse,' Cara said with a chuckle.

Asher smiled, not taking his eyes off the Lighthouse. 'I'm okay.'

Cara poked again at the fire. The embers crackled and snapped under the shifting wood. Eventually, she threw the stick into the fire. 'I meant what I said, you know, about Mia. It's not your fault.'

Asher closed his eyes and saw Mia's terrified face, blood dripping from the bolt protruding from her neck. 'They were after me, tracking me. If I hadn't gone to her, she'd still—' He paused, unable to bring himself to say the words as he suppressed tears forming in the corners of his eyes. 'It's my fault,' he whispered.

Cara sighed and looked towards the Great Lighthouse. 'You see that storm on the horizon?' she said softly.

Asher opened his eyes and saw the darkened clouds flash with unbridled energy, heard the thunder roll over the camp moments later. He nodded.

'You cannot force the storm away or reason with it. It will roll through regardless of whether you are there to stop it.' She placed a paw on Asher's knee. 'The best we can do is steer people to shelter, to endure the worst of it and come back stronger. We couldn't save Mia, but look around.' She gestured a paw at the hundreds of tents surrounding them. Asher followed her paw as it swept across the field. 'Look at all the people you've given hope to, those we saved from Otyrheim, from Highguard.'

'I feel like I'm leading them into the eye of the storm,' Asher scoffed.

'You are.' She chuckled. 'But they will endure it. To be free again, for the peace that follows, for their king.' She turned back to Asher and smiled, her eyes kind and caring. 'If you're going to lead your people safely through this, you have to forgive yourself for what happened to Mia. Endure that storm inside you and come out stronger.'

'I just—' He clenched his fists tight until the muscles began to ache. 'So many people have yet to face justice for what they've done. To me, to my people. I can't let them get away with it.'

There was a long pause as Cara stared down at the rings around her fingers, the silver glinting in the campfire as she fiddled with them. 'These rings belonged to my parents when they were alive. After I lost Luna, I became so angry all the time. It was the only way I felt I had any control over my life. I truly believed that anger gave me the strength to protect those I cared about... even if they feared me. My worst, most feral instincts guided me, and a lot of innocent people got hurt because of it.' There was a heavy pause as she took a deep breath, collecting herself. She looked up at Asher and stared hard at him with soft, mournful eyes. 'My parents died... because of me.'

Asher's chest tightened at the pain rising to the surface of his Vulpen friend.

She spoke softly, almost painfully. 'Holding on to rage won't bring those who are gone back. All it will do is bring more loss. You need to focus on the real reason we fight. To protect those we loved.'

'To protect those we love...,' Asher breathed.

'Yes.' She smiled. 'It will steady your arm and settle your breath. Only with a calm heart can you control that fire inside you.'

He looked into her eyes, and a warmth washed over him despite the frigid dawn breeze.

'Here.' She reached down, pulled one of her silver rings off her slender finger, and passed it to Asher. 'Take this, and every time you look at it, think about what I said.' She smiled at Asher expectantly, her palm open.

It was a simple yet beautiful ring, an inlay of darker metal swirling through its centre. Part of him felt terrible about taking something that belonged to her parents, something that had meant so much to her. But that was what made it special; that was what made the gesture squeeze his heart so tightly. Cara had become more than just a friend.

She was family.

'Thank you.' He nodded, taking the ring and slipping it onto his index finger.

Satisfied, Cara sighed and looked up towards the heavy overcast sky. Rain started to patter on the dirt around the fire, loud hisses bursting from the flames as Asher and Cara pulled their hoods over their heads. The sky was getting brighter, but the heavy clouds kept the morning light from shining onto the land below. All fires shrank until only embers remained. Tall columns of smoke rose from each like a forest of ash and clouds. Asher closed his eyes and listened to the rhythmic patterns of the rain.

The calm before the storm, he thought. *It's actually quite nice.*

Mia began to occupy his thoughts again, but now with Cara's words echoing in his mind. He still felt the anger, felt the fire in his chest surge with fury, but now he remembered not only her death but her smile, her eyes, her kiss. His thoughts then turned to Luce. They were no longer met with guilt or hesitation but anticipation and excitement. He wondered if she was thinking of him wherever she was.

The fire inside his heart had changed. It was still Folka's fire, but Asher's anger and vengeance no longer fuelled the power. Something new gave it life, something deeper, something he didn't have the words to describe.

'I really hope it's not raining when we attack the city,' Cara said with a huff, drawing Asher from his thoughts. 'I *hate* fighting in the rain.'

He opened his eyes and looked at her. She was gazing at the clouds above the high ridge to the north, a golden light glowing beneath. White Cliffe City—what they had all come for, its torches illuminating the heavy clouds in the morning sky.

'What's wrong with rain? Afraid you'll get your pretty tail soggy?' Asher chuckled.

'Shut it.' Cara laughed, punching him in the shoulder.

The pair laughed heartily together as the rain fell, a peaceful moment in a tranquil deluge. They were getting drenched and cold, but they didn't care. Asher wanted this moment to last for as long as possible.

A single horn bellowed from over the ridge. It trumpeted frantically, growing louder as it rapidly approached the camp. Asher and Cara leapt to their feet as the camp came to life, hundreds of groggy-faced Rabbethi erupting from their tents, some wearing armour, others in dirty tunics. A lone figure appeared on the ridge, a tall Rabbethi with a small horn in one paw. He sprinted down the gentle slope towards the camp, waving his arms and shouting.

'They're coming! They're coming!' he screamed as he reached the first line of tents. He sprinted through the camp, passing by dazed soldiers who dashed back into their tents to fetch their weapons and armour. 'They're pouring out of the city gates!'

Horsa and the earls emerged dressed in their armour with weapons by their sides.

'How many?' Horsa demanded to the scout.

'Thousands of them!' the exhausted Rabbethi rasped between heavy breaths.

Horsa's eyes went wide, and he made for his horse. Asher followed, as did Cara. They untied the reins from the wooden posts dotted among the tents and mounted themselves into the wet saddles.

'Ready the soldiers!' Horsa shouted to the scout. 'Bastards think they can catch us napping? We'll show them!'

The scout nodded and disappeared into the maze of tents and confused soldiers, the sound of a trumpeting horn echoing across the camp once more.

A chorus of other horns responded in understanding and panic, and a hive of activity erupted from every tent. Hundreds of Rabbethi began donning armour and strapping weapons to belts, grabbing bows and glaives from weapons racks before running to the bottom of the ridge. The earls separated and made for their forces to coordinate their preparations. Horsa, Asher and Cara galloped through the camp, their horses' hooves thudding into the wet mud. They climbed the ridge and stopped at its peak, gasping at what they saw.

'By the ancients,' Horsa breathed.

Pouring out of the city gates was a river of darkness. Thousands of bulbous red eyes and black hunched bodies poured out of the city like blood from a wound, spreading onto the plains before the city towards the camp. Peering through the rain and into the swarm, Asher could see hundreds of tall Rabbethi ears rising up and down above the hunched Shangari.

'There's Rabbethi in there!' Asher exclaimed.

'Must be the Third Sons,' Horsa said, spitting. 'Traitors.'

Asher watched in horror as more and more exited the city, a pit growing in his stomach, fear taking hold in his heart. There was just no end to them.

'It won't be long before they get here,' Horsa continued, scanning the open fields between them and the approaching horde. 'Where is your queen?' he barked, eyes locking onto Cara.

'I don't know!' she snapped back, a tremble in her voice.

The sky erupted with blinding energy overhead, flashing the world below in dazzling white for a fraction of a second. Asher's chest tightened as he grasped for his mother's necklace, his paw patting and scraping against his leather armour in an ever-increasing panic. A roar of thunder rumbled from every direction, reverberating deep within his chest.

'I-It's okay to be afraid,' he said into the rain, turning to Cara for reassurance.

Her eyes remained fixed forwards, a wide, blank stare on the black mass of gnashing teeth swarming towards them.

32

The Battle for White Cliffe

Rain hammered down as the two armies faced one another in anxious anticipation. From atop the low ridge, Asher stared through a wall of water over thousands of gnarled Shangari. They snarled and chattered from the other side of a sodden expanse, throwing insults and rageful slurs at the Rabbethi, thick saliva spraying from their long mouths. Their bloodlust was clear.

Standing among them and wearing the stolen armour of the city's royal guards were members of the Third Sons, forgotten children taken from their parents and forced into a life in the mines, all because they had two older siblings. Their eyes glared forwards in staunch determination, eager for freedom and vengeance.

Behind them lay the city of White Cliffe, the slated roofs peeking over the thick stone walls. Asher could just make out figures standing atop the city's gatehouse. One was tall and wearing a white robe shimmering with gold, a bushy red tail flowing in the wind behind them—Constance, the root of all Asher's sorrows, of all his rage. The fire in his chest burned at the thought of slicing her throat and watching her blood hit the dirt. He pushed the thought from his mind and refocused, looking at the others beside her. There were several more hooded figures, their white robes displaying significantly fewer golden details, ready to aid the high priestess in whatever twisted deed she deemed necessary. One figure stood out, however. Keeping guard behind Constance like an obedient dog was a colossal Medvedian clad in heavy-plated armour. Even at this distance, Asher could make out the gold etchings that coated the metallic surface across his chest. A white cape trimmed with golden threads billowed in the swirling maelstrom. Asher knew who it was—could feel it in his bones. The knight was back at his master's side. Beyond them, the square keep rose tall at the city's far end, watching over its inhabitants like a sentinel of stone.

Rain continued to thud against Asher's hood as he gripped the King's Bow tight in his paw, the power within humming gently at his touch. Cara stood beside him. Both had elected to dismount, preferring to fight on foot.

'Why does it have to be raining?' Cara grumbled, water dripping from the end of her snout.

'Because the ancients hate us,' Asher replied with a smirk.

'That's true,' she scoffed, a faint smile forming. It faded quickly, and she raised her head towards the dark clouds hanging heavy overhead. Asher watched the rain streak up her snout and across her cheeks towards her solemn eyes.

'I'm so sorry,' she breathed, not taking her eyes off the shadow above. 'I'm sorry about your father and your brother. I'm sorry about your people and Mia. I'm sorry I left you in the dungeon. I'm sorry my queen didn't come and that we all may di—'

Asher grabbed her arm and pulled her close into an embrace, wrapping his arms around her.

'It's okay,' he whispered. 'Despite all that's happened, I'm so glad we met. We're in this together, okay?'

Slowly, she wrapped her arms around him and lowered her head onto his shoulder, a modicum of her worries easing into his arms.

'Okay,' she whispered.

The pound of hooves echoed over the pounding rain as Horsa rode his horse along the front line of soldiers towards the pair, a royal blue cloak buffeting in the wind behind him like a victorious banner. A wave of cheers followed, and he raised his sword high into the air, inciting a reprisal of hoots and vigorous chest-thumping. Asher watched him closely.

Every time I see him, I'm sure he should be king, not me.

Horsa pulled on his reins, and his horse came to a stop beside Asher. Sheathing his sword, he gave a low bow from his saddle. 'Are you ready?' he asked, eyes locking onto Asher's in a composed sternness that Asher had not seen since their time in the Under Kitchen.

Asher wasn't ready, but he nodded regardless. Nothing could ever prepare him for what lay before them. It was both awe-inspiring and terrifying in equal measure.

'Why haven't they attacked us?' he asked, casting his eyes across the horde below.

'They don't want to charge up a muddy hill. We assembled much faster than they anticipated, so we now hold the advantage—a reckless gamble on their part.'

'We should make them come to us,' Asher said. 'Harass them with arrows and force them to attack.'

Horsa nodded. 'A sound strategy. Are you and the archers ready?'

Asher turned to the soldiers at his back. A mass of Rabbethi stared back at him, drenched from head to toe but with a fire in their eyes and bows in their paws. Horsa had taken the top archers from each earl's forces, mustered them together and placed them under Asher's command. Asher could see it in their eyes, the pride of fighting under the king's banner. There was also fear at what lay before them—an ocean of gnawing teeth, rusted blades and furious brothers and sisters—certain death.

Asher took a deep breath. 'I know you're all afraid. I feel your fear. I, too, feel the urge to run and hide. But we are Rabbethi! We are above such raw instincts! When our homes are threatened, we stand tall. When our loved ones are attacked, we fight hard.' He scanned their faces, watching as heads began to rise taller, chests broader. He smiled, feeling Folka burning proudly within. 'Fear does not make you a coward, nor does it mean you are not brave. Being brave is doing the next right thing in the face of fear, and you are the bravest men and women I have ever met. For you all answered the call, your people's call, my call. I am honoured to fight beside such brave Rabbethi today. Now—' He raised the King's Bow into the hammering rain. 'Are you ready to free our kingdom from the grasp of the Shangari scum?'

All present raised their bows high in unison, and cheers erupted from their ranks.

'The next right thing, huh?' Cara said with a smile.

Asher smiled, then turned back to Horsa. 'They're ready.'

'Good.' Horsa nodded, a proud smile across his face. 'On your order, we begin.'

Asher nodded, and with a kick into his horse's rear, Horsa was galloping down the line towards the flank where a host of mounted Rabbethi soldiers waited, their horses snorting and stomping in nervous anticipation. Asher understood their unease. It felt like he was standing on a cliff, teetering over the edge. He looked to Cara. She looked back at him, fur dripping and clinging to her slender frame. They both nodded in silent understanding, and she drew her long curved scimitar.

'Archers!' Asher cried, looking out over the torrent of black fur and blood-red eyes, noting where the tall flopping ears were congregating among the hunched Shangari.

In unison, all the archers pulled an arrow from their quills, nocked them and raised their bows towards the sky, drawing their bowstrings. Asher raised the King's Bow. Power surged up his arm in an instant, penetrating his body and colliding with the fire in his chest, becoming one. A sparking arrow of radiant energy materialised from the Shepherd Stone in the wood and grew as Asher pulled the string to his cheek. The arrow crackled against his fur, but he felt no pain. The fire within engulfed his eyes as his gaze drifted towards the city gatehouse, Constance watching the battlefield from atop like a sadistic puppeteer. Asher's rage began to burn as he thought about all she had done to him, to his people. The arrow responded in kind, coming to life with an increased ferocity in his grasp. Cara's words about anger and rage floated in the back of his mind, but at that moment, he was deaf to them—all he saw was Constance, and he wanted her to burn. He raised the relic to the sky.

'Loose!'

There was a rush of wind and a chorus of *thums* as hundreds of arrows whistled through the air. They arced high, holding for a moment at their peak below the clouds, before beginning their rapid descent upon the Shangari army. Asher then released his arrow. It soared through the air higher than the arrows of wood and feather and with such a velocity that it punched a hole into the darkness above, disappearing with a swirl of blackened clouds. Screeching commands echoed around the Shangari ranks, and those with shields raised them overhead. A deluge of arrows hammered those without, their bodies convulsing in a gruesome spray of blood before dropping like a grotesque pincushion. Screeches of rage echoed from the black horde, and where the dead had fallen, more quickly filled their space, clambering over their fallen comrades. None seemed to care about the dead, and the horde remained set on the prey before them, their bloodlust and hunger yet to be quenched.

Then it struck.

Like a celestial fury unleashed, a searing bolt of white light tore through the heavens. The arrow streaked towards the ground with unrestrained vengeance, finding its mark in the exposed chest of an unfortunate Shangari and crashing into it with a bone-rattling boom. The impact engulfed the Shangari in a blazing fireball, flesh and bone vaporised in an instant. All that stood in the path of this relentless force met the same fate—turned to ashes, erased from existence in mere seconds. The shockwave sent those nearby sliding along the sodden dirt as it blasted through the ranks. Silence descended over the battlefield as the echoing booms faded, leaving nothing behind but a smouldering crater and pitter-patter of rain. The army at Asher's back roared to life in a triumphant battle cry, stirred to life by the power of their king.

They could do it. They could win.

A figure among the Shangari stepped forwards, a humongous Shangari that towered over the others, his skin scarred in countless places, one eye coloured a milky white. Around his waist, skulls of varying sizes clattered erratically. Nin-Kilim, high chieftain of the united clans, raised a jagged black sword and pointed it directly at Asher, his one red eye narrowing on him with malicious intent. He screeched an ear-shattering screech that made all upon the ridge wince.

Like floodgates bursting open, the Shangari army surged up the hill towards the Rabbethi forces, a torrent of rageful hunger in their crazed eyes, their footsteps as thunder. Some slipped in the mud and were crushed by those behind who continued to stampede. A cacophony of battle cries rang out as they ran, and the soldiers at Asher's back began to shift nervously.

'Ready!' he commanded, drawing back another arrow from the Shepherd Stone. The power coursed through his body once more as the fire in his eyes brightened his sodden face. The sound of hundreds of arrows being nocked and drawn rumbled behind him.

'Loose!'

A fresh volley sailed through the air. More shields were raised in response, and more dropped dead, Shangari and Third Sons alike, pinned to the ground by a plummeting cloud of death. There was another flash of white, then an explosion of fire as Asher's arrow plummeted into the horde. Bodies scattered in all directions, leaving a void in the charging ranks. It was quickly filled as Shangari scrambled over their eviscerated comrades, their bloodlust overpowering any sense of fear.

Nin-Kilim and the front line were approaching fast. It wouldn't be long until they were upon the Rabbethi forces. A horn blew to Asher's right, and he turned to see Horsa and Athelbad at the far end of the ridge, a regiment of mounted soldiers around them, their long glaives lowered, eagerly awaiting the order to charge. Another horn sounded, and every soldier stepped forwards, shaking the ground underfoot as they formed ranks in front of Asher and his archers, their buffeting capes marking which earl they owed allegiance to. Lord Edgar paced back and forth with his mighty war hammer on the front line, bellowing at the oncoming horde in deep, bloodthirsty roars.

'Asher!' Cara yelled over the battle cries.

'Yeah?'

'I'm glad we met too!'

They both smiled, a look of understanding crossing their faces.

'Archers!' he yelled, taking a deep breath. 'Loose at will!'

A barrage of arrows began to surge through the rain. Arrow after arrow sailed overhead in a constant stream of pointed tips, and Shangari and Third Sons crumpled to the mud in sporadic waves, tumbling head over tail, their bones snapping and breaking as they rolled. The Shangari behind them paid no mind and swarmed over the bodies like a tidal wave, sprinting in a desperate plea for fresh blood. Asher raised the King's Bow and unleashed a torrent of crackling arrows, watching them sail high before descending like hammer strikes upon the charging army. Each one drained a little of his strength, but he did not relent. They crashed down upon the land, incinerating all with thunderous booms.

Still, they came.

Nin-Kilim led the way, a step ahead of his horde, his huge, jagged sword raised high in a gnarled paw. As the titanic Shangari collided with the Rabbethi front line, he brought his sword down on an unfortunate soldier, who raised his own to block it. It was useless. Nin-Kilim mowed him down in a spray of blood, his sword cutting through the man like hot butter, cleaving the soldier in twain. The colossal Shangari chief pushed through without breaking his stride, slashing maniacally into the Rabbethi ranks.

An instant later, the rest of the Shangari hammered into the Rabbethi line with a deafening crash. Screams and screeches echoed through the rain as the Rabbethi were pushed back by the initial force but were able to steady themselves and hold. The clang of metal against metal rang out, and the heavy scent of death began to emanate across the fields.

A horn sounded to Asher's left, and he saw Eawynne and Cedric mounted and surrounded by horsemen on the far flank, each equipped with long swords and small buckler shields strapped to their off-arms. They stampeded down the hill towards the Shangari flank, thunderous hooves shaking the ground. This was echoed to Asher's right as Horsa's forces also began their charge.

The horsemen slammed into the flanks of the black horde, cutting two deep wedges into the meat of the writhing bodies. The horses rapidly ran out of space to gallop, and both charges lost momentum. Horsa and his horsemen expertly swung their glaives from horseback, spinning them about their bodies with finesse and cutting down any Shangari that braved an assault. Eawynne's and Cedric's mounted swordsmen were not so skilled. Horses began to drop like flies in an awful wail of pain, their riders dragged from saddles and devoured in an instant. The horses met the same fate shortly after.

Among the torturous screams and wails of fallen soldiers, raucous laughter began to echo across the battlefield. Asher looked to the front line, through the sea of capes and tall ears, and found Edgar, the short, stocky earl of Ironsire, swinging his two-pawed hammer with an elegance unexpected of such a broad man and heavy weapon. The hammer sailed through the air, slamming into a Shangari with a crunch and sending it screeching across the battlefield. With the same motion, he brought his hammer down onto the skull of a Shangari wearing a scavenged iron helm. The metal imploded, denting as if made of mud. Blood squirted out of the eye holes like a berry pressed between the fingers, and the Shangari fell to the floor in a gurgling heap. Edgar raised his hammer and bellowed a deep, booming laugh, challenging all to him, relishing the heat of battle.

Closer to Asher, the cries of death began to draw nearer. A band of Shangari and Third Sons had managed to fight through the front line, slicing and stabbing as they went, and were now making a beeline for Asher. Lumbering close behind, the ground shaking with each gargantuan footstep, was the hulking mass of Nin-Kilim. He thundered forwards, killing all in his path. His saw-like teeth ripped throats as his blade sliced torsos in half. Some of the soldiers put up an admirable fight, landing a few glancing blows on Nin-Kilim's flesh, but were inevitably skewered by his vicious sword. Those untrained in war—farmers and volunteers—were not faring well. Before they could even raise their makeshift weapons, they were dead, stabbed and ripped apart with not much trouble. Still, they fought fervently, determined to do their bit and reclaim their home. As Nin-Kilim decapitated the head of a screaming farmer, he turned to Asher, his gaze landing on the bow in Asher's paw.

Then he smiled a wicked smile.

'Cara!' Asher yelled as his eyes met the Shangari chieftain.

Cara stepped before him in a protective stance, scimitar gripped tightly in her black paw, her black-and-red cape whipping around her. 'You're gonna have to go through me first, you mangey sewer bastards!' she screamed, her upper lip curling into a vicious snarl.

A pawful of Shangari and Third Sons broke through the ranks and scrambled towards Asher's position. With a burst of speed, Cara lunged downhill to meet them. She reached the first Shangari and stepped to one side, avoiding his downwards slice and bringing her scimitar across his torso, cutting deep. He was dead in a spray of blood, and she was running to the next. A Third Son came at her with a glaive, stabbing forwards with rapid speed. She batted the bladed tip away, spun along the shaft and extended her sword arm across the Third Son's neck. His eyes went wide as his head slowly slid off his still-standing body. The next attacker was on her, then the next and then the next.

She dispatched them all with skill, finesse and brutal efficiency, leaving nothing but bloody corpses in her wake.

But more were coming, and so was Nin-Kilim.

He cut down the last Rabbethi standing in his way with ease, ripping a huge chunk of flesh from the screaming soldier's shoulder, the metal armour providing little protection against Nin-Kilim's titanic jaws. The Rabbethi crumpled to the floor, gargling, and the Shangari chief placed a giant bare foot onto his head. He crushed it into the mud and continued up the hill, bloody sinew stretching underfoot before snapping and whipping back to the Rabbethi's flattened skull.

Nin-Kilim stared at Asher, then licked his crusted lips, sending shivers down Asher's spine. The titanic Shangari then noticed Cara standing defiantly between him and his prize. She growled at him with a wild fury. His grin faded into a snarl, and with a screech, he charged, sword raised high. Asher frantically fumbled with the King's Bow, drawing back the bowstring and feeling the power course through his body. An arrow materialised in his paws, and he aimed it towards the Shangari chieftain.

Cara readied herself, crouching low, her bushy tail flicking to and fro with anticipation. Nin-Kilim closed the distance, moving far quicker than anything his size had any right to. With a roar, he brought his sword down upon Cara with immense power. She dove to the side, rolling across the mud as the mighty sword slammed to the ground in an eruption of soil and water. Cara sprung to her feet and dashed for the recovering chieftain. He lashed at her with a backwards swipe, which Cara ducked and sliced her scimitar across his trunk-like calf. With a guttural screech, he fell to one knee but did not fall, leaning on his blade for support. Cara wasn't done. She attacked again, coming at his lowered form with a swipe for his thick neck.

CLANG!

It caught in the meat of Nin-Kilim's blackened blade. He swiped his sword aside with force, shoving Cara back and sliding across the slick ground. Despite the blood pouring from the wound in his leg, Nin-Kilim rose to his feet and lunged at Cara with a burning determination, the deep gash doing little to deter him from his prey.

Cara didn't wait and bounded forwards to meet him, snarling fangs bared, her scimitar held low, the tip skimming the wet ground. She brought the curved blade up across Nin-Kilim's bare chest, the momentum carrying her off the ground in a twirling swipe. The Shangari took the hit in a spray of blood, barely wincing through the obvious pain, but before Cara could land, his meaty fingers were around her, grasping her tight in his bloody grip, her sword falling from her paw. There she hung, her feet dangling above the ground. She gasped as he forced the air from her lungs.

Without hesitation, she plunged her curved blade in and through his gargantuan black bicep. He howled in pain but refused to relinquish his prize. She tried to pull her blade free, but it wouldn't move, the muscles in Nin-Kilim's arm tensing around the metal and keeping it held tight in his rotten flesh. Asher watched in horror as Cara was now weaponless and held firm in the chieftain's vicious grasp.

It was now or never. He had to take the shot.

Cara screamed as Nin-Kilim squeezed, his twisted grin growing at the sound of her misery. With a mighty heave, he threw her into the air and, with the same motion, arched his terrible black sword over his head. Cara was helpless as the jagged edge of the colossal blade sliced through the rain towards her.

Time slowed.

Flashes of lightning crawled along Nin-Kilim's mammoth frame, his manic grin eagerly awaiting his sword to bite into Cara's soft flesh. Cara fell slowly, her face a contortion of rage and regret. She was going to die, and there was nothing she could do about it. Asher tried to focus. He *had* to focus, but all he could do was stare at the sickening joy in Nin-Kilim's bulging red eye, the rampant malice that fuelled his actions. Asher could stop him right here and now. He could release his arrow and engulf the titanic chief in an inferno of fire and death, the monster that was Nin-Kilim becoming once more a mere tale to scare children at night. His heart begged him to do it. His rage demanded it. He pulled the bowstring taut and prepared to release.

But... Cara...

She was right there, inches away from Nin-Kilim's hulking mass. The fire would engulf her, killing her in a blaze of radiant flames. He couldn't let that happen—he wouldn't. He owed her too much. His kingdom be damned, his vengeance aside. At that moment, all that mattered was his friend. She had to live.

To protect those we love...

The wild energy flowing through him and into the arrow suddenly became narrow and sharp, a blinding white wire that sparked with condensed power. The flames that engulfed his eyes became focused, centring his vision like a lens on his target. He would not let loose this arrow in a wild rage to kill or hurt. Instead, he would use it to protect those he loved, to ensure their safety. That would be his focus. It was the right thing to do—the next right thing.

With his heart and mind finally one, his will clear, he released his breath and loosed the arrow. The bowstring twanged against the wood, and the bolt shot across the open space at lightning speed, the rain sizzling in its wake. It streaked past Cara, scorching her cheek and leaving a burning trail across her fur. Nin-Kilim's sword continued its descent, mere moments away from slicing the Vulpen agent in half.

Cara fell to the ground with a heavy thud, her body still intact, wincing at the sudden pain across her cheek. She looked up and gasped. The arrow had found its mark, plunging deep into Nin-Kilim's bare shoulder. Crippling shockwaves raked across his giant Shangari body, every muscle tensing as veins bulged to the surface. Muffled cries of pain emanated from Nin-Kilim's throat as his one good eye stared down at Cara with absolute rage. She picked up her scimitar and stood slowly, panting heavily, her cloak and armour caked in mud and blood. Collecting herself, she stared with hatred at Nin-Kilim's paralysed state. A smile began to form across her snout.

Don't just stand there, Asher thought as he ran towards her. *Finish him off.* The King's Bow had drained more of his strength than he had realised, every step feeling like he was slogging through waist-deep water. He doubted he'd be able to manifest another arrow without collapsing unconscious afterwards. Still, he pushed towards Cara, the bow slung over his shoulder.

Cara gripped her blade tight, met Nin-Kilim's stare and brought her scimitar back, holding it there briefly, clearly savouring the moment before she ended the malicious chieftain's life. A tiny movement caught Asher's attention.

One of Nin-Kilim's fingers was twitching.

'No...' he breathed, realising the danger.

Help me, Folka. Help me save her.

The fire within ignited into an inferno. With a rekindled power coursing through his veins, Asher took off sprinting across the bloody battlefield, blood and terror passing by in a drowned blur.

Cara thrust her blade into Nin-Kilim's abdomen. It stopped short, her wrist engulfed by the enveloping paw of the no longer paralysed chieftain. He stared at her, half-scorched, smoke rising from his shoulder, an enraged glow in his eye. He opened his mouth wide to reveal a mouth full of bloody, serrated teeth. A deep, growling chuckle hummed from the depths as thick wads of blood and saliva dripped onto Cara's black cloak. She struggled against his might, but it was no good.

'Do it then, you ugly bastard!' she screamed.

Nin-Kilim's maw descended through the rain, and... *CRUNCH!*

Asher's foot collided with the side of Nin-Kilim's head with a mighty impact. He had called upon every ounce of strength and put it all into his legs, leaping into the air and bringing his boot around as hard as he could. His foot met resistance at first as Nin-Kilim's bulging neck muscles strained against the impact. But as Asher leaned with his full weight, felt the fire in his heart burn bright, his eyes hot like bonfires, he felt his foot crack through skull and press into the much softer brain beneath. Nin-Kilim's muscles abruptly gave up, and his neck snapped around with a sickening crack. The titanic Shangari released Cara and stumbled back, gargled cries leaking from his long snout, now facing an impossible direction. He fell to his knees and crashed like a mighty tree into the mud, the impact shaking the hillside.

Nin-Kilim, high chieftain, was dead.

Asher and Cara stared at the corpse, waiting, making sure he was truly gone. After a moment, their nerves eased, and they looked at each other.

'Thanks,' Cara said through strained breaths as Asher helped her to her feet. 'He was a tough shit.'

'You're telling me,' Asher replied, feeling weak, the fire within his heart fading fast as his eyes returned to normal. 'I don't think I have anything left.'

They stood and gazed around the battlefield. Despite their chief's demise, the Shangari were still making ground. Even Edgar's laughter had stopped, and he now swung his heavy hammer with large, cumbersome swipes as he took retreating steps back up the hill. The Rabbethi ranks were shrinking. Horsa and some of the others mounted on horseback had managed to fall back to protect the Rabbethi flanks, but even they had suffered heavy losses and were now slowly becoming surrounded.

'This might be it,' Asher said, reaching for Cara's paw.

She looked down and smiled, grabbing his paw softly. 'At least we go together.'

Amidst the tumultuous storm, they found solace in each other's presence, their grasp on one another's paws growing stronger with every passing moment. Lightning flashed overhead, illuminating the dead and the dying. In the face of impending doom, Asher didn't reach for his mother's necklace. With Cara to guide him, he had discovered a newfound courage, and he closed his eyes, waiting for the thunder to roll overhead.

Horns suddenly erupted from the King's Wood. Asher and Cara snapped to the dense row of trees and watched in amazement as a thick volley of arrows sailed out of the shadows and hammered into the flanks of the Shangari army. Hundreds instantly crumpled to the floor in bloody heaps, skewered many times over. Another horn sounded, and a thunderous rumble exploded from the forest as hundreds of Vulpen horsemen in crimson-tinted armour stormed out from the treeline, smashing into the horde and sending Shangari and Third Sons flying through the air. Huge banners of red and gold flew with the charging horsemen billowing in the wind. The Vulpen face at their centre glared at the terrified Shangari army like a vengeful deity bringing forth a righteous army to smite them. The horde turned to face the new threat, but it was too late. Countless were trampled under hooves, while others were cut to ribbons by long curved scimitars, screaming as they fell. The Shangari at the front line faltered as the Vulpen army attacked their rear, their eyes darting between the Rabbethi and the new threat.

With a mighty cry, Edgar and his forces pressed the advantage and began advancing back through the enemy ranks, charging downhill, killing with renewed strength. Cara squeezed Asher's paw tight, her eyes fixed on the Vulpen Queendom banners flying high above their charging horses.

'She came,' she breathed, a broad smile growing across her drowned snout.

'She came...,' Asher repeated.

Victory was theirs.

33

A Familiar Place

'So this is your mother and father?' Cara asked within the dimly lit corridors of White Cliffe keep. The torches crackled in the silence as Asher gazed at the portrait, thankful the painting remained untouched during the church's occupation. In fact, most of the inner keep was much like how he left it. It was likely Constance had reserved the keep for herself and her loyal acolytes. The extra tables, candles, and loose scrolls supported this, with the lack of rotting meat, claw marks, and faecal matter indicating a lack of Shangari, for which Asher was very thankful.

He looked at his mother's portrait, his eyes drifting from her loving yet sad eyes to the necklace around her neck, the silver bow and arrow so expertly painted against her soft white fur. He instinctively reached into his mud-encrusted chest piece, pulled at the tarnished chain, and inspected the bow attached to the end.

I've still got it, he thought as if speaking to her, a small sense of pride filling him. After all that had happened, he kept his promise to carry her symbol and memory, her words and love. He smiled as he placed the chain back into his armour.

He then looked to King Hengist, his father, who gazed down at him with disappointed blue eyes. Asher stared back in defiance, a compulsive act that brought a pang of guilt. They had never gotten on, but his father had always tried, ever attempting to teach him the ways of ruling and court etiquette, despite Asher's clear disinterest.

I'm sorry I couldn't save you... that I wasn't a better son...

Then there was Henric. The first thing he had done when re-entering the city was search the keep for his little brother, but there were no signs of him. He had sent soldiers to search the docks for the entranceway that led under the city. They found it quickly within the ruins of an abandoned warehouse, thanks in part to the concentration of scampering Shangari, who fled into the water as soon as the soldiers arrived, their courage and bloodlust having died with their high chieftain. Thankfully, there had been no reports of Henric's body in the damp passageway or the strange spherical chamber within.

She must still have him, he thought as anger mixed with a mild sense of relief.

What worried Asher, though, was what else the soldiers didn't find in the underground chamber. The Silver Coffin, the mythical object in the chamber's centre, was gone. The soldiers found nothing of a glass orb or the shining box inside, just an empty spherical room with ancient murals, crackling torches and a walkway that led over an eerie abyss. They had discovered a hidden chamber behind one of the murals. Someone had managed to move the mural aside to get to the chamber beyond, which the guards had reported was empty save for a vacant pedestal at the far end. That troubled Asher deeply. What else had Constance taken, and why did she have Henric? Asher couldn't linger on Henric's image any longer. Guilt consumed his heart, and he turned away from his brother's young, inquisitive gaze.

I've let you down again. I'm sorry.

Cara coughed, and the lingering silence brought Asher's attention back to the corridor and his Vulpen friend, who was patiently awaiting a response.

'My mother died in a Shangari raid,' he said softly. 'And my father, he—' A lump formed in his throat as the memory came rushing into his mind. 'He died when the church attacked.'

'He would be very proud of you,' Cara said with a reassuring smile. 'They both would.'

Asher nodded slowly, for the first time in his life, believing it could be true.

'Thanks.'

They stood before the painting for some time, Cara admiring the artistry, Asher reliving old memories. Some were happy, others less so, but he tried to remember them all, valuing each as long-forgotten friends. He wondered what had happened to the portraits of Horsa. He had never seen them and guessed his father had torn them down, not wanting to see the face of betrayal in his home. What the betrayal was that had earned Horsa his banishment to the border, Asher would find out when the time was right. He fiddled with the chain around his neck as his mind jumped from theory to theory.

Heavy footsteps echoed against the cold stone floor from beyond the shadows of the dimly lit corridor. They drew closer until a black-furred Vulpen soldier emerged from the darkness, heavily plated in dark red armour, its curved layers of metal coming to sharp points, the edges trimmed black. A cape of crimson red flowed behind him as he marched. As he halted before Asher and Cara, he rested his paw on the pommel of a long curved blade sheathed by his side. He looked down at Asher with a passing glance before moving to Cara. Asher shifted uncomfortably, having expected more respect in his own keep.

The soldier addressed Cara. 'You have been requested to come—'

'You should bow to a king in his own castle,' Cara interrupted, narrowing her eyes.

The soldier was taken aback, any semblance of confidence immediately leaving his demeanour. His eyes darted to Asher and back to Cara. 'My apologies,' he said begrudgingly, bowing in Asher's general direction. It was so quick that Asher could have blinked and missed it.

'Better,' Cara said, raising her snout in approval.

He cleared his throat as he collected himself. 'You have both been requested to come to the throne room on behalf of the queen. Follow me.' With his disciplinary confidence returning, he turned on the spot and began marching away with haste, quickly fading into the shadows of the corridor. Asher and Cara followed after.

It didn't feel right following a stranger around his own home, especially as the soldier had to pause a few times to ensure he was going down the correct corridor. They passed by many more paintings of long-dead ancestors, their eyes following Asher as he stared up at them. There was no sense of belonging among these rulers of old, the architects of the kingdom, at least, not yet. Once the kingdom had healed, the church was truly vanquished, and his people's safety was secure, maybe he could stand proud alongside them.

The stone floor suddenly became soft and dull underfoot as the group trod along a wide blue carpet, their echoing footsteps becoming muffled. Shields with the Rabbethia sigil began to decorate the stone walls, and suits of Rabbethi armour with extended ear guards flanked the hallways, their old and blunted glaives standing tall beside them.

Asher slowed as he neared the double doors that led into the throne room, his heart sinking as he saw a patch of blood staining the stone wall. Memories of the grizzled old Harold flashed before him. He wished he could have come back for him, to carry him out of the castle and lead him to safety. There was no body, likely removed by Constance's acolytes to improve the air.

'I'm sorry, old friend,' Asher breathed. Harold was a man he would have done anything for.

'Asher?' Cara called from the doors, pulling Asher from his silent mourning. The soldier pushed one of the ornate doors open and stepped through, followed closely by Cara and then, hesitantly, Asher. The three entered the grand white stone hall of the throne room.

I guess this is my throne room now, he thought, letting the weight of that sink in.

The edge of the hall was illuminated by hundreds of torches fastened to the walls. Thick stone pillars flanked its length and rose high into the ceiling, where wide wooden beams crisscrossed into shadow. At the far end, a column of light shone through a vast circular window high above grand double doors, bathing a central space in a warm glow. Along the stone floor were faded patches of dried blood, memories of the last time he was here, memories he would rather forget.

In the centre of the hall, illuminated by the golden light and spinning with a sense of wonder as she stared up at the mighty pillars, was a familiar Vulpen agent.

'Luce!' Asher cried as his eyes landed on her bubbly face, his heart fluttering in his chest like a caged moth.

It had been so long. He had begun to question whether he would ever see her again. As king, there would be a lot of administrative duties to perform, and it could be months before he'd have the chance to visit Ignimarum again. His heart thumped as he thought back to his time in the Under Kitchen, how he had doubted Luce after Cara's fake betrayal, and how he longed to see her again regardless. She turned to them, and her beautiful smile grew even wider.

'Ash! Cara!'

The soldier halted by the closest pillar and beckoned the pair through, but Asher was already past the burly Vulpen, a broad smile across his face as he bounded for the bubbly Vulpen. Cara followed behind with a sigh, a slight smirk across her snout. Their footsteps echoed on the hard floor, bouncing off the pillars and disrupting the hall's stillness.

Asher and Luce embraced with arms spread wide. She buried her head into his chest, and he wrapped his arms around her shoulders, burrowing his twitching nose into her fluffy red fur. He had missed her smell, the gentle scent of rare orchids floating on a warm breeze. He breathed it in and sighed deeply. The fire burned in his chest, and it was a welcome change not to have it come from a place of anger or survival. It was love, a love he hadn't felt in a long time. Luce giggled as Asher released her.

'Luce, you have no idea—'

Luce grabbed his face between her soft black paws and pulled him down into a passionate kiss. Their lips locked, and Asher felt her warmth ebb into him, felt the passion in her heart flow into his very being. He closed his eyes and pulled her in close. He didn't care about the soldiers around them, didn't care that Cara was standing awkwardly beside them, desperately looking anywhere else but in their direction. He felt a wave of contentment surge through him. For the first time in a long, long time, he was happy.

A slow, exaggerated clapping began to echo around the hall, emanating from the far end, where two thrones sat. Asher and Luce pulled away, their wide smiles showing how much they had wanted to do that. The clapping continued, and Luce's smile faded, her eyes falling to the floor. Asher frowned, and he turned to the source.

His eyes travelled down the hall's length, landing on two thrones raised on a wide stone plinth and decorated with intricate engravings. His mother's shorter throne had swirling patterns that imitated the growth of vines and flowers, its back ending a good foot below the other. The other was tall and featured hard angular shapes, its back rising high and featuring the sigil of the kingdom at its peak. It had been his father's throne. Now, it was his.

'Such a touching reunion,' came a smooth, confident voice.

Lazing on his father's throne was a black-furred Vulpen, one leg hanging loosely over an arm. A thick plumage of crow feathers flowed from his upper shoulders, and a heavy red scar ran over his left eye, partially hidden by a grey eyepatch. A flicker of annoyance sparked in Asher at the sight of someone so casually lounging on his father's throne. Senator Corvo swung his leg off the arm and rose to his feet. He strolled towards them with a confident smile, his footsteps muffled by the long blue carpet trimmed with gold that ran from the hall's centre to the base of the thrones.

'Corvo!' Cara exclaimed as she marched towards her superior and friend. The two firmly grasped each other's forearms, smiles across their faces. 'Why aren't you in Ignimarum? Where's the queen?' Cara searched the hall as if Queen Tessina would appear at the mention of her name.

Asher could only see Vulpen guards lining the edges of the hall. None of his soldiers were anywhere to be seen. Folka's fire rumbled a warning within him.

I know...

'Sadly, she has other matters to attend to,' Corvo said, resting a paw around the handle of a long, sheathed dagger by his side. Asher had never seen such a blade before, though a sense of recognition itched at him like an insect bite just out of scratching reach. A sense of cold, oppressive unease washed over him as he studied it. Corvo continued, 'She has requested I perform this task in her absence.'

'What task?' Cara asked, her smile beginning to fade. In a heartbeat, the Vulpen guards began closing in, paws placed on the pommel of their long swords.

Asher felt a breath on his neck and heard Luce's voice in his ears. 'I'll see you soon.'

With that, she skipped towards the door he and Cara had previously entered. Before she disappeared into the shadows, she looked over her shoulder and gave him a signature wink. Confusion filled Asher as he turned to the guards closing around him. This was beginning to feel all too familiar. Despite his exhaustion, he let the flame inside seep into his muscles, readying them for whatever was about to happen.

'I'm sorry, Asher, but we don't feel you can be trusted with its protection,' Corvo said, turning to Asher with a condescending expression. 'White Cliffe is ours, and you're going to have to come with us.'

All at once, a chorus of metal echoed around the hall as guards drew their curved scimitars. Asher instinctively stepped back and looked to Cara, eyes wide, unable to fathom the possibility that she would betray him again.

'What are you doing?' Cara snarled, her lip curling to reveal sharp canine teeth.

'These are the orders of our queen,' Corvo responded calmly. 'Love them or hate them; you must obey.'

'I—' Cara stammered. 'She wouldn't...'

'Of course she would,' Corvo said, raising an eyebrow. He looked at her and sighed, softly placing a paw on her shoulder. 'I'm sorry, Cara. I know you've grown attached to His Highness, but this was always the plan. You must understand that. Just think how proud Tessy will be when you gift her the last of the Rabbethi kings. You helped him gather the Rabbethi army, had them weaken themselves against the Shangari. Now they're too weak to stand against us.' He chuckled. 'You have gifted her the whole kingdom.'

There was a long silence, the guards remaining ready, weapons pointed at Asher. The tension in the hall was so thick you could bottle it. Asher let more and more fire burn through his body, feeling the flames lick the back of his eyes. He turned to Cara, desperate for any sign that she didn't know, that she wasn't a part of this absolute betrayal.

She sighed, her whole body sagging, defeated.

No...

A smug smile grew across Corvo's mouth as he turned to Asher. 'I am thankful that great oaf of a warden didn't kill you in one of his little fights. I gave him specific instructions to keep you alive, but he's never been one for orders—tends to be a bit rough with his playthings, even the important ones.'

Asher glared at the spymaster with a vengeful rage, unable to speak the words he felt in his heart. The fires in his eyes were pushing to the surface, begging to be unleashed. Corvo leaned close to the enraged Rabbethi, his one good eye narrowing as he looked deep into Asher's very being, his face twisting into a bitter scowl. 'You think that power of yours is the only divinity in this world?' he hissed. 'You have not earned it, have not suffered for it. Only in *her* shadow will the strongest fires burn.'

'What?'

Corvo stepped back, his confident smile returning, and he turned to the despondent Cara. 'Be a dear and relieve the king of his weapons. Careful not to burn yourself.'

Cara nodded slowly. She turned to Asher, her eyes soft, the look of sorrow across her face.

'Please, Cara,' he pleaded, feeling as though his heart was being ripped from his chest all over again. 'We're in this together, right?'

'I'm so sorry,' she whispered.

She suddenly turned on the ball of her foot and jabbed an open palm hard into the startled Corvo's throat. A horrible wheezing sound was forced out of his snout as his eye bulged in pain. With lightning speed, she reached into his cloak and pulled out a small glass vial of mysterious black liquid.

'Hold your breath!' She threw the vial onto the ground, spinning to shield her eyes. Asher inhaled deeply just before the glass container smashed into a thousand shards, the liquid spilling onto the white stone floor. A plume of black choking fog erupted around them, filling the immediate area. Coughing and wheezing erupted all around.

Asher peered into the inky blackness, searching desperately for his Vulpen friend.

'Cara—!' he began before doubling over in a spluttering cough, his lungs trying to escape their ribbed prison. A paw latched onto his arm and yanked him through the cloud. Before he knew it, he was emerging out of the darkness and stumbling behind Cara. She looked back at him, tears threatening to fall down her cheeks.

'Run!'

34

Between Family and the Abyss

Suits of armour and paintings of kings long dead sped by in a blur as Asher and Cara flew through the inner workings of the royal keep. Asher led the way, remembering the route without much thought, instinct guiding his feet. Behind, muffled footsteps thudded in pursuit. Angry shouts and vicious curses echoed through the halls, growing faint as the soldiers had neither the experience nor the patience to remember the keep's burrow-like layout. Nevertheless, Asher and Cara continued at full pace. They bounced off the stone walls as they rounded each corner at great speed, their padded footsteps echoing around them as the carpet ended, replaced with hard stone.

Asher suddenly stopped, ears twitching, his senses heightened by the fire burning through his body. Footsteps were approaching fast from the shadows of a side passage. He drew the red ribbon dagger and readied himself in a boxing stance.

'What is it?' Cara asked in a hushed voice as she drew her scimitar.

'I don't know. Could be trouble.'

Horsa burst forwards, stopping suddenly before them. His eyes were wide, his breathing heavy, and his leather armour was littered with new tears and cuts. A spray of fresh blood coated the surface.

'Asher!' he yelled, relief washing over his face.

'Horsa!'

They embraced, Horsa's arms wrapping tight around him. Asher held on, not wanting to let go.

'Are you alright? What's going on? We were all celebrating with the queen's soldiers. Before I knew it, they were slaughtering us where we stood. I ran for the keep to find you.'

'They attacked us too!' Asher exclaimed, parting from the veteran soldier. 'They're claiming the kingdom is theirs. I-I don't think we have the numbers to fight them.'

Horsa's head snapped to Cara as if noticing her for the first time, and he eyed her with fresh suspicion. He took a few cautious steps back, his paw gingerly lowering to his sword pommel.

'Don't give me that look!' Cara growled. She stared daggers at the guarded Rabbethi, her sharp canine teeth glinting in the torchlight. 'I just gave up *everything* for Asher. My friends, my family. My mother...' Tears began to well at the corners of her eyes once more, but she forced them back, maintaining her death stare at Horsa.

Horsa turned to Asher, and Asher nodded, his eyes lowering to the floor.

'I'm... sorry,' Horsa said, lowering his guard. 'I know what it's like to be turned on by those you love.' Quiet fell upon the corridor, the crackling torches mounted on the walls underlining the uncomfortable silence. Cara turned away.

'What do we do now?' Asher asked.

'You need to get out of here,' Horsa said with a hard look.

'I can't leave! I'm the king! My people need me!' Panic was taking hold. So many looked to him now as a symbol of hope—to lead them in this dark time. He couldn't just abandon them. Too many had died to get him where he is now.

'If they catch you, or worse, kill you, then we'll have no chance of taking the kingdom back. Please, I beg of you, go to Fenrath. High King Alasdair is a good man. He's always sympathised with us Rabbethi. He may be able to help, but it won't be for nothing. He'll want something in return, and you won't have much choice but to accept whatever it is.'

'But what about you?' Tears were beginning to form in the corners of Asher's eyes. Horsa was the only family he had left. Asher turned to Cara.

No, that's not true anymore.

Still, he couldn't bear the idea of losing Horsa after only just finding him.

'I have to stay here and do what I can to keep the people of our city safe,' Horsa said. 'Besides, there's still that crazy bitch that wants to release a god, right?'

Horsa chuckled.

Asher did not.

'I don't want to lose you,' Asher began, the words forming a lump in his throat.

Horsa brought him close, gently resting his forehead against Asher's. 'We will see each other again, I promise,' he whispered. 'When a Rabbethi king sits upon the throne.'

Asher looked into his eyes as they parted and saw tears.

Horsa then turned to Cara. 'Take care of him, alright? That's the king of Rabbethia, you know.' He looked back at Asher and smiled. 'He's family.'

Cara nodded. 'With my life.'

'Good. Good...' Horsa took a deep breath, collected himself and drew his sword. He then walked past the pair towards the shadows behind them. Before he vanished from sight, he called over his shoulder. 'When a Rabbethi sits upon the throne!' He was gone, his footsteps picking up speed as they faded into distant echoes. Asher stared into the darkness.

'When a Rabbethi sits upon the throne,' he repeated, quieter than the crackle of the torches.

They continued for some time through the maze of the inner keep, not stopping as they ran down the winding corridors of stone. Cara followed closely behind Asher, her breaths growing more and more laboured. Asher, however, was barely winded. What little strength Folka's fire had left was slowly releasing into his muscles, giving him the energy he needed to keep going. It was like nothing he had ever felt before. Who knows what he could do at full strength?

A single wooden door came into view as they rounded a final corner, waiting for them at the end of a long passage. Light leaked around the rim, silhouetting the simple door. They bounded down the corridor, their footsteps echoing loudly all around them. Discretion was no longer their concern. They needed to get out of the keep and out of the city fast. They crossed a junction in the passage, and Asher stopped. Cara continued on a few paces before turning.

'What is it?' she asked, stepping beside him.

'She's there,' he growled, his Rabbethi ears picking up a conversation about Tessina from somewhere in the shadows. Without hesitation, he began marching towards the guards, the fire inside taking in the rage he felt in his heart, growing.

He felt a paw on his shoulder, stopping him. 'What are you doing? We need to get out of here,' Cara urged quietly.

Asher pulled his shoulder from her grasp. 'We could end this right here, right now! We kill her, and the bloodshed ends.'

He couldn't let Cara talk him out of this. He knew he was right. He had to take this opportunity, so he took off before Cara could protest further. His eyes burned, his senses heightened, his muscles tensed. He would fall upon the unsuspecting guards like a storm.

As he drew closer, he found a group of Vulpen guards standing in front of a wide set of spiralling steps. But they were not just any guards. Their armour was a deep black and engraved with beautiful patterns that swirled and flowed as they reflected the dim torchlight. There were four of them, and each had a red cape hooked to their shoulders, trimmed with golden thread. These were royal guards, Queen Tessina's personal force.

The first guard peered into the shadows of the passageway, standing a little straighter as he strained a pointed ear to listen. He shifted uneasily, placing a paw on the pommel of his sword. Not hearing anything, he relaxed and lowered his paw.

Asher appeared from the darkness, leaping at him with a speed unlike any other, his knee crunching heavily into the Vulpen's snout. Blood exploded as the guard's face crumpled inwards, coating the corridor and the other Vulpen in hot crimson. The guard flew through the air, colliding with a wide-eyed guard standing behind. She was pinned to the wall, crushed by the weight of the other guard, who now lacked any semblance of a face. Blood erupted from her snout, and she was unconscious. The two bodies slumped to the floor in a heap, one with blood trickling from her snout, her eyes rolled backwards, the other with brain leaking from their helmet.

Two to go.

The others blinked dumbfounded at this sudden assault, at the Rabbethi with a white fire burning in his eyes. Asher stared back with nothing but malicious intent. He would not let them stand in his way.

One grabbed a horn from his belt and pressed it to his lips, taking a deep breath. Asher was on him in a heartbeat, filling the horn with his fist and punching through, forcing the horn down the terrified Vulpen's throat. His eyes bulged as he choked on the metal, his paws desperately clawing at his throat. Asher pulled the red ribbon blade from his chest and, with a swift motion, slit the guard's throat, ending his suffering. Blood poured from the wound, and the Vulpen's strength quickly faded. He, too, slumped to the floor, dead.

One left.

The last guard stared at her fallen comrades with wide eyes, then back to Asher. With the cry of someone with nothing to lose, she lunged, attacking with desperate swipes and stabs. But with the fire burning through him, the Vulpen's onslaught appeared sluggish and cumbersome. He dodged the attacks with ease before stepping into the guard's space and plunging his blade up and through her snarling jaw. She froze, her arm raised high, ready to bring her sword down upon him. Blood began to flow from the corner of her mouth, through her canine teeth and onto the stone floor. Her eyes rolled backwards, and she collapsed, her scimitar clattering to the floor. Asher pulled his blade from her throat. He wiped it clean against her crimson cloak as Cara emerged from the darkness.

'That was... impressive,' she breathed in disbelief. 'But we need to leave. You know there'll be more and—'

'That bitch needs to die!' Asher snapped, his heart still aflame. 'If you're not going to have my back, *leave*!'

'Asher, I... She's my...'

But Asher was gone, sprinting up a wide spiral stairwell, his fury carrying him upon wings of vengeance. Tessina would pay for this betrayal, and Asher would ensure it was by his paws. Footsteps echoed faintly behind him. He knew he had been too harsh with Cara, knew the conflict she must be feeling inside, but now was not the time for sentiment. Once the bloodshed ended and the fighting stopped, he would apologise.

Higher and higher he went, the twisting stone stairs a blur beneath him, the fire coursing through him, preventing him from becoming dizzy. He eventually arrived at a lone wooden door. A cool wind passed around the door's rim as Asher unslung the King's Bow, and he burst into the cloudy afternoon light.

There was screaming, so much screaming.

The sound of battle raged across the city as Vulpen soldiers turned on their Rabbethi allies. He was on the vast square roof of the keep, where he found Queen Tessina standing at the far edge. Instead of her usual delicate silk dress, she wore a metal-plated suit of armour, shaped perfectly around her slender frame and etched with fine golden details mimicking the dance of flames. A crimson cloak rested over her long tail as it swished and flicked at her feet. Beside her stood Imperatrix Fira, the captain of the guard and the agent Flora's mother. Her white fur contrasted vibrantly against her curved, black-plated armour, and her pupilless red eyes stared at Asher with a calm, collected coldness, her thoughts and intentions unreadable. Upon her back rested a colossal greatsword, the likes of which Asher could never hope to lift.

She tilted her head towards Tessina as Asher entered the rooftop. Tessina nodded but did not turn. Instead, the Vulpen queen remained with her gaze fixed over the ocean, its shimmering water stretching out from the base of the cliff upon which the city proudly stood. By the docks, three Tail o' Wars sat heavily in the water like fat sows, with hundreds of smaller black-and-red vessels drifting around them like buzzing flies.

Asher raised the bow towards Tessina, the crackling energy scorching his cheek as he pulled the bowstring taut. 'Tessina!' he cried.

All at once, a chorus of bow strings sounded from every direction. A score of Vulpen archers took aim, their arrows prime to pierce his body many times over. Asher didn't care. He refused to take his eyes off Tessina.

'It seems like but a hop and a skip before you'd reach Ignimarum,' the queen said unperturbed, a wind carrying her calm voice over the screams far below. 'It would take no time at all, wouldn't you say?' She nodded over the sea towards a group of vessels sailing west. 'Look.'

Asher glanced in the direction and noticed a large fleet of Rabbethi ships sailing towards the Great Lighthouse, their blue-trimmed hulls skimming across the calm waters, the Rabbethia sigil proud on the full sails. There was something strange about the leading ship. Keeping the bow trained on Tessina, Asher strained his eyes and made out the shape of something large and spherical aboard the deck. Inside was some kind of steel box; no, not steel.

Silver.

'It appears we have both failed in some regard.' Tessina sighed. 'You have cleared Constance and the Shangari from the kingdom but failed to capture her. I have taken the kingdom from you but failed to serve justice upon my crazed sister.' She turned to face him, her eyes narrow and hard.

'Why are you doing this?' Asher demanded. 'I thought we were allies!'

'Why?' she snapped, taking a step forwards. 'Because prey cannot be trusted! Because prey are cowards! Their only instinct is to run into holes and hide. When they are needed, they *flee.*'

'We are not prey,' Asher growled.

Tessina lifted her snout and began pacing back and forth slowly. 'Oh, but you are. And we...' She gestured to her Vulpen guards surrounding her. 'We are predators. I am simply restoring the natural order.'

Asher followed her with his bow, the arrow continuing to crackle.

'When my sister attacked Ignimarum all those years ago,' she continued, 'we fought hard against her zealot church acolytes. There was so much bloodshed, and many noble Vulpen died defending the city. Alas, they forced us deeper into the city and trapped us within the palace.' She stopped, and her eyes became blank, her mind lost in the whirlpool of a terrible memory. With a deep breath, she continued, 'We sent countless ravens to your father, our closest ally, seeking aid and pleading for reinforcement. But as the days passed by, we heard *nothing*.' She spat the last word, snapping her head to Asher, her eyes now full of rage. 'We started to run out of food and water, my husband grew sick, and we gave up hope. In that awful, cold darkness, we waited for death.' A sudden, unexpected smile cracked her lips. 'But then a miracle happened! Our beloved seamstress Mathilde died. What a wonderful woman—even in death, she proved more useful than her station.' She subconsciously licked her lips, a hunger sparking to life within her eyes. 'We knew it was forbidden, but we *had* to survive, had to hold on. My sister would have driven the queendom to ruin if she had gotten her way. It also just felt...' Her eyes snapped to Asher. 'Natural...'

'You're a monster,' Asher breathed, his stomach churning at her words.

'What would you have done in our situation? Starved? I doubt it. All you Rabbethi care about is self-preservation!' Her teeth glinted in a vicious snarl.

Asher didn't blink, suppressing the instinct to cower before the queen's predatorial presence. He kept the arrow aimed directly between her eyes.

Her snarl slowly faded, and she calmed herself. 'It was the last meal my husband ever had. He died that night in my arms, as thin as your people's honour. Four more days I endured, trapped with a pawful of my court, the body of my beloved cradled in my arms, not knowing whether Cara was alive.' She took a deep breath and began walking back to the keep's edge. 'Eventually, a patrolling Tail o' War returned carrying enough brave Vulpen soldiers to break the siege and remove my twisted sister from the city. From that day, I decided that prey could not be trusted, that Rabbethi could not lead a people.' She turned and smiled, raising her arms wide. 'And thanks to you, they never will again! With the kingdom under my control, I can ensure the safety of those at the border, manage the population properly and deal with criminals... permanently.'

Asher felt a sudden presence at his back as Cara emerged from the stairwell. How long had she been there? He couldn't tell, but he was thankful to have her with him. She stepped forwards.

'Tessina... Mother. How could you?' she asked, unable to hide the betrayal in her voice.

Queen Tessina suppressed a startled gasp, seemingly unprepared for Cara's sudden appearance. 'Cara, darling. We'll talk about this later. Maintaining order will be challenging, but with my favourite agent by my side, I know we can do it. Together.' Her mouth formed the imitation of a loving smile, but her eyes remained cold and calculated. 'I need you, my most worthy child.'

'This is wrong. What you're doing is wrong. You must know this!'

Tessina's smile dropped, her eyes narrowing, her tail flicking erratically. 'Stupid girl! I knew you were too weak to handle the truth. Where's that savage predator I used to love? Where's that wild creature that killed without mercy? That slaughtered prey without ever asking questions?'

Cara looked at her thoughtfully, a deep sorrow welling in her eyes. 'She died with my parents.' Her gaze dropped to the stone floor.

Tessina's smile returned. It was a wicked smile without remorse or compassion. Her voice became smooth as silk. 'And now I'm all you have left, darling. You have no family, no friends. You're all alone, and you only have yourself to blame. Remember why?'

Cara's head snapped up to meet her cruel stare. 'Please, don't...' she pleaded, her voice trembling.

'You killed your parents in cold blood! The only people who loved you, and you slaughtered them!'

'Enough!' Asher suddenly cried. He didn't want to hear any more of Tessina's lies, any more words of poison and malice. He just wanted her gone. Stepping past Cara, he narrowed his eyes, focusing all his rage and anger into the arrow at his fingertips. It surged with fresh energy. He would not control this arrow. He would let it burn bright and scorch Tessina's cold, empty heart until there was nothing more than ash and dust. Imperatrix Fira sprang into action, reaching for the greatsword at her back and planting her foot as she made for Asher.

Time slowed as he released the bowstring. Everything went silent save for the thumping of his own heart and the crackle of fire within his eyes. Yes, he was probably going to die, but at least his kingdom would *finally* be free.

Pain.

Horrific, mind-numbing pain erupted from his lower back, and the arrow sputtered out of existence, the raging inferno in his heart fading as if doused by an all-encompassing cloud. It was cold, and it began to fill his entire body, sucking the life from his very being. Dark whispers started to echo in his mind, whispers not his own. Glancing over his shoulder, he found a heavily panting Corvo leaning against the door frame, his black paw reaching out, tendrils of black smoke wrapped around his fingers. With the last of his fading strength, Asher looked into Corvo's cold eye and saw nothing but an inky blackness.

Corvo smiled. 'Gotcha.'

Asher collapsed, his life fading as an icy claw began to smother the fire in his heart.

'Asher!' Cara screamed.

She reached for him, catching him in her arms as the blade in his back fell from its mark and clattered to the stone. Without hesitation, Cara bounded for the keep's edge as a storm of arrows rained upon her. One pierced her side, and she screamed, the shaft embedding deep into her flesh.

'Don't hit my daughter, you idiots!' Tessina yelled.

Then, Cara leapt.

The next thing Asher knew, he was falling. The edge of the keep grew smaller and smaller as he and Cara plummeted towards the ocean below, the wind coursing through his fur, his ears trailing wildly above him. His whole body was surrendering to the numbing cold, the blood in his veins like icy water from the Outer Rim. The only warmth he felt was from Cara, who held him tightly in her arms, the soft fur of her neck pressing gently into his face. He could hear her heart beating—felt its strength with each thump. The thunderous crashing of waves was growing louder and louder. With the last of his strength and the fire in his heart all but gone cold, he wrapped his arms around her and looked into her eyes.

She was crying.

'It's okay to be afraid,' she cried, looking down at him through the rushing wind, squeezing him tighter.

'Just do,' he breathed with a weak smile, the weight of his eyelids becoming too great, 'the next right thing...'

Epilogue

Grey clouds hung low in the evening sky, threatening to unload their weight over the calm waters of the Cinder Sea. Splashes of salty brine cascaded in a spray over the wooden deck of a small vessel as it skimmed across the gentle waves. Its hull was a deep red, the railings painted an inky black, and upon the stern was the name *The Jackdaw*. With a northwesterly breeze bloating its dark sails, it maintained a steady speed as it sailed away from the burning White Cliffe city.

Its only crew member was sitting cross-legged atop the small space of the crow's nest, high above the deck. She was confident in her ability to set the ship on a steady course and so had finally decided to write her long overdue report. On the railing beside her, a raven cawed expectantly. The sailor reached into her black cloak and pulled out a slither of dried meat, passing it towards the excited bird, who snapped joyously. She didn't take her eyes off the parchment on the floor, even as the raven's sharp beak nearly sliced through her red-furred fingers. She scanned the words she had written.

I have him.

We should make land on the Northern Continent in a few days.

I will keep you updated as often as I can.

Your beloved daughter.

She nodded, satisfied with her work, and rolled up the parchment, wrapping a red ribbon around it and tying it off into a pretty bow.

'That'll keep her happy for a while,' she said, smiling at the raven. The raven pecked once more at her cloak, tilting its large head as its eyes searched. 'Stop it! You'll get more when you get home,' she scorned as she tied the letter to the bird's black legs. 'Right, off you go.'

With a caw, the raven flapped its large black wings and took off into the wind, rising high above *The Jackdaw* and disappearing into the clouds.

With a yawn, the sailor stood and stretched her lean muscles. It had been a long few days, easy but long. Sneaking out of the keep and stealing a ship had been no trouble at all. There had been a couple of minor obstacles, but she had disposed of them quickly, leaving their bodies near sewer grates to blend in with the victims of the Shangari. So far, the sail north out of Rabbethia had been unbearably tedious. She had so wished for pirates to try to capture her, if anything, just to provide a little excitement. At best, she would have made some exciting new friends and, at worst, sparring practice, but the waters had remained calm and the winds favourable, with no such fun ever appearing. She remembered her newly acquired guest and smiled. With him, there would be fun and danger aplenty.

She leapt over the side of the crow's nest and effortlessly clambered down, using the ropes and pulleys to slow her descent. With a silence any Muuraki would be proud of, she landed gracefully on the deck and casually strolled into the cabin. It was simple inside. A desk and chair faced an open circular window at the back, through which a gentle breeze rolled into the room. Barrels of supplies stood stacked in a corner beneath shelves of bottled spirits, carefully secured with small lengths of chain.

The cabin creaked as she skipped to the bed in the opposing corner. She giggled at the unconscious Rabbethi lying upon it. She had removed his damaged leather armour and carefully tended to the wound in his lower back. It wasn't a deep wound, but it had been stubborn to heal. The ointments she had used seemed ineffective, and the area around it was cold and already beginning to rot. She had never seen such an injury before and had to call upon every inch of her knowledge just to stem the bleeding. She knew he would need further, more advanced healing to recover fully.

For now, the young Rabbethi rested peacefully on her cabin bed. He shivered, and she pulled the blanket up to his shoulders, tucking him in. He was a handsome man. The patch of fur around his eye reminded her of oak. She decided her favourite tree was now oak. A part of her toyed with the idea of keeping this Rabbethi all to herself and running away beyond the Rimwall Mountains where no one could find them, not even her mother.

Best not, she thought, kissing him lightly on the forehead with her long Vulpen snout.

'Rest well, my little Ash. We have a long way to go.'

Thank you so much for reading *The King's Bow.* This is the first of many stories to come, and I hope you enjoyed reading it as much as I enjoyed writing it. If you did, I would be forever grateful if you could leave a review on the platform(s) of your choice. Be sure to signup to my newsletter to stay updated on future projects.

The warmest and kindest of regards,

Jamie

www.jamieroe.com

Printed in Dunstable, United Kingdom

63832687R00265